VAN TERRA III:
BLACKOUT

Rory North

For Grandma.

You will be missed.

Content information available at
rorynorth.com/content-warnings

Cover art by Rory North.

The Janus System

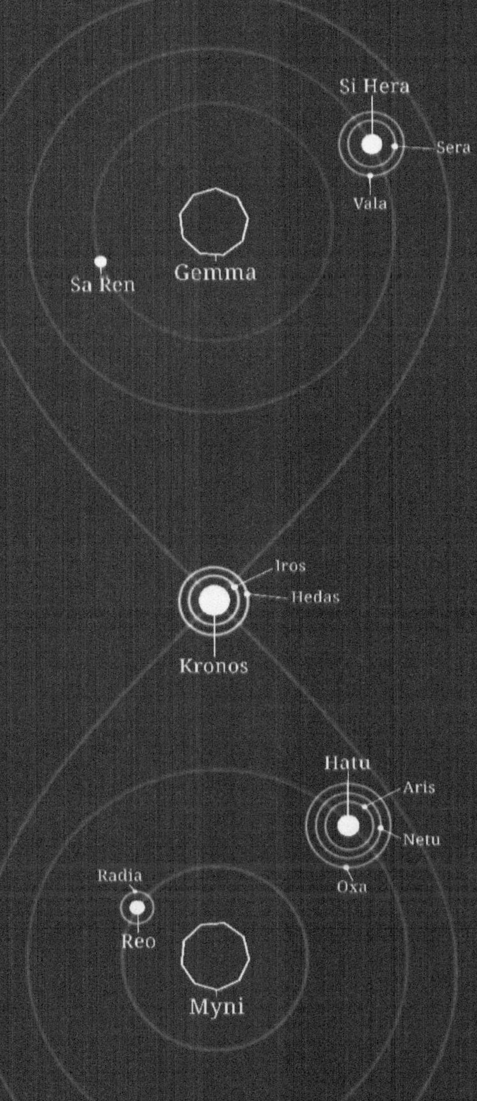

Chapter One
Steering The Course

Three days, five hours, twenty-eight minutes.

That was how long Jasper had until she'd be escorted to her execution.

It had been just over two months since her sentencing. The Earth date was December 3rd, and she couldn't care less what the Kronos date was. At the moment, all she cared about was the narrow window of time today that she had to speak to Dr. Charon Steer.

Dr. Steer was kept near the north edge of the prison, a considerable distance from the center where Jasper's cell was. But they weren't always so far apart. Jasper had glimpsed him occasionally leaving the dining hall while she was being escorted in for her work shift. After all, why hire employees to come work in a prison full of dangerous criminals when you could make the prisoners do all the work instead? The lucky ones were even paid a fraction of a jano a day. That was sure to get them far if they were ever released.

Jasper spent her first few weeks at the Shark Tank hoping to be put on a shift with the scientist, but of course, she wasn't that lucky. She did finally manage to get her hands on a copy of the work schedule, at which point she realized the next few weeks didn't look so good either. Steer was mostly given work in the medical wing, given his skillset. That forced Jasper to come up with a Plan B.

Today, Steer would be in the infirmary while she was in the kitchen.

Before the guards came to fetch her for her shift, Jasper practiced her breathing. A mental timer clicked on as she finished sucking in a deep breath, and she was briefly grateful that she'd been kept solo in her cell since her sentencing. No nosy cellmate to ask what she was holding her breath for. Or to steal one of the few flimsy hair ties she was allowed to have, like the woman she'd been paired with before her sentencing had.

Five minutes, thirty-two seconds. New record, and longer than she theoretically needed, even once her plan was actually in motion and she wasn't simply sitting cross-legged in a quiet cell. Assuming her estimates weren't too far off, that was. An anxious part of her insisted it still wouldn't be enough, but there wasn't really anything she could do at this point but hope.

The door at the end of the hall clanged open, and the sound of footsteps followed. No matter how quickly Jasper jumped to her feet, how quietly she waited by the door, perfectly still, hands in the air to show she was unarmed, the guards were always a little rougher than necessary as they yanked her out of the cell. Today was no different.

"Hey guys," Jasper said as they began the journey down the hall. "How's the family?"

"The closer we get to your execution date, the more annoying you get," the guard at her right grumbled. His grip on her arm tightened, wrinkling the bright red material of Jasper's prison jumpsuit. The material was reflective, making it easy to spot any prisoners who made it outside of the prison with searchlights. Not that anyone ever made it outside the prison.

Jasper restrained a grimace of pain. "Thanks."

While they walked, she scanned the neighboring halls with her x-ray vision. She did it every day, everywhere she went, and had long past memorized the sections of the prison that mattered. She scanned again anyway, burning every last detail into her memory, ensuring nothing had changed.

Her various vision modes and advanced computing abilities were all she really had at the moment. A network shield over the prison prevented any communications that weren't sent through the prison's specially coded channel from going in or out. Even with her cybernetic components, Jasper had no way of sending messages or accessing the net. Same went for anyone who somehow managed to sneak in a smartsphere or similar device.

On top of that, any files stored in Jasper's memory card had been wiped with a magnetic pulse on her way in, just as Starr had done when she'd tried to take video evidence of his involvement with the child-abducting bounty hunters. But she'd known this was likely to happen, and she'd known about the network shield. She'd planned around it. Planned as much as she could. And for the things she couldn't plan, she'd come up with a dozen different ways to handle every possible scenario. At least, she hoped she'd thought of every possible scenario.

It the prison kitchen, Jasper was left in front of a pile of mushy root vegetables and instructed to chop them up and toss them in boiling water. Perfect. Plenty of opportunities here for an unfortunate accident that would send her to the infirmary. She certainly wasn't looking forward to more pain, but it was time to get this nightmare over with.

Once the guards were no longer hovering over her, Jasper lifted her left arm—not wanting to risk damaging any of the cybernetic components in her right, though they'd *probably* be fine—and plunged it into the boiling water.

Oh, fu—

Jasper yelped in pain and yanked her arm back out, drawing attention from other prisoners and the closest guards.

"I splashed boiling water on myself," Jasper informed them plainly.

"How the hell did you manage that?" one of the guards demanded as he stormed toward her. He grabbed her arm and examined the nasty burn overtaking her skin. Then, with a sigh, he said, "I'll take her to the infirmary. But she's a level five. I'll need seven to come with me."

Jasper was admittedly still smug about being assigned the highest danger level in the Shark Tank's prisoner ranking system. More smug than she should have been, given how much harder it made it to get things done. Her status came with constant supervision from multiple guards and a pulser patch on the back of her neck that, if triggered, could make her fall unconscious at a moment's notice.

A second guard nodded. "Who do you want?" he asked.

"We've got enough extra perimeter guards," the first answered. "Grab some of them."

Jasper's nails dug into the unburned part of her forearm as the guards led her out of the kitchen, hoping to distract herself from the intense pain farther down. *You've felt worse. You've felt worse. You've felt worse.*

Her eyes were scanning the infirmary the moment she entered. Dr. Steer was one of a very few prisoners authorized to give first aid to others, and he was the only person scheduled in here right now. He'd have to be the one to treat her.

"Steer," the lead guard said as he dragged Jasper forward, causing her to stumble. "Where are you?"

A man emerged from a doorway leading to rooms for prisoners who required a longer stay in the medical wing. He had the vibrant red skin of an East Kronosian, completely black eyes, and long white hair pulled up in a simple bun, and he was accompanied by guards of his own. Only two. Unlike

Jasper, the man was hardly a threat to anyone, locked up in here for being a spy rather than any acts of violence or spectacular mayhem.

"Treat her burns," one of Jasper's other guards ordered. "Quickly, please. We'd like her to get back to work."

Jasper rolled her eyes as she was shoved in the direction of a cold metal bench. She settled onto it while Steer retrieved a small bag from a nearby shelf.

"Well, if it isn't the infamous Van Terra," Steer said as he opened the bag. "Did someone attack you?"

"Nah, I'm just clumsy sometimes." Jasper's gaze darted to the guards. They were chatting amongst themselves nearby, and while they threw frequent glances her way, they didn't seem too concerned with whatever words she and Steer were exchanging.

So, voice lowering, she said to Steer, "I need your help."

Steer frowned as he pulled a tube of medication out of the bag. "Beyond what I'm doing right now?"

"You worked at Sky Labs."

Steer's hands froze for a moment. Then, he uncapped the tube. "I did."

"They put a serum in me and it's killing me." Jasper swallowed. "I found a man named Dr. Androm who worked there, too. He gave me his files hoping I could find someone who can tell me what to do. It seems you're the only option I have, short of a Ouija board."

If Steer didn't know what a Ouija board was, he didn't say so. He took Jasper's wrist, sending fresh pain dancing across her nerves, and squeezed a neon yellow ointment onto her burned skin. "Do you remember the exact serum you got?" he asked.

"Version beta-three, according to Androm," Jasper told him.

Steer nodded. "We were able to develop a counteragent for that one. It's called ThetaEight. The subjects we tested it on all had good results."

"Ah, well, I guess I escaped the lab before they got around to that." Jasper grimaced as Steer began rubbing the ointment in. There was an odd combination of intensifying pain from the pressure on her burn and a cooling rush that didn't entirely counteract it. Like chewing on jalapenos and mints at the same time.

"All formulas developed at Sky Labs are kept in storage after testing," Steer continued. He pulled away from Jasper and returned his attention to the first aid bag, where he began digging around for something else. "At least a little bit of everything is kept on hand at all times, so if you can get in there, you don't have to worry about recreating it. It will be ready to go. Administration instructions should be there, too."

"Oh, finally. A little bit of convenience." Jasper flexed her hand, watching the neon sheen from the ointment reflect the overhead lights.

"Besides the part where you have to break into Sky Labs." Steer glanced over at her. "And get out of here."

Right.

Steer continued. "I was arrested before I got to verify any long-term effects of the counteragent, but they should have that data now, and we'd developed similar formulas in the past. It's pretty straightforward to make a counter to the types of serums we were giving test subjects. Thankfully." His expression darkened, though his hands kept moving through the bag. "I expect that once you take it, the ongoing processes caused by the original serum—like the cellular regeneration that keeps you from aging—would cease immediately."

Jasper nodded. Dr. Androm had told her the same thing on Reo. Her body would pick up aging right where it had left off.

Steer lifted a roll of bandages from the bag. "That also means your advanced healing would drop off quite a bit. But the serum's already made some permanent changes to your physiology. Those won't be so easily undone."

"I'll still have super strength?" Jasper asked, perking up slightly.

"A little. Some of that will diminish more over time, but it'll be gradual." He paused. "You won't be what you were, but you won't be entirely human, either. Plus, you'll still have your cybernetics, of course."

"But I'll age? And I won't be dying?"

"Correct."

That was all that mattered.

While Steer set to work bandaging her arm, Jasper asked her next question as quietly as she could manage. The two of them were getting more frequent glances from the guards, who seemed to be getting impatient. "So, you were with Earthguard. I don't suppose you know if they've made any progress dealing with Starr recently?"

Steer shook his head. "I have no way of contacting them, nor them me. Not without risking valuable information falling into the government's hands. I have no idea what their status is." His eyes lifted to briefly meet hers. "You know of them. It sounds like you've met some?"

"I think just Dr. Androm, personally, though he didn't seem long for this world. Another agent rescued my…friend from Starr, but she was killed in the process. Her name was Kara Callisto."

Steer shrugged. "Androm's name does sound familiar. He might have been brought into the labs shortly before I was arrested. Not sure about Callisto, though. But agents only tend to know the names of people on the same mission as them."

"Any idea how I could find other agents?" Jasper asked.

Steer shook his head. "Good luck. Contacting them is impossible if you're not up to date on the secret codes and drop locations. I honestly think your best bet would be to somehow get recruited."

Jasper huffed. She had no interest in working *for* Earthguard. She just wanted to know if they had any strategy whatsoever, or if they were shooting in the dark with their attempts at stopping the abductions and experiments.

"You've spent a long time on death row, for the Shark Tank," Steer noted with a raised eyebrow. He tore the wrapping around Jasper's arm off from the rest of the bandage roll and fixed it in place. "I think the record before you was three pentasols."

Jasper shrugged as she pulled her arm back to examine it. "I'm high-profile. From what I've heard, Starr's really hyping the execution up." She only hoped that the team was…managing as well as they could, emotionally speaking.

"Hey, what's taking so long?" one of the guards finally asked. He took a few steps toward the two. "Weren't you just supposed to give her ointment and wrap it up?"

"Sorry. The ointment needed a little time to set before I could put the wrap on." Steer rose to his feet. "She's ready to go."

Jasper followed his lead, suddenly aware of the dull ache lingering in her arm. "Thanks, doc."

"Try not to get hurt again."

Jasper waved her good hand dismissively as she walked toward the waiting guards. "Sure thing."

Unfortunately, sometimes getting hurt was part of the plan.

Chapter Two
Grim Outlook

The crumpled remains of Grim Machine's body had long stopped smoking under the jungle rain. Most of his lights had gone out. Most of his software had crashed. But a periodic chirp—accompanied by a pulsing blue glow—signaled that some part of his system was still running, still fighting, even so many pentasols after Van Terra's attack. Still, it was all the robot could do to perceive the darkening jungle around him. Movement was impossible, and so was sending a signal for help.

Tonight's rain shower faded not long after it had started. The only thing coming down from the sky after that was the glow of the full moon Radia. Countless stars dusted the black around it, illuminating countless unknown worlds that the robot would likely never see. But somewhere among those stars was the home of his creator.

Amidst the chorus of jungle animals, the chirping and croaking and buzzing, a mechanical sound arose. Clanking metal, beeping and clicking, robots muttering strange curses to each other as they traversed the dense landscape.

Blinking lights, this is a terrible place.

Zap this entire operation.

Grim needs us. But all my drives, why did it have to be a jungle?

A second, sharper beam of light dropped down from the sky, originating much closer to the planet's surface than the moon. It swept back and forth over the jungle, keeping pace just ahead of the robot search party.

Eventually, the searchlight landed on the pile of Grim Machine.

"There he is," a familiar voice boomed from within the light's source, a hovering silver-white crescent-shaped spacecraft. The craft was one of the fleet's smaller ships, with only the space of a small apartment on the inside. "Have a nice nap, Grim?"

The grimbots flew into a frenzy as soon as they were within reach of Grim Machine, tearing off their own components and swapping them in for Grim Machine's broken ones. Two bots kept themselves whole, stepping in to make repairs when the rest could no longer function using parts they could no longer move themselves.

Finally, Grim Machine could speak again. "Meg," he grunted.

Meg clicked her tongue over the speaker. "Poor thing, out here all alone. I hope you know we sent bots out to search for you as soon as we lost contact with you. I wasn't able to get a cruiser out here until a few days ago, though."

Grim Machine's primary processor didn't do much with that information. He was too focused on the bots still putting the final touches on his exterior. "Why are my grimbots doing this?" he demanded. There was more than simple curiosity in his tone. Maybe bits of his programming needed patches. "They're destroying themselves—"

"Doncha know? They were made and given to you for this very reason, though they made good henchbots, too. Too bad there weren't enough around to save you after your last fight. You never really needed them until then."

Additional internal processors whirred within Grim Machine's body, a few still coming online, his reaction time still picking up speed. He'd been programmed to protect the grimbots. His ever-evolving algorithm had led to him taking revenge on anyone who damaged or destroyed them.

But he was also programmed to listen to Meg. To take everything she said as gospel. As far as the robot was concerned, she was the highest power in the universe.

Grim Machine's visual field shifted down to examine the three remaining grimbots. Two in perfect condition, one missing an arm sacrificed to bring him back. The rest were hardly more than scraps, though they could probably be used as bases for new machines. Their memory was likely to need resetting, though. They wouldn't be as intelligent—as useful—as the bots whose algorithms had been trained over several starcycles in combat and chaos.

"Don't worry, Grim," Meg said, voice still chipper as ever. "We'll get ya some more. In the meantime, though, we need your help. The war is far from over."

Grim Machine's thinking algorithms finally handed him one of the most interesting pieces of information yet for him to examine. "You're—here," he said slowly. "In the Janus System." He focused his attention on the hovering cruiser. "Are you actually in there, Meg?"

"Not in this cruiser, no."

"But you're nearby?"

"You know I'm a high-profile target, dear. For my own safety, I can't tell you yet. But you'll get to see me in person soon. And I'm *really* looking forward to it."

It had been starcycles since Grim Machine had last seen her. Last seen anyone from her team, really. Every once in a while, an engineer was sent out to make repairs or upgrades—the most recent being the extensive process of giving him the ability to transform into a tank—but beyond that, Grim Machine was left to do his own thing in the Janus System. He occasionally received specific instructions and random tasks but generally operated under one ongoing order: create chaos.

The space cruiser's overwhelmingly bright searchlight dimmed, allowing Grim Machine's visual sensors to detect the hatch sliding open in its underside. A high-focused gravity beam locked onto Grim Machine and his surviving grimbots and pulled them up.

The receiving room of the cruiser was plain, sleek and the same silver-white as the exterior. A screen took up most of the space on one of the walls, but while it was on, it only showed an empty blue quartz desk in a bright, clean office.

A voice spoke from just off camera. "So, Grim, are you ready to help me bring order to the Janus System?"

"Order?" Grim Machine's mouth turned into a frown to express his confusion, the gaps in his understanding. "My commands for the past few starcycles have been to incite chaos." He wasn't sure he was equipped to do much else.

"And you've done it beautifully. Paving the way for us to step in." Meg chuckled. "And there is still plenty of chaos to come."

"What about Skybreaker? Will she be hosting more races for me to participate in?"

"The races are done. You'll be helping her in other ways, but you can worry about that later. I'm sure your tank form will still be useful, though."

Grim Machine couldn't disagree with that, even if Meg's plans for the future were vague. Her grand plan didn't matter to him, really. All he needed to know was his role. It was all he was programmed to need.

So, he asked, "What do you want me to do now?"

Chapter Three
Rock Paper Bomb

The atmosphere in the prison cafeteria was the same as ever the day after Jasper burned herself. Faint scratching of plastic utensils on trays, chatter amongst the prisoners that was rarely polite, occasional barrages of insults or threats of violence. The usual.

More often than not, Jasper's meals were served to her in her cell. But on the days she was escorted all the way to this side of the prison to work, she was left to eat here in the cafeteria afterward. Her ankles were cuffed to the table, of course, and there was nothing remotely sharp or dangerous she could use to attack anyone.

But there wasn't much to stop others from hurting her. Which happened to be what she really needed.

As Jasper shoved a bite of some sort of unseasoned mashed root into her mouth, a fellow prisoner walked by: a yellow-skinned, webbed-fingered, amphibious guy by the name of Mog whom Jasper had developed a particular dislike for. And given her talent at being annoying, it hadn't been hard to make him feel the same way about her. Their last altercation had ended with several threats of violence on his part.

A follow-through on those threats was exactly what Jasper needed right now. Another self-inflicted injury, no matter how accidental she claimed it to be, would be suspicious. She couldn't risk those suspicions compromising her plan.

"Hey, Mog!" Jasper exclaimed through her mouthful of mashed root.

Mog stopped in his tracks and turned to face her, annoyance already simmering in his expression. "I warned you to keep out of my sight, Van Terra."

Jasper swallowed and grinned at him. "Aw, you can act like you hate me all you want, but I know you like me deep down. Come on, why don't you join me for dinner?"

"I'd rather watch you choke."

"I know why you're so mean, Mog. You do like me—and everyone else you threaten to murder—but you don't know how to make friends." With a shrug, Jasper shoved another bite in her mouth.

Mog gestured to a couple of the guys who'd been walking with him. "I've got plenty of friends."

Jasper laughed through her food. "No, those are people you find valuable, so you've intimidated them into hanging out with you. But you know you can't intimidate people like me. So, you threaten to kill me instead." She swallowed, then wagged her fork at him. "You know that in a fair fight, I'd have you on the ground in a heartbeat."

"You're nothing compared to me."

"I don't believe you."

Before the Shark Tank, Mog had been a powerful drug lord. And he still had connections that could get him those drugs smuggled in, giving him something he could bribe other prisoners and guards alike with. And he wasn't the kind of person to let someone like Jasper get away with insinuating that she was stronger than him.

So, just as Jasper expected, Mog—whom the guards tended to look the other way around, thanks to those bribes—was able to produce a shard of sharp glass from his pocket. God knew where he got it from, or what kind of infections it might give Jasper if her upcoming wound went untreated, but she hadn't come up with any better ideas.

Mog moved to swing. Jasper couldn't take any chances. He'd likely get one hit in before guards were forced to intervene, and it had to land where she needed it to. She lifted her right arm into the path of the glass. She didn't feign fear, or show pain, or give any indication that she intended to dodge the shard at all. She simply stared Mog dead in the eye as his weapon sank into her skin. Blood welled. Dripped onto the table. The floor.

"What the hell—?"

Mog's confusion was short-lived. Guards grabbed his arms, grabbed Jasper, and the shard of glass clattered to the tile below. Despite the fact that Mog had physically incited things, Jasper knew exactly what would happen next.

"Mog, sit down, or you'll be escorted back to your cell," one of the guards ordered. His head turned, and he barked commands at the others. "Take Van Terra to the infirmary to get that patched up. Then, she goes straight to solitary confinement."

Jasper let the guards drag her away from the table, away from the meal that she would have liked to get a few more bites of, even if it was bland as hell. Oh, well. A few bites of prison food probably wouldn't make or break her ability to get out of here.

As they left the cafeteria, Jasper wrapped her left hand around her bleeding wound, acting as if she were simply trying to stop the blood and not preparing herself to flip a switch hidden among the circuitry beneath her skin.

She traced the path she and the guards took against the mental map she'd constructed of the Shark Tank. Well, the map of the parts that mattered. Like the giant outflow pipe that went deep into the ocean. The water was filtered and chemically treated first, the bare minimum to meet ocean-dumping regulations, so it shouldn't be too gross. But it certainly wasn't drinking quality.

Oh well. Beggars couldn't be choosers.

The pipe's end point was far too deep into the ocean for Jasper to survive the swim, and it ended in a grate that would have been a challenge to break through even if she could make the journey. Thankfully, the bomb that her *lovely* friend Sarena Trench had so kindly planted months earlier would make a new exit point for Jasper to slip out through. Assuming Jasper could trigger the damn thing.

From the nearest access point to the outflow pipe that she'd identified, it would be a one-minute journey to the exit. And then a two-and-a-half-minute swim to a point in the water beyond the Shark Tank's long-range weapons and radar.

Jasper clutched her wounded arm, spilling blood on the tile as she walked with the guards, counting doors and halls and preparing herself for the moment where she'd need to act. Bracing herself for the pain. Even worse pain than what she was feeling right now.

The guards led her around another corner, and up ahead was the split where Jasper would need to break away from them.

"Can you walk any faster?" one of the guards demanded when they were about halfway down the hallway. He shot Jasper an annoyed glance.

"Believe me, I'm trying," Jasper muttered. Biting back cries of pain and doing her best to hide her movements from the guards, she ran a thumb along the inner mechanical components of her arm until she found what she was looking for.

First, the switch she'd programmed to connect to the bomb.

Jasper winced as she flipped it. This spike of pain was minimal, thankfully, and she was quickly distracted from it by the slight tremor that shook the floor below.

The guards stopped. "What the hell was that?" one at Jasper's right asked.

"Might be a seaquake," another replied, the one who had snapped at Jasper moments earlier. "Let's get her secure. Then we can ask command if they know anything."

They continued on. Almost to the intersection. Almost. Jasper's fingers continued to move, her search growing more frantic as she tried to find—

There. The electrokinesis trigger. Her only hope of making it through the guards between her and the pipe. Even with it, she had no chance of making it out of any of the real exits. The power would fade too quickly, and she'd probably collapse from pain before making it very far if it didn't.

Jasper pressed the trigger just as she and her escorts stepped into the intersection. Before any of them could attempt to drag her in the direction of the infirmary, opposite the way she needed to go. For a moment, all she knew was blinding pain.

And then it faded enough for her to watch the electricity explode from her body.

Pink arcs of lightning sent the guards flying back with shouts of pain, smacking into walls and floor with resounding thuds. It was all Jasper could do to run, face twisted from the electricity coursing through her own body. Not as much as was leaving, not as much as was striking anyone in her path, but enough to hurt.

The surge of electricity was also more than enough to fry the pulser on the back of her neck. As she ran, she was able to yank the patch off without triggering it and toss it aside. One more problem solved. Just a dozen more to go.

Jasper only had a few minutes before the electrogenesis would fade. A few minutes to find her way into the outflow pipe. She followed the map burned into her memory. There were three hallways between her and her destination.

She took the first corner and found only the typical number of guards posted in the next hallway. They immediately surged toward her. She swung her arm to quickly direct the bolts of electricity their way, and they went down fast.

By the time Jasper reached the next hall, emergency lights had come on. At least, she assumed they were emergency lights. The ceiling was flashing with every shade of neon. That sure was one way to let people know something was up. Or encourage a dance party.

It had certainly worked to mobilize the prison's guards. A squad of ten came around the opposite corner, blocking her path. Jasper slowed her pace and forced a laugh as she strolled toward them. "Sure, group yourselves together. Make things easier for me." She flung out both her arms. A massive storm of pink light knocked her opponents back.

As soon as the guards were down, Jasper grabbed her bleeding arm again and let out the cry of pain that had clawed its way into her throat. "God, that's bad." She tipped her head back and swallowed. "Come on. Come on. Almost there."

Her pace slowed significantly as she reached the next corner. The hallway she needed. The hallway packed with well over twenty guards.

Jasper glanced at her arm, at the scattered pink arcs jumping across her skin. They were already starting to slow, to fade. She had to get these guards down fast. With a cry that she hoped was intimidating and not revealing of how badly she wanted to collapse, she charged toward them. Flung her arms out again. The lightning storm escaped her body with ferocity, jumped from guard to guard, eagerly crashed through every person in its path.

Jasper staggered to a stop in front of the pile of collapsing guards, breathing hard. To her dismay, three managed to get themselves upright quickly. Despite the pain on their faces, they were drawing pulse guns. Moving toward her.

Jasper ducked, grabbed a pulse gun off a nearby unconscious guard, and chucked it at the closest approaching enemy. It smacked him square in the forehead and knocked him onto his back. He groaned but didn't make any attempt to get back up.

The move took the other two guards by surprise long enough for Jasper to lunge forward, kick one in the stomach, and roundhouse the other in the jaw.

Her path to the outflow pipe was clear. Almost. The only thing in her way now was a locked door. Jasper grabbed an ID badge off one of the fallen guards and used it to unlock the maintenance room in the middle of the hallway. She yanked open the door with her good arm and staggered in. A few hopefully clean towels were folded in a stack on an overhead shelf. She grabbed one and tied it tight around her bleeding arm.

Footsteps thundered nearby. And with her body's electrical output faltering, Jasper had little to defend herself with. She dropped to her knees, twisted the small handle in the floor, and lifted the hatch that blended in almost perfectly. The sound of rushing water reached her ears. She slid into the darkness without hesitation.

Her feet hit hard cement while the hatch clanged back into place above her. Not that that would stop the guards from figuring out she'd come down here and following. But they wouldn't follow for long.

Jasper crossed the tunnel she'd landed in toward the massive pipe running under the prison. Another hatch awaited her, this one much harder to open. She twisted the handle with a grunt and dragged it open with shaking arms. By the time the gap was wide enough for her to squeeze through, she was on the verge of collapse. At least she didn't have to swim, yet. Just hold her breath and let the painfully cold and lightning-fast water sweep her out of the prison.

It was harder not to hesitate before this leap. But the thunder of footsteps above kept Jasper moving. She closed her eyes, sucked in a sharp breath, and dove into the cold current.

Chapter Four
I Survived The Shark Tank And All I Got Was This Stupid Jumpsuit

The world was whipped away from Jasper the moment she hit the water. She barely kept the air in her lungs, barely kept her consciousness from fracturing. She knew somewhere in the back of her mind that the pipe would take her toward the edge of the prison and then straight down, but she had no idea which way was up, which way she was facing. Her eyes stayed shut tight against the pressure of the water. Not that seeing would have helped any.

She could tell when the pipe's direction switched, though, mostly by the way her stomach climbed into her throat at the sensation of plummeting. Her lungs burned, already begging for fresh air. She was only thirty seconds into the journey. Halfway through the pipe.

In the cold and disorienting dark, Jasper reminded herself what she was fighting for. The team was waiting for her. Starr was still alive. Skybreaker was still planning to break apart the Janus System, innocents be damned.

You. Can. Do. This.

One moment she was shooting through the water, the next she was drifting. Jasper forced her eyes open and looked up. Far above her, glimmers of the setting sun danced at the ocean's surface. She couldn't go up yet, though. She had to get out of range.

Her own blood clouded the water around her as she forced her arms to move, to push herself away from the Shark Tank. There weren't any actual sharks in Kronos's waters—wealthy assholes had imported some from Earth for the novelty of it, then hunted them all right back out of the ocean. But there were other predators. Things that would come her way if they caught the scent of her blood.

Jasper was rapidly running out of energy. And oxygen. She kicked harder. Put all the power she could muster into her strokes. Moved up, moved forward. Counted the time.

Finally, she dared to move up to the water's surface. She broke it, sucked in a deep breath, and immediately went back under, bracing herself for the potential onslaught of bullets or blaster beams, swimming as fast as she could in case an attack came. But there was nothing.

Well, not quite *nothing*. The prison's alarm was blaring in the distance, piercing the evening air and warning everyone in the vicinity that something had gone wrong. Jasper turned herself to face the prison and poked her head out of the water again, briefly, just long enough to watch a few flying cruisers lift into the air. They'd be armed with snipers and heat scanners, but as long as Jasper stayed at least a few feet below the surface, they wouldn't be able to find her.

There was just the issue of, well, breathing.

Jasper continued to swim away from the prison. The search party would expect her to head directly for the nearest shoreline, even though swimming that far was impossible for pretty much anyone. Even Sarena had been exhausted just going between the prison and the floating platform that was relatively close, and her body was adapted for this.

Instead, Jasper went at a different angle, in the direction of well-trafficked ship routes. An area filled with cargo ships, leisure vessels, and fishing boats. People getting as close to the prison as was legally allowed. They might search for her over there, too, but once she was lost in traffic, finding her would be much harder.

The reason the area was heavily used by such a wide variety of watercraft, despite its proximity to the Shark Tank, was the formation of currents that kept this part of the sea relatively safe, compared to other regions that saw more storms and rough waters. It also meant that once Jasper couldn't see the prison's search cruisers in the sky, she'd be able to float on her back for a while, rest, and let the currents take her in roughly the right direction.

She swam hard, making quick stops at the surface and throwing frantic glances at the sky for nearly an hour before she finally felt safe enough to shift into a back float. Night was falling fast, and searchlights would be needed to see her at this point. Those would be relatively easy to avoid if she could get under the water quickly. The downside was that fast-sinking sun also made the world even colder.

Thankfully, an abundance of thermal vents in the water kept the oceans relatively warm, even when Kronosian winter set in. Emphasis on *relatively.* And that fact certainly didn't stop the night air from biting at Jasper's skin. Shivering, she reminded herself that she didn't have much farther to go. She just needed to stay afloat until she could commandeer a small watercraft. Hopefully she had enough remaining strength to overpower a few people. She might be able to trigger the electrokinesis again, but at this point, the pain might make her pass out, too. Last resort, she supposed.

With the cover of night making her feel safer, Jasper grabbed the next piece of driftwood that floated by and used it to support herself so that she could rest her eyes. She never stayed asleep for long, but occasionally drifted in and out of consciousness, torn between desperately needing rest and not wanting to let her guard down.

The final time she closed her eyes, it was dark, and they reopened to a blinding morning sun cutting across the rocking waves, illuminating the sea, circling birds, and...

Distant ships.

A weak smile crossed Jasper's face. Fresh hope sparked in her chest. She was going to make it.

She kicked toward the ships. Occasional aircraft passed by, making her heart quicken, but while she braced herself to dive back under each time she saw one, none of them ever veered her way.

Despite the increasing number of ships in the area, Jasper still spent most of the day in the water. Many that she started to approach proved to be way too big for her purposes, forcing her to go in wide circles around them and continue searching for something else. The surface of the water had begun to reflect the reds and oranges of the setting sun by the time something really promising came close. Jasper kept as much of her body under the water as possible as she summoned a little of her lingering energy and pushed herself toward the small fishing vessel.

As the approaching boat bobbed up and down on the waves, Jasper eyed the fishing lines extending into the water. The two men on board. She could probably take them, even in her weakened state, but she would need the element of surprise. She circled around to come at the boat from behind, carefully watching the backs of the men's heads to make sure they didn't turn.

She made it all the way to the boat's rear. Now for the hard part: getting in quickly.

Jasper lifted her hands to the back of the boat, sucked in a deep breath, and pulled herself up. Pain flared in her arm. Well, all of her body, but mostly her arm. She yelped in pain and grabbed it as she stumbled haphazardly into the boat. "Oh, god, that hurts!"

The men were on their feet in an instant, facing her with wide eyes.

"Sorry! Didn't mean to startle you." Jasper's gaze darted around the boat, assessing her options. "Well, I guess I kind of meant to startle you. But not like that."

"Who the hell are you?" one of the men demanded.

"Don't even worry about it." Jasper grabbed one of the spools of fishing line lying on the driver's seat and charged the men.

They were strong, but they clearly had no combat training. Within minutes, Jasper had them on the ground and tied up in their own fishing line. She straightened up and looked over her work. Resting her hands on her hips, she said, "Again, I'm really sorry about this. I didn't have a lot of options for getting to shore."

"That's a prison uniform!" the man on the right exclaimed. "Good Gemma, did you break out of the Shark Tank?"

"Wouldn't you like to know?"

The man on the left's eyes went wide. While his friend's mouth hung agape, he said, "You broke out of the most secure prison on the planet?"

Jasper shrugged. "What, like it's hard?"

The men continued to protest and shout questions at her while she dug around for the boat keys, forcing Jasper to put some tape over their mouths before starting the engine and setting off.

"Promise I'll untie you and all that jazz before I leave!" she shouted at them over the wind. "I really just need a ride."

Jasper quickly forgot about the men on the floor behind her as she raced toward shore. Her fatigue, her hunger, her thirst, it was all catching up with her. The thirst was solved by one of the water bottles she found while digging through the men's supplies, but the other problems weren't going away anytime soon. And neither was the throbbing pain in her arm. With the amount of time she'd spent in the water, there was no way it wasn't getting infected without intervention.

Just make it home. Dax can fix it.

It was dark by the time she pulled into a harbor. The night was cold, but it was probably safer to crawl home in the dark, anyway. Before climbing off the boat, she took a pocketknife from one of the bags and approached the bound men.

"Be nice and give me a thirty-second head start, all right?" Jasper sliced through the fishing line. She'd let them handle the tape themselves—it would be a good distraction and might actually give her that head start she needed. Still clutching the stolen knife, she hopped out of the boat and jogged off the pier at the fastest pace she could muster.

She slowed to a pained walk after only a block, and she was on the verge of collapse by the time she ducked into a clothing store to grab stuff that could hide her prison uniform. Black cargo pants and a baggy gray poncho-style shirt. She was tempted to snatch a black overcoat, too, but resisted the urge to go for her usual. The last thing she needed was to be recognized right now. In fact, it was tempting to take her hair down to mix up her look even more, but with it soaked from the ocean and likely a tangled mess, she decided to keep it in its ponytail.

Jasper paused by the store's front windows and scanned the street outside. Nothing beyond the usual evening crowds. People getting off work, picking up groceries, shopping if they had money to spare. The neon glow and grime of the lower districts in all its glory.

No police. No citywide manhunt for her. It seemed Starr didn't want the public knowing she'd escaped. He must have been confident search patrols would catch her out in the ocean. Or thought she was already dead.

No, he wasn't careless enough to assume that. He'd search until he found her or a body. But if he could prevent the public from knowing about it, of course he'd take that route. How embarrassing would it be for him if word got out that Van Terra had escaped the freaking Shark Tank?

After slipping out of the store, Jasper dragged herself to the subtrain station entrance across the street, staggered down the stairs, and hurried onto the waiting train just before the doors slid shut. She sank into a seat and let out a shuddering breath. Her shoulders sagged. It would probably be ten minutes before they reached her stop. She'd have to resist the urge to pass out until then.

She didn't fall unconscious, but she did zone out for a while, only snapping out if it when someone spoke directly in front of her. "Um, are you all right?"

Jasper glanced up and found a woman standing over her. "Huh? Yeah, I'm fine."

"It's just—" The woman pointed toward Jasper's arm. "Looks like you're bleeding."

Jasper glanced at the dark red stain growing on the sleeve of her shirt. Oh. Damn. She did her best to cover it with her hand and shot the woman a wary glance. "It's fine."

"Are you sure? I could help you get to a hospital—"

"It's *fine*," Jasper repeated, the words both strained and harsh. The woman pressed her lips into a thin line, nodded, and moved away. Would she assume Jasper simply couldn't afford medical care? Or had she picked up on the fact that Jasper had other reasons to avoid attention?

The train slowed. Jasper glanced at the screen displaying the stop name and was relieved to see it was hers. She climbed to her feet, nearly collapsed but didn't, and hurried out with the crowd. Up the station stairs. Across streets and sidewalks.

She finally collapsed in the alley behind the apartment.

Jasper made one attempt, two attempts, to get back on her feet before resigning herself to crawling toward the vent where she'd left her grappling hook. Then, her struggle with the grate began. Clinking echoed through the quiet alley. Lights from passing vehicles lit the world around her up briefly before fading, her presence going completely unnoticed each time. Finally, the damn thing came off. Jasper had to take a full minute to catch her breath before reaching her left arm into the vent and grabbing the grappling hook. Her gaze darted up to her bedroom window. It seemed much farther up than she remembered.

One last round of pain. One last fight. Then she could give up and let the team take care of her. Assuming they didn't throw her right back out the window. They probably weren't too happy about being left out of her plans.

Jasper lifted the hook, aimed as best she could with her shaking hands, and pulled the trigger. The window shattered. She squeezed her eyes shut against the shards of glass that tumbled down. Once the air was clear, she gave the hook a slight tug to ensure it was caught on something. Then, bracing herself for another spike of pain, she pressed the trigger again to pull herself up. She was momentarily blinded by the flashing in her vision that followed, dancing lights brought on by the most intense pain she'd felt since activating her electrokinesis at the prison.

The next thing she knew, she was on her bedroom floor in a pile of broken glass. Well, that had to have woken someone up. Any second now, someone would come running in—

"Jasper!"

Jasper forced herself up off the floor enough to tip her head back. Grace stood between her and the bed, the blankets disturbed behind her, her hair a mess and bags under her eyes.

Jasper had never been so happy to see her in her life. "Grace?" She pushed herself up a few more inches. "What are you…?" *Why are you in here?*

Okay, Jasper, maybe worry about the fact that you're bleeding and soaked with ocean water and still creeping closer to death, first.

"Oh my god, it is you." Grace rushed forward and dropped to her knees in front of Jasper. "You're—" She lifted a hand toward Jasper's face.

"Alive, at the moment." Jasper lifted her arm, revealing the blood-soaked fabric. "Um, I hate to cut our reunion short, but—"

"Dax!" Grace screamed, rising to her feet again. She started toward the bedroom door. "Dax! Thea! Holly!"

Jasper sank back into the carpet and rolled onto her side. The full force of the pain she'd managed to keep at bay overwhelmed her, locking her in place, pricking her eyes with tears, and making every second before the team came in nothing short of excruciating.

Chapter Five
Back in Business

The moment Grace heard footsteps in the others' bedrooms, she turned around and ran back to Jasper, who'd gone entirely limp on the carpet. "Jasper," Grace stammered as she dropped to the ground next to her. "Jasper, please, don't die—"

"I'm not dying," Jasper muttered into the carpet. "Not yet, anyway."

Grace reached for Jasper's face again, then pulled her hand back, not wanting to make the pain worse. Best to let Dax handle this.

Holly came rushing into the bedroom first, but Dax and Thea were close behind. While they gathered around, Grace helped Holly pull Jasper to her feet. Holly was quick to peel off her blood-stained poncho, revealing the even more soaked Shark Tank prison uniform underneath.

And it wasn't just blood, Grace realized as she fully processed that Jasper's hair and clothes were wet through and through. "God, you're drenched."

Jasper grimaced. "Yeah, the ocean'll do that."

"We need to get you into something warm before you freeze to death." Holly guided Jasper into a sitting position at the edge of the bed. Dax was next to them a heartbeat later, one hand hovering above Jasper's shoulder. A blue glow radiated from his palm.

Holly hurried to Jasper's closet next and yanked the doors open. "Someone grab a meal bar from the kitchen," she directed as she began digging for clothes. "And water. And bandages."

"That should jumpstart her. I'll get bandages so I can finish up," Dax said. He started toward the door.

"Meal bar," Thea added as she followed.

Grace was frozen for a moment, feeling like it was wrong to leave Jasper right now but also knowing the others were right to be scrambling around. Jasper needed more than just their presence right now.

"I'll, uh, get water," she stammered. She backed toward the door slowly, watching for a few more moments as Holly carried a pile of clothes over to Jasper. Then, she forced herself to turn and hurry to the kitchen.

When Grace returned a minute later with a glass of water in hand, Thea and Dax were already back, and Holly had gotten Jasper into completely new clothes. As she finished pulling a long-sleeved black shirt into place, Jasper's head turned, and her long wet hair tumbled down past her shoulders. Grace froze, the sight of Jasper's hair down taking her by surprise.

Holly stuck out her hand. "Water, please."

Grace hurried forward and handed the glass over. Holly held it to Jasper's mouth, all but forcing her to drink. Jasper's eyes rolled, but she didn't lift a hand to take control of the glass. Was she even capable of doing that right now?

"Can Dax take a closer look at my arm now?" Jasper asked quietly when Holly finally pulled the glass away. "It feels like it's on fire."

Holly nodded. "Get in there, Dax. And Jasper, you should eat."

Jasper groaned. "I feel nauseous."

"When was the last time you ate?"

"Uh, dinner yesterday?"

"Take a bite." Holly took the meal bar from Thea and began unwrapping it.

Dax settled onto the bed next to Jasper, placed a hand on her arm, and grimaced. "This is bad." His other hand moved to her shoulder and emitted a soft blue glow. After a moment, he said, "Okay, the good news is it feels like your body's responding pretty well to the first wave I gave you. Not as fast as I'd like, but I was expecting worse."

Jasper took a small bite of the bar Holly held out to her. While Dax focused on her arm and Holly continued to try and get her to eat, Grace and Thea watched anxiously.

Finally, Dax moved on to bandaging up the arm. "I've jumpstarted the process as much as I can. Bleeding should stop in a few hours. Just be careful not to reopen it. Like I said, it'll be a few days before it gets anywhere close to fully healed, assuming I'm even judging your healing time correctly." He finished bandaging and leaned back. "So, uh, the Shark Tank—"

"Jasper, what the hell were you thinking?" Holly blurted. Grace jumped, Thea's eyes went wide, and Dax winced.

Jasper sighed. "I know, I know. I owe you guys a much longer explanation, but—"

Holly had her arms around Jasper in the blink of an eye, her face buried in her shoulder...sobbing?

"Oh," Jasper said, looking absolutely stunned. "Holly. Crying. That's new." Her face twisted into a grimace. "I appreciate the show of affection, but that kind of hurts—"

Holly pulled back abruptly. "We thought you were going to die, Jasper!" She wiped an arm across her face, but it didn't do much to get rid of the tears streaming down. Thea and Dax looked as surprised as Grace felt.

Jasper's expression softened. She glanced at the others. "I—I know you guys need the full story. I did learn something that's going to save me. But I don't have the energy right now—"

"Get some rest, Jasper," Thea said, cutting her off. "We understand." She glanced at Holly. "Right?"

Holly nodded and sniffed. "Yeah. Get some sleep, dumbass."

Jasper managed a weak smile, but her pain and exhaustion didn't leave her eyes. Voice quieting, cracking, she added, "Can you all...stay in here tonight?"

Jasper's bed was plenty big enough to fit everyone. Grace wondered if Jasper had realized yet that she'd been sleeping in here when the grappling hook came crashing through the glass. Had been sleeping in here since the day Jasper was arrested. The team had been having frequent visitors over to discuss plans, and Grace figured it was easier to just stay in Jasper's room than move in and out of the "guest room" that had become hers. They could have made Jasper's room the guest room, but...that didn't feel quite right. And admittedly, their guests weren't the only reason Grace had decided to stay in Jasper's room.

Grace hesitated at the edge of the bed, watching as Jasper climbed into the center, clearly still in pain judging by her slow, jerky movements and the winces flashing across her face. Dax slid in from the other side and rested a hand on Jasper's shoulder, and Thea settled in behind him, propping herself up on a few of Jasper's many pillows.

"Go ahead," Holly said behind Grace, quietly.

Grace climbed in and found herself in roughly the same spot she'd been sleeping in before Jasper came crashing through the window. Jasper laid on her back, eyes already shut, but as Grace tried to make herself comfortable next to her, Jasper's head turned toward her. Her eyes opened for a brief moment, and the weakest semblance of a smile crossed her face before she was out.

Holly climbed in under the blankets behind Grace, and Grace felt a strange comfort in the feeling of being surrounded. And the sounds of the others' breathing. It briefly reminded her of the sleepover they'd had on Cutthroat's deck the night they watched the alignment of Hatu's moons.

Grace couldn't be sure, but she thought she was the last to fall asleep. Jasper was out instantly, and though Grace was concerned, she hoped that meant Jasper was getting some well-needed rest. The others' breathing patterns became slow and steady over the next few minutes.

Finally, sleep took Grace, too.

Grace seemed to be the first to wake as well. But she wasn't the first to get up or even move. She lay perfectly still in the light of the morning sun, anxiously watching an unconscious Jasper lie equally unmoving in the dawn's rays, save for the rise and fall of her chest.

Eventually, Holly stirred first and hopped out of bed. "I'm gonna go get breakfast started," she said to anyone who was listening. "Hopefully she'll be feeling well enough to eat."

Thea and Dax were apparently awake by that point, because they began moving, too. Thea climbed out of bed and followed Holly out. Dax took a moment to check under the bandage on Jasper's arm before heading after them.

That was enough to make Jasper stir, but her eyes remained closed. Finally, after a couple of minutes, Grace spoke.

"How are you feeling?"

Jasper opened one eye. "A lot."

"Bad, I'm guessing?"

"Physically? Yes, terrible. But waking up and seeing you instead of that prison cell?" A small smile crossed Jasper's lips. "Best feeling in the world."

Grace's face flushed. Despite Jasper's easy—albeit a little sleepy—expression, despite the fact that things should have been just as they were before, there was that *thing* that happened right before Jasper was taken.

After a painfully tense moment, Jasper laughed. Grace's brow furrowed. "What?"

"Holly cried and the rest of you didn't." Her tone was clearly teasing, and there was a smirk at the corner of her mouth.

"I—I was just so shocked," Grace said, laughing slightly herself. "I still am, I think. I hope this isn't a dream I'm going to wake up from."

"Me neither."

"Besides," Grace added. "I cried when they arrested you."

Jasper smirked again. "That's not the only thing you did."

Right. Grace cleared her throat and shifted her gaze toward the ceiling. "Yeah, I, uh—hope that was okay. That I kissed you, I mean."

"Grace, you know how I feel." Jasper pushed herself up with a groan. "There's, um—a lot going on right now, though. Physically. And mentally. And emotionally. And maybe spiritually, too, my first cellmate was a little preachy. Anyway, point is, right now I just want to be…around you. With you. And with everyone. But I'm not sure I can handle much…intensity, yet." She grimaced.

Grace nodded. She'd waited months for Jasper. If Jasper needed her to wait a little longer, she could do that. And she wasn't sure she was ready to rush anything either. She'd never felt this way before in her life. It was…overwhelming.

"Wanna head out to the kitchen?" Jasper asked. "I thought I heard Holly say something about food."

"Sure thing." Grace slid off the bed. "Need help walking?"

Jasper landed on her feet next to Grace with a grunt. "I'm alright."

Still, it was a slow walk to the kitchen. Grace resisted the urge to help her, or move too close, or—

"You don't have to treat me like I'm contagious," Jasper said with a laugh.

Grace managed a weak chuckle in return. She eased closer as the two neared the end of the hall, but still not close enough to touch.

Jasper shot her another glance. "You're injured, too."

Grace fought back a grimace. "Not as bad as you."

"That's not saying much. Did you get into a fight?" Jasper's expression darkened.

Yes. A lot of them. "I just got scraped up pulling some people from a car accident. I'm fine."

To Grace's relief, Jasper dropped the matter after that. And as they entered the kitchen, she laughed again. "I wasn't dreaming, was I?" she asked. "Holly, you cried last night. Over me. Your annoying, exasperating, insufferable leader."

Thea was pulling dishes from the cupboard, Dax was digging around in the fridge, and Holly stood at the stove warming something up in a pan. Holly huffed and turned around. "Well, yeah, Jasper, maybe I cried a little. Sorry for caring about your safety!"

"I'm the one who should be sorry." Jasper's tone softened. She settled into a seat at the counter. "To all of you. But I had to do this, and...I really didn't think you would let me go if you knew."

"You were trying to save your own life. Of course we understand." Holly turned back to her pan. "Now shut up before you make me cry again," she muttered quieter.

"So, speaking of you trying to save your own life," Thea said, setting a stack of plates on the counter. "Are you ready to tell us what you found out in the Shark Tank?"

"Yessiree," Jasper replied as Grace sat down next to her. "There's a cure waiting for me in Sky Labs. It's called ThetaEight. Should be sitting on a shelf in their storage room."

Holly shot her an incredulous look. "Oh, just sitting on a shelf? Yeah, I bet we'll be able to walk right in and take that."

Frowning, Dax turned away from the fridge. "So, in order to fix you, we have to...break into Sky Labs?"

"We will," Jasper confirmed. "It won't be easy, but it's not impossible. I already have a few ideas. I need to know all the resources at our disposal, though." She leaned forward. "What's been happening the past couple months? We still got Cutthroat and Sarena?"

Grace and the others exchanged glances. Thea spoke first. "Cutthroat seems pretty on board with helping us, still," she said slowly. "Sarena...I think she's with us, though she's been busy with pop star stuff."

"And she complains a lot when she's here," Holly added with a roll of her eyes.

Dax came to the counter with a bottle of Nova Cora and a jug of water. "And we've got Aymes."

Jasper raised an eyebrow. She shot the Nova Cora bottle a look but didn't reach for it. "Aymes Bell?"

"Yep. He showed up right after you got arrested saying he wanted to help. He's been a bit secretive the past couple weeks, but I think he's been working on a few plans of his own. And practicing his abilities."

"Still, the only people who go in and out of the labs are heavily vetted scientists and security guards, right?" Thea asked. "We can't scam our way in like we do most other places."

Holly nodded in agreement, eyes narrowing. "And even if Cutthroat and Sarena bring their henchpeople to help, too, I'm not sure we can brute force our way in and out. We might find what we need, but Governor Starr will send backup the moment there's trouble, won't he?"

Jasper pursed her lips. "Can we cut their comms? Thea?"

Thea considered for a moment. "They'll have the best security systems money can buy. With enough prep time, I could get you maybe ten minutes. I wouldn't count on more than five, though."

Jasper lifted an eyebrow. "Well, then we'll have to keep them from finding out there's trouble until it's too late." She swept her gaze over the team. "I think Holly should come in with me with her shapeshifting. And to avoid drawing too much attention, it should be just the two of us."

Grace's heart quickened at the thought of the two of them going in alone. Memories of her own escape from Sky Labs flashed in her mind. She didn't remember much of the inside, but there had been a lot of guards. A lot of shooting.

"What can the rest of us do from outside to help?" Thea asked. "Besides my hacking, of course."

Jasper rubbed her forehead. With a slight groan, she said, "I don't know. We'll need a quick escape."

"Cutthroat could bring the Astronomer escape pods," Grace suggested.

Thea nodded. "And I know you only want you and Holly, but Sarena's persuasive voice might help."

Jasper rested her elbows on the counter, pressed the tips of her fingers together, leaned further forward. Grace watched her brow furrow in concentration, watched her think. Come up with a plan, like she always did.

"I have a better idea than Thea getting into their cameras and risking their techs catching us in their system," Jasper finally said. She straightened up. "Let's have Aymes send in a bug. Remember the way Ringmaster used to make animal spies with birds and stuff?"

"And Sarena?" Grace pressed, really wanting there to be another person to fight with Jasper and Holly if things went bad.

"I still just want me and Holly on the inside. We'll keep her on standby. I plan on slipping out unnoticed, but we'll have Cutthroat ready an escape pod, too."

"And the rest of us?"

"Also on standby." Jasper glanced at Grace and gave her a reassuring smile, apparently seeing her anxiety all over her face. "If this goes well, we won't need help."

Grace nodded. At the beginning of all this, she would have loved nothing more than to stand on the sidelines and watch the team do all the work. Now, the thought made her anxious. But she had to trust Jasper. Jasper had broken out of the Shark Tank, for stars' sake.

She could get in and out of anything.

Chapter Six
Dark Skies

While the plan Jasper laid out over the next half hour or so sounded fairly straightforward, Grace was still intimidated by the whole idea. Old memories were resurfacing with more ferocity now. Her narrow escape. The scientist who'd saved her getting shot. Meeting Syrus Starr.

Jasper's confidence could only get them so far.

"When are we doing this?" Holly finally asked, twirling a fork between her fingers. The team had long since cleared their plates of breakfast but had been too occupied with planning to move onto cleaning things up. Grace, Jasper, and Dax sat at counter seats, while Holly sat on the edge of the counter and Thea paced on the other side, scrolling through data on her tablet.

Jasper lifted her right arm and gave a slight wince. "Ideally, tomorrow. I don't want to push myself, but I can't sit around waiting to fully heal when that might not happen. At a certain point, I'm just going to keep getting worse." As she rubbed her shoulder, she switched topics. "So, what's Skybreaker been up to?"

The reminder of Skybreaker's very existence made Grace's stomach turn. She blew out a heavy breath of air. "Killing people. Mostly villains, but...not always."

Jasper's jaw clenched. "How many?"

"About one a week, for the villains. Some who survived the races started turning up dead around the star system pretty much right after you were arrested." Grace glanced at Thea. "Could you bring up some of her messages?"

Thea nodded and pulled a smartsphere from her pocket. While she set it on the counter and brought up a holoscreen, Jasper asked, "Messages?"

"She left messages with the victims' bodies," Grace explained. "Police tried hiding them from the public, but Thea was able to pull files from the precincts. Skybreaker too, apparently, because she leaked them herself about a month in. Oh, and then bombed one of the precincts involved in the coverup."

Thea nodded as she brought up an image of a bloodstained sidewalk. The body responsible wasn't in view, but a message scribbled on the pavement with some kind of marker was. *I will continue to destroy. If you are in my path, change the world before you are no longer in it.*

"Short but sweet," Jasper muttered.

"Not all of them are, uh, quite so cryptic," Grace said as Jasper continued to study the message. "Some of the others made it clearer she intends to kill anyone she considers a villain unless they start using their power for good."

"Well, I don't know much about these particular villains, but I'm not opposed to using that strategy on Starr and the other elite. I assume it gets worse?"

"Yeah, well, she started setting fires to some chain stores, too. Mota Marts, for example. Leaves behind similar messages taking about what a plague the company is on the planet." Grace's hands tightened into fists on the table. "That got a lot more people hurt."

Jasper sighed. "I almost get it. I've fantasized about burning down nearly every Mota Mart I've walked into. But not while innocent people were inside. God, why doesn't she just...do it at night while they're closed, at least? Or better yet, go after the headquarters and their CEO, if she really wants to hurt the company."

"No idea," Grace replied. "But it seems like she's not brave enough to do anything in the upper districts. Maybe she's worried Starr will figure out it's her if she does."

Jasper nodded slowly. "Could be. He might not even care much about Skybreaker right now. But attacking the upper districts would change that." After a long moment, she sighed again. "I just wish I knew why she's working with him in the first place. What does she need from him at this point?"

"Believe me, I wanted to ask her. But even when I got to her fires fast enough to save people, she was always long gone."

Jasper shot Grace a look that bordered on horrified. "You were trying to go after her?"

"Doesn't matter." Grace shrugged. "Never even got close." Despite Jasper's reaction, she wished she'd gotten closer to Skybreaker. Maybe it was stupid, but Grace was certain she could handle a short fight with her. And with Holly, Dax, and Thea prepared to intervene, with the various plans the team had come up with in case of an encounter, they might have even been able to capture her.

"She's still working for Starr, then?" Jasper asked, pulling Grace from her thoughts.

Thea chimed in. "Yep. Still accompanying him pretty much everywhere as Subject Eighteen. I guess she's acting as his bodyguard. Seems like an intimidation tactic on his part."

"He's been giving a lot of big speeches lately," Dax added. "Talking about crime reform and squashing big criminal operations."

Jasper raised an eyebrow. "Really?"

Holly let out a short laugh. "Yeah, he was really counting on your execution to hammer that point home."

"Speaking of, there's been no word on the news about your escape, yet," Thea said. She dismissed her sphere's holoscreen with a wave of her hand and returned it to her pocket.

"Well, they won't be able to keep it under wraps forever, right?" Jasper laughed. "I mean, they have no one to kill on camera in a couple days."

"Yeah, Starr doesn't have much time to come up with a way to spin this."

"Well, I guess we'll see what he says." After a moment's consideration, Jasper continued. "Anyway, I wonder what Skybreaker's waiting for. She seemed to have big plans. I thought for sure she'd have taken some kind of action against Starr by now."

"Maybe she was waiting for your execution," Grace suggested.

Jasper frowned. "Maybe. I don't know, something just doesn't seem right." She shook her head. "Guess we'll just have to wait and see." Then, glancing up, she asked, "I'm assuming Starr emptied out that lab on Reo?"

"Yep," Thea answered. "It was cleaned out within hours. No idea where Starr took the weapons and cyborgs. I'm trying to dig up information, but I haven't found anything on satellites or cameras anywhere, yet."

Holly slid off the counter and began picking up the dirty plates scattered across it. "We are low on groceries. Thea, Dax, and I were planning on running out to grab a few things today." Her gaze darted to Grace. "Grace, you up for keeping an eye on Jasper?"

Grace nodded. "Yeah. I got it."

"Call us if she starts dying or anything."

"Will do."

As the three began pulling on shoes, Jasper's face lit up. "Hey, can you guys grab a Christmas tree while you're out?"

Holly paused and shot her a blank stare. "A what?"

"Oh, right, that's coming up." Dax glanced at Thea. "I didn't realize they celebrated here." Thea shrugged.

"It's not just Christmas on the Earth calendar," Jasper replied. "Kronos's winter is aligning with Earth's winter! Well, Earth's northern hemisphere and Kronos's southern hemisphere, which is where most of Kronos lives—look, my point is, the human communities here have made the Christmas holiday an actual thing when the seasons line up like this, so they should be selling generic winter holiday decorations in most stores now. I haven't celebrated Christmas in...a long time." Some of the enthusiasm slipped from Jasper's expression. But she replaced it a moment later with a wide smile. "Come on, we should make the apartment a little festive!"

"Okay, fine, we'll get a tree thing. But only because you almost got executed." Holly shrugged on her jacket and grabbed the door handle. "We'll call Cutthroat, Sarena, and Aymes too. See if they have time to come by later and discuss the plan for Sky Labs."

As the three filed out and closed the door behind them, Grace glanced at Jasper. "What is Christmas, exactly?" she asked. "I've heard of it, but I don't know exactly what it is besides a holiday."

"Humans coming to space started spreading it out here over a century ago," Jasper explained. "Technically, it's a religious thing, but out here on Kronos that all kinda got dropped. People just care about decorating and giving gifts and caroling. You'll see once we get closer."

"What day is it?"

"Uh, the Earth date is December twenty-fifth. I'll have to take a look at the calendar and see what Kronos day that is."

"Oh, I can figure it out," Grace told her, straightening up. "That's just about three weeks away."

Jasper nodded. "Like I said, I haven't been able to celebrate since I was back on Earth. It'll be nice to have people to celebrate it with again." She smiled.

Grace returned the smile. "Well, whatever you need us to do to make it a good holiday, just let us know."

"You don't all have to be extra nice to me just because I almost got executed," Jasper replied with a short laugh.

"That might be hard to do." Despite Jasper trying to brush the matter off with a joke, Grace felt her throat tighten. Her voice quieted. "It was a hard couple of months. I mean, I'm sure it was much worse for you, but..."

"I know." Jasper swallowed. "I'm just glad we're all together again."

Grace nodded. "Me too."

She found herself leaning in again and stopped herself. Jasper was in pain, Jasper had been through a lot, Jasper needed to rest. So instead, Grace slid off her stool. "Did you want something to drink? I could pour some of the soda in a cup for you." She glanced at the Nova Cora bottle Dax had left on the counter.

Jasper waved a hand. "You can put the Nova Cora back. I'm good for now. Water would be great, though."

Grace obliged. Then, she settled in on the couch in the living room, opened her tablet, and began scouring news channels.

"Any news about me?" Jasper called from the counter.

Grace shook her head. "Still nothing." She switched from news to some game show that involved people being dunked in tanks of neon goo and turned the volume down, letting the broadcast fade into background noise.

"So, what all have you guys been up to while I was gone?" Jasper asked. "You mentioned talking to Cutthroat and Sarena and Aymes. And Dax said something about Aymes practicing with his powers?"

Grace blew out a breath of air, mulling over the work the team had been doing. The work they'd thrown themselves into after Jasper was taken to the Shark Tank. "Yeah, we've been pretty focused on Starr. Once we're done with Sky Labs and ready to focus on him directly, we can go over everything we've learned. Thea's been working on cracking the palace tech, and the rest of us...well, we had a few ideas."

Chapter Seven
Previously On Van Terra, Part 1

One month after Jasper's arrest, Dax found himself staring down rows of hospital beds. A leaky faucet somewhere nearby put out a persistent dripping noise, an off-beat accompaniment to the beeping of machinery. There was a faint smell, too, like someone had left food in a corner somewhere and let it go bad.

Dax rubbed a hand along the stiff long-sleeved black undershirt he was wearing, finding both it and the matching pants beneath his outer layer slightly uncomfortable. But Thea knew what she was doing, and if the wiring and circuitry hidden in the cloth could somehow give her information about his powers—and how to improve them—he would take her word for it.

Slowly but surely, he was expanding the distance at which he could heal. And he was learning how to apply his power to multiple people at once. What he really needed though was more practice transferring the healed ailments to others, if he was going to be of any use in a big fight. It wasn't exactly easy to find test subjects, though.

"And you said you've volunteered with us before, Dasher?" the nurse next to Dax asked.

He nodded, absentmindedly adjusting the volunteer nametag with the fake name he'd offered upon checking in. He used a different one at each hospital. "A couple times earlier this month."

"Great. We'll just have you walk down the aisle and take meal orders." She held out a clipboard, the sheet on top containing a list of names and several food options to choose from.

"Sure thing." As Dax accepted the clipboard from her, he added. "Sorry if you mentioned this earlier, I didn't catch it. What kind of patients are these?" He shot a glance down the aisle ahead of him.

It wasn't an odd question to ask. Any volunteer with an ounce of self-awareness would probably behave a bit differently among people dealing with broken arms or common viruses as opposed to those with terminal illnesses.

"It's a trauma wing," the nurse replied, her voice lowering. "They're all expected to recover, eventually, but many will have long-term complications."

Dax pressed his lips into a thin line and nodded. The longer someone had an injury or illness, the harder it was for him to do anything, he'd come to learn as he'd spent more time with long-term patients the past few weeks. Permanent damage was incredibly resistant to whatever energy he poured into people's bodies, and amputated limbs seemed impossible to affect at all.

"Any questions?" the nurse asked.

Dax hesitated a moment, then said, "I think I'm good. I was curious, though... Have you heard the rumors about Remedy going around?"

"The superhero?"

Dax's heart skipped a beat at being called that. It was...technically true, he supposed, but after so many years being considered part of Jasper Van Terra's team, it just didn't seem *right*.

The nurse continued, her voice quiet but eager. "Yes, my friend is a nurse at once of the hospitals he visited. He's real! I'm sure it must be impossible for him to heal everyone, I just wish..." she trailed off and sighed. "I wish he could."

"I wish that, too." Dax flexed his free hand at his side. He'd tried to do an entire hospital, once, instead of just one wing. Just a week after Jasper's arrest. He'd made it through half a floor before passing out. The rest of the team had to carry him home, and he'd slept for sixteen hours afterward.

Dax surveyed the beds again, feeling bad for the patients all crammed together in one room. There were private rooms elsewhere in the building, but it was still a lower district hospital. People who had less money were put in big rooms together to reduce their bills to something they might actually pay off eventually.

The nurse left to attend to other matters, and Dax set off down the aisle. As he circled food options on the clipboard, he would point the finger resting under the board toward the patient and channel his power toward them. No one seemed to notice the faint blue glow at his fingertip. But within a few days, their doctors would *hopefully* realize that the healing process was coming along faster than it should have. Dax tried to balance the energy he was putting into each person, not using up too much of his strength while still giving individuals enough of a boost to actually make a difference. Hopefully, it would be enough to prevent at least some permanent damage, for a few patients.

At the far end of the room, Dax eventually came to a stop in front of the youngest patient yet. A young Kronosian boy with velvety blue fur and large batlike ears. Around ten years old, maybe? The woman at the boy's bedside—his mother, presumably—looked up as Dax approached. Her fur was redder in tone than her son's.

"Hey there," Dax said, causing the boy to look up from the ancient-looking tablet he was watching something animated on. "Want anything to eat, Verren?"

Verren looked to his mom, who smiled encouragingly. "You hungry, sweetie? I think I heard someone order an ichthy mash."

Dax nodded. "We have that."

Verren perked up. "I'll have that," he said, glancing back up at Dax.

As Dax circled the corresponding option next to Verren's name, he eyed the cast on the boy's leg. Could he pour enough energy into him to heal up the bone in a matter of minutes rather than days? He didn't want to try something like this on deep wounds that had already been stitched up, fearing the stitches would get stuck and cause more trouble during the removal process, but this boy's bone had already been set into the correct position. All he needed was time.

Time, or...

Dax pushed most of what he had left into this final burst of energy, mentally channeling it from the tip of his finger to Verren's leg. The light never left his finger, its glow remaining hidden behind the clipboard as he shifted it to hide the glow from view. He wasn't sure why the glow stayed on his skin when some kind of power was clearly being transferred away from him to the person he was healing. Maybe Thea would be able to figure it out.

So far, it seemed that the more energy he put into healing someone, the more severe that wound or sickness would be when he inflicted it on someone else. Which meant that this broken leg could be one of his most severe attacks yet, if he chose to use it. But the energy pattern—a term Thea had started using—would fade from his body's memory after a few days if he didn't inflict it on someone.

Dax turned away from Verren and crossed the aisle to the final patient. He took the woman's order, gave her what healing energy he could, then left the wing to hand the clipboard off to the kitchen. After that, he slipped out of the hospital and headed south down Violet Avenue, which had earned the lovely nickname Violent Avenue for reasons that weren't hard to guess.

As he walked, Dax tapped his comm to unmute it. "Leaving the hospital, Thea. You seeing any data yet?"

"Yep. I'll take a closer look when I'm done running this poke on the palace network."

Dax nodded absentmindedly, wondering if this poke would be any different than the dozens of others Thea had attempted. They were supposed to give her a sense of how many security measures the Governor's Palace had on its wireless systems, but so far, she'd only hit dead ends. She'd already thrown out the idea of going there in person to try to tap into their systems directly, but Dax and the others had convinced her not to resort to something that dangerous. Not yet.

Dax continued toward the rundown convenience store Thea had flagged as the headquarters of an up-and-coming gang calling themselves the Gunheads. The windows were all boarded up, and the glass front door had been replaced with a metal one. The gang was a small group so far, with only about twenty members. Far too many for Dax to handle alone, maybe even too much for the team without Jasper, if they were caught by surprise.

So, Thea had identified their patrol patterns—the patrol in question covering about ten blocks—and the time of day when there were the fewest members present inside the base. The gang as a whole still had a lot to learn about managing territory, it seemed.

"I'm on the balcony of the bar across the street," Grace said over comms.

Dax glanced in that direction and gave a single nod. "Thanks. But...I want to try doing this myself first."

"Roger that, Remedy. Good luck."

Dax smiled. "Thanks, Superangel. I'll call if I need you."

Grace's distant figure gave him a thumbs up. There was an awkwardness to how she moved the arm that suggested another new injury. Probably from her fight with those bank robbers this morning. They hadn't been superpowered, but there had been a lot of them.

Part of Dax wanted to run over and heal her up immediately, but he needed to save his energy for the fight he was about to walk into. Besides, if it were really bad, Grace would have said something. So, he turned, walked up to the front door of the convenience store, and tugged on it. Locked. He could just make out the faint sound of voices coming from inside the building. He took a moment to steel himself. Then, he knocked.

Silence fell on the other side of the door. A moment later, footsteps approached, and the door cracked. "What the hell do you think you're doing, man?" The man on the other side of the door was tan-skinned and looked almost human, save for his unnaturally long limbs.

Dax rolled his shoulders. "You the Gunheads?"

The man's eyes narrowed. He started to push the door shut again, but Dax had already slipped the blade of a dagger into the gap. "Five of you in there right now, right?" he asked, his voice coming out strangely chipper. He didn't think he'd be any good at sounding intimidating, so he didn't bother. He knew he sure didn't look it.

The Gunhead switched tactics. He pushed the door open farther, grabbed Dax's wrist, and yanked him into the building.

Four men were gathered at a table in the middle of the lobby. Shelves half-filled with food and vehicle maintenance equipment were shoved up against one wall, and wrappers littered the rest of the floor. At least half of the overhead lights were out. Some from dead bulbs, others due to being shattered completely.

The other men were playing twin suns, but they quickly dropped their cards on the table and rose to their feet as the fifth member dragged Dax toward them. All five wore similar clothing: black underlayers with metal mesh jackets and pants over top. Their boots looked like they were completely made of steel. Great for foot protection. Not so great for moving fast.

"Well, what do you think we should do with this guy?" the Gunhead who'd greeted Dax asked. "He's apparently too good to mind his own business."

"Other people's business is so much more interesting than mine, though." Dax lifted the hand that wasn't being held in a vice grip by the gang member. His fist clenched.

The men at the table collapsed one by one, each gasping or yelping in pain as they went down. The man next to Dax shouted in alarm. He reached for the dagger in Dax's hand, and Dax wasn't strong enough to pull his arm free. Instead, he focused his power on the man, this time pulling something more specific than the random assortment of fractures and wounds he'd healed earlier. The moment the man yanked the dagger free from Dax's grip, Dax pushed a multitude of fractured hand bones onto him.

The Gunhead screamed, and the dagger dropped. For a moment, all Dax could do was cringe at what he'd done. He had no qualms about it in theory, but actually watching someone's bones break, their insides churn with illness...it wasn't easy. Not for him, anyway. The first few times he'd used this aspect of his power, the adrenaline of the fights he'd been in had somewhat distracted him from his discomfort. But now that he was getting more comfortable with being front and center in combat, he had this new struggle to grapple with.

Then, despite his obvious pain, the Gunhead was diving for his dagger as it skidded across the floor, and Dax needed to act. He went for the blade, too, and the man switched directions. He grabbed Dax with his uninjured hand and shoved him hard.

The man was stronger than Dax had expected. Dax flew back a few feet, then his back hit something hard poking out of the wall. The light switch. And just like that, the world went black.

And then he saw it. The blue glow. Not on his own hands, but in the man's broken hand, faintly emitting from under his skin. Dax probably wouldn't have noticed it if the lights hadn't gone out.

So that's how the glowing worked when things were reversed.

The glow faded, and footsteps started toward Dax in the dark. He needed something more debilitating to keep the man off him. He recalled healing the young boy at the hospital, putting so much of his energy into healing the leg. He grabbed for that energy pattern, its imprint in his mind, and he shoved it back at the Gunhead.

The glow was a bit more noticeable this time, though Dax still doubted it would have been visible in full light. It was at the bottom of the man's pant leg...maybe if he weren't wearing pants?

A heartbeat after the glow began, there was a sickening crack, and the man screamed again and collapsed. Doing his best to ignore the churning in his stomach, Dax fumbled behind him for the light switch, and the interior of the gang's headquarters brightened again.

"Stop harassing and stealing from the people who live around here," Dax said. "Or I'll come back with my friends."

He walked out the front door, leaving it unlocked. "All clear," he said into comms as he emerged. "I might not have to fully heal someone to inflict their injury on someone else, but I think it makes a difference. Like, it doesn't take as much energy. That last leg break I threw out felt a lot easier."

"I'll check the output data and see if I can verify that," Thea replied.

Dax crossed the street, and as he reached the sidewalk on the other side, Grace glided down from the balcony above, wearing her full Superangel costume. A bruise that had appeared a few days earlier still clung faintly to her jaw, and there were some fresh scrapes on her cheek. Dax had to resist the urge to throw his healing power at her, knowing she'd protest that it was a waste of energy on such minor wounds.

"Word's already spreading about what you did at the hospital," she said. "A kid whose leg was broken after falling off a balcony yesterday walked home without so much as a fracture today."

Dax smiled. "They use the name Remedy in the news?"

"Yup." Grace managed a faint smile back, but it didn't do much to combat the fatigue in her expression. "Hey, if we get the others to start doing hero stuff in the news, we could come up with a team name."

Dax thought for a moment. "Jasper and the Neoworms."

"Ha. That sounds more like a band name than a hero team name."

"Maybe. She'd like it though."

Grace turned her head toward the sky, her expression turning wistful. "Yeah. She would."

Chapter Eight
Previously On Van Terra, Part 2

Even hours before sunrise, the Governor's Palace was busy. Holly lay on her stomach on a roof nearby, catching glimpses of ships approaching and leaving the palace through the sky traffic passing between her and the building. The palace's iridescent exterior, dark blue stained-glass windows, and white-flecked matching blue dome still managed to be ridiculously shiny even without the full light of the sun overhead.

Holly shouldn't have been here. Not being able to sleep was a decent enough excuse for walking around at night, but coming all the way up here? As if she were actually going to *do* anything?

Except...there were a lot of rather plain-looking workers walking in. There was a security check, sure, but it seemed to amount to looking at people's faces and making sure they matched their ID badge. The extensive background checks were performed long before anyone set foot in the palace. Catering and cleaning crews were all carefully vetted.

But once someone was approved on paper...would it really be as easy as borrowing their face and slipping in with the rest of their coworkers? Holly shifted her binoculars to the air traffic stream. A carrier with the logo for a cleaning service was slowing, preparing to make the turn toward the palace.

She rose to her feet slowly, part of her brain screaming at her to move before its other half could reconsider. Thea's pokes had all been failing, and so had her attempts at social engineering a way in. Maybe she'd trick a palace employee into giving her access codes eventually, but they'd ignored her phishing attempts so far. And while her hacking skills were fantastic, her technopathy didn't do much long-distance. She'd have to put herself in danger to enter the palace and access their systems directly, and even that didn't guarantee success.

But Holly, who could hide behind another face…she might be able to find something. Get out a piece of tech that Thea could use to make a connection with the rest of the palace's systems, maybe.

Holly raced down the building's fire escape and across skywalks, keeping an eye on the cleaning company vehicle above as it veered toward the palace. The closest skywalk to the palace didn't extend all the way to the building, what with it only being accessible by air traffic and all. But as she drew closer, she noticed that not every vehicle was given clearance to fly directly to the palace. Most were landing on a parking pad hovering just at the edge of the traffic stream. Directly above the skywalk she was on.

It was a high jump. But as Holly had learned in the past few weeks, her physiology was even more flexible than she'd once thought. She made her form more similar to that of one of the lower Kronosian species, her legs lengthening, focusing on strengthening the musculature there alone. When she pushed herself up off the skywalk, she easily went up ten feet.

It wasn't quite enough to land on the parking pad, but it was enough for her to grab its edge. She couldn't truly increase her overall strength when she shapeshifted like this, but she could redistribute it on a cellular level. In this temporary form she'd created, while her arms looked about as muscular as her legs, they were actually significantly weaker, with random tissue giving the illusion of muscle rather than true muscle.

Holly reversed the shift in strength and pulled herself up onto the pad. There were lights over, of course, but if Holly kept to the edge with a layer of black fur over her body, she was all but unnoticeable. She added a pair of large ears to ensure she resembled a common Kronosian species, then began surveying the parked vehicles.

The cleaning carrier was touching down near the north end of the pad, and palace security teams seemed to be moving up and down the parking spots, checking vehicles one at a time before allowing them to continue on to the palace. While some guards surveyed the insides of carriers and poked through supplies, others compared ID cards to faces and examined paperwork.

There weren't any teams near the cleaning company vehicle at the moment, so Holly hurried over to it as employees piled out and waited for security to come check them in. One woman lingered at the edge of the group, reading something on her smartsphere's holoscreen. She was the same species Holly was currently pretending to be, only with brighter magenta fur.

Holly grabbed the woman's arm, clapped a hand over her mouth, and pulled her around to the other side of the vehicle. "I'm not going to hurt you," she said quietly. Then, she slowly removed her hand from the woman's mouth, and when the woman didn't scream, Holly relaxed slightly.

"Who are you?" the woman whispered, her voice shaky.

"Not your business. What's your name, and how much do you make in a day's work?" Holly asked.

"Jella. And, uh, fifty janos."

Yikes. That was all the palace cleaning crews got paid? "I'll transfer five hundred to you right now," Holly said, pulling out her smartsphere. "If you give me a little information. Oh, and let me borrow your ID card. And your uniform. And your face."

Five minutes later, Holly was climbing into the cleaning crew vehicle with the rest of the employees. Jella was on her way home after Holly had jumped back down to the skywalk with her, promising to have her ID card returned to her by the end of the day so she could come back to work tomorrow.

The carrier vehicle went directly to a palace landing pad this time, and the crew was led into the palace without so much as another glance from security. One guard remained with them to lead them to an elevator and send them down a few floors, but after that, they were on their own. When they reached their destination, Holly stepped out of the elevator and surveyed the hallway they'd entered.

"Jella!"

Holly turned, recognizing the name the woman she'd shapeshifted into had given her. "Yes?"

The woman who'd spoken—who seemed to be the cleaning crew's manager—held out a mop and a bucket. "Get the offices down that hallway today." She nodded toward the hallway behind Holly.

Holly accepted the cleaning instruments. "Sure."

"Watch out for AstraSweeps. Apparently one of them has some kind of bug and isn't returning to the charging docks with the rest. Just put it up on a table if you see it."

AstraSweeps? Holly just nodded. She'd probably be able to figure out what one was if she saw it.

She turned around and headed into the first room in the hallway. Just an office with shiny quartz floors and a big fancy desk. She eyed the desk carefully as she mopped. What the hell was she even looking for, though? She didn't know enough about computers to know what would help Thea.

You got in. You know you can get in with the morning crews. That's something.

Still, Holly kept an eye out as she moved from room to room. After running through five more offices, she found herself in a break room. And smack dab in the middle of the floor between the tables and the kitchen area was a roughly laptop-sized, square-shaped...thing?

Holly set the mop and bucket down and moved forward. It was some kind of machine, for sure. Red in color. Its corners were rounded too, and there was a tiny screen on the top displaying the text *signal lost. sweeping cycle paused.*

Was this the AstraSweep? A tiny robot that swept? As Holly bent down to pick the thing up, she nearly stopped to smack her own forehead. She'd seen these things before, back when she'd been a kid in the Faye Penthouse. They'd been a bit bigger than this one, though, and they'd had a bunch of buttons. And they hadn't ended up getting used very much. She suspected her parents preferred the aesthetic of cleaning crews in neat uniforms to the zigzagging robots.

"Here you go, little guy," Holly said as she set the cleaning robot on one of the break room tables. Part of her wanted to roll her eyes at her own words. It's not as if the thing could hear her. Or care, if it could.

Holly turned to face the kitchen, and her brow furrowed. There was a toaster, a refrigerator, a mini oven, and a stovetop. But not a button or dial in sight. "Why don't any of these appliances have buttons?" she muttered.

Footsteps entered the room to her left, making her start. "Sorry, Jell," the man who'd entered said. "Didn't mean to startle you. I'm taking my break a little early." He pulled some kind of food wrap from his pocket, tore off its outer plastic, and tossed it in the mini oven. After closing the door, he pulled his smartsphere from his pocket. The holoscreen popped up, he tapped something on it, and the mini oven came to life with a hum.

Holly blinked. She wanted to ask how the guy had done it but didn't want to risk blowing her cover if it was supposed to be something everyone here knew. She scrambled for an idea and found one. "Hey, I left my sphere in one of the other offices—think you could run that for thirty seconds for me when you're done?"

"Sure." The man turned. "What are you heating up?"

Shoot. Holly glanced around the sparse break room, looking for an idea. She spotted a few cups upside down on a dish drying rack. "Um—just some water. My throat's a little sore. From the temperature changes, you know.

Always happens to me this part of the starcycle." She moved forward and snatched up one of the cups.

"Oh, sure, that happens to my brother," the man replied while Holly filled the cup at the sink.

When the mini oven beeped to announce that the man's food was done, he took it out, then held the door open for Holly to place the cup of water inside.

This time, Holly moved closer so that she could see his holoscreen while he activated the appliance. The man launched an application with an icon of a gold star on a black background, with gold lightning dancing around it. He tapped "mini oven 9928" in the menu that opened, then selected the number thirty from a list of options that followed.

Well, that explained how to use the damn things. But there really weren't any buttons? Not even as a backup? What if your sphere died, or you forgot to bring it with you to the break room? Or there were connection issues?

Holly forced a chuckle. "I still can't believe these things. Wish I could afford one."

"Right?" the man laughed. "I'm saving up to get my wife one of the AstraSweeps for Christmas, but I think an AstraBake is a ways away."

What a creative product naming system. Holly raised an eyebrow. "You celebrate Christmas?" She immediately kicked herself. She had no idea what Jella's relationship with this man was. What if she was supposed to know that already?

Thankfully, the man didn't seem put off by the question. "Yeah, my wife's ancestors are from Earth. They passed the tradition down to her and, well, our kids love it. I mean, pretty much everyone throws a party for it these days, but we actually do the gift thing, too."

Right. Christmas had become...trendy, for lack of a better word, on Kronos in recent starcycles. For the elite, it was another excuse to throw big parties. For the lower districts, it was a bright spot in a somewhat dreary existence.

The mini oven beeped again. Holly took the cup out and, not really seeing any other option, took a sip. "Thank you," she told the man.

"Sure thing. I'll find an office to eat in so I don't bother you while you're mopping." He waved a hand and walked out of the room.

Holly unmuted the comm hidden in her ear. "Thea, you awake and on comms, by chance?"

"Wide awake," Thea replied. "I build robots when I can't sleep. I imagine you're up to something a little more exciting?"

Holly couldn't help but smirk. "You say that like building robots isn't exciting."

"Not so much when you've done it a million times."

"Fair enough. Hey, have you ever heard of an AstraBake?"

Chapter Nine
Previously On Van Terra, Part 3

Thea threw every box labeled AstraSmart she saw into the shopping cart. By the time she was halfway through the electronics store, she'd already accumulated an AstraBake mini oven, an AstraToast, two AstraSweeps, an AstraBlend, an AstraHome Sphere Hub—whatever that was—and an AstraCool mini fridge.

"AstraSmart was the Janus System's fastest growing tech company last starcycle," she told Holly and Dax as she reached up to grab an AstraPlay speaker. "And their sales are still skyrocketing."

Next to her, Holly folded her arms, while Dax leaned forward to study a different variation of the AstraPlay. "I still don't get the appeal," Holly said. "How is pushing a button on my smartsphere better than pushing a button on the actual thing I'm using?"

Thea shrugged. "Well, you can control stuff from rooms away. Turn your oven on before you get home, turn up the volume on a speaker from the next room, that kind of thing." She glanced down at the box she'd grabbed. There were two key features listed on the box. The first was local connection, so that you could control the speaker from another room. That would be relatively safe, and nearly impossible to hack from a distance.

But the net connection feature…that could be her way in. The devices, for some strange reason, needed constant net access to function. The box said something about always giving you the latest software updates, for your protection. But it also meant if your toaster lost connection to the internet, you couldn't, well, *toast*. And what reason would anyone ever have to turn their toaster on from another room, anyway? Let alone while away from home.

"Okay, fine," Holly said with a huff. "But can't the device itself still have buttons? So I can use it the normal way too?"

"I agree that would make for a much better product." Thea tossed the box in the cart, then grabbed the cart's handle. As she moved further down the aisle, she added, "But the real issue is all the potential security vulnerabilities."

"And how sure are you that those exist?" Dax asked, jogging to catch up to the cart. He tossed another box in, something labeled Astra Sync. Were those...headphones?

"No idea," Thea told him. "AstraSmart could be a company employing the best engineers and any technopath they can find to ensure their code is uncrackable. Or, it could be run by an egomaniac who cares more about looking cool and cranking out new products than writing good code, and who sells ridiculous appliances to rich people by somehow convincing them that everyone else thinks they're classy." She paused at the end of the aisle to examine more products. "Based on the research I've done on the CEO so far...well, I'm leaning the latter."

They eventually took their hoard to the front of the store and checked out the old-fashioned way—they had plenty of money to spare these days, thanks to some side gigs Thea had running online, and the store wasn't part of a particularly large chain, so it was possible the owners weren't The Worst.

Within thirty seconds of returning to the apartment, Thea had half the appliances out of their packages, and half of those cracked open with wires spilling out. A minute later, there was a thud on the balcony, then Grace was walking into the living room in her Superangel costume.

"I'll have a roast and some vegetable mashes ready in about half an hour," Dax told her as dropped onto the couch.

Grace pulled her mask off and leaned back. "I was thinking about just eating a nutrient bar and heading back out, honestly."

"Don't be ridiculous," Holly snapped. "You've been out all morning. Eat some real food and sit down for a while."

Grace grimaced. "I know, I know. I just...like being out there. It's..."

"A nice distraction?" Dax offered.

Grace pressed her lips into a thin line. After a moment, she nodded.

"I don't think your body's going to let you keep doing that indefinitely," Thea pointed out. As the words left her mouth, she glanced down at the mess around her. Did she have room to talk when she passed out each night with eyes blurry from code, hands shaking from plugging in wires? When she'd buffed her smartsphere's waterproof casing so that she could keep working in the shower instead of…thinking?

"Well, maybe we could play a game of twin suns or something?" Grace suggested.

"I'd love to, once food's ready," Dax said.

Holly folded her arms. "Sure, if it'll keep you out of trouble."

Thea picked up one of the AstraSweeps, waving her other hand dismissively as she did. "You guys play without me. I've got work to do."

"Really?" Holly asked, her narrowed eyes turning on Thea. "After the conversation we just had?"

"Okay, but this actually might get us closer to taking Starr down!"

"And do you really think half an hour's going to make a big difference?"

Thea sighed. "All right, all right, I'll join you guys after we eat."

While Dax resumed blending up vegetables with a hand mixer, Thea dug into the sweeping robot's insides, Holly began playing a game on her tablet, and Grace launched a news broadcast on her smartsphere.

"—Starr's latest message after the vigilante Superangel was seen in the Silver District today."

Holly glanced up. "I haven't heard a single news station refer to you as a 'hero' in at least a month. Starr's really wants them to convince people you're dangerous."

Grace nodded, her eyes narrowing as the reporter continued.

"Heroes enforce the law, working side by side with police to maintain order."

Thea rolled her eyes. It had been a long time since Kronos had had any true heroes, from what she'd heard, but surely people knew that wasn't true, right? If it were, heroes would just sign up to be police officers. They wouldn't have code names and costumes to hide their real identities.

Maybe things worked differently here than they did on Earth. But given the way people cheered for Superangel when she appeared, Thea had a feeling that wasn't in case.

"On her vlog this morning, pop star Sarena Trench released a statement about her friendship with Superangel after videos of a concert from earlier this season began circulating again."

"What?" Grace yelped at the same time Holly cursed.

"Why wouldn't she coordinate with us on any statements?" Holly demanded.

Thea gestured with the screwdriver in her hand. "She hasn't exactly been the most cooperative. She cares more about fixing her image than making any progress against Starr." Even though she'd seen with her own two eyes what kind of army he was building. The horrible weapons.

"I haven't been in contact with Superangel lately," Sarena said. "As many of you know, she did save me during a Van Terra attack on the set of Star Conquerors when she was new on the scene, so I did have a good relationship with her then. She seems well-intentioned, but that doesn't mean she can't do real harm with her actions. I hope she does the right thing."

"I don't get it," Dax said. "Despite what Starr's been saying, people in the lower and middle districts love Superangel. Sarena wouldn't lose many fans by continuing to support her."

"You make it sound like she cares about her fans," Holly replied, eyes rolling. "All she cares about are elite parties and brand partnerships. And keeping her name on the list of the top ten wealthiest celebrities."

"Obviously, the people of the lower districts deserve to be just as safe and healthy as those in the upper districts," Sarena continued. "Which is very important to me, and something I talk about on my upcoming album *The Birth of a Revolutionary.*"

"Ha!" Holly's cold laugh echoed around the room. "She's calling it *that*? That's the stupidest thing she's done yet. She can't possibly think that making net posts about how poor people deserve food makes her a revolutionary, can she?"

Grace sighed and turned the volume down on her broadcast. "I'd love to ask her about that next time we see her. Assuming she's not ditching us entirely."

"I won't let her abandon us now. As much as she sucks, she's very useful." Holly glanced back down at her tablet screen and resumed her game. "And if she wants to be a revolutionary, I'll be more than happy to help her with that."

Dax dumped a fresh pile of vegetables into a bowl and shrugged. "Talking about revolution is very trendy right now. Actually doing it is not."

Thea pried another circuit board free from the AstraSweep and found the connection she was looking for. She grabbed a cord attached to her laptop and plugged it in. "Well, if anyone could make it trendy, it would be Sarena," she said. "Her fans nearly flattened a Mota Mart last week trying to buy an exclusive album re-release." A loading symbol appeared on the screen in front of her.

"Not even a new album," Holly muttered. "A stars-damned *re-release.*"

Surprise flashed across Grace's face. "Seriously? I missed that. Was there damage?"

Thea shrugged. "Just some knocked over shelves, smashed merchandise, and broken bathroom sinks, for some reason."

"Huh. I think Sarena might be useful for more than just her powers."

"Jasper had that thought," Holly said, glancing up at Grace again. "But I don't think she likes the idea of throwing innocent people into the crossfire. The most she's done is get that old Starchatter editor Omic Attom a healthy dose of online harassment after putting out that mean article under his name." She shuddered. "Yeah, Sarena's fanbase isn't an enemy I would wish on most people."

Grace shrugged. "I think there's still ways we could get some use out of them without getting anyone innocent hurt. If Sarena's willing to put her reputation on the line."

Holly snorted. "Good luck with that."

The loading symbol vanished from Thea's screen, and chunks of text began loading in. As the higher part of Thea's brain kicked in, processing the code in a way that was more by feeling than by logic, a smile spread across her face.

Chapter Ten
Back To Your Regularly Scheduled Programming

About a month after Holly and Thea had discovered the hacking potential of the AstraSmart network in the palace, Grace and Jasper sat on the couch and watched a terrible game show broadcast until the rest of the team returned with groceries. They also brought home Cutthroat, Aymes, Sarena—with her orange hekten Blitz perched on her shoulder—and a tree. Sort of.

When Jasper hurried to greet them at the front door, she ignored the others and immediately zeroed in on the not-tree. "Holly, this is just a fake plant!" She exclaimed as she took it from Holly's hands. "And it looks like someone shrunk a maple tree." She glanced at Thea and Dax. "You two know what Christmas trees look like, right? Didn't they have any in the stores?"

"We didn't see any. They might not get put out for a couple more pentasols," Dax replied with a shrug. "Christmas is widely celebrated here, but it's not as big and all-consuming as it was in the states on Earth."

"Boo. Did you at least get lights? Ornaments?"

"What for?" Holly asked blankly.

"For decorating—oh, never mind." Jasper sighed. "This is clearly something I'll have to handle myself."

Thea and Dax moved into the kitchen with the groceries. Sarena cleared her throat. Aymes waved awkwardly. While those two were dressed in more casual clothing, Cutthroat wore his usual layers of purple and black leather, though his black overcoat would have likely prevented anyone glancing his way from recognizing him.

"Hello, Jasper," Cutthroat said as he slid off the coat. "Good to see you in one piece."

"Oh, right." Jasper shot the three newcomers a quick glance before carrying the tree into the living room and setting it on the ground next to the couch. She straightened up and turned. "How are you all?"

"How are we?" Cutthroat raised an eyebrow. "You just escaped the Shark Tank. How are you?"

"Fine."

"Recovering from serious injuries!" Dax called from the kitchen.

"But fine, besides that." Jasper collapsed back onto the couch next to Grace. "Thanks for not disappearing on the team. We could really use your help."

"I'm still on the fence about helping you," Sarena said.

"I heard," Jasper muttered. Her head turned. "Aymes, I'm glad you decided to turn up, too."

Aymes nodded. "Me too. However this ends up turning out. I'm doing more good out here than I was in an upper district university."

"What, you trying to get a medal for being a good person, or something?" Sarena asked with a roll of her eyes. The comment went ignored.

"How's your mom?" Jasper asked.

"Good." There was a flash of a grimace in Aymes's expression. "Thinks I'm still enrolled."

Well, that didn't seem to really be Jasper's business. She didn't have any useful advice for Aymes in that department, anyway. Turning to the others, she asked, "So, did my team mention the plan to you guys?"

"They said something about breaking into Sky Labs," Cutthroat replied, scratching at his beard. "A few months ago, I would have called it crazy, but I guess you know what you're doing, given what you just pulled off."

Jasper nodded. "This should be much simpler. And Holly and I will be doing most of the work. Aymes, I will need your eyes and ears, though."

"I can get you a spy into the labs," Aymes replied. "Think a fly will do the trick?"

"It should. There are lots of those down in the sewers, and a few getting into the labs wasn't unheard of while I was there. There were usually a few in the cell block, anyway." Jasper folded her arms. "My last big concern is Skybreaker. If she happens to be in the labs, or gets called in, it'll be hard to fight her, just me and Holly. And getting backup in will be pretty much impossible without making things worse."

"Well, Starr has a rally planned tomorrow," Thea said from the kitchen as she emptied the last shopping bag onto the counter. "Based on what we've seen the last couple months, Subject Eighteen will be there."

"All right, let's start the break-in at the same time the rally starts, then," Jasper said. "And Thea, I want you ready to kill their comms to give us an extra few minutes to get out if anything goes wrong."

"Got it," Thea said. "Best way to do it without risking tipping off their system is to do an area-wide blind kill. But that'll take out your comms, too."

"That's fine." Jasper waved a hand. "You'll immediately work on getting us back online?"

"Sure. Our comm system is much simpler, so I can probably get it back up before Sky Labs gets theirs back online. But no guarantees. It'll be a close race. They probably have at least one technopath."

"I can have an escape pod ready in case you need to get out fast," Cutthroat said. "But I want to know what we're doing after this. There's been a lot of talk about a pretty ambitious takedown of Governor Starr." His gaze flickered briefly to Aymes.

Sarena yawned and patted Blitz's head. "Yeah, I'm gonna need to see some real payoff soon, or I'm dipping."

"You've been saying that for months," Holly muttered.

"And? I'm serious, the whole debacle with supporting Merama against the Fayes and calling Superangel my friend put me in some serious hot water. You know how I've maintained such a big fanbase for so long? By staying out of politics!"

"Lots of people have been praising you for helping Merama and Superangel disrupt the system," Thea said, brow furrowing.

"Yeah, and a lot of rich people have gotten mad at me! Those are the ones who give me the most money!"

"Do you really need more money?" Holly asked. "If you kept your money in reasonable investments and stopped buying starships, I'm pretty sure you could live off what you have. Not to mention all the crap you steal as South Siren."

Sarena huffed. "You wouldn't get it."

"Sure."

Jasper pursed her lips. Her head tipped to the side. "Sarena, do you want things to stay as they are, or not? Because you seem to be sitting pretty happy in the current system."

Sarena whirled on her. "I want the Tide District fixed. And…I guess the other lower districts, too. Look, I have a lot of money, but I don't have 'fix every problem in the lower districts' money. I'm not a gazillionaire like that Astra CEO guy."

"Yeah, you can't do it alone. Fair enough." Jasper raised an eyebrow. "So, your solution is to pander to the wealthy and avoid talking about the problems you want to fix? Or publicly supporting the people who are making real progress like Merama?"

"Like I said, if I advocate for change, I'll lose what power I *do* have."

"Right. So, you're not going to accomplish anything ever."

Sarena's hands clenched into fists at her sides. "Well, I was under the impression you had a better idea on how to fix things."

"I do. But I'm pretty sure you're only here right now because all those bodies that have been turning up have you scared. You know Skybreaker still wants you dead, and you know we're the only people who are really trying to stop her."

"Well, I'm willing to help, so who cares why I'm here?" Sarena exclaimed. "Just tell us all what your big plan is!"

Jasper smirked. "Let's get me fixed up. Then we'll talk bigger plans." Her head turned. Her eyes locked with Grace's. "Hope Superangel's ready, because we're gonna need her."

Grace nodded. "I'm ready."

"So, I get Holly has her shapeshifting," Cutthroat said slowly. "But how are you planning on getting yourself into Sky Labs? It's not enough to not look like yourself. You'll have to be someone the rest of the staff recognizes."

Jasper laughed. "Oh, believe me, I have the perfect disguise."

I. SKY LABS

Chapter Eleven
Not Again

Jasper had skipped the Nova Cora entirely her first day back. She'd been deprived of it in prison, and while it was tempting to take the energy boost, she'd decided to hold off a little longer.

The morning of the lab heist, though, she downed half a bottle.

"You sure your arm's good enough to do this today?" Holly asked as Jasper returned the rest of the bottle to the fridge.

Jasper threw the door shut and straightened up. "This shouldn't be a physically intensive job, if things go according to plan."

Holly's eyes narrowed. "And if things go south?"

"I'll make it," Jasper told her firmly. "And like I said, I have no idea if my arm is actually going to heal much more with how much damage the serum has done. Now, I'm going to go get dressed. You ready?"

"Everyone's just about ready, I think," Holly replied.

Jasper's gaze darted toward the living room, where the others were gathered. "All right, all right, I'm hurrying."

"Take your time," Holly said. "Just, you know, don't forget that the rally starts in half an hour. So maybe hurry a little."

"Great. Thanks."

Twenty-eight minutes later, the break-in began.

Jasper crouched at the edge of a grate leading down into the sewers, Holly at her left and Sarena at her right. The alleyway they stood in was quiet, but traffic roared at the far end, and music was blasting in one of the apartments far above.

Jasper had on a white overcoat, with the hood pulled up to hide her face in shadow. Holly was in her usual human form, for the time being. On the other side of the grate stood Aymes, his brow furrowed in concentration.

Grace shifted her weight from foot to foot next to him, looking as anxious as Jasper felt.

Finally, silver fly zipped out of the grate and flew into Aymes's hand. He made a fist around it. "All right," he said. "I've got the route with the fewest number of guards mapped out. And two employees called in sick today. We can use one of their identities."

"Hopefully," Jasper said. "Are either of them researchers?"

Aymes nodded. "One. Evy Bluepool. He's a biologist."

"Perfect. Thea, can you get us a visual?"

"Yup, found him," Thea answered over comms. "Sending an image to Holly. I found an old vocal sample, too, from a lecture he gave at the University of Kronos ten years ago."

Holly drew a sphere from her pocket and held it up. The sphere's holoscreen popped up with an image: a Kronosian man with light gray fur, large batlike ears and a snout to match, and sharp teeth. A clip of him saying something about cellular regeneration played.

Holly quickly took on man's form. As the last patches of her new layer of fur settled into place, she reached into the bag of clothes they'd brought along and grabbed a lab coat to throw on over her plain black outfit. Hopefully, it would be enough for her to blend in.

Jasper took a deep breath. "All right, let's get in there." She lifted the grate out of the ground and set it aside. Then, she jumped into darkness. Her boots thudded against the floor of a sewer tunnel. A moment later, Holly landed next to her. Above them, someone slid the grate back into place.

Jasper pulled back her hood, exposing a white wig pulled up in a ponytail and the bright green contact in her right eye. "Ready?" she asked.

"Whenever you are," Holly replied, gesturing for Jasper to lead the way. She'd managed to shift her vocal cords precisely enough to make a pretty good match for Bluepool's voice from the recording.

The two walked quietly through the tunnels, hearing nothing but occasional chittering from crawlers and a distant, low hum. Jasper hadn't been inside the labs since her escape all those years ago, and she'd only been close once to snatch a scientist to interrogate when she went after their files. She'd certainly thought up plenty of plans to break in, to destroy them, to blow the place to bits. But she'd never come anywhere close to following through.

Apparently sensing her inner turmoil, Holly whispered, "Are you sure you'll be okay in there?"

"Yup," Jasper replied nonchalantly. What choice did she have?

They reached the spot in the wall where the main Sky Labs entrance was hidden. According to Aymes, the same security procedures that Jasper had observed during her last venture down here were still in place. After a painfully tense moment, a hidden intercom came on, and a security guard's voice echoed through the tunnels.

"Well, this is a surprise. Dr. Bluepool, good to see you up and about. I thought you called the office and said you had food poisoning?"

"It got out of my system faster than I expected," Holly replied.

"Ran into her on the way down here," Jasper added.

"And I thought you were at a rally with the governor today, Eighteen." The guard sounded more curious than accusatory, to Jasper's relief.

"I planned to be there in person," she told him. "But something's come up, so I've got a hologram out there for now."

"Is there something we can help you with?"

"Yes, actually." Jasper glanced at Holly. "I need something from lab storage. Dr. Bluepool said he could help me grab it."

"All right. Hope you get it sorted out." The intercom clicked off. A moment later, a gap appeared in the tunnel wall, and the door slid open. Jasper and Holly strolled in. They passed a handful of guards who simply nodded at them as they walked by.

"All right," Jasper muttered under her breath into her comm once they were past the guards. "You got a clear visual, Thea?" Instead of risking Thea getting caught trying to hack the Sky Labs security system, Jasper had a button camera hidden in plain sight on the front of her coat.

"Clear as can be," Thea replied.

"And Aymes, you're seeing the camera feed, too?"

"I've got it," Aymes confirmed.

"Great. Lead the way, then."

Over the next few minutes, Aymes gave quiet directions into Jasper and Holly's ears. "Left at this intersection. All the way to the end of this hall. Through that door on your left—"

At every checkpoint, security waved them through without issue. But as smoothly as things were going, as decent a job as Jasper was doing keeping herself together, no plan could ever go perfectly. And once they got close to the cell block, it became a lot harder to keep up the façade.

As they passed one of the branching corridors, a distant shout echoed off the walls. There was something hauntingly familiar about the cry, something

Jasper couldn't quite put her finger on but that made her blood run cold anyway. A few more shouts followed a moment later. Then, a few thuds.

"Sorry for the disturbance," a security guard said as they passed. "One of our residents is on her third escape attempt this week."

Residents? Was that what they were calling the prisoners now? Jasper didn't respond, so Holly nodded at the guard. "Hope you're able to get her under control soon."

She was just playing a part, but the words still made Jasper's jaw clench. Her seemingly endless days in that cold, dark cell were clawing at the back of her mind. Those days strapped to a hospital bed. Those days being operated on, cut open—

No time for the parade of memories haunting her now. Jasper did what she was best at. Pushed the emotions down to feel later.

She and Holly stopped in front of the door to the storage room. Like with his coworkers, the guard only asked a couple of questions, didn't seem to actually care much about the answers, and let them in.

The sight on the other side was overwhelming. Shelves and coolers were packed into every inch of space on the walls. Bottles and boxes filled the shelves. A variety of colors, confusing diagrams, walls of text on labels, long and complex chemical names...

"How are we supposed to find this thing?" Holly hissed as Jasper strolled forward. "We can't stand in here all day, the guards—"

"I know, I know!" Jasper snapped back. She turned in a slow circle. Too many colors. Too many words. Too many—

"You said it's called ThetaEight, right?" Aymes asked. "I found it already. North wall, lower shelf near the left side, somewhere between that big purple box and the empty beakers..."

Jasper's head spun. She had to force herself to think, to process his instructions. She and Holly moved to the shelf he described and began searching. Jasper was barely reading the labels, despite her best efforts.

Dax spoke up. "Jasper. Take a deep breath for me."

Jasper nodded and did as he asked. Next to her, Holly grabbed a small bottle and held it up. "Found it."

Jasper took one more deep breath. "Okay. We're good." She took the vial from Holly and examined it. Stared at the label. Stared a little too long. The thuds and shouts they'd heard earlier echoed in her mind again.

Holly moved in close. "Jasper? You okay?"

"It's not enough to just take this," Jasper whispered. She glanced up. "We have to destroy this place."

Holly's nostrils flared. "How do we do that? *Can* we even do that? That wasn't the plan, we aren't prepared—"

"Holly, I think you're forgetting that blind destruction is actually easier than sneaking in and out of a place." Jasper shoved the vial into her coat pocket. "And relax, I'm not dumb enough to try something right now. But we have to come back. Soon. I let this place go on too long."

"Jasper," Holly muttered. "I agree that blind destruction is easy. But if you want to save those prisoners, too, things are going to get a lot more complicated.

Jasper cursed under her breath. Holly was right. They couldn't just blow the place up. Not yet.

"Let's try to get a look at the cell block before we go, then," Jasper said. "See if we get any ideas. Get a recording of the layout on my camera." She met Holly's gaze. "Is that okay?"

Holly pressed her lips into a thin line. After a long moment, she nodded. "Okay."

As they started walking, though, she seemed to be having second thoughts. "What do we say if they ask why we're over here?"

Jasper shrugged. "Tell 'em to mind their business."

"Sure, that'll work great," Holly growled.

"Aymes, help us to the cell block," Jasper said as they left the storage room. She braced herself for objections or concerns from the others, but no one made any comments.

"All right," Aymes said. "Start heading back the way you came."

At the cell block entrance, a guard at the right side of the heavy metal door simply nodded at the two as they approached. "Subject Eighteen. Dr. Bluepool."

"Anything we can help you with?" The guard on the left side asked. Jasper wasn't entirely sure whether she imagined the hint of suspicion in his tone.

"Just taking a look for Starr," Holly replied. "He has some new project ideas and asked me to see if there are any promising candidates."

That was good enough for the guards, apparently. The left guard scanned his badge on a box by the wall, pressed a few buttons on the keypad, and the doors slid open.

Jasper and Holly entered a narrow corridor. A familiar-looking corridor. A chill ran down Jasper's spine, and she was unable to stop herself from shuddering. The sound of the doors clanging shut behind her didn't help. At the end of the corridor, they took a corner and found themselves starting down a longer hallway lined with cells. Jasper swallowed her memories, the ghosts haunting her, and started forward.

She studied the cells as they walked, ignoring the glares and occasional shouts of anger from the prisoners. "Maybe we could break these all open in rapid succession," she muttered to Holly. "Place some small bombs, tell everyone to back up against the walls..."

"These bars have to be galaxium," Holly pointed out. "Bombs strong enough to destroy that are going to damage everything in a huge radius. Including people. We need to get into the electronic control system and open the doors that way."

Thea chimed in over comms. "Okay, so when you say 'we,' you mean me. And I don't know if I'll be able to manage that without causing a dozen other problems," she said. "Whole facility will probably go into lockdown."

"Well, can we override the lockdown?" Jasper asked quietly, her pace falling a bit behind Holly's. She tried to avoid looking at the prisoners' faces as they passed, did her best to ignore the insults they spat at the people they thought were Subject Eighteen and one of the scientists that experimented on them.

"Maybe. But you'll still be stuck fighting a lot of guards. And these prisoners probably aren't in great physical condition. I don't know how you plan to get them out—"

"Jasper!" Holly hissed, cutting Thea off. She'd stopped in front of one of the cells a few feet ahead and was staring into it with wide eyes.

"What?" Jasper hurried over to her, then turned to glance at the prisoner Holly was staring at. She froze when she saw the girl in the cell.

Not again.

Chapter Twelve
By Any Other Name

The girl in the cell was…twelve? Give or take a couple of years? Jasper wasn't entirely sure. She was too distracted by the fact that the girl had her face. Well, the face she used to have.

Another clone.

How many of me are there?

And she really did look exactly as Jasper had when she was younger. Her dark hair was cut to her shoulders. No weird eye colors, no obviously metal limbs. Jasper hoped she hadn't endured any of the researchers' experimentation yet. She was so much younger than Jasper had been when she was brought here.

"Eighteen," the girl spat. She clearly wasn't fond of the older clone she thought was standing in front of her.

"Oh. Right. Uh, listen, I'm not really Subject Eighteen." Jasper moved close to the cell bars, dropped to one knee, and lifted the green contact just enough to expose the brown iris underneath. "I'm the original. The one and only Jasper Van Terra. And my friend here is also in disguise."

The young girl raised a skeptical eyebrow. "Uh, okay. Why are you here, then?"

"Just taking a little behind-the-scenes tour." Jasper straightened up. "What's your name, kid?"

The girl shrugged. "I don't remember. A bunch of stupid numbers and letters. But they usually call me Twenty-Eight."

"Well, what do you want to be called?"

The girl considered for a moment before answering. "Can I change my name to Flamethrower?"

Jasper was tempted to laugh and say "hell yes"—Flame would be a cute nickname, right?—but Holly shot her A Look. "Uh, maybe for your middle name," Jasper said. "You should probably go by something a little more...unassuming."

"Hey, guys?" Sarena sounded pretty annoyed. "Hello? What's happening? Aren't you supposed to be getting the hell out before someone realizes you're not supposed to be there?"

"Just a minute," Jasper muttered back.

"There was a character in a book I read named Rose," the girl said slowly, seeming not to notice Jasper's comment.

Holly folded her arms and lifted an eyebrow. "They let you read books in here?"

"Yeah. Something about them not wanting me to go crazy."

Jasper was tempted to ask if she'd been taken to the lab yet, but further questioning would have to wait for later. "All right," she said. "If you want to be Rose, you can be Rose. Now, whaddaya say we bust you out of here?"

"Jasper!" Holly's head snapped toward her. "How are we supposed to do that now? We're not prepared—"

Jasper waved a hand. "Shh. We can get one small child out. Especially one that's tried to escape before." She glanced at Rose. "You are the one who's been making escape attempts, right?"

"Yup." Rose beamed. "And I've gotten pretty close. I took a wrong turn in the vents last time. That's how they got me."

Vents. Jasper glanced up and briefly scanned the walls with her x-ray vision, quickly identifying the ventilation shafts. Well, for someone as small as Rose, that likely was the best way out. But it would be a tight fit, even for her.

"Do you know the way out through the vents?" Jasper asked Rose.

"I do now," Rose replied. "I just have to wait for a chance to get back in. I broke into them while I was in the bathroom last time, but now they'll probably cover them up before they let me go in there."

"Okay, maybe we can find another entry point to get you into the vents." The grates here in the cell block were too small, but Jasper had noticed some bigger ones while they were walking around earlier.

"How are we supposed to get her out of the cell block?" Holly asked. "Asking the guards to get her out for us would be pushing our luck."

"Would it?" Jasper asked. "Our disguises are believable, we already have a cover story, and a researcher like you should have no problem grabbing a prisoner. It's not like we're going to try to walk her out of the building."

"But the guards are going to want to accompany her."

"I've got a plan. Trust me on this." Jasper really only had the foundation of a plan, but it would have to be enough. She wasn't leaving Rose in here for even one more day. "Rose, we'll be right back."

Rose looked skeptical, but she nodded and moved to the small cot in the corner of the cell to sit down. Jasper and Holly returned to the cell block entrance.

"What's the escape plan if this fails?" Holly whispered.

"Same as it was before. Thea will kill comms, and we'll run," Jasper replied. Her voice lifted as the guards turned toward them, noticing their approach. "We need to grab one of the prisoners. Bluepool has a few blood tests to run."

"All right, I'll come with you," one of the guards replied.

He led them back into the cell block, and when Jasper gestured to Rose, he tapped his card against the box by her cell. The barred door swung open, and she was free to walk out.

Jasper grabbed Rose's arm, and Rose shot her a murderous glare. Smart kid. Not bad acting, either. With a feigned glare back, Jasper said, "Doubt she'd beat me in a fight, if it came to it."

The guard smirked. "I'm sure you're right, but protocol is protocol. You qualify as four guards, so I'll have to be the fifth." He shot Holly a look. "No offense, Dr. Bluepool, but you don't meet the requirements."

One of Holly's ears twitched. "I know."

All right, fine. One guard with them wouldn't be the end of the world, for now. But Jasper needed to get Rose into a vent without him calling for backup.

"Straight to the labs, I assume?" the guard asked as they made their way back out of the cell block.

No, no, not that. But where else could they possibly have an excuse to go with Rose? Jasper opened her mouth, but before she could think up a diversion, Aymes piped up over comms. "There's an employee break room that's sort of on the way to the labs. That would be a good place to get Rose in the vents."

As his suggestion came through, something zipped through the air above Jasper. Her gaze darted up just long enough to glimpse a silver fly shining in the fluorescent lights.

"Damn flies," the guard muttered. "Sorry, were you going to say something, Eighteen?"

"Yeah, we actually needed to drop by the break room real quick."

"I'd like to grab a coffee before we get started," Holly added.

The guard chuckled. "Sure thing. I could use one, too."

"Who's Rose?" Sarena demanded again. "Could someone tell us what's happening?"

"Let them focus on getting out without getting killed, Sarena," Cutthroat growled in response. Sarena audibly huffed.

Jasper followed Aymes's directions to the break room, leading the way with a confidence that she hoped would keep the guard convinced she was the real Subject Eighteen. They reached the break room a few minutes later and were greeted by a few gray tables, matching chairs, a small kitchen that was remarkably clean, and a large screen on the far wall. It wasn't quite as sterile looking as the rest of the facility, but it wasn't exactly cozy either. Jasper turned her head slowly as they entered, taking the space in.

"I have an idea," Aymes said as they entered.

"I'm open to suggestions," Jasper muttered. *Please give me suggestions.*

A fly zipped down from the air above and landed on the guard's face. The guard lifted a hand to swat it away but never followed through. His hand dropped. He staggered to the right.

"Whoa, you feeling all right there?" Holly grabbed the guard's shoulders and guided him to one of the chairs.

The guard groaned. "Just...a little lightheaded..."

"Here, I'll get you some water."

"You got the kid, Eighteen?" the guard asked, his words slurring together as he glanced at Jasper.

"Yeah, I got her. Try to relax." Turning away from him, Jasper quietly asked, "Wow. What did you do, Apprentice?"

"While you were in the storage room, I had the fly slip into a vial of a strong sedative. Sinks in right through the skin. That guard will be completely out in a minute or so."

Smart thinking. Jasper raised an eyebrow as she watched the guard's eyes drift shut. "Were you going to warn us not to touch it?"

"Sorry, didn't think I needed to. Also, I'm not going by Apprentice anymore," Aymes added.

"What's your name, then?"

"Uh, still working on it." Aymes cleared his throat. "Now, this should buy you a few minutes, but whoever's watching cams will probably send someone to check on this guy pretty quick. Make sure you look like you're actually worried about the guy."

Right on cue, Holly came over to the table with a glass of water from the sink. "Well, how do we get Rose in the vents without them seeing us?" she hissed.

"Give me twenty seconds," Thea chimed in. "Since it's just one camera in there, and you won't need long, I can use your comms as a jumping off point to put out a signal that will disrupt the camera feed. That'll trigger even more security to come check things out, but they won't be able to see what happened while the camera was down."

While Thea worked on that, Jasper moved to the guard's side and waved a hand in front of his face, hoping that would be interpreted as concern by whoever was watching. But she didn't want to look too upset, either, figuring that Subject Eighteen probably wasn't the most touchy-feely type.

Admittedly, she was starting to lose steam. Finding Rose had distracted her from her memories a little, but they still loomed over her, ready to pounce if she let her mind wander their way. She sighed and resisted the urge to sink into one of the nearby chairs. She feared that if she sat down, she wouldn't be able to get herself back up.

Thea spoke again. "All right, cams are down."

"A couple of guards are on their way to you," Aymes added. "You've got about two minutes."

Jasper turned to Rose. "Okay, you said you know where you're going?"

Rose hesitated a moment. "I think so." She sounded considerably less confident than she had in her cell.

Jasper shook her head. "They'll find you, block your escape, and force you back out."

"She should have someone with her to guide her," Holly said, resting a hand on her hip.

"There's no way we'll be able to fit—" Jasper started.

"I could shapeshift into a smaller form," Holly cut her off. "And getting to a safe exit point shouldn't take long. Aymes can help. We'll be fine."

"And me?"

"You look like Eighteen. You can just walk out. Hell, they might question me if I try to go with you, since I'm supposed to be working. I was going to pretend I felt sick again, but it'd still be weird if we left at the same time."

"Right. Okay." It was a good plan, actually. And Jasper didn't like the idea of one person staying behind to avoid suspicion, even temporarily. "I'll meet you two on the outside."

Jasper helped the two into the vent entrance above the refrigerator. Holly first, then Rose. Once they were in, she checked on the unconscious guard one more time before strolling out of the break room and toward the front entrance.

It wasn't long before she ran into guards.

"Eighteen!" one exclaimed. "Can you tell us what happened in the break room?"

Jasper paused. Her gaze flickered to the end of the hall. Her escape was just around the corner. *So close. So damn close.*

She frowned. "You mean with the guard? He said he wasn't feeling well, so we stopped in the break room to get him some water."

"It looked like he passed out while you were in there with him."

"Yeah, we were going to call for medical staff, but then he came to. Seemed fine when we left. He said he'd sit down for another minute then head back to his post." Jasper shrugged nonchalantly. "And I dropped Bluepool and the kid in the labs already."

"You did?" The guard on the right glanced at his colleague. "Did you catch that on cams?"

"Not before we came to investigate." The other guard shrugged. He seemed far less concerned.

"Weird coincidence that the cameras had issues at the same time that the guard you were with started feeling sick," the first guard said, turning back to Jasper.

Jasper feigned concern. "You're not wrong. The kid might have pulled something, but like I said, she was surrounded by guards when I left her. Could be another failed escape attempt on her part."

"Wouldn't be surprised," the first guard muttered. "I'll head to the labs and check in." To the other guard, he added, "Go check on the guy in the break room. Maybe take him to the labs and have a doctor look at him."

Jasper took that as a sign to get moving. She strolled forward, past the guards, so close to the exit—

The first guard spoke again. "Eighteen, it might be better if you stay here until we get to the bottom of this."

Jasper whirled around. "Would love to. But Starr's expecting me. I'd rather not keep him waiting any longer than he already has."

Apprehension flashed across the guard's face. "Right, of course not. Certainly wouldn't want to keep you from him—"

"And whatever happened, you better figure it the hell out and hope Starr doesn't catch wind of any problems."

The guard's eyes bulged, and he nodded. "Right. We'll get this sorted out fast." The guard on his left actually looked worried now, too. The two turned around and scurried away from Jasper without another word.

Relieved to have that interaction over with, Jasper turned and continued toward the exit at a pace that was quick but not suspiciously fast. Hopefully. She took the corner, nodded at the guards waiting by the exit, pretended to be totally at ease as she waited for them to open the doors and see her out.

"See you soon, Eighteen," one guard said as she passed through the doors.

"Yup."

The moment the doors clicked into place behind her, Jasper broke into a sprint.

Chapter Thirteen
Rose Vented

As she flew around the corner, Jasper heard a creak—the exit doors reopening—followed by a shout. A distant blare of an alarm. They were on high alert now, and all she could do was hope that Holly and Rose had made it out.

And that she'd be able to make it out.

She was already slowing, lagging, feeling the burn in every muscle in her body. Footsteps joined the chorus behind her, forcing her to stop and scan the area for a less direct path away from the labs.

Aymes's silver fly came to the rescue once again. "Access tunnel to your right, just ahead," he told her on comms. The small insect zipped to the handle of a hatch Jasper had missed on her initial sweep.

She nodded and grabbed the handle. Twisted it open with a grunt. She'd had so much more strength and speed that day she'd first escaped Sky Labs. Her mind went to the vial in her pocket. Even once she was healed, she would never fully get that back.

Jasper slipped through the hatch, pulled the door shut behind her as quietly as she could manage, and started up the ladder on the other side. "Where's this taking me?" she asked.

"An alleyway on Cygni Avenue."

"Great. And Holly and Rose?"

"Still in the vents, but they're close to the surface."

"They're okay?"

"Right now, yes."

Well, that wasn't the most reassuring thing he could have said, but Jasper would take what she could get. She switched her focus to forcing her shaking limbs up the ladder without slipping, on getting closer to the distant light of the surface world.

Once she was outside, Jasper tore off the white wig and popped out the green contact. "Take me to the grate Holly and Rose will be coming out of," she ordered as she tossed them into a trash bin.

The fly that had led her up here zipped off, and she followed. Aymes guided her through a maze of back alleys to the side of one of the buildings that stood directly over Sky Labs. An entrance to the ventilation system poked out between two dumpsters. Jasper moved to stand next to the vent grate, heart thundering.

A shadow passed over her. She glanced up as Grace dropped down from the sky and landed next to her. "Sounds like everything went okay in there?" Grace asked as Jasper's head turned.

"It did today."

"You're really going back in?"

Jasper's jaw clenched. "I have to. We have to stop what they're doing down there."

"Everyone's still a little confused about the detour you two took. Who's Rose?"

Jasper turned to stare at the vent again. "You're about to find out." Distant clangs and thuds slipping through the vent grate gradually grew louder, kicking Jasper's heart into high gear. She slid her hands into her pockets to hide their trembling.

Relief washed over her when the grate popped out and a smaller version of Holly crawled into view. She returned to her normal size as she climbed out, stretching and grimacing. "Ow. Keeping myself that small for that long was a little harder than I thought."

A final thud came from the shaft, and then Rose was pulling herself out. She squinted into the bright sun and lifted a hand to shield her eyes as she climbed to her feet.

"Uh, Grace, this is…" Jasper swallowed. Turned. "This is Rose."

"Oh." Grace stared at the young clone, multiple emotions warring in her expression. Jasper was having a hard time reading exactly what was going on there beyond shock. A moment later, though, it was all gone, replaced by a warm smile. She dropped to one knee. "Hi, Rose. I'm Grace."

Rose blinked a few more times, lowered her hand, and stared at Grace for a long moment. Finally, she said, "Okay. Cool."

Grace laughed a little and straightened up. "So, what now?"

Jasper wasn't sure if she meant what they were doing at this moment in time, or in general. After checking that her comm was unmuted, she decided to answer the former. "Let's all meet back at the apartment."

Everyone responded in affirmation. Aymes's silver fly vanished in a flash of light, leaving Jasper, Holly, Grace, and Rose to walk by themselves back to the apartment. Comms went quiet, and none of the four had much to say amongst themselves, either. While that seemed to be mainly due to exhaustion on Jasper and Holly's part, and thoughtfulness on Grace's, Rose simply looked to be too in awe of the world around her to say or even think much of anything. Her head swung back and forth, her wide eyes devouring everything in front of them.

It put a small smile on Jasper's lips. This was one of the uglier parts of the city, of course, being down in the unmaintained lower districts. But to someone who'd spent their entire life in an underground lab, she could see the appeal of the neon signs and the sun gleaming on windows and the air traffic and the blue sky far above.

"It's even better than the pictures," Rose eventually whispered.

Jasper chuckled. "If you like this, you should see...literally anywhere else."

Twenty minutes of walking and a short subtrain ride later, they strolled into the apartment and found everyone else already waiting in the kitchen and dining area. A news broadcast played on a holoscreen in the living room nearby. After a moment, Jasper realized it was a clip from Starr's earlier rally. He stood at a podium, with Skybreaker—dressed in her gray Subject Eighteen uniform, of course—at his side.

Starr's voice boomed through the microphone in front of him. "We'll be making an exciting announcement soon, the pinnacle of our work developing anti-crime programs—"

"Mia, mute the holoscreen," Jasper ordered.

The apartment fell silent. All eyes moved to the four. Dax paused midway through pouring glasses of water at the counter. Thea sat on a stool on the other side, working on a laptop. Cutthroat, Sarena, and Aymes played a card game at the dining table.

Jasper stepped aside, offering everyone a good look at the smaller version of her in tow. "Rose, everyone. Everyone, Rose. As you can see, she's another clone of me. Let's not make a big deal out of it, okay?"

Sarena shrugged. "All right." Aymes and Cutthroat nodded. Thea offered a thumbs up before returning her attention to her screen, and Dax gave Rose a small wave and a smile.

Jasper cleared her throat. "Okay. Cool. Now that that's out of the way, let's discuss tomorrow's plan."

Holly's eyes went wide. "Whoa, we're planning something for *tomorrow*? Do you even have a fully formed plan?"

"I do." And this time, she meant it. Jasper cleared her throat. "We're busting out the Sky Labs prisoners and destroying the place."

"That's crazy!" Sarena exclaimed.

"She's pulled off crazier," Cutthroat pointed out. He set down the hand of cards he'd been holding and leaned back in his chair. "But even if we somehow get all those prisoners out, what will we do with them? We certainly don't have room to keep them here, they probably don't have homes, and the government's not gonna do them any good." He raised an eyebrow and added, "And before you ask, no, you can't use my ship. I don't have the food or resources for more people at the moment."

Jasper shot Sarena a look. "I actually have something else in mind."

"I already hate it," Sarena muttered.

"You don't know what it is."

"I can guess."

"You know it'll be good for you."

"I beg to differ."

Jasper shrugged. "Well, maybe we can negotiate some of the details."

The rest of the team looked confused, but they didn't need to hammer out that part of the plan right now. Jasper had to lay out the main framework of what would go down in the lab itself so that they could get prep done tonight. She opened her mouth to continue but stopped when she realized Rose had disappeared from her side. "Where—?"

Jasper turned as Rose scurried into the living room and jumped onto the couch. As she settled into a seated position, she said, "Holoscreen, switch to channel eighty-seven."

"The program running that sphere is named Mia," Jasper told her. "If you want to give commands, you have to use—"

"Mia. Channel eighty-seven."

The sphere was quiet for a moment as Mia processed Rose's demand, and then the screen switched channels. A broadcast Jasper vaguely recognized as an animated show about a spacefaring detective—or something along those lines—began to play.

Rose lit up. "This is my favorite episode!"

"They let you watch broadcasts down in the labs, too?" Jasper folded her arms. "Sounds like you got better treatment than I did."

"I got better treatment than most of the prisoners. Still sucked, though." Rose rubbed her arm, a faraway look creeping into her eyes.

Before Jasper could decide whether to question Rose further on that, Sarena spoke up. "Uh, she's not going to be a handful, is she?" she asked. "Babysitting's not exactly one of my strengths."

"If she's anything like Jasper, she'll definitely be a handful." Holly put her hands on her hips, but despite the annoyed tone, the expression on her face hinted at a smirk waiting in the wings.

"We'll keep her out of trouble," Jasper said with more confidence than she probably should have. "Let her watch TV for now while I lay out the plan."

"Right." Sarena leaned back in her chair and threw her feet up on the table. "How are we getting those prisoners out, exactly?"

"What we need is a distraction. A big one. And more brute force than we can muster alone on short notice. Disguising myself as Skybreaker gave me an idea." A slow grin spread across Jasper's face as she turned toward Thea. "How hard would it be for you to hijack the race broadcasting signal?"

Thea raised an eyebrow. "You want to use it to send out a message?"

"Yep."

Thea stretched her arms, cracked her knuckles, and began typing. "Give me a couple of hours. Skybreaker hasn't touched it since Reo, so it might be left vulnerable."

"Uh, I think I see where you're going with this," Holly said. "But now that Skybreaker's made it pretty obvious she wants to kill everyone, how can we expect anyone to actually show up?"

"Plus, no one's gotten any of the money or rewards she and Ringmaster were promising," Aymes pointed out. "That was the main motivation for turning up at all, in the first place."

Jasper exchanged a glance with Thea. "Think you can round up enough money for the villains who were in the top three after Reo? And maybe a little bonus for everyone else so they know we're totally and completely serious about giving out a reward this time?"

"I'm sure I can come up with a persuasive amount," Thea answered. Her typing pace picked up. "At least, something that will stay in their accounts long enough for them to think its worth coming back for more."

While Thea worked on that, Jasper laid out the rest of the plan. The others didn't look too skeptical, by the end of it. In fact, they were all nodding along as if they agreed it was a good idea.

"I think this will work," Cutthroat said. "Though, I do worry about getting the numbers we need on such short notice."

"I guess we could postpone it for a few more days," Jasper conceded reluctantly. Sky Labs had been running for decades. Maybe even longer. If waiting a few more days improved their odds of getting everyone out, it was worth it.

"That will give you more time to recover, too," Dax pointed out. "From that description we saw on the bottle, it looks like it'll take a couple days for the ThetaEight to really get working in your system."

Good point. Jasper drew the vial out of her pocket and held it up. "Better get it in me now, then." She turned it to read the instructions on the back. "It needs to be injected straight into a vein. Looks like we'll want to use half the bottle." With a small sigh of relief, she added, "No reported side effects after a ten-year study."

"I'll grab a needle," Dax said.

While he went to fetch a needle from their medical supplies, Jasper moved into the living room and sat down on the couch next to Rose. Grace followed, while Holly sat down at the table with Sarena, Cutthroat, and Aymes.

"What's this show called?" Jasper asked.

Rose's gaze stayed fixed on the screen. "Uh, Detective Cosmonight."

"Are we going to take her wherever we take the rest of the prisoners we rescue?" Grace asked quietly.

Jasper swallowed. "I'm not sure yet." As she turned to study Rose, something the girl had said earlier flashed in her mind, when they were talking about the vents. *I broke into them while I was in the bathroom last time, but now they'll probably cover them up before they let me go in there.*

It took Jasper a moment to figure out why the statement was setting off alarm bells in her brain. The cells all had their own small bathrooms attached to them. There was no reason to have guards accompany Rose to a different bathroom, unless she was already being taken somewhere else in the facility.

"Maybe give it a few days before you start prodding her about lab stuff," Grace whispered, seeming to sense what was on Jasper's mind. Jasper nodded quickly.

A moment later, Dax entered the room with a needle in hand. Grace stood so that he could take her place next to Jasper on the couch. Jasper shrugged off her coat and pulled up the sleeve of her shirt.

"You ready for this?" Grace asked as the tip of the needle moved to the skin of her forearm.

On impulse, Jasper reached up to squeeze Grace's hand. "Ready as I always am."

Surprise briefly flashed across Grace's face, quickly replaced by a small smile. "Well in that case, I think you'll be just fine."

The needle sank beneath the surface with a slight pinch. Something warm spilled into Jasper's veins, beginning its race against the ice in her blood.

I hope you're right, Angel.

Chapter Fourteen
Reach For The Sky

That night, Grace returned to her former bed in the guest room. Though, guest room probably wasn't the right thing to call it anymore. It really was hers, and it had been for months. Still, after spending nearly half that time in Jasper's, it was strange to be back.

Still, she was glad no one had asked to stay the night, as she would have volunteered herself for the couch regardless of her exhaustion. Cutthroat had returned to where he had the Astronomer docked in a quiet part of the atmosphere, and Sarena had apparently convinced him to let her stay in one of the ship's rooms. Aymes, meanwhile, still had a lease on a small apartment near the University of Kronos campus.

Grace spent the hours that followed anxiously tossing and turning instead of sleeping, thinking up a dozen different ways things could go wrong at the labs in a few days. And with Jasper. What if ThetaEight ended up having unexpected side effects that didn't appear in the other test subjects? Or what if just…didn't work at all?

She did manage a few bursts of sleep here and there, but she was still exhausted by the time she dragged herself out of bed the next morning and ventured out to the living room. Thank god they'd persuaded Jasper to wait a few more days before attacking the labs.

Jasper was already in the living room, wrapping the tree Holly had brought back with a string of lights. "It's not the most Christmas-y," she said as Grace approached. "But I'll get this place whipped into shape over the next few weeks. And there will be parties hosted around Kronos—hopefully some by humans who actually know what they're doing. Maybe we'll have time to go to one or two." Jasper glanced up. "What I really want is to show you Christmas on Earth, someday."

Grace smiled. "I'd like that." Glancing at the tree, she asked, "How's Rose?"

"Still sleeping." Jasper straightened up. "She kicks like crazy in her sleep. I've got a small bed scheduled to be delivered later today for her."

It didn't take long for the rest of the team to turn up in the living room, and then it was time for the first step of the plan, the preparation of their secret weapon for when the day came. For the broadcast, they used Aymes, who claimed to be acting on behalf of Ringmaster. He disavowed Skybreaker's previous use of his former partner's broadcast channel. Hopefully, that would be enough to persuade everyone that Skybreaker had nothing to do with this.

Thea sent the broadcast out right away, giving all interested villains a couple of days to get to Kronos and prepare to inadvertently get involved in a prison break. That was just the beginning of her task, though.

"I can disable the signal now to prevent Skybreaker from sending any messages to sabotage us, but I'll need to constantly be monitoring it to keep her from getting it back online," she explained as her hands danced across her keyboard. "I've got a software pinging it for its status every ten seconds, and a backup algorithm ready to kick in and fight her until I can get in myself."

Dax's brow furrowed. "If she does figure out what we're doing, do you think she'll come up with a way to stop the villains from showing up?" He glanced at Jasper.

Jasper shrugged. "I mean, we are using the villains in a way that puts them at risk, which she should be on board with. But she's also playing the part of someone who wants to defend Starr, and by extension, the labs." She paused and thought for a moment. "Of course, she's only pretending to work for Starr. She undoubtedly wants to see the labs destroyed eventually. Maybe she'll let us get away with it. Especially if she's close to...whatever it is she has planned with Starr."

"Assuming she figures out that's what we're attacking," Grace pointed out. They wouldn't be putting out the race map until the morning of to prevent Starr or anyone else from realizing the labs were in its path.

"She might suspect it." Holly's arms folded. "Especially after finding out someone with her face was walking around the labs pretending to be her yesterday."

"I'm sure she'll at least consider it a possibility that the labs are our target." Jasper rose to her feet, pressed her palms against the coffee table, and leaned forward. "And if she brings in reinforcements, we'll just need to keep the focus on the other villains. Get in and out of the cell block as fast as possible." She glanced up, her gaze briefly meeting Grace's. "Even if she does decide to intervene, we'll have her outnumbered. And any one of the racing villains is going to be way more powerful than a lab security guard. All we can do now is hope it'll be enough."

The next two days flew by, with most of the time spent training together.

Sarena wasn't around nearly as much as Cutthroat and Aymes, claiming she had final prep work to do for her new album, but she did get in a few good sessions with them. Rose, in the meantime, mostly watched broadcasts and devoured incredible amounts of food. She also tuned in for the planning. Grace wanted to talk to her more, to try getting to know her, but she didn't seem interested in long conversations with anyone. Not even Jasper.

The day before everything would go down at the labs, rather than admitting Jasper had escaped prison, Starr announced that the execution was being put off due to "medical reasons" and that there would be more information next pentasol. Whether that update ever came was anyone's guess. Did he think he could recapture her in less than a week?

The question still weighed on Grace's mind the following morning while the team prepared to head out. Who all did Starr have looking for Jasper? Did police know? Or only Subject Eighteen?

On the bright side, Jasper's arm had healed up fairly well. A little faster than the average human, a little better than how it'd been healing before the ThetaEight injection. Still not as good as her healing had once been, but it was good enough for the plan. Good enough according to Jasper, anyway. Dax did warn her as they started for the front door that there was a chance the wound could reopen if she went too hard on her motorcycle, to which she responded with an enthusiastic, "Reopen, shmeopen."

With that promising statement, Jasper threw open the apartment's front door. Grace followed, and the others came behind her. Thea with her bag of equipment, Dax and Holly in costume ready to handle their part of the plan, Aymes and Cutthroat and Sarena—and Blitz—ready to race.

They split outside the building. While the others headed off to get into position or grab their own vehicles, Grace and Jasper went to the back alley where Jasper's motorcycle waited. Grace grabbed the helmet Jasper had picked up for her the day before and slid it on. This one was white with a dark blue visor and tiny gold wings painted on the sides, something that actually matched her Superangel uniform.

"Ready, Angel?"

"Yup." Grace wrapped her arms around Jasper and tried not to dwell too much on the sensation of being close to her. "You?"

"Hell yeah."

Jasper revved her engine, but before she could take off, a small figure came running into view at the end of the alley. As the figure—dressed all in black and wearing a black motorcycle helmet with a red rose painted on the side—came closer, Grace realized it was Rose.

Jasper cut the engine. "Rose? What are you doing out here?"

Rose stopped a few in front of them. "I wanted to ride on your motorcycle with you! And help you with the plan."

"Some other time. Today's too dangerous."

"I already spent my entire life down there. What's another day?"

"Today it's going to be full of villains and we're going to be trying to destroy it."

Grace frowned. "Rose, where did you get that helmet?"

"Stole it from a shop down the block."

"You're really something, huh." Jasper waved her hand in a polite but firm shooing motion. "But you'd better get back inside. I promise you'll get to join us on a mission one of these days."

"Jasper," Grace said under her breath. "I don't think promising a kid that is a great idea."

"Well, she should at least be able to fend for herself." Quieter, Jasper added, "And I really just want to get her back inside."

Rose's shoulders sagged. With a huff and a muttered, "Fine," she turned around and ran back out of the alley.

Grace glanced up at the rising sun, at the golden glow bouncing off the buildings around them. The engine roared again, and she and Jasper raced into the city streets. Toward the lab that had made them. A little more literally, in Grace's case.

They caught up with the others near the entrance to the lab. Cutthroat on his cart, Sarena on her motorcycle, and they'd both rounded up some other decent vehicles for a few of their pirates and sirens. Aymes, meanwhile, had crafted a motorcycle from his silver energy.

Thea nearby monitoring the race. Holly and Dax off somewhere preparing the prisoners' escape. Grace and Jasper on Jasper's motorcycle.

And something new racing through Jasper's veins.

Thea was also preparing to brute force her way into the lab cameras. Not just for monitoring, but for recording as well. The alarms her attack would raise wouldn't matter—security would be far too busy with the pack of villains being directed through the heart of the facility.

"Okay, let's do this," Jasper said, slowing the motorcycle as they neared a subtrain station entrance. "Thea, play the recording."

All around the block, Thea's drones came out of hiding, emerging from storm drains and dumpsters and ledges inaccessible by foot. Together, they projected a holographic message Aymes had recorded the day before, announcing the race's imminent start. Grace scanned the area as his hologram spoke, picking out villains who were flying toward the starting point, coming down from traffic above and emerging from alleys. The racing crowd gathered in front of the station entrance, sending pedestrians scattering.

The recording neared its end. "Villains! Your race begins in three, two, one—"

Grace tightened her arms around Jasper.

"—go!"

The motorcycle shot forward. While the villains went down into the corridors connecting subtrain platforms, where they would continue on into access tunnels that would eventually take them to the hidden Sky Labs entrance, Jasper turned toward some fake construction tape blocking off a road ahead. Detour signs that Holly and Dax had thrown up only minutes ago.

She and Grace slipped past the fake construction signage and dropped through a hole blown open in the street into the sewers. The landing wasn't too painful, but the thud reverberated uncomfortably through every bone in Grace's body.

"I need updates," Jasper said.

"Sarena and I are near the middle of the pack," Cutthroat said. "Aymes isn't far behind us."

"Dax and I are about to go into the parking garage," Holly added.

"And the first racers are getting close to the lab entrance." Thea paused for a moment before adding, "The few cameras down here in the sewer and access tunnels aren't great, but as soon as they're through the front door, I'll break into the lab cameras."

A stream of water on the concrete below splashed against the walls as Jasper cut through it. Lights flickered. Grace tried to focus on the mission ahead and not the tight space, the darkness, her longing for the sky and fresh air. Her hold on Jasper tightened even further.

Thea spoke again a minute later. "They seem a bit confused by the wall. Looks like they're double-checking the map we sent out."

"Come on," Jasper muttered. "Come on, go for it..."

"We're almost there—" Cutthroat started.

Thea cut him off. "Oh, a new guy just rolled up. Looks like he's firing a blaster cannon—"

A distant boom echoed through the tunnels.

"He got the doors partway open. Other villains are joining in. They should be inside in just a few more seconds."

"Perfect," Jasper said. Grace could practically hear her grinning. "Let me know once most of the villains have made it in."

She and Grace circled random tunnels a few times until Thea gave the go-ahead. When they reached the doors to the labs—the same doors Jasper had escaped through decades earlier, that Grace had fled through only four years prior—they had been blown wide open.

The first few hallways were empty. Signs of destruction, cracked walls and shattered lights and leaking pipes, were accompanied by distant engines, firing blasters, shouting. But underneath the layers of chaos, Grace saw something familiar. Something that brought memories of running to the surface. Memories of sheer terror.

The comm in Grace's ear cracked, distracting her from the way her hands were starting to shake. "We have a slight problem," Thea said.

"Problem?" Jasper repeated. "What, is the small army of supervillains we mustered struggling to plow through the ordinary security guards?"

"Yes, actually. Looks like the Sky Labs guards have been given those new high-powered blasters we saw on Reo."

Grace's heart skipped. "What?" She didn't even try to keep the horror out of her voice. How were they supposed to fight those?

"And the cell block has gone into lockdown with extra galaxium panels," Thea continued. "Racers have gotten stuck in a fight with the guards just outside."

"Well, those fancy blasters can probably handle the galaxium, right?" Jasper asked. "We just have to nab some from the guards."

"And get close without getting shot."

"Sure." Jasper made it sound easy. She took a corner and came to a halt in the middle of the next corridor. "Okay, Sarena, Cutthroat, Aymes. Can I get updates?"

"Lab's locked down tight, too," Cutthroat said. "Not sure how we're going to get my bombs in."

"Sarena's voice isn't enough to get through?"

"No, she screamed at the panels a few times and only made a dent."

"Go get yourself one of those high-powered blasters, then. That oughta do the trick." Jasper's hands tightened and untightened around the motorcycle handlebars. "Aymes?"

Grace lifted her gaze to the end of the hall, bracing herself for any guards that might pop up out of nowhere.

"I've circled the perimeter," Aymes responded. "There's not much besides the labs and the cell block. A few offices, a computer server room, some rooms that look like training rooms, and a small weapons closet. One random empty room, not sure what that's for. But a few bombs from Cutthroat and it'll all go down easy. And—uh oh."

"Aymes? Is everything okay?"

"Skybreaker's here. Just came in the main entrance. Headed your way."

Chapter Fifteen
More Thorn Than Rose

As far as Jasper was concerned, Skybreaker was a ticking time bomb. No matter where in the labs she and Grace went, Skybreaker would find them. All they could do was try to accomplish as much as possible before the inevitable showdown. Jasper swerved at the next intersection and shot down the hall to the right.

"Where are we going?" Grace asked. Her arms tightened around Jasper.

Jasper ignored her heart's quickening rhythm. "Cell block."

"Already? I thought we were waiting for the all-clear from the others."

"We don't have time for that. Not with Skybreaker here." Jasper took a left next, slowing just enough to make it around the tight corner without crashing. Even so, she and Grace passed within inches of the wall before Jasper straightened them out.

"Thea," Jasper said once they were upright again. "Any lone guards near me?"

"Afraid not," Thea replied. "Most are in big groups either fighting villains at the cell block bottleneck or defending the lab. But there is a group of three coming from the entrance side toward the cell block. Cut through the northeast section and you'll run into them."

That would have to do. "Angel, I need you to nab one of their blasters while I distract them," Jasper said, head turning briefly to glimpse Grace in the corner of her eye. Of course, Grace's helmet hid her expression.

"Got it." Grace sounded confident, but Jasper couldn't be sure.

"Don't get shot," Jasper added. "I'm not sure your wings could take a single hit from those new blasters, and I don't want to find out the hard way."

As she and Grace neared where Thea expected them to run into the guards, Jasper switched to x-ray vision. If Grace was going to have any chance of succeeding, they needed to come at the guards from behind.

Oh, they were really close. Jasper took a painfully sharp left to avoid entering the same hallway as them. Grace's yelp of surprise made her wince. She forced herself to keep up her speed, to move fast enough to pass the guards in the parallel hall and meet them at the next intersection.

The guards heard her coming and started to turn around, but they didn't move fast enough. Jasper slammed into the guard at the rear and sent him crashing through his colleagues. They all went flying into the air. Their body armor—which would likely prevent them from taking much damage, so better not to count on them being down long—cracked against the floor as they landed. Grace immediately leapt off the motorcycle and dove for the nearest guard's blaster. She snatched it from him without a problem, but as she rushed to get back on the motorcycle, another guard sat up and took aim with his weapon.

"Angel!" Jasper shouted. She grabbed Grace's arm and shot forward a few feet, just far enough to yank Grace out of harm's way. The dark blue blaster beam cut through the air behind Grace's head and struck the wall.

An explosion of debris rained down on the floor and flooded the air with dust. The hole left behind in the wall made Jasper's eyes go wide. "I didn't think they'd set them quite so high. Damn."

Grace scrambled onto the motorcycle behind her. "Let's not let them do that again."

Jasper slammed the gas. The echo of another blaster shot shook the hall behind them, but they were already taking the next corner, and the guards had no hope of catching up on foot.

Another corner, another corner, the sounds of firing weapons and shouting increasing in volume, another corner—

And then they were rolling up to the battle. Many of the villains had been forced off their vehicles to fight the guards, who were doing everything they could to block the villains' attempt to break through the galaxium panels that had dropped down to protect the cell block. The cell block that they had to pass through to win the race. There were a few faint dents and scorch marks in the panels, but no serious damage yet.

The good news was that it didn't seem like every guard had a high-powered blaster, just a few. And in the chaos, they seemed hesitant to fire for fear of hitting their colleagues instead of villains. There were still plenty of blaster shots going off, but the power levels weren't intense. Villains took hits and kept fighting, some seeming completely unfazed.

"Let's give them a hand," Jasper muttered. She reached out a hand behind her, and Grace placed the stolen blaster in her palm. The motorcycle slowed. Jasper cranked the power dial up the rest of the way, aimed carefully, and fired.

The beam blew the galaxium wall wide open. Jasper swallowed as she lowered the weapon. Something that could obliterate galaxium like that...

What a terrifying amount of power to fit in her hand.

Villains quickly returned to their vehicles, eager to get to the front of the pack. Jasper came to a halt on the motorcycle, letting them flood the cell block and take up the attention of the guards waiting inside before she and Grace made their move.

Finally, once the chaos on the other side of the galaxium panel seemed to have reached an appropriate level, Jasper turned her head. "Superangel, you ready to save some prisoners?"

Grace slid off the motorcycle, yanked off her helmet, and put on her Superangel mask in its place. As she drew her sword, she said, "Sure am." Her chin went up just the way Jasper knew it would, that confident expression blazing across her face. Jasper never would have dreamed she'd see that expression so often on the woman she'd rescued from jail the day they met.

Jasper caught the helmet Grace tossed to her. "See you on the other side then, Angel." She quickly fastened the helmet to the side of the motorcycle. At this point, she'd originally planned to help the others plant bombs to speed things along, but the better move now was to distract Skybreaker. Stop her before she could stop the prison break.

"Anyone got eyes on Skybreaker?" Jasper asked as she turned the motorcycle around.

"She's headed toward the cell block," Thea replied.

Of course she was. Jasper sighed. "Great. Thanks."

"You don't sound very thankful."

"I'm not."

Jasper passed through a couple of hallways before the roar of another engine rose in the distance. She slowed and listened to it approach, rapidly growing louder until the motorcycle responsible came flying around the corner.

Skybreaker came to a halt and leapt off the motorcycle—a smaller, less flashy one than what she used when actually playing the part of Skybreaker.

Staff already drawn, she swung as she came flying at Jasper. No helmet today. Just her gray Subject Eighteen motorcycle suit.

Jasper ducked and jerked the handlebars of her own vehicle to the right, dropping the motorcycle low to the ground. Skybreaker flew over her head, twisted in the air, and landed on her feet in the middle of the hallway.

"Wow, right into it, huh?" Jasper stepped off the motorcycle as it skidded to a halt and strolled toward Skybreaker, drawing her stolen blaster. As she twisted the dial to a lower power setting, she added, "No 'Hey, how are you?'"

"Hey. How are you?" Skybreaker pointed the staff toward Jasper and unleashed a burst of electricity. White electricity.

Jasper flung up her arms and crossed them in front of her face. The blast struck her and sent her sliding back a few feet across the slick tile. Pain coursed through her body, but it wasn't enough to stop her from moving. Her arms lowered as the arcs of lightning dancing across her skin quickly fizzled out.

"Great, thanks," she told Skybreaker. She raised the blaster and fired.

Skybreaker was dodging before Jasper even squeezed the trigger. Jasper's jaw clenched. She fired off more shots in rapid succession. To Skybreaker's right, her left, above her, at her feet—

Skybreaker dropped to her stomach and rolled to the right, narrowly missing the lowest blaster beam. She jumped back to her feet in a heartbeat. Her staff twirled in her hand.

"Your lightning's white today," Jasper noted.

"I always use white when I'm playing Eighteen. The green would be a little too obvious."

Jasper lifted an eyebrow. "You used green when you fought us at Reo."

"And I destroyed the cameras," Skybreaker replied. "Blamed it on your tech." Her hand tightened around her staff, and lightning began dancing along its length.

Hoping to distract her a little longer—and maybe get a hint at what she was planning—Jasper asked, "Can you explain to me again how getting innocent people killed in fires aligns with your plans to fix the Janus System? I fail to see how I'm any worse a person than you are."

Storm clouds rolled into Skybreaker's expression. Jaw clenching, she said, "I'm trying to fix the Janus System for future generations," she growled. "The current population is a waste of space. They let things get this bad, and now it's impossible to make things better without burning it down and starting over."

"No one living today had anything to do with generations of the Starr family ruling." Jasper adjusted her grip on the blaster, but didn't aim, didn't give any indication that she intended to fire.

Skybreaker shrugged. "Well, they still had their chance to fight back. Any idiot can take a look at the world and see that the lower class far outnumbers the elite. They were too scared to strike or protest in any meaningful way. Not willing to sacrifice their small comforts for a better society."

Jasper's finger slid a fraction of an inch toward the trigger. "You could still wipe out the elite and the upper districts instead. Why does anything in the lower districts have to be destroyed to make things better?"

"If you knew what was coming, you would understand. Starr's time will come. In the meantime, I have to start bringing down the foundations. The violent criminals. The chain stores cranking out profits for their owners."

"A handful of stores is barely a dent to those companies. But the people scraping by whose lives you burned away—"

"You don't understand." Skybreaker's eyes narrowed. "You're not strong enough to understand. The world doesn't change without sacrifice."

"I think I do understand. For whatever reason, you can't attack Starr yet. You don't dare draw his attention by attacking the upper districts." Jasper lifted the blaster slightly. "But you like destroying things. Killing villains and burning stores to the ground makes you feel like your making progress, even if you aren't really hurting the big guys, yet."

The faint arcs of electricity dancing along Skybreaker's staff became bigger and brighter. But before she could swing, a thud came from somewhere above the two of them. Both of their gazes darted up, scanning the ceiling for any indication of the sound's source. In the same instant, they found the vent grate in the upper wall. The large vent grate. Not large enough to fit either of them, but a child—

Jasper's body went cold. No. No way was she here.

Another thud. The grate flew out of the wall and nearly smacked Skybreaker in the face. She barely deflected it with the staff in time.

Rose's face popped out of the ventilation shaft.

Skybreaker's eyes narrowed. "Janus-28. I'm assuming I can thank Van Terra for your escape a few days ago?"

"It's Rose, you electric idiot."

Despite Jasper's utter terror at the sight of Rose back in the heart of Sky Labs, far from the safety of the apartment where she was supposed to be, she bit back a laugh. Skybreaker raised an eyebrow. "All right, you little gremlin. I think it's bedtime." She raised the staff.

Jasper lunged without thinking. Skybreaker whirled to face her instead. Lightning began running up and down her staff, but before she could direct it at Jasper, Rose pushed herself from the vent and dropped on top of her. A flash of bright light lit up the hall.

"Rose!" Jasper took another step forward, heart skipping beats at the sight of the arcs of lightning racing over Rose's skin. But to her surprise, Rose climbed to her feet without a hint of pain in her expression. In fact, she seemed entirely unfazed by the electricity.

Skybreaker lifted her staff. "Come on, what was it, Rose? You're not getting out of here. If you don't go back to your cell, you'll just make things worse for yourself."

"You're forgetting something." Rose lifted her hands, palms facing Skybreaker. Her eyes narrowed. "Roses have thorns."

Two circles opened up in Rose's palms, each emitting a neon green glow. And then the glow was a pair of blaster beams, both aimed at Skybreaker. Skybreaker ducked. The beams pierced the wall and clouded the air with debris. They didn't match the power of the new blasters from Reo, but the sizable holes they left behind still surprised Jasper.

Skybreaker was back on her feet a heartbeat later, wide eyes looking Rose up and down. "They started putting cybernetics in you already?"

Rose's brow furrowed. "They started those years ago."

Something briefly danced across Skybreaker's expression, something that looked a lot like shock. And horror. And disgust. "Starr said they were just doing blood tests," she muttered.

And then the only thing on her face was annoyance, and Skybreaker was swinging her staff again. Rose darted out of the way and blindly fired another beam from her right palm, forcing Skybreaker to delay her next attack.

Jasper's comm crackled in her ear. "Bombs are all planted," Cutthroat said.

The plan. *Focus on the plan.* "Angel," Jasper said under her breath, backing toward her motorcycle, her gaze fixed on Rose. "Status?"

"I'm leading the prisoners. We're following the path the villains cleared. We're already out of the labs. Should be to the meeting point in less than ten minutes."

Jasper's gaze darted between Rose and Skybreaker, who'd fallen to a standstill and were sizing each other up. Her foot bumped against something. Her motorcycle. Quietly, she reached down and grabbed the handlebar.

"I already broke out once," Rose said, chin lifting. "And I'm leaving again."

Skybreaker shook her head. "There's nothing for you out there. Not yet."

Jasper lifted the motorcycle and swung a leg over it. "Okay, Thorn. It's about time we cleared out."

Both heads turned toward her. Skybreaker started running toward Jasper, summoning more electricity to the surface of her skin, staff spinning at her side. "You're not going anywhere—"

Jasper shot forward. Skybreaker let the electricity explode from her body. Anticipating the attack, Jasper swerved away from Rose, planning to circle back around and grab her before driving off. But the burst of lightning went farther than she expected, and Skybreaker's electricity overwhelmed her, making her lose control and sending her veering toward the wall.

Barely able to think through the pain, Jasper forced the motorcycle to turn back on her intended path. Of course, now Skybreaker knew where she was going, and Jasper needed a new plan to get herself and Rose out.

A green blaster beam narrowly missed Skybreaker's face and sent her stumbling backward. Rose darted forward and jumped onto the back of the motorcycle, quickly latching onto Jasper. Skybreaker lunged toward them, swinging at the motorcycle, bringing more electricity with her, but Rose was able to force her to back off with another blast.

The surprise of Rose and her cybernetics was throwing Skybreaker off enough to make up for Jasper's inability to get the upper hand on such short notice. Still, the next wave of electricity grazed the motorcycle and brought it to a shrieking halt.

"Go!" Rose shouted. "I'll keep an eye on her!"

Jasper was dismayed to realize the engine had shut off entirely. She got it to start up again just fine, but the occasional flurry of white sparks that jumped out of every visible gap made her nervous. *Please don't catch on fire. Or explode.*

Once she and Rose had made it a few halls away from Skybreaker, Jasper slowed and listened. There was another engine in the distance, but it was getting quieter. Was Skybreaker retreating?

Jasper glanced back at Rose. "Why did you come?"

"To help."

"This was insanely dangerous, and you're a kid." Jasper shook her head. "How did you even get in here?"

Rose rolled her eyes. "Through the vents. Duh."

"But how'd you get here from the apartment?"

"Bus."

Great. She was resourceful. That was, unfortunately, not surprising. But it was something to worry about. *Something to worry about later.*

Jasper followed the path of destruction back to the cell block and passed through the now quiet hallway. The cells were all empty, their doors flung open. At the other end of the hall, wall after wall had been blown through, all the way to the edge of Sky Labs and into the sewer system.

"We got all the prisoners out?" Jasper asked as she left Sky Labs for the last time.

"Yup," Grace answered. "Just reaching the meeting point."

"I can confirm there's no prisoners left in the labs," Thea added.

"Is Skybreaker still in there?" Jasper asked.

"She just went out the main exit. Which means I don't have eyes on her anymore."

Jasper's hands tightened. "Everyone else?"

"I've got Sarena and Aymes with me, and we're ready to set off the detonators as soon as you give the word," Cutthroat said.

"Roger that. Give me a few."

Jasper stopped in front of a service elevator and hopped off the motorcycle. Rose slid off on the other side and wordlessly helped her roll the motorcycle in. They took the thing up to street level and stepped out into the storage room of some city building or another. There was an exit just down the hall, and then they were free and clear. Jasper led the way into a nearby alley, where she rested the motorcycle against the wall before leaning back next to it. Rose hurried to her side.

"Thea," Jasper said. "Send me the camera feeds for the cell block, the main lab room, and the entrance."

Thea didn't question the command. A moment later, three boxes popped up on Jasper's internal screen.

"All right, space pirate. Blow that place to hell."

A distant tremor shook the ground below, and flames overtook Jasper's vision.

Chapter Sixteen
Penthouse Sweet Penthouse

The villains made easy work of the walls past the cell block, clearing a way out of the labs and into the maze under the city. They plowed through the guards, too. Grace faced little resistance as she rounded up the prisoners and led them out. With what remained of security struggling to fry much bigger fish now, Thea had no trouble brute-forcing the doors open remotely. It was unlikely the prisoners knew who Superangel was, but they were more than happy to follow her out.

The crowd was big, nearly thirty people in total, and most of them weren't exactly in great condition, limiting ladders and stairs as an option. Grace followed directions Jasper had given her earlier to a service elevator. It was used for bringing down larger maintenance equipment, but it still only held half the group. Grace sent half ahead and went up with the second half a few minutes later, silently hoping the entire time that the others would be safe at the top.

She and the others emerged from the elevator, regrouped with the rest of the former prisoners in the maintenance room it spat them out in, and filed out of the back of the government building that housed the room. Waiting outside were Thea, Dax, and Holly. And a stolen bus. Holly wore an equally stolen transit employee uniform. As Grace approached with the prisoners in tow, she adjusted the cap on her head. "All right, get 'em in fast."

The escapees didn't need to be told twice. They hurried in as fast as they could manage, with Dax waving a glowing hand at a few here and there to heal up the worst of their ailments.

Grace stopped next to Thea and folded her arms. "We're still meeting the others at Sarena's apartment, right?"

"Yep. Except Jasper, who should be here any second," Thea replied.

"Try this second!"

Grace, Thea, and Holly turned as Jasper wheeled her motorcycle down the sidewalk toward them. Walking beside her, looking...bored? was Rose.

Holly gestured angrily to Rose the moment she saw her. "What the hell is she doing here?"

"Wish I could tell you." Jasper set a hand on Rose's shoulder as they joined the group. "But she did help me fight Skybreaker. Oh, and she's got blasters in her hands."

"She didn't think to mention that sooner?"

Rose shrugged. "You didn't ask."

"Why would we ask that?" Holly exclaimed.

Rose shrugged again.

"Are either of you hurt?" Dax asked, shooting a glance their way.

"Nope." Jasper glanced at Thea. "But Skybreaker hit my motorcycle with her electricity. It seemed okay on the way here, but there were some sparks earlier that have me a little worried. Could you take a look at it?"

Thea waved a hand dismissively. "Sure, sure, when I have a minute later. I have a lot to do today."

"Great, thanks," Jasper muttered.

The last of the prisoners climbed into the bus. Jasper dragged her motorcycle in next, and Grace and the others followed behind. Holly took the driver's seat. Grace slid onto the bench behind her. Once Jasper had secured her motorcycle on the other side of the aisle, she took the seat at Grace's right. Thea and Dax sat behind the motorcycle, and Rose joined them, apparently to pester them with questions about stars-knew-what.

Jasper watched Rose for a long moment, a distant look in her gaze. Grace wasn't entirely sure if she was actually looking at the young clone of herself or just spacing out. "So, what was that about blasters in Rose's palms?" Grace asked quietly.

"Oh, yeah, the blasters must be built into her arms. Her palms open up and fire the beams." Jasper turned her head forward and tipped it back as she sank further into her seat. Her eyes drifted shut. "I thought—she's so young. I was hoping they hadn't done anything like that to her yet." Her brow furrowed. "Skybreaker seemed surprised too, when she found out. And I think she might have been...angry that they did that to her."

"You think Skybreaker cares about Rose?" Grace frowned.

Jasper shrugged, eyes still shut. "I don't know. She was trying to get Rose to go back to her cell, but she was saying it was for her own good...who knows what she's thinking? She's a crazier version of me, and I'm already not all the way here."

Grace didn't have a response to that. She turned her head to stare out the window as the bus took to the air and moved up through traffic toward the upper districts. Twenty minutes of flying brought them to the top of a sapphire blue building. Holly landed them on a massive balcony jutting out from the building's highest floor.

Grace rose to her feet and took a deep breath. Fighting in the labs was far from easy, but the part of the plan she was really dreading was what came next. A grand speech about rescuing the prisoners that Thea would record and broadcast to the world.

At least she'd be doing it with Sarena.

Grace turned around to address the exhausted faces that filled the bus. "Wait here, everyone. We'll get you all inside in a moment."

Jasper stood up next to Grace with a yawn. "Can't wait to crash at Sarena's place for a while. I bet her furniture's nice and comfy. Oh, and she's probably got good food, too. Maybe a private chef…"

"She made it very clear we're not staying," Holly muttered as she shut off the engine and opened the bus door.

"We'll see about that." Jasper followed Holly to the door. Thea, Dax, Rose, and finally Grace filed out after them onto the balcony. Grace brought along the bag with the remaining pieces of her Superangel costume. As she stepped off the bus, the door into the penthouse slid open, and Sarena stepped out to greet them.

Well, maybe greet wasn't the right word.

"Hey, did you nerds get lost or something?" Sarena rested a hand on her hip. "What took you so long?"

"Sorry, giant buses don't exactly move as fast as motorcycles," Holly replied coolly.

"Whatever. Can we just get this over with already? I hate everything about this plan."

"Why?" Thea asked as she began fiddling with her smartsphere. "We're going with the sanitized version that will save you from Starr's wrath."

"*Might* save me from Starr's wrath. What's to stop him from just lying right back and saying we busted them out of prison or something?"

"If he's smart—and he sure seems to be—he'll assume we recorded video of the labs that we could drop whenever we want," Thea replied. "Which we did. He tries to claim we rescued legal prisoners, we reveal the full extent of the labs and their connection to him."

"I'm still not convinced he's just going to let us get away with this," Sarena said.

"If he wants to avoid dealing with the heat of Sky Labs, then he should."

Jasper cut in. "Besides, this is going to make you look really good."

"There are a million better ways I can do that, but whatever." Sarena's eyes rolled. She turned and started toward the door inside.

Cutthroat and Aymes appeared in the doorway as the group approached. Cutthroat folded his arms. "Since Aymes and Dax are the nicest of this little group, why don't we have them bring the prisoners in while Grace and Sarena record their video?"

"Great idea," Jasper said. "Maybe I can grab them some snacks." She glanced at Sarena. "So, if you just want to give me directions to the kitchen, I can handle that myself."

Serena rolled her eyes again and strolled past Cutthroat and Aymes into the penthouse. While Aymes and Dax headed back to the bus, everyone else followed her in. They entered a wide, well-lit living space dominated by teal, orange, and silver. Two couches and several chairs surrounded a coffee table. Blue and green plants grew out of scattered pots, a chandelier glittering with diamonds hung from above, and a few wide archways led into other parts of the penthouse. Against one wall was a massive aquarium housing Blitz, whose darker orange rings had appeared around his spikes, marking him as Sarena Trench's beloved pet rather than South Siren's infamous sidekick.

Rose tagged along behind Jasper as she went off in search of food. Cutthroat moved to one of the chairs and settled in. The idea of him watching them record made Grace even more apprehensive, but she swallowed her nerves and followed Sarena and Thea to the center of the room. Holly plopped into a chair near Cutthroat.

Thea set her smartsphere on the coffee table and opened the camera screen. After a few moments of making adjustments, she aimed it toward the balcony door. "We'll start recording as they come in. You two ready?"

"Of course I'm ready," Sarena replied in annoyance.

Grace nodded. "I'm good." *I hope.* She picked up her Superangel mask and placed it on her face.

"Good." Thea glanced up. Her gaze settled on the open doorway behind Grace. Grace resisted the urge to glance back.

When voices and footsteps approached, Thea lifted a hand and began counting down with her fingers. *Three. Two. One.*

Grace's mouth opened. The words she'd half-practiced to herself all morning tumbled out. "Hey there, Janus System. This morning, I infiltrated a secret lab hidden under the streets of Kronos. This lab was holding abductees from around the galaxy, and they were being experimented on illegally."

Grace swallowed before continuing. "I've brought these people to a friend of mine to get sanctuary for now." Her head turned. Thea panned the camera toward Sarena.

Serena flashed a smile that seemed surprisingly genuine. "I'm lucky to have a home that has more space than I know what to do with. When Superangel reached out, it only seemed right that I host these escaped abductees until they're able to find some way to move on."

Grace nodded. "I think we can all agree that it's terrible that people were being held in these conditions right under our noses." She folded her arms. "And believe me, I won't stop until I figure out who's responsible and bring them to justice." The team hadn't decided yet exactly when they would reveal Starr was behind Sky Labs, but the video footage would be ready once they'd come up with ways to head off any strategy Starr might use to dissociate himself with the labs.

"And...cut," Thea said. The camera blinked off. "Great job, guys. I'll get that ready for upload." She hopped onto the nearest couch—earning a glare from Sarena that she didn't notice—and grabbed a laptop from her bag.

Sarena headed off to presumably help get the escapees settled. Not sure what else to do with herself in the meantime, Grace sat down next to Thea and watched her work. Holly began scrolling through a news feed on her sphere's holoscreen. Cutthroat leaned back and closed his eyes.

Jasper and Rose returned not long after with armfuls of food. As they joined Grace and Thea on the couch, Thea raised an eyebrow at her screen. "Huh," she said. "Starr has a big announcement that's supposed to be airing soon. Maybe he'll address your lack of, you know, getting executed."

Jasper leaned toward her. "How soon?"

"Ten minutes."

"And how soon until you get that video of Grace and Sarena up?"

"I was planning about an hour," Thea replied. Raising an eyebrow, she added, "Unless you have other ideas."

"No, that's fine. Let's see what Starr has to say." Jasper leaned back and thought for a moment. Next to her, Rose popped open a container of chocolate lunberry cake and dug in. Before Grace could think of anything to add, or wonder much about Starr's impending announcement, Sarena, Dax, and Aymes returned.

"Alright, alright," Sarena said as she reached the seating area. "Everyone's settled and eating. You can all get out now. Just call me whenever you're ready to do something else that makes me look good."

"Their setup is actually comfortable, right?" Jasper was surprisingly stern. "You didn't just cram them all into a closet?"

"It's pretty good," Dax said. Aymes nodded in agreement.

"Also, we're not leaving yet," Holly said. "Starr's about to make an important announcement, apparently. We should all watch the broadcast."

"It's just one thing after another with you people!" The exasperation in Sarena's tone made a few nearby plant leaves wave back and forth. Still, she picked a chair and sat down. Aymes and Dax found seats, too. Thea set up a holoscreen and brought up the governor's channel. A countdown played on the screen.

When the countdown ended, the image changed to an empty podium. It only took a moment for Governor Starr to step into view, Subject Eighteen at his side.

"Citizens of Kronos, it is an honor to address you this morning," Starr said. "Today, we take an important step forward in our efforts to reduce crime here in the Janus System."

Jasper lifted an eyebrow. "Is he just…not addressing my disappearance?"

"Maybe he's hoping whatever this news is will distract everyone," Grace suggested.

Thea nodded. "I mean, people are talking about Jasper on the net, but if the government just continues to ignore the situation, it's not like anyone can do anything about it." She tapped a finger against the coffee table next to the sphere. "And a distraction might help."

Starr continued. "Our star system has long lacked heroes willing to take a stand against the many villains who harm and terrorize our people. And those few who have declared themselves heroes in recent years, or even participated in a handful of seemingly heroic acts, have acted outside of the law.

"Their reckless activities may seem helpful to some." Starr paused. "But it is unsafe to let them continue as they are. And we certainly shouldn't be relying on them. Without guidance from our police forces, figures like this will do more harm than good, and many will get hurt in the crossfire of these vigilante activities."

Jasper frowned "Well, it seems like he's making a pretty clear statement against Superangel."

"He's trying to be subtle, though," Thea pointed out. "He knows a lot of people like her. He doesn't want to turn them against him, so he has to gradually lead them to his point of view."

"Today, I can finally give you a hero fit to be your protector." Starr stepped aside and gestured to someone off screen. A figure moved forward to take his place at the podium.

Starr's hand lowered. "Citizens of the Janus System, meet Captain Cora."

Chapter Seventeen
Players and Pawns

A stunned silence fell over the room. Jasper was the first to finally break it. "What the hell?"

"Looks like someone got a promotion," Holly muttered.

Captain Cora was a man in neon orange body armor, which was plastered with logos for various Kronosian corporations. The most prominent was the bright pink-and-blue Nova Cora logo smack in the middle of his chest. Another covered the front of the helmet tucked under his arm.

Captain Cora had pale blue skin, buzzed dark hair, one violet eye, and one silver cybernetic orb to replace the eye he'd lost.

Captain Cora was Bruce Wright.

Jasper glanced at Grace, who was undoubtedly recalling the same day she was. The day they'd met. Their encounter with the Sky District's chief of police who had arrested them and thrown them in the same cell.

Starr was still talking. "Funded by generous businesses from across Kronos, businesses who care about their communities and all of our citizens—"

Jasper let out a short, cold laugh. "Yeah, right."

"—Captain Cora will use state-of-the-art body armor and high-tech weaponry to combat villains in ways that ordinary police officers can't."

"I'm guessing he's got those fancy new blasters," Dax said.

Thea nodded. "Undoubtedly."

Grace's brow furrowed as she stared at the screen. "I don't get it. If Starr wants a new hero to defend Kronos and make himself look good, why not have Subject Eighteen do it? She's actually got an enhanced body and better cybernetics."

Jasper could only guess at Starr's intentions, but she was pretty good at guessing. "She's supposed to be Starr's right hand," she said. "His personal protector. This new hero on the other hand...he's supposed to protect everyone. Of course, he's really the personification of protecting the elite. And corporate Kronos as a whole." And even if Starr did trust Eighteen, he probably recognized her personality didn't make her a good candidate for a corporate-friendly hero.

Holly snorted. "Yeah, Starr can go on about Captain Cora being for the people all he wants. The only people someone like that is going to be protecting are people in the upper districts."

"I'm sure that won't stop some people in the lower districts from falling for his plan, though," Jasper added with a sigh. The gears in her mind were already turning, searching for ways they could make Captain Cora look bad. And, by extension, Starr.

"Do we need to worry about him, you think?" Grace glanced at Jasper.

Jasper chewed her lip for a moment. "Well, he's another player in Starr's game. Could just be a pawn, could be something bigger. But this seems like Starr trying to add another layer to protect his image." The image they were trying to tear apart. "With the missing criminal execution still on a lot of people's minds, he needs something like this."

Sarena raised an eyebrow. "We could handle him, couldn't we?"

"Sure," Jasper replied. "I'm not sure it's worth the time or energy right now, though. I think for the time being, Captain Bruce Wright Cora is going to keep doing the cop stuff he was doing before, just with more firepower."

"When we inevitably take the fight to the government, he'll be one of the prominent figures we'll be fighting," Aymes pointed out. He folded his arms. "It will help our cause if we can make him look bad beforehand."

Smart kid. He was picking this stuff up fast. "I agree," Jasper replied with a nod. "But I think we can wait a little longer on that front, is all. There's no reason to add more pressure to our plans just because Starr put a cop in a capitalism-fueled superhero uniform."

Aymes nodded slowly. "Fair enough."

The room fell quiet for a moment, letting the sound of Starr's broadcast dominate again. But Starr seemed to be wrapping things up. "I hope you can all rest easy tonight knowing you have a new protector, a champion dedicated to preserving our beautiful city-planet, and the other worlds of the Janus system."

Jasper rolled her eyes.

"This announcement won't mean much to people without quick results," Cutthroat said. "And Starr knows that. We may not need to worry about Captain Cora right away, but I'm sure he's going to try and do something big, quickly. Something along the lines of taking down a big villain."

"That shouldn't interfere with our plans," Jasper said.

"No, but the more goodwill he earns with the people, the harder it will be to turn them against him later."

Cutthroat had a point, but Jasper still felt there were bigger priorities than rushing out to kick Bruce's ass. As much as she wanted to, it would have to wait.

Focus on what's killing you fastest.

Nothing was killing her right now. Not quickly, anyway. Time to stop focusing on protecting herself, on running from her problems, and get on the offense. Focus on the biggest pieces. The biggest pillars holding Starr up. The rest would fall into place, in time.

"Why'd they give him such an ugly costume?" Rose asked as the camera zoomed in on Captain Cora waving to the crowd.

"Ugly costume for an ugly hero protecting an ugly city," Jasper replied. Rose laughed at that, and the sound put a smile on Jasper's face. She was glad the kid seemed to be lighthearted and happy, for the most part. Despite everything she must have gone through in the labs. It had taken Jasper a long time to laugh again after she'd made her escape.

With all of Starr's talk about vigilantes being dangerous and on the wrong side of the law, the team would also need to step up their game in molding Superangel into someone the people could rally around. And while Jasper was dismissing the other's concerns about Captain Cora for now, a confrontation between the two so-called heroes seemed inevitable.

Thea stood up. "While we're all here, we should talk about the next phase of our plan."

Serena groaned. "Can't it wait? It's been a long day."

"It's barely noon."

Holly, Dax, and Grace moved to stand next to Thea as she brought up a holoscreen projection on her smartsphere.

"So, the presenter becomes the presentee," Jasper said under her breath. Next to her, Rose tore open a bag of spherical chips. She held it out, and Jasper plunged a hand in to take a few.

"So, what are you guys planning, anyway?" Rose asked.

"Oh, nothing big. Just making Grace into a superhero, going up against Governor Starr, ending his ring of bounty hunters and dangerous experiments, exposing his true nature to the galaxy and the Interstar Council, and overthrowing the government." Jasper popped one of the chips into her mouth.

Rose grinned. "That sounds awesome."

Jasper chewed and swallowed. "It will be." Despite being chips, the seasoned meat flavor and unusual texture made it feel like she was eating a nice meal. "Wow, these taste expensive."

"They are," Sarena muttered.

Thea cleared her throat and gestured to the 3D model of the Governor's Palace she'd brought up. "Ready when you are."

Jasper leaned back on the couch and nodded. "Take it away."

"So, while you were away, we began assessing the Governor's Palace and developing some potential ideas for a siege plan." Thea reached out and gave the model a slow spin. "I'm still gathering intel on what we're dealing with inside, but we already know we'll need to make a few trips outside Kronos. And the other things we're dealing with will likely keep taking us around the star system, too." She glanced at the others.

Dax cleared his throat. "The Astronomer is nice, but it's also big. We have to park way out of the way, and even then, it can be hard to avoid drawing attention. Especially when visiting cities."

"If we had something smaller, we could run our errands more discretely," Grace said. "It'll also make getting to any warps we hear about easier, if Starr's still hunting those down."

"And we'll be less obvious than Jasper on that damn motorcycle," Holly added, quieter.

"So, in order to move forward, we should first get our hands on a smaller spaceship," Thea concluded. "Something small and fast we can take around any planet." She waved a hand, and the smartsphere's projection switched to a map of the Janus System. A few red dots appeared across the various planets and moons. "I've identified a few places where we could potentially get our hands on one. Military bases, transport operations, engineering facilities—"

"No need," Jasper cut in. Sure, the locations Thea had picked out would offer ships that were good. Great, even. Small, fast, armed. But there was a better option. An option that quite possibly no one else in the galaxy knew about, besides her.

Holly frowned. "What do you mean, no need? You don't think a ship would help us?"

"No, you guys are right, having a small spacecraft is a great idea." Jasper smirked. "But I already know where we can get one. The best one."

Chapter Eighteen
Eighteen

A video of a burning Mota Mart played on the holoscreen. Some chemical had been spread to turn the flames green, and another rambling message about destroying the elite was written on the side of the building in neon spray paint. Syrus still hadn't found a high-quality clip of that green lightning people claimed this villain wielded, but the reports seemed believable.

Syrus Starr was not afraid of Skybreaker. Not of any of the villains that wreaked havoc on the streets of his city. Most of them knew better than to get in his way, and he had ways of dealing with those that didn't.

But while Skybreaker had kept from troubling him much so far, there was an undercurrent to their plans that suggested something bigger. Something that might eventually be directed at him. Plus, while she was only attacking the lower districts, those Mota Marts did belong to a powerful man. And he was getting antsy.

As the news clip ended, an assistant walked through the open door into Syrus's office with a tablet in hand. They glanced briefly around the room, at the neatly organized shelves and display cases and the pristine black wood desk. "Sir, the reports from security are done. Nothing out of the ordinary from the footage for Subject Eighteen's room."

Syrus reached out a hand to accept the tablet. "Thank you." His bodyguard had given him no reason to doubt her yet. The lab researchers had planned every second of her training, her education, and his interactions with her, all to ensure loyalty to him alongside her drive to destroy Van Terra.

But he hadn't made it this far by being anything but overly cautious. Every ambassador that entered the palace was scrutinized. Every security guard was questioned on protocol daily. Every piece of evidence connecting Syrus to his underground work was secured. Or better yet, burned.

And every second of footage in Eighteen's room in the lab was carefully studied.

Her psychological programming was supposed to be perfect. But the lab rarely got things right on the first try, and she was the only clone from the Jade Project to be raised to adulthood. He had to double check, triple check, just to make sure. But in this case…

"Nothing," he muttered as the assistant left the room. He scrolled through the report on the tablet screen, detailing every minute of Eighteen's activities over the past pentasol. Nothing out of the ordinary. Nothing incriminating. And the last of the footage that had been transmitted from Sky Labs before it burned had showed her defending it tooth and nail.

She seemed eager to please. Could she have learned to act like that in the environment she'd been raised in? The training simulations based on Van Terra's memories had taught her a lot about deceiving people.

Well, she'd been reliable so far, and if she truly wanted him dead, she'd had plenty of opportunities. Opportunities she wouldn't have much longer, with the progress made on his new army. He could spare a dozen of his new soldiers to defend him around the clock. Neither Eighteen nor Van Terra would stand a chance against him then.

Speaking of Van Terra…

Syrus dismissed the video clip he'd been watching and started a call with the Tide District police chief he'd spoken with the night before. The turquoise-skinned man answered quickly.

"Governor Starr," he blurted. "How are you?"

"Fine, Chief Cephalo. How did your meeting with those fishermen go?"

"Great, sir. They accepted the money. No one should be hearing about…well, you know."

"Good. Thank you." Syrus knew better than to blindly trust that the men who'd seen Van Terra would keep their mouths shut. He'd assigned some of his security detail to tail them. He did hope that the money would be enough motivation to keep them quiet, though. He hated making more messes in the process of cleaning up. It was miracle enough they'd gone directly to the police without blabbing to a dozen other people first.

Syrus ended the call and leaned back in his chair, his mind still on Van Terra. With Sky Labs destroyed, his idea of pulling one of the clones from storage to take her place in the execution was no longer possible. All of the clones besides Eighteen and Twenty-Eight were essentially dead anyway, only kept alive through tubes and cryogenics in case the biologists needed tissue samples. But one could have been propped up long enough to make it believable.

Well, it hadn't been a great long-term plan, anyway. Van Terra was sure to make it publicly known sooner or later that she was free. The upside of admitting her escape first would be the ability to initiate a system-wide manhunt with a handsome reward. If every citizen were actively on the lookout, it might finally be possible to find her.

The downside, of course, was admitting her escape.

II. BLUE MOUNTAIN RESORT

Chapter Nineteen
Slippery Slopes

The light dusting of fresh snow wasn't bad, but the bitter cold nipped at all of Jasper's exposed skin as she and the team trekked up the mountain slope. And this was the hemisphere's *summer* weather. This landscape would be near impossible to survive in the winter.

It wasn't quite the peak of summer in the Si Heran mountains, so there were still a few dark hours during the planet's rotation. Like right now. On top of that, there was a thick blanket of clouds hanging overhead, with only a little of Vala's moonlight visible at the horizon. Jasper would have much preferred to come later in the day, both to sleep in and to wait for things to get a few degrees warmer, but Cutthroat had insisted they get an early start. Jasper couldn't imagine waiting a few more hours to get the ship would make much of a difference, but whatever. They did have quite a ways to hike.

Cutthroat had flown the entire team out to this mountain in the Astronomer. This far from the cities, it was easy for him to park the massive spaceship without being seen, once they actually found a clearing big enough. But the team was right. They would need a smaller ship going forward.

Back on Kronos, Sarena's personal assistants—yes, assistants *plural*—had agreed to take care of the Sky Labs escapees and keep the penthouse locked down. Pirates and sirens would be staying with them to help, and that combined with Sarena's security system would hopefully be enough to keep the place safe if anyone did decide to come after the former prisoners.

And although there was plenty of reluctance on everyone's part, Rose was accompanying them up the mountain this morning. The team had tried to make her stay back at the penthouse, but she'd managed to sneak onto the Astronomer and hide in a storage closet, avoiding discovery until they were far from Kronos. Attempting to get her to stay on the ship seemed equally futile, so they'd brought her along on the trek through the slopes. If she was going to be running around trying to help regardless, she'd be safer in the middle of the group.

Plus, the mission was likely to be danger-free. Jasper knew better than to expect no issues at all, but their destination was remote, and there was no reason for anyone else to be near it—no one else could possibly know it existed at all.

During her time in the Si Heran resistance, Jasper had flown quite a few spaceships. And she'd seen the prototypes for many more. They were all kept here in these mountains, far away from prying eyes. Ships kept in this particular hangar were in varying states of completion, last she'd seen them, but there were sure to be at least a few that were ready to fly.

"Jasper, are you sure this place is still here?" Holly asked as they continued up a particularly steep hill.

Jasper nodded. "It'd be pretty hard to get rid of without blowing the whole mountain up."

"And these super high-tech, very expensive spaceships are just sitting there untouched?" Holly's skepticism was thick in her tone, even with her breathing growing a little ragged. They would need to take a break soon.

"The base requires a bunch of codes to get in. And that's assuming you can even find your way to the entrance." Jasper threw a quick glance back at Holly before returning her gaze to the next peak. They'd be cresting this one in only a couple more minutes.

"Only resistance members know the codes," Jasper continued. "And all of them but me were killed. I'm the only person alive who can access these ships." She paused, letting the group that had grown a little spaced out get into a tighter formation. It also gave her a moment to access a satellite map and double check their location.

Jasper glanced back again. Her gaze moved over the group, making sure no one looked too exhausted. "We're close. It's underground, so we won't be able to see it, but the ground above it will be visible at the top of the hill after this one."

She didn't move on yet. A minute for everyone to catch their breath would be fine. No need to rush.

The wind picked up, making Jasper grimace, but Cutthroat glanced up with an oddly...serene expression. "Clouds are moving out," he said softly. "Finally. They come and go fast this time of year."

"You've been out here?" Jasper asked.

"Not these mountains specifically, but the range to the north," Cutthroat replied. "A lot of ships crashed up there a few winters back when storms were particularly bad. Some braindead businessman tried to use the usual shipping routes anyway and lost a lot of cargo in the process. Plenty of pirates went in to clean up after."

Jasper followed his gaze upward, and sure enough, the clouds were dissipating fast. But rather than stars lighting up on a dark background behind them, shifting colors began to appear in the sky.

"Give it a few seconds," Cutthroat said.

Grace moved to Jasper's side as the sky lit up with a neon rainbow aurora, reflecting even more colors than the ones from Earth Jasper had seen pictures of. Beneath the sky, peak after peak of snow-coated rock nearly glowed in the new surge of light. Patches of dark green forest cut through the white further down the mountain slope. Miraculous monuments of life in a place that had every reason to be dead.

"It's beautiful," Grace said after a moment.

"I think that's an understatement, somehow." After a long moment, Jasper reached out to grab Grace's hand. It would have been better if they weren't both wearing gloves, but the reassuring squeeze from Grace was nice all the same.

Holly, Dax, Thea, Rose, and Aymes all looked up in awe as well. Sarena—who'd left Blitz behind in the warm Astronomer—didn't look as enthused at first, but the longer she stared up at the northern lights, the more her expression softened.

A minute later, the team pressed on up the mountain. Rose picked up her pace quickly, bringing herself to Jasper's other side.

"Hey, Thorn," Jasper said to her. "Willing to spare any of your snacks?" Rose held out the container she'd been eating from during the hike. Jasper snagged a few chips coated in a spicy blue sauce.

The horizon hinted at the morning sun by the time they neared the top of the next hill. At the top, Jasper stopped and stared at the sight that waited in the valley below. Her hand pulled away from Grace's so that she could gesture angrily to the scattered clusters of buildings, the distant crowds, the first rays of dawn reflecting off parked vehicles and spacecraft.

"There's supposed to be nothing out here!" Jasper exclaimed.

Thea caught up on Grace's other side and raised an eyebrow. "Well, there's something."

Jasper mind raced while Thea pulled a tablet out of her bag. Had someone else known the base's location after all? A surviving resistance member, or a spy, or—?

"Blue Mountain Resort," Thea read aloud.

"A *resort*?" Could it be entirely unrelated to the secret hangar, then?

Thea brought up a map of the place. "There's rooms, restaurants, slopeboarding lifts, hot tubs—"

Ooh, a hot tub sounded so nice right now. Jasper had to remind herself to stay focused. Though, maybe if they had time after getting a ship...

"—cabins, a handful of shops," Thea continued. "And a few other small attractions."

"Well, Jasper, glad you were super-duper confident that no one else knew where this secret base was," Holly said. She folded her arms as Jasper glanced back at her. "What now?"

Jasper rubbed her forehead. Forced herself to think. Maybe the situation wasn't as bad as it looked. "The hangar is pretty deep underground. It's still likely no one knows it's there. But of all the places to build a mountain resort..."

"To be fair," Thea said. "This is one of the few places in these mountains tame enough to build anything at all." She tapped the screen a few times. "Looks like quite a few parties bid on the land. A lot of people wanted to put something here."

"Well, can we confirm that the hangar and spaceships are still underground before I make the trek to the entrance?" Jasper asked.

Thea nodded. "Sure, I can take some scans, but we'll need to be right above where the hangar is supposed to be."

Jasper's head turned so that she could study the resort again. "I think we'll need to get right to the heart of all that."

Thea pulled up a map of Blue Mountain Resort and held it out to Jasper. Jasper's eyes flitted between the map and the valley below before she finally pointed to a spot on the screen. "Here, looks like this building is where we'll want to be."

Thea took the tablet back and zoomed in. Did a little tapping, a little typing. "That's a hotel, but the first floor is mainly used for events, apparently. So, most of the rooms could be empty at the moment."

Jasper shrugged. "And if there is something big going on, we'll just have to find a way in." Her earlier confidence gradually returning, she grabbed Grace's hand again and started toward the resort.

"Great. All downhill from here," Holly muttered behind them.

It quickly became apparent that there was, in fact, something big going on. The air was thick with the sound of far more shouting than would ordinarily be expected at a presumably expensive resort, and the crowds were much thicker than they should have been, too. There also seemed to be a lot of bright signs stuck up on posts to direct people around, but they were unreadable from this distance.

They eventually reached a winding stone path at the edge of the resort property that led them through scattered cabins toward bigger buildings near the main entrance. Jasper squinted at the first discernable group of people that appeared in the distance. "Are those people wearing costumes, or do rich people just dress really weird these days?" The clothes looked like a strange blend of high-tech space wear and fantasy armor.

"Must be an event of some kind, right?" Dax asked.

"Maybe the crowd will be easy to blend into?" Grace suggested. She glanced at Jasper. "Easier than just a bunch of rich elites on vacation, anyway."

Cutthroat let out what sounded like a very skeptical hum. "We should probably figure out what's going on before we get our hopes up."

"Yeah," Aymes added. "Maybe someone could check out a sign or a banner or one of those neon flyers that seem to be floating around."

Jasper threw him a look and raised an eyebrow. "Send one of your birds or flies, why don't you?"

"That might draw unwanted attention. It's unusual to see animals out here."

Right. "Fair enough."

The people got closer, the details on their clothes became visible, and Jasper realized there was something familiar about some of the outfits. Before she could put her finger on it, Sarena gasped.

The rest of the group stopped and turned to face her. She stood frozen at the back of the party, eyes wide. "Oh, no. No, no, no. I'm out."

"Why?" Jasper glanced around. There was no indication of danger. No sign of anything that could hurt them. "What's happening?"

Sarena let out a loud, pained groan. "It's StarConCon."

Chapter Twenty
StarConCon Conquerors

Jasper was a little relieved to see that everyone else looked just as confused as she felt. Sarena's complaint was met with blank stares, and a few of the others exchanged glances.

"StarConCon?" Holly repeated. "Whatever that is, it sounds stupid as hell."

Sarena pulled up the hood of her coat and pulled the drawstrings tight, partially hiding her face. "It's the Star Conquerors Convention," she elaborated. "Not an officially sanctioned one, otherwise I'd probably get roped into going. Just a bunch of the show's craziest and richest fans throwing a convention on their own."

"This doesn't seem too bad, though," Dax said, glancing around.

"If that catch wind I'm here, they'll be on me in a frenzy." Sarena buried her face in her hands.

Jasper shrugged. "No biggie. Well just throw a quick disguise on you."

Sarena peeked at Jasper through her fingers. "Okay, I also don't want to be around a bunch of crazy people. Can I just wait on the ship?"

"You want to hike all the way back by yourself?"

"Yes. Gladly."

"You'll be fine," Jasper replied with a dismissive wave of her hand. "Besides, we might be able to use this to our advantage."

"I'm not revealing myself as Sarena Trench."

"We'll see."

"What are you planning?"

"Don't worry about it."

"Whatever it is, I'm not doing it."

Jasper turned. "I said, 'we'll see.' Now come on, we don't have all day."

"Ooh, ooh, can I take a look around?" Rose jumped up and down a couple of times. "I love Star Conquerors."

Jasper frowned. "Aren't you a little young to be watching that show?"

"They let me watch it sometimes in the lab."

"Well, I'm not sure those people know much about childcare." At least Rose's experience had been better than a year in a cell with no entertainment whatsoever. That would probably be less healthy than a couple of slightly mature television shows.

Rose offered a small shrug in response. "Some of the scientists loved it. They snuck in episodes at work when they didn't have too much to do."

"Oh, how heartwarming. Those evil scientists who tortured children are just like the rest of us!"

Thea brought the resort map back up on her tablet. "Looks like we'll have to take the lift a little ways up the slope to get to the hotel."

"Lead the way," Jasper told her.

Sarena kept her face hidden as best she could with her hood and a pair of sunglasses as they walked through the crowd of excited Star Conquerors fans in costume. They also passed some groups of people dressed in ordinary clothes. Fancy and expensive clothes, sure, but not costumes. They ranged from completely disinterested to mildly annoyed by the show fans mingling around them.

A few minutes of walking brought the team to the lift. An employee approached them as they stepped into the line. "You got tickets?" he asked.

"We're just trying to get to the convention center at the hotel," Jasper told him. "We're not slopeboarding."

The employee shook his head. "Doesn't matter. You need tickets for the lift regardless."

Jasper nudged Sarena and shot her A Look. *Your time to shine, pop star.*

"Already?" Sarena huffed. "I thought we'd have a little more time before this went downhill."

"Come on, Sar," Jasper pleaded in response. "You can get us on the lift."

Sarena sighed and removed her sunglasses. "They're my security team."

The employee frowned. "Security...team?"

Sarena's voice lowered. "I'm Sarena Trench."

"Oh! You are! Oh my stars, I can't believe it!" In contrast to Sarena's, the man's voice jumped high in volume.

"Shhh!" Sarena waved her hands frantically as she shushed him. "We can't have the whole resort knowing."

"Yeah," Jasper added. "It's a secret. Huge secret. She's going to make a surprise appearance."

The employee nodded eagerly. "Of course. Completely understand." He leaned forward, and his expression changed, his brow furrowing. "Is that...white hair under your hood?"

"It's a wig," Sarena told him quickly. "Trying to keep this a secret, remember? Now, can we get on the lift, or not?"

The employee nodded again. "Uh, if it's not too much trouble, though, could I... get your autograph?" He reached into the pocket of his snow pants and pulled out a pen and a resort pamphlet. Sarena shot Jasper a desperate look, a silent plea in her eyes.

"It's just one teensy little autograph." Jasper gestured to the man. "Least you could do, considering how helpful he's being."

Sarena mouthed the words "I hate you" before accepting the man's pen and pamphlet. As she scribbled down her name and handed the items back, she said, "And remember. Keep this a secret." This time, as she spoke the words, Jasper could tell she was pouring her power into them. The employee was completely mesmerized as he nodded yet again.

After that, he left the team to check the tickets of the people who'd joined the line after them. When they reached the front, Jasper, Grace, and Rose squeezed into one lift chair. Dax, Holly, and Thea took the one behind them, then Sarena, Cutthroat, and Aymes brought up the back of the group.

Rose leaned forward to peer at people coming down the snowy slope on boards below. "Does anyone have anything we can throw at them?"

Jasper laughed. "Why do you want to do that?"

"It'll be funny."

Jasper glanced at Grace, who looked to be holding back laughter herself. When Jasper's eyes met hers, she cleared her throat. "We should probably avoid drawing attention to ourselves right now," she said.

Rose sighed. "Fine." She began kicking her legs back and forth. Her hands moved into her coat pockets to pull out pieces of candy she'd stashed away.

They hopped off the lift at the first stop. The line of chairs continued upward to higher slopes for more intense boarding, but the resort's buildings and other attractions ended here. A path led away from the slopes and into the cluster of buildings that included the hotel.

Entering the building's lobby felt like stepping into an oversized—and probably overpriced—cabin. Dark wood interior, animal heads hanging on the walls, paintings of forests, lots of browns and reds and dark greens. And the star of the show was a massive fireplace alight with purpley-blue flames.

A pillar of stacked stones held a map and directory. Thea made a beeline for it, and the others trailed behind. Sarena fell into pace next to Rose as they walked, just ahead of Jasper and Grace. "So, kid, you said you watch my show?"

Rose shoved another piece of candy in her mouth and nodded.

"Who's your favorite character?"

"Captain Denner," Rose answered through a mouthful of chocolate.

Sarena frowned. "Don't you like Livia Starbright?"

Jasper snorted. Of course Sarena would obsess over whether some random kid liked the character she played. She found her fans annoying, but that didn't mean she didn't love having them. As long as they kept their distance.

Rose shrugged. Swallowed. "Eh, she's alright."

Sarena's eyes narrowed. Rose glanced up at her and began laughing maniacally. Jasper grinned.

"Kids these days," Sarena muttered as she stormed up to where Thea stood. The others caught up and gathered around.

Thea tapped the directory. "I think this room's our best bet. G7. There's an event in there soon, but if we hurry, I should be able to do what we need to do before people start coming in."

The rest of the team followed her into one of the halls leading away from the lobby and quickly got caught up in a thick crowd. Jasper took the lead and shoved her way forward. "Outta my way, people, or I'm gonna start throwing elbows."

Rose lifted her fists. "Yeah, outta our way!"

They made it halfway down the hall before someone stepped directly into Jasper's path, forcing her to stop. The woman's eyes were fixed on Sarena. For a moment, Jasper feared they were about to see the frenzy Sarena had been afraid of, but then the woman said, "Hey, nice Luna costume."

"What? I'm not wearing a costume." Sarena glanced down at her winter hiking outfit, the sunglasses she still wore reflecting the hotel lights. Gaze darting back up to the woman, she added, "Besides, don't you think I look more like Livia?"

The woman looked her up and down. "Uh, sorry, I don't really see it."

As the woman walked off, Jasper muttered, "Really couldn't help yourself there, could you?"

"How could she not see it!" Sarena exclaimed indignantly, eyes still on the woman walking away.

Holly shot her a look that was somewhere between confused and annoyed. "Aren't you worried about blowing your cover?"

"Well, apparently I don't need to be."

"We don't have time to deal with your ego. Come on." Jasper pressed forward. At the end of the hall, she took the corner to the right and nearly took a fist to the face.

The woman throwing the punch barely avoided grazing Jasper as she hit her target, another fan wearing a costume for the same character she was. At first, Jasper thought that might have been why they were fighting, but then the shouting began.

"You're insane if you think Luna is actually going to marry Jevsier!" the puncher shouted.

"Their relationship is perfect!" the other fan screamed in reply.

"It's the most toxic thing I've ever seen. Luna and Denny should be together!"

The second fan slapped the first. The first rubbed her face. "Weak. Just what I'd expect from a Lunny truther. The writers would never do that."

"Whoa, I didn't realize there was so much violence at these things." Jasper was beginning to wonder if she should come to more of these events, if only to watch people like this.

"Yeah!" Rose exclaimed. She pumped a fist in the air. "Fight! Fight! Fight!"

"Like I said," Sarena muttered. "Crazy people."

"This is the same fanbase that destroys stores when Sarena releases new merch." Holly folded her arms as the first woman threw another punch, only to miss. "Are you really surprised?"

On the other side of the hall, Jasper spotted the door to room G7. Next to it was a lone security guard. His eyes were on the two women, but he wasn't moving to do anything about the breakout of violence. Yet.

Jasper cupped her hands around her mouth. "Come on, Lunny truthers!" she shouted. "Are we just going to let her get away with attacking one of our own like that?"

That incited a round of shouts and boos from the crowd. A few of the fans nearest to the fight moved forward, egged on by the growing chants Jasper had encouraged. Sets of fists went up. Some people nearby began shoving each other.

Rose was still chanting at the women to continue their fight, and the number of people standing still to watch the action—and block traffic—was growing by the second. Only a few more moments passed before the guard stepped away from the wall and started toward the chaos.

Jasper took the chance to dart forward and slip through the door to G7.

Chapter Twenty-One
Jingle Most Of The Way

Room G7 held a small stage, which in turn held a long table and several chairs. Between the stage and the entrance were twenty or so rows of additional chairs. While Jasper paused to assess the space—scanning for alternate exits and potential weapons—Thea made a beeline for the stage, already opening her laptop as she ran.

Jasper turned back to the door, where the others were filing in. "Cutthroat, Aymes, can you two stay outside and keep watch?"

"On it," Aymes replied. Cutthroat nodded and joined him in slipping back out. The door fell shut with a heavy thud that Jasper could only hope didn't draw much attention on the outside. Judging by the shouting coming from the hallway, she probably didn't have much to worry about.

As Jasper moved to join Thea—Grace, Rose, Dax, Holly, and Sarena in tow—she noted the room's decorations. Coniferous trees dragged in from outside standing tall in the corners. Silver and pink tinsel along the walls. Strings of rainbow lights along the ceiling. "Hey, looks like they celebrate Christmas at this resort," Jasper said, pace slowing so she could study the room further. "Maybe we should hang around a little while after I find us a ship."

Dax's brow furrowed. "Uh, sure, but it seems a little off from the Christmas I remember on Earth."

"Whaddaya mean?"

"Well, they spray painted the trees pink." Dax pointed to a spot above the doors they'd entered through. "And that painting of Santa makes him look like a fantasy elf. And his reindeer are humanoid aliens with antlers. How are they supposed to pull a sleigh?"

Jasper shrugged, less interested in the finer details of the decor and more excited about participating in holiday festivities for the first time in about six decades. "Well, holidays taken from other planets rarely get perfectly translated. As long as they've got the spirit of things…"

Sarena stared up at the painting Dax had pointed out and frowned. "Is that not an accurate depiction of the lore? I used to perform at a lot of Christmas parties. I always sang that song about the adventures of the glowing-antlered hero of the north."

Jasper frowned. "Yeah, that's not—never mind."

But before she could continue pushing her plans to look into the resort's holiday activities, Thea waved a hand. "Hey, I've got my scans pulled up." Her finger moved to point at her screen. Jasper rushed to peer over her shoulder and squinted at the shapes, trying to make sense of them.

"Big hollow area under the base," Thea explained, gesturing to a dark mass in the center of the screen. "And look at these smaller objects here. Could be—"

"Spaceships," Jasper finished with a nod.

"So, you wanna go straight down?"

Jasper shook her head. "Base is impenetrable from above. I'll go in the front door. But I'll have to take the lift up to the top of the mountain and hike a bit. It's a long walk from the entrance down to the actual hangar."

"I think there's a faster way, if you want to call up your motorcycle from the Astronomer." Thea switched from her scan of the underground to a map of the mountain. "They're called snow corridors. Mostly used for maintenance vehicles and the like, so there shouldn't be any traffic. They run from the base of the mountain up past the highest point of the resort." She glanced up at Jasper. "Should cover all the ground you need and keep you away from prying eyes."

Perfect. Jasper touched the comm in her ear. "Cutthroat. How fast can you get me my bike?"

Cutthroat responded with a heavy sigh. "Doesn't it have automatic driving?"

"Yeah, but it'll take—" Jasper flipped to her own map on her internal screen. "—like, twenty-five minutes to get here."

"Well, we're not in that much of a hurry, are we?"

It was Jasper's turn to sigh. "Fine, I'll summon it off the ship." Even just an escape pod from the Astronomer would probably draw too much attention, anyway. Not that a self-driving motorcycle *wouldn't* draw attention, but you had to take what you could get sometimes.

"What should we do in the meantime?" Grace asked, moving closer to the stage. Behind her, Dax, Holly, Rose, and Sarena also took steps forward, waiting for Jasper's answer.

"I vote we get the hell out of this place," Sarena said before Jasper could speak. She threw an apprehensive glance back at the door. "If they figure out who I really am, I'm never gonna make it out. And even if they don't, I can't take another minute around those weirdos."

"Those weirdos are the reason you're rich," Holly reminded her.

"We'll regroup outside, and you guys can find a place out of the way to wait for me," Jasper said. "Before we leave though, Thea, can you check if the Blue Mountain Resort has any events happening today—?"

"Hey, you've got people trying to get in there," Cutthroat warned over comms. "Security's headed our way, too. I don't think we can keep them out without starting a fight."

Jasper rolled her shoulders. "Okay, let's get out."

"You got an exit strategy that doesn't involve walking into security?" Cutthroat asked.

"Yup. Let 'em in."

Sarena's eyes went wide. "What?" she yelped.

Jasper ignored her. "Thea, pack it up. Once the crowd floods in, it'll be easy to slip out."

"Can't we go out the window or something?" Sarena protested. "I don't want them anywhere near me—"

The doors swung open.

"Nope," Jasper said cheerfully as she hopped off the stage. "Let's roll." Behind her, Thea zipped up her bag and moved to follow.

A moment later, the crowd poured in. Jasper and the others met them in roughly the middle of the room. While most people were focused on finding seats for whatever panel was about to take place here, a few people in security uniforms were moving a little quicker. And they were headed toward Jasper.

"Hey, what were you doing in here?" one of the guards asked as he and two of his colleagues approached.

Jasper's head tipped to the side. "What do you mean? We came in with everyone else."

"But I saw—" The guard stopped and frowned, apparently doubting his own eyes under Jasper's unwavering confidence. It was easy enough to bulldoze through his hesitation. Jasper ignored the guard's orders to "hold on just a moment," and within seconds, she and the others had vanished into the crowd of fanatics trying to find seats.

The team regrouped with Cutthroat and Aymes in the hallway. From there, they moved outside the building and followed a path to a quieter area between the hotel's conference center and a mini market. While they'd escaped the crowds, there were still plenty of people in costume wandering the resort grounds. Jasper lowered her voice as she laid out their next steps.

"Alrighty, my motorcycle is en route," she told the others. "I'll head out to the hangar, grab a ship, and meet you guys at the edge of the resort property."

"Where will you exit the hangar?" Cutthroat asked. "The resort isn't in the way, is it?"

Jasper shook her head. "The hangar door opens in the side of a cliff below the resort. It can only be opened from the inside."

Sarena's arms folded. "Why don't we just come with you to the hangar?"

"The hangar has an intense security system, and trying to guide you guys through without anyone getting hurt will take forever," Jasper explained. She waved a hand dismissively. "It will be easier if I go by myself. You all wait up here. I'll come pick you up soon."

Sarena groaned. "Please don't leave me here."

"Too late." Jasper turned. Before walking away, though, she added, "And keep a close eye on Rose. All of you."

"Hey!" Rose said indignantly. "What's that supposed to mean?"

"It means you're a troublemaker. "Jasper shot her a glance and raised an eyebrow. "Which I generally consider a compliment, but it's also something I can't really deal with right now."

Rose rolled her eyes. "I can handle myself. I don't need babysitters."

"Don't think of them as babysitters. Think of them as your personal security."

"I'm not an idiot."

"I'm no one's personal security," Sarena added, sounding just as indignant as Rose.

Cutthroat waved a hand. "Let's get a move on, Van Terra. I'd rather not be here all day."

"All right, all right." Jasper moved away from the group and started toward the edge of the resort to wait for her motorcycle. As she neared an area where paths and buildings gave way to snow and trees, she checked on the motorcycle through her internal camera feed. Almost halfway. She trekked into the forest and made a slight adjustment in the steering to bring it her way. Eventually, its engine became audible in the distance.

The motorcycle slowed a little as it rolled up to Jasper, but it was still moving pretty fast. She mentally willed it to brake and frowned when it didn't immediately respond. After a few more seconds, it jerked to an abrupt stop, rolled forward again, then made another sudden stop next to her.

"Yikes," she muttered. Thea still hadn't had a chance to examine the vehicle after the blow it had taken from Skybreaker. Well, it had made it all the way here, so it should be able to manage getting Jasper to the hangar. Hopefully. She put on her helmet, swung a leg over the seat, and hit the gas.

As Jasper set off north, she pulled up a map to find the snow corridors Thea had mentioned. The resort grounds disappeared behind her, and the world became nothing but snowy forest terrain. Dark blue-green conifers dusted with white. The glare of the rising sun bouncing off icy hills. The faintest hints of neon in the sky above, the only remnants of the vibrant aurora they'd seen earlier.

The landscape remained as ordinary forest for only a few minutes. Then, towering walls of snow appeared through the gaps in the trees ahead. Taller than many of the resort buildings. It didn't take Jasper long to spot an opening in the side of the snow wall.

A click signaled that someone's comm was unmuting. Thea spoke. "Hey J, I looked into the event schedule you were asking about. There is stuff going on today we can discuss later, but I've also got some bad news about the snow corridors—"

"Uh, hang on," Jasper cut her off as the sound of engines reached her ears. She scanned the surroundings, heart racing. Her head turned. Her eyes darted toward movement in the trees behind her. Skybreaker? Other villains?

Nope.

A herd of snowmobiles.

There was momentary relief, then confusion. Jasper frowned as she realized the vehicles were following her. "What are these people doing?" She was moving slowly enough that the snowmobiles were narrowing the gap between them and her, allowing her to notice that the vehicles were painted and decorated like spaceships. Many even had fake wings jutting out the sides, ranging from fairly high quality craftmanship to crappy pieces of cardboard fastened on with tape.

"It's a racing contest," Thea explained. "The vehicles are decorated like ships from Star Conquerors."

"Why are they following me?"

"They must think you're the race leader. You're a few minutes early, but you went right past the starting point. And the race is supposed to go through the snow corridors. Not as far up the mountain as you're going, but still."

"Well, no biggie. I'll just get them off my tail." Jasper turned her attention back to the snow wall ahead and hit the gas. She was nearly to the wall's opening when the motorcycle jerked suddenly to the right. Jasper swerved the other way and fell into a frantic zig-zag pattern. She had to slow significantly to get back in a straight line.

"Damn it," she hissed. "My motorcycle's acting up. I can't go very fast." She needed to get far away from these people before she reached the hangar.

Jasper arrived at the snow wall. She passed through the opening, and besides a strip of pastel sky above her, the world turned white.

Chapter Twenty-Two
Let It Snowmobile

Walls of tightly packed snow rose high into the air on either side of Jasper, leaving her a narrow, winding path to travel up the mountainside. To her dismay, the snowmobile racers followed her into the corridor. And they were getting closer with every second. The vehicles were surprisingly fast, for snowmobiles. Whatever was wrong with Jasper's motorcycle certainly wasn't helping.

"I need someone to get these people off me!" Jasper exclaimed into her comm. "I can slow down a little, but we don't have more than ten minutes before we reach the base entrance—"

A bright beam of blue light burst through the ground, sending a spray of glittering snow through the air. Jasper yelped in surprise and swerved away from the snow shower. The beam had narrowly missed her.

"Jasper?" Grace's voice was thick with concern. "Are you okay? What was that?"

"I'm fine." Jasper sighed. "I forgot about the lasers."

"Lasers? How do you forget about lasers?" Holly exclaimed.

"Well, we used to fly right over them! They were meant to stop anyone hiking the mountain on foot." Jasper slowed, delaying the approach to where the laser triggers were even more densely packed. "Which means they're easy to dodge in a vehicle, but I don't want to take any chances with these people. The lasers shouldn't do more than lightly burn some skin, but still."

"Didn't Thea say maintenance vehicles use these corridors?" Cutthroat asked. "Why are lasers going off now?"

Jasper's jaw clenched. She didn't have time for lengthy explanations, but... "Well, most of the outside security measures were designed to go into hibernation after a few years of no access to the hangar. To save power."

Another blue laser fired from beneath the snow. Jasper swerved again. The motorcycle locked into the tight right turn for a moment too long, nearly sending her careening into the snow wall. She cursed as she pulled the vehicle back into a straight line.

"Jasper?" Dax asked.

"I'm okay. Anyway, Thea's scans might have triggered the lasers. They had equipment looking for radar and radio waves and stuff that would activate a high-alert mode if it sensed potential infiltration." She'd have to permanently disable all that while she was in the hangar to avoid any problems in the future.

Jasper risked another look over her shoulder. Even with the lasers firing, the snowmobiles were still moving at full speed. They must have thought the blue beams were for show rather than something that could hurt them. She slowed further to all but close the gap between her and the racers. "Hey, you all need to get the hell out of here!" she screamed at them. "You're not supposed to be following me."

One of the leading drivers glanced at another to his right. "Wow, she does a really good Commander Moonweather impression!" he shouted.

Jasper groaned. Back to trying to lose them, she supposed. She pushed the motorcycle as fast as she dared and began to slowly inch ahead. Painfully slowly. On her internal screen, she pulled up the map of the snow corridors again. Her hand moved under her coat to the blaster at her side and drew it out. No choice but to waste some time on a detour.

X-ray vision. A few quick mental calculations to determine the angle. Then, Jasper turned tight to lower herself, aimed at the ground far ahead, and fired the blaster rapidly until she triggered a laser. Its light exploded from the snow-dusted ground and struck the snow wall to the left. While the lasers weren't as powerful as blaster beams, they had a slightly wider area of effect, making them a little more efficient for what Jasper was trying to do. Plus, the angle would be a little awkward with her blaster at this distance. Triggering the laser instead was much easier.

It worked. A narrow section of the wall caved in, and the pile of snow left behind made for the perfect ramp to launch her out of the snow corridor.

And right into another one.

Jasper fired several more blasts behind her to collapse another wall into the path, blocking the way back down the mountain. Then she kept moving, waiting for the snowmobiles to continue to follow. Once it looked like they were all behind her—or at least most of them—she collapsed the wall ahead, too.

"Jasper," Grace said over comms. The faint hiss of wind mixed with her voice. "I'm on way to help."

"Great," Jasper replied as she activated the motorcycle's anti-gravity. "All you have to do now is rescue the racers from the caved-in snow corridor."

"What? What happened?"

"I trapped them somewhere safe. They'll be fine, they just need to be pulled out." Jasper approached the wall to her right, barely paying attention to the snowmobiles slowing and stopping, the confusion and alarm growing behind her. Hopefully, the snow would be tightly packed enough for her to get up the wall.

It was. And then she was on top of the snow walls, staring out at a maze of corridors racing and crisscrossing up and down the mountainside. The light of the suns that were both visible in the sky now bounced off the snow, flooding the hillside with a warm glow and forming deep shadows in distant valleys across the mountain range.

Jasper raced along the tops of the snow walls for a while before dropping back into one of the corridors. She had to dodge a few more lasers popping out of the ground, but she was almost to the hanger entrance, and getting in from there would be a piece of cake.

She may have overexaggerated the security system to the others a bit. It was intense, sure, but with a working fingerprint and codes, there was nothing to worry about. Once the security door had been passed through correctly, the lasers and any other security measures would be disabled automatically. Unless someone tried to break into the hangar from another point, but there was no way that was going to happen.

The slopes of the snow walls went down. Trees once again became visible up ahead. As Jasper reached the end of the snow corridor, she spotted a sign fastened to one of the trees, warning that she'd reached the edge of Blue Mountain Resort property and that dangerous drops lay beyond this point. She slowed to navigate the steep slopes and densely packed trees that followed. It didn't take more than five minutes of that to finally reach her destination. At the very edge of a very, very steep cliff stood a stunted pine tree that looked to be on the verge of death.

It had looked like that for decades, maybe even longer. It wasn't a real tree, but a very convincing fake that held the controls to the hangar entrance. Jasper stopped next to the tree and dismounted her motorcycle. She ran her hands up and down the bark, feeling a sensation she hadn't felt in a long time. Or maybe it was an entirely new feeling, tinged with memories from another time. She let her hands linger longer than necessary before locating the knot and running her thumb along the upper edge until she found the hidden switch. It clicked as her thumb brushed over it, and a section of the tree bark slid down to reveal a small panel of buttons and a fingerprint scanner. A red light blinked at the top of the panel. Good. The place still had electricity.

Though to be fair, the lasers had suggested as much, too. There were generators in the base that were meant to keep it powered long after everyone in the Resistance had been killed. The place would still be running on its own for decades more. Maybe even a century or two.

Jasper punched in the long code that was still burned into her brain, then pressed her thumb against the fingerprint scanner. The red light turned green. Something rumbled deep in the ground below. She turned to watch a large, square hole open up in the ground nearby. Snow tumbled into darkness as the door slid open. Jasper left her motorcycle leaning up against the tree and walked to the gap. Now for the fun part. Well, she thought it was the fun part. All the other Resistance members had always hated this. Jasper had no idea why.

She jumped into the void.

In the pitch black, she could only hear the sound of the water splashing, and then feel it as she was completely submerged in the deep pool she'd landed in. At the bottom, the current pulled her into the slide that spiraled down into the base's entry room. The water drained out of a grate in the slide near the end, leaving her on top to pass through a set of dryers like a vehicle in an autowash.

The person who'd designed this base was dead by the time Jasper joined the Resistance, so she never got the chance to thank them for making one of the best things she'd ever experienced.

Jasper came to a stop at the end of the slide, climbed to her feet, and brushed off her coat. Perfectly dry. Sometimes space wasn't that bad. She quickly ducked into the control room sitting just off the entryway, disabled the lasers and a few other outer security measures, then hurried back out and moved on to a long hallway.

At the south end of the base was the hangar, with a runway on the far side leading to the opening in the cliff she'd mentioned to the team earlier. There were three different tunnels branching off the hangar in other directions. The one leading to the entrance that she was walking now, one leading to a storage area, and one leading to temporary quarters.

There were a lot of ships to choose from. Right off the bat, Jasper eliminated about half of them based on size. Many were only meant to carry one to three people, and quite a few others had more room than the team needed. From there, it came down to figuring out which ships had a lot of speed and stealth. Some of the spacecraft were equipped with extra heavy weaponry, but that wasn't something Jasper felt the team needed out of this. The Astronomer already had plenty of bombs and cannons.

After walking past a dozen or so ships in varying shapes and sizes and colors, she paused in front of a sleek black one, considering it. Before she could make up her mind whether to hop in, though, she turned around, and a slightly smaller one caught her eye. A narrow, triangular spacecraft. Iridescent. Small but powerful thrusters at each side.

Jasper remembered this one. She'd never gotten to fly it, but she'd seen it go out for a handful of stealth missions. It was one of the last ones built before the Resistance's end. One of the best. She moved to the hatch at its side behind the wing, punched in the pin used for all the ships, and tapped the open button. The door slid open with a creak. Dust clouded the air in front of her, making her cough a few times.

She crept into the ship's quiet exterior. Lights flicked on automatically. The ventilation began to hum. Something beeped. "Still in tip-top shape, I hope," Jasper murmured as she stepped in. She took a moment to examine the seats in the back and analyze the storage space but moved on quickly. The cockpit called to her. And as she slid into the pilot's seat, a feeling she hadn't felt in a long time washed over her. The flying car, being limited to the atmosphere, just wasn't the same. And they'd been flying plenty on the Astronomer lately, but being at the controls was different. The apprehension. The anticipation.

The flight.

Jasper flipped a couple of switches, grabbed the large lever to her right, and slowly pushed it forward. A smirk crossed her face as the engines came to life with a roar.

She scanned the control panel until she spotted the button for the hangar doors. A few more security codes and another fingerprint scan later, and a horizontal beam of light appeared at the far end of the hangar, cutting through the black. It gradually expanded as the door opened. Daylight washed over Jasper's face.

She broke into a wide grin. The sky had been calling to her. And she was finally going to answer.

Chapter Twenty-Three
Flight Risk

The sun was blindingly bright, the air was bitterly cold, the crowd was annoyingly loud, and Rose wanted to be on a motorcycle with Jasper, not wandering aimlessly through the resort with the rest of the group.

Holly was grumpy but mostly quiet. Thea was cool but also quiet. Dax was...fine. Nice enough, Rose supposed. Grace's wings were interesting, but hadn't used them much around Rose, yet. Cutthroat was pretty cool but a little too serious, and Sarena was annoying. Obnoxious. Whiny. The last person Rose expected someone like Jasper to let hang around. Surely she was useful in some way, but Rose had yet to see it.

Jasper was the coolest person in the group—though the space pirate was a pretty close second—but she didn't even want Rose tagging along on what was supposed to be an easy mission. Rose would prove she could keep up, eventually.

But right now, she was hungry.

"Can we get something to eat?" Rose asked.

"There's food back on the Astronomer," Cutthroat replied. "It shouldn't take Jasper long to get a ship, and then we'll head back."

"But I want food now." Rose folded her arms. "Why can't we just get a snack real quick? We're just standing around, anyway."

"I'm not paying for the resort's overpriced food."

"But Sarena's rich."

Sarena scoffed. "This place isn't worth my money."

"We're criminals!"

"And we're trying to avoid drawing attention to ourselves." Cutthroat sighed. "Just be patient. We'll leave soon."

Thea made a concerned noise. Tapping her comm, she said, "Hey J, I looked into the event schedule you were asking about. There is stuff going on tonight we can discuss later, but there's also some bad news about the snow corridors—"

Something interrupted her, and the others gathered around, worry showing on their faces. Rose looked around aimlessly, studying nearby buildings, not really paying attention to whatever conversation she was missing out on over comms. Oh, that building right there was a mini market. Maybe she could grab something inside.

Finally, Grace spread her wings, catching Rose's attention. "I'll go see if I can get those snowmobiles off Jasper's tail so she can focus on getting to the hangar."

Damn. Something exciting was happening, and Rose was missing out. Again. Weren't the blasters in her hands enough for the others? She could totally keep up with them on missions.

Rose glanced at the rest of the team. Thea was focused on her tablet screen again, and Dax was peering at it over her shoulder. Holly had popped in a pair of headphones and didn't seem to be listening to anyone. Sarena was pacing back-and-forth and throwing anxious glances at anyone in costume who got too close. Cutthroat, however, had an eye on Rose. Getting away from him would be the challenge.

Okay, forget running. Time for plan B. "I have to go to the bathroom," Rose announced.

Cutthroat cast the others a weary glance and sighed. "All right, I'll take you. I think there's one in the building we were in." He nodded toward the conference center.

"You're going back in there?" Sarena exclaimed as the two began to walk.

Cutthroat rolled his eyes. "We'll be right back. She's just using the bathroom."

"Well, good luck."

They returned to the thick crowds populating the building. That would make it easier to slip away from Cutthroat, Rose thought for a moment, but she ultimately decided that going into the bathroom first would give her a little more time. All she needed was to run over to the market, grab a snack, and then run back to where the rest of the team waited.

"In here." Cutthroat stopped next the bathroom entrance. "Try to hurry, please."

"Yeah, yeah." Rose waved a hand as she walked in. She immediately bumped into an East Kronosian woman in a very expensive-looking white fur coat.

"Watch it, young lady." The woman turned to her friend next to her and sighed. "That's one of the worst things about these people. They let their kids run around unsupervised. If I'd known this was happening this weekend, I would have rescheduled our trip—"

Rose rolled her eyes and darted past the woman. Another person in line—this one in a Star Conquerors costume—exclaimed, "Hey, there's a line, kid!"

"I'll be real quick, I just need to blow my nose!" Rose darted into a stall as someone else stepped out, pulled the door shut, and climbed onto the toilet. Her hands moved to the bottom of the window above it. "Sucks to suck, old man," she muttered to herself as she lifted it open. The screen behind it popped out of place easily.

Rose could barely squeeze through the window frame, even all the way open, but she made it through the gap and fell a few feet onto the cold ground with a thud and a grunt. She hopped back onto her feet and raced toward the mini market.

Inside, she was ecstatic to see how much food was packed onto the shelves. Her eyes went wide as she moved through the aisles, sights set on stuff that was far from a healthy meal: chocolates made with spices from across the star system, sweets that were all sugar and fruit, chips in every flavor under the sun. The complete opposite of the bland nutritional mush she'd been given in Sky Labs.

Rose grabbed a package of sugar-coated fruit spheres and a bag of chips coated in a spicy green powder. Even in the days since her escape from the lab, indulging in whatever she could find at Jasper and Sarena's apartments and on the Astronomer, she hadn't been able to get enough of this stuff. With her snacks tucked casually under the arm, she headed for the door. *Act casual,* she thought, *and no one will pay me any attention...*

"Hey!" an employee at the counter shouted as she neared the door. "You gotta pay for that, kid!"

Every adult in Rose's vicinity turned to stare at her.

Rose shoved the snacks into her coat pockets and broke into a sprint. The closest adults didn't react fast enough to grab her as she passed, and the ones that did try to chase her couldn't match her speed. Cold mountain air washed over her as she dashed out the door. She was almost in the clear—

"Hey!" Another store employee followed her out and pointed at her. "Someone stop her, she's shoplifting!"

More eyes turned on Rose. Oh, great. She needed a way to move faster than she could run, or someone was bound to catch her eventually. As nearby adults started toward Rose, she switched directions and headed for another nearby building: an equipment rental shop.

Rose flew inside, nearly crashing into a couple on their way out, and headed straight for the slopeboards. She selected one that looked about the right size for her and picked it up. On a nearby shelf, she found a pair of slopeboard boots. Magnets on the bottom fastened them to the board, strong enough to keep them attached on a ride down the slope, but they would disconnect under a hard enough impact to prevent injury.

Someone tapped Rose's shoulder. She yelped and whirled around, finding herself face-to-face with an employee. "Excuse me kid, you got a parent with you?" they asked. "Guardian? Supervisor?"

"Uh, no, but I got this." Rose swung the board and smacked the employee in the side. Not painfully hard, just enough to send them stumbling into the nearest shelf and give her a chance to run.

She went out the rental shop on the opposite side that she'd entered through, hoping that people over here were less likely to be after her. No one paid her any immediate attention, so she paused long enough to squeeze her feet into the slopeboard boots. Just as she'd pulled the second one on, two men came running around the building's corner toward her. Resort security guards.

More running. Rose had better endurance than the average person, but she was still getting sick of the chase. And the slopeboard boots were slowing her down. She focused her attention on the lift in the distance, marking an entrance to the slopes where she could make her getaway. *Not much farther,* she told herself.

Frequent glances back warned that the gap between her and security was closing slowly but surely. To buy herself a little extra time, Rose grabbed a chair outside a café as she passed and threw it backward into the guards' path, forcing them to slow and go around it.

Finally, she was passing the lift. She raced past a man getting off, earning a shout of annoyance that she ignored. She tossed the slopeboard she'd stolen onto the ground and hopped on. As she gained momentum, she glanced back again. The guards had stopped at the top of the hill, realizing they had no chance of catching up on foot. Rose grinned. "Take that, suckers!" she shouted.

She picked up speed. Faster. And faster. Shoot. It was so much harder to steer this thing than she'd expected. Rose made a slight adjustment, hoping to move more toward the middle of the slope. She was getting the hang of it, but not fast enough. Another attempt at steering sent her speeding to the left. She yelped and tried to correct herself, but it was no use. Within seconds, she was off the slope and in the forest.

The snow became thicker and higher, slowing Rose somewhat, but she still had no control. For several minutes—which felt like much longer—she narrowly missed trees and flew over short drops in the landscape before flying into a clearing and hitting a snowdrift. Her boots snapped off the slopeboard as she crashed face first into the freezing white. Shivering and groaning, Rose tried to push herself up. The snow beneath her began to fall, rapidly moving down like sand in an hourglass. Rose frowned. Where was it going?

She didn't have to wonder long. All the snow beneath her gave way, and then she was falling with it. Tumbling into darkness.

Rose screamed as she fell. Cold, hard stone slammed into her. As pain jolted through her body, all she could focus on was the crunching sound in her coat. Great. Her chips had likely crumbled into dust. The fruit spheres were probably all smushed, too.

The last of the snow settled around her. Rose rolled onto her back and stared at the light far above her. Far enough that she wouldn't be climbing or jumping out. She pulled off the slopeboard boots and pushed herself onto trembling legs.

"Hello?" Rose called into the shadows. "Anyone here?" Why couldn't the others have given her a comm? Sure, she was supposed to have someone with her at all times, but what if she'd been kidnapped?

She'd have to make an argument for her own comm later. For now, she needed to find a way out of this place. She slowly moved away from the hole she'd fallen through and realized it wasn't just piles of snow around her. There was rubble, too. She seemed to be in some underground facility that had caved in long before her arrival.

There didn't seem to be a point in continuing when she couldn't see, but Rose had nowhere else to go. She tried a few more steps forward and another shaky, "Hello?" This time, she got a response in the form of a distant clang. A very ominous clang. She froze. For a long moment, all she could hear was her own hard breathing. She didn't dare make any other noises.

Another clang reverberated through the hall ahead. Then, a single glowing point of light appeared in the distance.

Before Rose could decide what to do, a light directly above her clicked on. Then one ahead, then another, and another, slowly leading down the hall toward the source of the sound. The source of the glow. A seven-foot-tall humanoid constructed of silver metal.

An android.

"Intruder detected." The android's voice was on the fritz, and a burst of static followed its robotic statement. Its arm began to lift slowly. Rose raised her hand quickly in response and opened up the blaster in her palm. Neon green light flashed.

A semi-transparent sphere surrounded the android, shielding it from Rose's blast. Then the android lifted its arm the rest of the way, and an orange glow warned that it also had a blaster ready to fire.

But unlike the android, Rose had no shield. And the hallway was too narrow for her to dodge. Panic made her freeze over. Should she try firing again? Run the other way? Hope that the android's blaster components were as deteriorated as its voice box? She managed to back up slowly, move back into the beam of sunlight, but that was all she could bring herself to do.

Something new inside Rose whirred to life. There was an unfamiliar sensation of movement in her feet, but something about it vaguely reminded her of the way the blasters activated in her palms.

The android fired.

Rose shot upward.

For a moment, she was back in the sun and the light. Then the flames shooting out of the bottom of her feet vanished, and she was falling. Back into the underground facility. Back into the path of the android.

Rose landed on her feet this time, rolled, and jumped back up. The android was walking toward her now. Its arm lifted to fire again. Escape was possible. But Rose's fear of the enemy was subsiding, replaced by determination. If she couldn't defeat one measly robot, how was she supposed to be a valuable member of Jasper Van Terra's team?

Rose strolled forward and rapidly fired off blasts from both hands. The first clashed with the android's next attack, sending a shower of green and orange sparks across the floor. The next two bounced off the android's shield, but the fourth was enough to break it. The fifth struck the android in the chest and sent it flying back.

Rose charged forward and kept firing. One blast took off the android's firing arm. Another broke open its outer casing, fracturing it from one leg up through its neck. Finally, Rose melted the components in its chest. The android collapsed into a pile of smoking, melted metal.

Rose's sigh of relief echoed around the dim hallway. She glanced down at her shoes. They were torn open in the bottom where the thrusters had come out of the bottom of her feet. Dang. She'd liked these shoes.

Well, she had a way out now. Rose went back down the hall to the spot under the gaping hole in the ceiling. To the light pouring down. She willed her feet thrusters to come back on. The action came as naturally as firing the blasters in her hands. She shot out of the underground and into the air.

The being-in-the-air part felt a lot less natural.

In the panic that came with suddenly being high above the ground, Rose twisted her body so that she shot away from the hole. Then, she turned the flying blasters back off. Dropped. Went crashing into the snow. The collision with the ground wasn't too hard—not for her, anyway—but it still smacked her with enough pain to make her gasp.

Worth it. She could fly. She could freaking *fly.* That must have been what that last surgery had been for. Maybe if Jasper's team hadn't rescued her and blown the labs up, she would have been given instructions on how to use the thrusters soon.

Rose climbed out of the snow and brushed the powder off her clothes. Okay. Now, she just needed to find her way back to the others. She turned in a slow circle, taking in the snowy landscape around her. The endless trees in every direction. The complete lack of signage or buildings or any indication of the resort nearby. She wasn't even entirely sure which way she'd come from.

Getting back might be harder than expected.

Chapter Twenty-Four
Onward and Upward

Cold wind danced over Grace's skin, ruffled her metal feathers, and whipped her ponytail around as she soared over the snow corridors, searching for movement. It didn't take long for her to spot the holes blown in the sides of the corridor walls, and then the collapsed piles of snow and the snowmobile drivers trapped between them.

No one looked hurt, to Grace's relief. But they were clearly terrified. There was no apparent way out, with only steep slopes and high walls on every side. She wasn't sure Jasper could have been any nicer about it, given the circumstances, but part of her still cringed at the sight.

There were twenty to thirty racers in total. Grace was probably capable of carrying each snowmobile out, but it would take forever going one by one. It would be faster to just clear out one of the snow walls, like Jasper had, and have them drive themselves back to the resort grounds.

Grace drew her mask from her jacket pocket and slipped it on. Once it was secure, she dropped down so that she could talk to the racers before clearing a path. Hopefully, she'd be able to calm them down a bit.

"Everyone stay where you are!" she exclaimed as she landed. "I'm going to get you to safety."

"Oh my stars," one of the closest drivers said with wide eyes. "Are you Superangel?"

Grace nodded. "I am."

"How did you find us?" a nearby woman asked. "And why are you out here?"

Shoot. Grace racked her brain for a quick explanation. "I was following Van Terra. There were rumors that she's in the area," she said. "I think she was the one driving around on the motorcycle. I'm not sure what she's looking for, but you all seem to have followed her by mistake. Just a bit of a mix-up."

The drivers began freaking out again.

"Van Terra? Out here?"

"Did she escape prison?"

"We're lucky she didn't kill us!"

"Why hasn't the government said anything?"

"Whoa, whoa, there's nothing to be afraid of. I won't let anyone or anything hurt you." Grace lifted her hands. After a moment, she added, "Van Terra doesn't really go after civilians, anyway."

Thankfully, that was enough to settle the crowd, for the most part. They still looked apprehensive, but they stayed quiet and remained in place while Grace moved toward the snow pile blocking them at the rear. The walls were too tightly packed to bring down without weapons, but this snow looked loose enough for her to handle.

"Now, everyone stay back. I'm going to clear the way over here." Grace spread her wings and sucked in a deep breath. Then, she beat her wings against the air as hard as she could, aiming the current in the direction of the snow pile. The blast pushed some of the snow out of the way, but it wasn't quite clear enough for the drivers to get through.

A second beat of Grace's wings took care of the rest.

She glanced back at the drivers over her shoulder. "Do you need me to guide you back to the resort?"

After a long moment of silence, someone shouted, "Yes, please!"

The next push of her wings took Grace to the air. One by one, the snowmobiles roared to life, and the drivers began moving underneath her. Grace scanned the landscape ahead and set off on the fastest path to the resort buildings in the distance.

"Hey, we've got a problem," Cutthroat said. "We lost Rose."

"What?" Jasper exclaimed. "How? Where? Why? When?"

"I took her back into the conference center to use the bathroom, and she vanished from there. She was complaining that she was hungry before that, so maybe she went looking for food."

"Seriously?"

"I'll find her," Grace said. Maybe she shouldn't have sounded as confident as she did, but Rose could have only gone so far, right? Once the drivers below began rolling back onto resort grounds, she began circling the area, searching for any signs of movement outside of the buildings.

"I'm in of all the resort's cameras," Thea said. "No sign of her around here, but I'll keep looking."

Food. Rose had mentioned wanting food. "Thea." Grace kept scanning as she spoke. "Can you tell me what food options are available around where she disappeared?"

"Well, there's the mini market nearby." A tapping sound came from Thea's comm before she continued. "Yeah, that might be where she went."

"Can you give me directions?"

Following Thea's instructions, Grace made her way to the mini market. She dropped to the ground in front of the door and ran inside. All eyes moved to her. Maybe it was the fact that she was frantic and out of breath. Maybe it was the fact that she'd been flying. Maybe it was the Superangel mask. Regardless, may as well make use of all the attention.

"Has anyone in here seen a small girl?" Grace asked loudly. "Pale skin, short black hair? Human? From the Solar System?"

The employee at the front counter narrowed their eyes. "Oh yeah, she was in here. She stole a bunch of stuff and ran out."

That sounded like Rose. "Do you know which way she went?"

"I tried following her, but she went into that slopeboard shop on the other side of the main walkway," the employee replied. "Security showed up, so I left it to them, but I haven't heard anything since."

Great. If Rose had gotten her hands on a slopeboard, she might have gotten a decent distance from the resort grounds. But on the other hand, if it was just food she was after, she had no reason to go that far from the team. Right?

Unless she got carried away running away from the security. Which was a very Jasper-clone thing to do.

"Okay, thank you!" Grace waved a hand as she ran back out of the market. Her wings went out, and she went back into the air. She flew over the rental shop and kept moving toward the slopes.

It wasn't something on the ground that caught her attention, but something in the air. Something child sized. Something that looked suspiciously like a flying Rose.

Grace flew toward the figure. Yes, definitely Rose. Flames were shooting out of her feet, keeping her in the air.

"Rose!" Grace exclaimed. "Since when can you fly?"

"Uh, well, I don't really know how to control it," Rose replied, sounding nervous for the first time...ever. At least, in the short period of time that Grace had known her. "I've been stuck up here for a while. And there's this beeping in my brain that I think is a low fuel warning."

As if on cue, the flames went out, and Rose began to fall. They flickered on and off a few times, catching her briefly before she dropped again. Rose shrieked.

Grace swooped down and easily scooped her out of the air. She adjusted her grip so that she had Rose in one arm. With the other, she touched her comm to unmute. "I've got Rose. We're in the air just east of the resort."

"On my way to you," Jasper replied.

Grace turned to face the upper slopes of the mountain. "How close are you?"

"Very close. I can see you."

"Really? I can't see—oh, wait, is that you?" Something was shimmering in the air, barely visible. But before long, Grace could just make out the outline of a spaceship. Panels across its surface reflected the sky above and the forest below.

As it neared Grace and Rose, the panels gained color, becoming iridescent. The ship stopped and hovered in the air in front of Grace and Rose. Grace couldn't help but grin. "That's a pretty awesome looking ship."

"Right?" Jasper exclaimed in response. "Hang on, I'll open the hatch so you two can fly in."

A door panel behind the wing slid open, and Grace carried Rose in. It closed behind them, and Grace set Rose down carefully before dropping to the ground herself.

Jasper appeared in the doorway. "Wanna try flying?"

"I have no idea how," Grace told her. "I've never driven or flown anything. Ever." It kind of sounded fun. But it also sounded terrifying. She had always been secretly amazed that there weren't way more vehicle crashes in all the traffic on Kronos.

With a shrug, Jasper leaned against the doorway. "Alright, well, I'll teach you one of these days when we have time. I've been meaning to teach you how to drive too."

"Hey, is anyone going to ask if I'm okay?" Rose demanded, folding her arms. "I fell into this underground tunnel and had to fight an android!"

Jasper's brow furrowed. "Jerry?"

"I don't know," Rose replied. "Is Jerry made of metal and capable of firing blaster beams from his hands?"

"Yep, sounds like Jerry. You must have been in one of the base's outer halls, near the living quarters."

"Oh," Rose said. "Well, sorry. I kind of obliterated Jerry."

"That's fine. No one liked him." Jasper turned and stepped back into the cockpit. "Now, let's grab the others and figure out lunch. I'm starving."

They landed the ship in a clearing not far from the resort and met the rest of the team there. As the others gathered inside the ship and assessed its interior, Thea made an announcement.

"There's a Christmas feast lunch at the resort," she said. "I got us tickets."

"Perfect!" Jasper exclaimed with a grin. Everyone else groaned. Or at best, seemed indifferent. Jasper's expression quickly turned to exasperation. "Oh, come on, we've been hiking all morning. Don't act like you guys aren't at least a little hungry. Those meal bars aren't exactly satisfying."

"I'm hungry," Grace said quickly. "And we're pretty far from anything else."

"A good meal before we head out isn't a terrible idea," Cutthroat conceded.

"What are we doing after that?" Sarena asked. "And how fast can we get away from here?"

Jasper clapped her hands together. "We'll discuss next steps while we eat. Thea, do you have something to share with the class?"

Thea nodded. "A new target."

"Awesome. I love targets."

After spending a little more time checking out the ship and taking a few minutes to rest, the team headed through the trees back to the resort grounds and made their way to the conference center they'd been in earlier. A grand dining hall waited in the center of the building, where they had to show their hacked tickets to security before making their way to their seats.

"There's still StarConCon attendees here?" Sarena muttered under breath as she side-eyed some people passing by in costume. "There's no Christmas in Star Conquerors!"

"You guys did a Christmas episode, though," Holly pointed out.

"Yeah, and I wish we didn't. I want to wipe that abomination from my memory." Sarena flung up her arms in frustration. "It's not even canon!" As a woman dressed like Sarena's character walked by, with the addition of a Santa hat on her head, Sarena shot her a glare. "And Livia would never wear such a ridiculous hat!"

Dax frowned. "Why do the Santa hats here have jewels and crystals on them instead of white fur?"

Jasper shrugged. "Close enough. Anyway, I love that there's convention people here. They're making all the regular fancy rich people uncomfortable. And that's what Christmas is all about."

"That can't be right," Holly muttered under her breath. "It makes no sense to center a holiday around that."

Grace glanced around, taking in the festive bejeweled clothing that many people in the room were wearing, including waitstaff. Strings of star-shaped lights hung from the ceiling, shining in every shade of neon. Gold and silver statues of antlered aliens with hooved feet were scattered across shelves and tables throughout the dining hall. Faint music played in the background, a serene blend of strings and bells and something vaguely electronic.

The team reached their seats and settled in. Thea set a sphere in the center of their table. "While we wait for food, let's talk about what we're dealing with next. Kiv Astra." She tapped the top of the sphere to project an image of a man into the air. East Kronosian. Reddish-pink skin that was paler than most members of his species. White hair cut close to his head, matching his goatee. Black eyes marked only by violet pupils.

"He's the CEO of AstraSmart," Thea continued. "They make all sorts of fancy appliances that are controlled via smartsphere and have to be connected to the net to work. The code's not exactly well-written, but despite that, AstraSmart products are all over the Governor's Palace."

"And you think you can hack them?" Jasper asked, perking up.

"Yes. But I need more information. I got enough out of cracking the devices open to be certain I can do this, but I need details about the company's server-network interfacing that I can't get in the device code itself."

"Makes sense to me," Jasper said. "I think." She clasped her hands together and leaned forward. "So, how do we get to Kiv Astra?"

"Well, he spends most of his time these days on Iros managing his new project," Thea replied.

"Iros?" Aymes repeated, surprise flashing across his face. "Where Ringmaster's carnival was?"

"Yep." Thea swiped a finger across her sphere's holoscreen. The image changed from Astra to an amusement park. It looked kind of similar to the old carnival Ringmaster had run, but there were a lot more rides—bigger ones, mostly—and several large buildings behind the park that hadn't been there before. Was that a mall?

Thea continued. "The government seized it after Ringmaster's disappearance and auctioned it off. Astra's the one who bought it," she explained. "A lot of it was rebuilt because of, you know, all the destruction and whatnot. He also added a ton of new features and rides. There's also a mall, giant hotels, restaurants, all kinds of junk."

Dax leaned in and stared at the picture, eyes wide. "They built all that in the past few months?"

"Yep. Astra's pretty damn rich, after the success of AstraSmart the past few years. And all the money he dumped into getting this thing up and running quick seems to be paying off. It's pretty popular."

Jasper frowned. "Are we planning to interrogate him? I don't want Starr finding out and getting suspicious." Voice lowering, she added, "I don't want to give him any hints that we're planning on making a big move soon. Or scare him into throwing out his AstraSmart devices."

"If all goes according to plan, we won't have to deal with Astra directly," Thea assured her. "I just need to get into his system and steal some files."

"And you think he'll have that on him at Iros?"

"Yeah. He's pretty much living there right now, but he's still in regular contact with his factories on Kronos. They have to be sending him code to review, even if he doesn't understand it as much as he pretends to in interviews, based on what he's been approving in these devices." Thea shook her head. "Seriously, I was writing better code within months of touching my first computer. And we'd barely invented those on Earth!"

A waitress stopped next to the team's table. Thea quickly dismissed the holoscreen projection.

"Who's ready for food?" the waitress asked. The massive diamond hanging at the end of her fuzzy red hat swayed as she lifted a tablet to take their orders. Colorful lights from above reflected off the other gems circling the hat's base.

Jasper grinned, her concerns about Astra and Starr vanishing from her face. The excitement that took its place was contagious, and Grace couldn't stop herself from smiling, too.

Chapter Twenty-Five
Friends in High Places

Janus hadn't spent much time in formal wear, and she still wasn't entirely sure how she felt about it. The suit she had on tonight was a deep emerald green, with a light shimmery gray shirt underneath similar in color to her Subject Eighteen suit, and a pop of bright green on her tie to match her right eye. She looked damn good, at least, but that didn't mean she was looking forward to the upcoming dinner. Quite the opposite, in fact.

Politicians were only on Governor Starr's side as long as he continued to feed them, to give them money, to let them write the laws in their favor. And, most importantly, as long as he kept enough public opinion on his side. That last part might not seem like it should have mattered to the elite, but the Starr legacy was not unbreakable. Centuries of the family's rule could be brought to an end if the right person got it in their head that they could take his place. Sway the rest of elite and the public to their side, convince the other families they could do better.

And with the army Starr was building, with the soldiers on his side, an uprising like that would not be without blood.

So, today was about impressing the elite. Reminding them. Warning them. But Janus wasn't the warning—no, Starr was still keeping the extent of her abilities under wraps. And Janus, of course, was keeping the true extent of her upgrades from him.

Tonight, the warning would come in the form of Captain Cora. He'd give a demonstration of his upgrades, and then they'd all have a big fancy dinner and pretend that the man's very existence wasn't a threat on Starr's part.

Janus left the bathroom and rejoined Starr in the hallway. In the time she'd spent putting her hair up, Captain Cora had arrived. He looked Janus up and down as she moved to stand on the other side of Starr.

He hadn't said anything yet, but Janus was pretty sure he recognized that she was a clone of Van Terra. No one else who'd gotten close to her had said anything, either, and the white hair and distance she kept from cameras had apparently been enough to throw the general public off, so far. Not that Starr seemed to care if people figured it out—he would have been much more careful if he did. Was it meant to be another subtle threat?

"Ready?" Starr didn't glance at either of his escorts as he checked the watch on his wrist. Without waiting for a response, he said, "Let's go." He, Janus, Captain Cora, and the team of security guards that were practically pointless next to the cyborgs set off down the hallway.

"Don't forget who the star of the show is tonight, Subject Eighteen," Captain Cora muttered.

"Sure thing, Captain," Janus told him, doing her best to keep the "Captain" part from sounding too sarcastic. She wasn't sure why the man had decided to dislike her so quickly after meeting her—though her snarky comments about his costume might have played a role—but she did her best around Starr to be polite to the man. It helped to remind herself that she'd get to kill him someday. Someday soon.

The dining hall where tonight's events would be taking place was three floors down. Janus had taken this path before, and she zoned out during the walk, not coming back to the present until a hand on her shoulder snapped her out of her thoughts.

Starr. Janus glanced at him, but he waited until Captain Cora had passed into the dining hall just a few feet ahead before speaking, his voice low. "There was an incident at Blue Mountain Resort on Si Hera about an hour ago."

Janus raised an eyebrow. "Incident?"

"Snow walls collapsed around some snowmobile drivers. Superangel rescued them. No one was hurt, and it shouldn't make much news. But rumor has it Van Terra was there."

"Any video footage?"

"Nothing concrete. Some blurry shots of Superangel up in the sky, but I'm not worried about that right now."

It wasn't hard to pick up what Starr was implying. Van Terra had been in the Si Heran mountains. It sounded like they didn't need to worry about a public stir, but it was worth wondering what she'd been doing there.

"I don't want the public seeing any more of her," Starr continued. "At this point, I just want her dead. Trying to keep her alive long enough for a public execution isn't worth the risk, regardless of what we could learn from her."

His eyes narrowed. "And I have the council to deal with, now. Rumor has it they're coming to Kronos next pentasol."

Janus nodded. "I'll start tracking her again." Killing Van Terra was part of her own plans anyway. No villain, no criminal could be left alive in the Janus System. Certainly not one who loved chaos as much as Jasper did.

Maybe she could have been helpful taking down Starr, if the timing had been a little different. But Janus had a feeling she was more likely to ruin everything than help at this point.

Janus started to move toward the door, but Starr wasn't done. "Something new is happening, too. There was already support for Superangel, but it hasn't clashed with any of my operations or stopped things from running smoothly up here. Until early this morning."

Janus suspected she knew what he was referring to. It wasn't in the news, of course. It'd been hidden. Suppressed. But Meg had mentioned something about it when she requested that they have a video call that night. She turned. "What is it?"

"There was a riot at a factory this morning," Starr told her. "Mostly the usual complaints about pay and hours and work conditions, but a few people were wearing Superangel costumes. They're starting to rally around her as a symbol of revolution."

Starr glanced into the dining hall behind Janus, his gaze fixating on something in the distance. "This is part of the reason I'm bringing Captain Cora out now," he continued. "We need to crush Superangel."

"You want me to help with that?" Janus asked.

"When the time comes, you'll stand by as backup. But you're not meant to be the symbol he is." Starr's attention was back on Janus, his eyes locked with hers. "You're my right hand. You're more than him. He's meant to fight Superangel, and you're meant to fight Van Terra. The real threat. We both suspect Superangel is being guided by Van Terra, anyway. A fake puppet hero."

Janus swallowed her annoyance. *Just like Captain Cora.*

Starr finally started walking again, and he and Janus entered the dining hall together.

The demonstration was boring, which was an impressive feat for something that involved weapons. The dinner was even more boring. But at least at the end of it, Janus had something to look forward to. At the end of the dinner, Janus got to go home somewhere new.

Her own apartment.

Starr had finally let her move out of Sky Labs—not that he had much choice, given its destruction—and into his own home. Her place in the Governor's Palace was more spacious. More isolated. She didn't dare assume she had more privacy, though. Hidden cameras and bugs were to be expected.

And, as with the camera in her head, they could be worked around.

Janus moved slowly through the apartment after dinner, having nothing better to do with the time before her scheduled call. There was the kitchen, mostly white, accented with silver and red. Not her first choice, but she wasn't going to complain. Her bedroom was also rather plain, and so was the bathroom. Just the bare essentials for her.

The closet held only the weapons Starr had given her. Her Skybreaker suit, her staff, and her motorcycle were all hidden deep in the underbelly of the city, for the moment. Far away from Starr's eyes. Or any of the eyes working for him.

There was a beep in Janus's skull. An incoming call, on a signal that would block any prying from Starr's techs. She collapsed onto the white couch in the living room and answered. Meg's video feed appeared on her internal screen. "Evenin' Skybreaker. How are ya?"

Despite referring to it as a video call, Meg wasn't actually on screen. She sat just out of view, and the occasional tapping suggested she was typing on a keyboard.

"I'm good," Janus told her. "Is it true you're in the Janus system?" One of the techs who'd called into Janus's brain the day before to check her protective code had mentioned Meg's arrival.

"Yes, I'm here, but I can't disclose any more information right now."

"I didn't realize you were going to act so soon."

"You sound apprehensive."

"Excited," Janus deadpanned. "But I try not to get my hopes up."

Meg chuckled. "Don't worry, we'll be acting soon. I'm just trying to decide what I want to do about the council."

"Starr seems to be thinking a lot about that, too."

"Well, we know that his general plan is attack the moment they try to strip his power away." More typing on Meg's end. "Maybe we let them fight it out and then step in afterward, eh?"

"That seems reasonable." And it would give Janus more time to think. To plan. She had no intention of trading Starr for Meg. Of continuing to be someone's tool. Her would-be-masters both tried to convince her they considered her an equal. But as skilled as they both were at manipulation, Janus was better at seeing through it.

"Is there anything you wanted to talk to me about tonight specifically?" Janus asked. This was all still rather vague. Didn't really justify a call over a message.

"We recovered Grim Machine."

Janus raised an eyebrow. "Does he have orders?"

"He'll be working for you for the time being. Basically your new henchman. Or should I say henchrobot?"

Janice didn't think she needed a henchman, nor did she really want one. In fact, she wanted Grim Machine as dead as the rest of the villains. But she supposed the extra muscle might come in handy, for now. As long as he was obedient. "What are my orders, then?" she asked.

"I know what Starr and the council want, but there's a wild card that's come to my attention," Meg replied. "Jasper Van Terra."

"Yeah. Starr wants me to kill her."

"Do you know what she wants?"

Janus offered a slight shrug. "Revenge on him. We don't know exactly what she's got planned, but he's tired of dealing with her."

"Is he scared?" Meg asked.

Janus leaned back and fought off a yawn as she sank even further into the couch. "He's pretending not to be, but I think he is a little scared. She came pretty damn close to getting hard evidence on his trafficking scheme a while back."

"Well then, I'd like to keep Jasper alive a little longer. I do want to know what she's planning. She's...interesting. Think you can take her alive?"

"We're pretty evenly matched right now," Janus told Meg. "Maybe with a few more upgrades..." She paused a moment before asking, "Have you considered my proposal?"

"I love your proposal, hun," Meg said with more enthusiasm than Janus was expecting. "But that's Sky Labs tech, and last I checked, that place got blown to bits."

Damn it, Van Terra. You couldn't have waited one more week to blow that place up? Swallowing her anger, Janus said, "With your system's tech, I figured it'd be easy for your people to recreate."

"We have the technology, but the details of making something like this work with your biology are complex. If I order my team to start now, it could take seasons to get a working prototype. It would go much faster if we had the lab's blueprints."

"The lab's databanks were designed to resist impact and heat. The data might have survived," Janus told Meg. She didn't like to get her hopes up when the chances were this slim, but it was hard not to in this case. "It's too dangerous right now for Starr to send his people back in to check, but I bet I could get through the rubble."

"But do you think you can do it without getting caught?" Meg asked. "Starr's probably still monitoring the area, right?"

Janus's jaw clenched. "I could have Grim Machine do it."

"That'll do. We've just got to finish a few upgrades to his software, and I'll send him down."

"Great. Anything else?"

"That's all, for now. Have a good night, Sky."

"You too, Meg."

The call ended with a click. Janus had more questions for Meg, but they'd be hard to ask without raising suspicions. Meg was the type to keep those she'd employed in the dark about the big picture and only provide details that were necessary. And Janus was having a hard enough time dealing with that from Starr, already.

Chapter Twenty-Six
The Spirit of Things

"Can I get you all started with some drinks?" the waitress asked.

Grace glanced at the waitress briefly before returning her attention to Jasper, who looked eager to place her order. "Yeah, we'll take one of those giant jugs of eggnog." Jasper pointed toward the nearby table, where people were pouring themselves drinks from a massive silver jug.

The waitress's brow furrowed. "Do you mean blugnoog?"

Confusion crossed Jasper's face, mirroring the waitress's expression. "What's blugnoog?"

Holly groaned. "Jasper, did you even look at the menu?"

"Well excuse me, I thought I knew Christmas food and drinks! Apparently not." Jasper folded her arms. "Also, they want us to scan a code on the table with our smartspheres just to see the menu, and that's too much work."

Grace tapped the sphere Thea had set out and loaded the menu. She glanced at the description of blugnoog. "A blend of Hatuan milks flavored with spices from the desert lands in the planet's northern hemisphere."

"Sure, give us a jug of that," Jasper said, sounding mildly disappointed. "And maybe a Christmas turkey for the table."

"If you're looking for roasted avians, we've got northern goswings and blue-crested lunarants," the waitress replied.

"We'll take one of each."

The waitress checked that no one else wanted any other offerings from the menu before moving on to the next party to take their orders. Jasper let out a small sigh but didn't make any more comments about the dining options.

Grace cleared her throat. "Hey, Thea, how are Mia and Chloe's bodies coming along?"

Jasper perked up. "Oh, yeah, I don't think I've seen you work on them since I got back! I miss those funky little robots."

"Androids," Thea corrected. "And I didn't get much done while you were gone, to be honest. I was mostly trying to work out ways to get into the palace systems. But I think I'm finally close to finishing the main components on their new bodies."

It was true, Grace hadn't seen much of the android bodies while Jasper had been away at the Shark Tank. But Thea had still managed to spend nearly every night working until she passed out, often in the kitchen or living room, lines of code that none of the others could understand scrolling across her screens.

"Well, I can't wait to see them." Jasper pushed her chair back from the table and rose to her feet. "I'll be right back. Just gonna run to the bathroom real quick."

As Jasper walked away, there was enough of an air of mild disappointment still clinging to her to put a twinge in Grace's chest. But an idea popped into her head that quickly wiped the feeling away. "Hey, Thea," she said, eyes lingering on Jasper's back as she approached the dining room exit. "Is there anywhere nearby that sells Earth stuff?"

"Uh, depends on what you mean by 'nearby'. There's a big store called SolGoods in a city at the base of the mountain, but it's definitely not within walking distance." Thea raised an eyebrow. "Why do you ask?"

"I have...a plan. Someone's going to need to fly down there and pick up a few things. Someone who knows what Earth Christmas is actually like." Grace quickly explained her idea. Part of her feared that the others would think it was too much effort—especially Sarena and Cutthroat—but they all agreed without protest. Jasper's time in the Shark Tank must have garnered her more sympathy than Grace had expected, even from those generally annoyed by her antics.

The plan also involved distracting Jasper. That would be Grace's job. Grace and the others were just barely able to finalize the details of the plan when Jasper returned.

Jasper dropped into her chair and gestured wildly with her arms. "Guys, some lady tried selling me Tristar while we were waiting in line for the bathroom. That company is a plague." A small frown touched her mouth as she took in the other's faces. They must have looked a little too much like they were hiding something, because she asked, "Uh, is everything okay?"

"Everything's fine," Grace said quickly, reassuring Jasper with a smile. "That's crazy that Tristar reps are here, though."

Food arrived not long after that, and the roasted birds tasted incredible. The blugnoog was a little strange, but not bad. Jasper must have really liked it, though, because she drank half the jug by herself.

As food was served, a group of musicians with stringed instruments, bells made of an iridescent metal, and horns carved from what seemed to be animal bones gathered in front of the dining hall's fireplace and played soft background music. Jasper occasionally shot them perplexed—and borderline annoyed—glances.

Grace leaned toward her. "Is the music anything close to Christmas music?"

"It'd be better if it wasn't." Jasper raised an eyebrow. "It sounds like they were given upside down sheet music."

When the waitress returned a final time to collect their dishes, she nodded toward the band. "The music's lovely, isn't it?"

Jasper shrugged.

The waitress didn't seem to notice Jasper's disinterest. "I do wish they'd play my favorite Christmas song, though."

"And what would that be?"

"The Red-Nosed Angels From the Great Beyond."

Jasper scoffed. "That's not a real Christmas song."

"And how would you know?"

"I'm literally from the planet where Christmas was invented."

The waitress rolled her eyes. "That's nice. Have a great night." She picked up the last cup off their table and walked away.

"Thanks, I will!" Jasper called after her as she stood from her chair.

"I'm glad prison didn't take away your ability to cause a scene," Cutthroat said as the rest of the team got to their feet.

"You can take Van Terra out of the drama, but you can't take the drama out of Van Terra." Jasper tossed a few jano bills onto the table and started toward the exit. Grace and the others hurried to follow.

As Grace caught up on Jasper's right, Jasper sighed. "Well, the search for a decent Christmas party continues. Kronos will probably have some that are more accurate to Earth culture. There are way more humans living there."

"Sorry this one wasn't what you'd hoped," Grace told her.

"Thanks, Angel." Jasper turned her head to grin at the others over her shoulder. "But I don't need a perfect party when I've got you guys."

Holly groaned. "Ugh, is now really the time to get sappy?"

"What, afraid you'll start crying again?"

"Shut up," Holly muttered. Grace caught a hint of flush creeping into her cheeks as she lowered her face.

The team reached the front doors of the building and stepped out into a surprisingly dark resort. Grace frowned. "How is it already almost dark again? I thought it was summer this side of the planet."

Cutthroat pointed up. "Big storm just rolled in. Look at those clouds."

Grace tipped her head back, and her eyes widened. From horizon to horizon, most of the sky had been overtaken by a thick blanket of near black clouds. A flurry of white was the only thing interrupting the darkness, a snowstorm that...somehow wasn't touching them?

"Looks like the resort's got a pretty impressive forcefield," Thea said, already pulling up an informational page on the resort's net site.

Sarena turned in a circle, eyes going wide. "What? Will we be able to leave?"

"Yes. It's more of an umbrella than a full-on forcefield. We'll run into the storm at the edges, but we can walk through it to the ship."

"Storm should pass pretty quickly, anyway," Cutthroat added. "Like I said, the clouds come and go fast this time of year."

The sight of the resort in the darker lighting was actually kind of beautiful. Lights in every color hung on strings outside buildings and illuminated the pathways. The glittering lights reflected rainbows in Jasper's dark eyes as she turned to take it all in.

While Jasper moved toward a nearby lightpost to examine the fake glowing flowers and glittery vines spiraling up its metal surface, Grace stepped closer to the others and lowered her voice. "Everyone ready?"

The others nodded or voiced their confirmation. They hurried off to board the ship before Jasper could ask questions. Of course, it didn't take her long to notice their disappearance, but Grace jumped in with an answer before she could even ask what happened. "The others went to grab some supplies at a store nearby. I told them I wanted to walk around the resort and look at the lights," she said quickly. "Wanna come with me?"

"Sure." Jasper only looked flustered for a moment before flashing a smile.

"Hey, Grace," Thea said over comms as Grace and Jasper started down the path. "Don't respond, just letting you know I temporarily blocked signals on Jasper's comm. We'll let you know when we're landing."

Grace resisted the urge to confirm she'd heard the information and instead focused on the sights around her. After about ten minutes of pointing out some of the resort's weirder decorative statues to each other—along with a few of the more outlandish convention outfits walking around—Jasper paused and glanced at Grace.

"I think we should take off the first day in Irosland," Jasper said. Her hands slid into the pockets of her coat. "We could all use a break and a little fun. I'm not sure if it's a good idea with everything going on, though. You got any thoughts?"

"Absolutely," Grace said, maybe a little too quickly. "I don't think one more day will change things much. And you especially deserve to relax when you can."

"Yeah. I'm...still pretty exhausted," Jasper admitted. "I don't want to burn the rest of the team out, either. Sounds like you guys didn't get much rest while I was gone."

Grace laughed weakly. "Can you blame us?"

"Guess not," Jasper replied with a sheepish grin. The two continued walking. "Anyway, I want to check out that amusement park thingy."

"Sure. Sounds fun." After a moment, Grace added, "You think you're feeling up for it, physically?"

"Hope so. I have been feeling better since I took the ThetaEight. It's just all the pressure of everything else making me tired right now, I think." She shot Grace a sideways glance. "And I want as much time with you as I can possibly get."

Grace's heart quickened. Doing her best to sound casual, she replied, "Me too."

As their walk continued, Grace asked Jasper for more details about how Christmas worked on Earth. Jasper was midway through explaining a strange tradition involving socks full of gifts when Thea spoke in Grace's ear. "We're coming in on the east side."

Moments later, Jasper looked up at the sky and squinted. "Oh hey, there's our ship."

"Yep. Let's go." Grace grabbed Jasper's hand and ran toward the descending spacecraft.

The outside of the ship looked just as it had earlier, but a complete surprise greeted the two when they stepped inside. Silver and red tinsel was strung across the walls, with a handful of wreaths and paper snowflakes along for the ride as well. A few tiny reindeer statues stood in one corner, fuzzy red stockings were pinned above the entrance to the cockpit, and standing against the back wall was the star of the show: a Christmas tree.

"Wow, you guys decorated that thing fast," Grace said, admiring the tinsel and ornaments and lights wrapping around the tree. A golden star was perched at the top.

"It came like that," Holly replied plainly.

The ship wasn't the only thing that got a makeover. The others had changed clothes as well. Cutthroat had a massive bag slung over his shoulder and had—begrudgingly, it seemed—allowed someone to give him an actual, white fur-lined red Santa hat. Sarena wore...well, her very expensive-looking dress was red and white, which was probably the best they could have hoped for.

Dax and Thea, meanwhile, had put on red-and-green elf costumes, even going as far as to complete the look with pointed shoes and caps ending and bells. Holly had joined them in the look, but she'd avoided the hat and stuck to her black combat boots. Aymes's brown clothes were on the plainer side, but he had on fake reindeer antlers, and his nose had been painted red. Grace wasn't exactly sure what that was about. Jasper had explained a fair amount of Christmas stuff, but she clearly hadn't covered everything.

Rose had the most impressive costume. She'd gone a similar route to Cutthroat, but rather than sticking to just a hat and bag, she had a full-on Santa costume, complete with a huge fake white beard.

Grace grinned. Her smile spread even wider when she saw the look on Jasper's face.

"You know who Santa is, Rose?" Jasper asked as she took in the costume.

Rose shrugged. "I'd never heard of him before, but there was a giant mural of him in the Christmas section at SolGoods and I thought he looked cool."

From what little Grace had gleaned about the way Earth celebrated Christmas, Santa was beloved, but "cool" wasn't exactly a common descriptor. Well, as long as Rose was excited, she wasn't sure it mattered. The more the team got invested in helping Jasper celebrate the holiday, the better.

Jasper turned again to face another corner. "And I see we have some...cartons of gasoline?"

"It's for my thrusters," Rose explained. "Thea helped me figure out how to refuel."

"They aren't powered by bioelectricity like the rest of our cybernetics?"

"Apparently not."

Thea chimed in. "I'm guessing they're more of a prototype. A working one, thankfully, but they just don't seem as refined as the rest of the cybernetics you three have." Her gaze flickered briefly to Grace.

Dax held up a box wrapped in with snowflake-patterned paper and topped with a silver bow. "Jasper, we got you a present, too, if you want to open it—"

"Hold on, it's not Christmas yet," Jasper said as she took the gift from his hands. "Any and all gifts wait until December twenty-fifth."

"Uh, what's the Kronos date on that?" Aymes asked.

Jasper shrugged. "Do the math yourselves." She crossed the small space to the tree and set the present underneath it.

Sarena put her hands on her hips and shot the tree and its accompanying gift a look. "I don't think that's going to stay in place while we fly."

Jasper waved a hand. "We can tie everything down. It'll be fine." She looked up, and a more genuine smile overtook her expression. "Thank you all. You absolutely nailed it." Her eyes landed on Grace, and she offered a small nod of understanding, a small acknowledgement that she'd deduced who planned all of this.

Grace nodded in return and smiled.

III. IROSLAND

Chapter Twenty-Seven
Arrivals

Another one of Astra's changes to the former site of Ringmaster's carnival was the addition of several luxury hotels. Hotels that had surprisingly good net security, given who owned them. Thea was insistent she could get the team rooms, but after watching her shout at her laptop for ten minutes—and nearly throw it across the ship at one point—Jasper told her she had a better idea for accommodations.

They returned to the Astronomer in the new ship, then took the Astronomer to the atmosphere outside Iros, arriving the morning after their adventure at Blue Mountain Resort. From there, the team—with the added inclusion of Cutthroat's two pirates Hook and Steele—left the Astronomer behind in the atmosphere and flew down to Iros's surface in the new ship, which Jasper had decided to call the Comet.

"We're not going to vote on it?" Sarena had complained when Jasper announced the name.

"I got us the ship, I get to name it," Jasper replied before strolling into the cockpit to fly them off the Astronomer's dock. "Them's the rules!"

They flew over the moon's glittering crystal crust for a while before passing over the new Irosland. A newer, shinier, and much bigger Ferris wheel stood where the old one once had. Roller coasters and other rides covered far more ground than the original carnival. And right next to the park stood the giant mall Astra had crammed in on top of everything else.

The park itself had more than just thrilling rides. It was a theme park, now, based around one of Astra's other ventures: Astra Entertainment. The production studio churned out half-assed cartoons directed at children, though many were popular with older audiences, as well. Rides at the park were now based on the company's shows and movies, and actors in costumes roamed the park to take pictures with guests.

Jasper flew them past all that to a building directly behind the mall. When they approached the parking lot of the building in question, Holly buried her face in her hands. "Jasper, is that a goddamned MoonCo?"

"Of course," Jasper replied. She grabbed a lever and pulled it back, putting the ship into a hover. Turning the pilot's chair around the face the rest of the team, she added, "They sell food, furniture, and clothes. They'll have everything we need while we're here."

"And employees that will kick us out."

"Have you seen those giant playsets and sheds they sell? We can hide out in those until everyone goes home."

"Pretty sure the employees check those," Holly countered.

"Not if one of us poses as a new employee and tells everyone they already checked." Jasper tapped the side of her head. "Remember how easy understaffed stores are to infiltrate? This particular location has lots of job listings posted on the net. They need people."

Holly groaned. "Fine. But I'm not playing employee."

"That's fine. I was thinking Sarena should do it, since her voice will make it easier to pull off."

Sarena shot Jasper a glare. "I am not pretending to be some lowly store employee so that we can sleep in display beds for however long we're going to be here!"

"Display beds?" Jasper lifted an eyebrow. "I was thinking we would bust open some sleeping bags and hang out in the tents in the camping section."

"That's worse!" Sarena folded her arms. "No way am I doing that. I'm buying myself a hotel room."

"Not unless you're buying rooms for the rest of us."

"Not a chance."

Jasper leaned back in her chair and raised an eyebrow. "We need to stick together, just in case Skybreaker shows up, god forbid. Or some other asshole comes and attacks us. A lot of people don't like us right now."

Sarena sank off her chair to the floor and groaned. "Fine!" she finally exclaimed. "Whatever. Can't be worse than playing that nerd in that candy commercial."

"Oh, I remember that commercial! That was hilarious." Jasper grinned as she turned back to the ship's controls. "I liked the part where you said, 'No one smashes starjoys like me!'"

Sarena groaned again while Jasper brought the ship down at the back of the MoonCo parking lot. They certainly weren't the biggest vehicle parked in the lot, which would help with blending in. On the off chance someone did come snooping, though, there was no reason to worry about the ship being invaded or stolen. Jasper had given the rest of the team the entry password and added their fingerprints to the database. Without those, the Comet was impossible to access. Worst case scenario, someone called in a towship, but Thea could track it if it came to that.

As Jasper emerged from the cockpit, Sarena moved to the small fishtank the team had picked up before leaving Si Hera, opened its lid, and let Blitz crawl up her arm onto her shoulder. "Don't worry, buddy," she cooed. "We'll get you a bigger tank soon."

Nearby, Cutthroat chatted quietly with his men, who looked pretty much just as Jasper had remembered them. Hooke's lavender skin was mostly covered by black leather, and his short, darker purple hair was neatly combed. Steele's body was covered in silvery reptilian scales, and he wore mostly dark blue and silver, complete with a blue leather hat over his bald head.

Jasper clapped her hands to get their attention. "All right, team, let's roll!" She led the way out of the ship and into the parking lot. It wasn't bad back here, but closer to the building, the place was packed to the brim with vehicles and people with shopping carts.

"Is it always this busy?" Sarena grumbled as she surveyed the crowd.

"Yes. Which will make it easier for us to slip in." Jasper adjusted her coat and strolled forward. "Let's go."

"You're not planning on trying that 'hey our mom's inside' strategy again, are you?" Holly asked as she caught up on Jasper's left. The others followed behind them.

"Uh, I was thinking about it," Jasper replied. "Why?"

"I've heard they've gotten more strict about security." Holly glanced back. "And I think that lie's even more unbelievable now than it was when there was only five of us."

Right. The original team, plus Sarena and Blitz, Aymes, Cutthroat, and two of his henchpirates. "That's okay," Jasper said, her mind working. "I have a plan B."

When they reached the entrance, Jasper flashed a smile at the employee standing guard. "Hi, we wanted to look into getting a business membership for our small business. Where can we go to do that?"

The employee turned and pointed toward a desk nearby, where a giant sign reading "Membership" hung overhead. "Right over there."

Jasper shot Holly a raised eyebrow. Holly sighed.

The team filed in past the employee, strolled right past the membership desk, and headed straight for what lay at the center of the store: the outdoor section. Camping equipment, sheds, playsets. As they approached, though, something else caught Jasper's eye. Something that might help them avoid notice while the store was still open. She veered into the cleaning aisle and stopped in front of a wall of paper towels.

Grace stopped at her left a moment later, eyes wide as her head tipped back. "I've never seen so many paper towels in my life. Is all of this really going to get bought?"

"Eventually. But not today. And where other people see paper towels, I see the building blocks of a fortress." Jasper reached out and plucked one of the packages of towels off the shelf. They were lined up in a complex pattern that let people pick packages randomly out of the middle without the whole wall collapsing, though employees undoubtedly had to fill in gaps throughout the day to keep it stable.

Behind the front wall though were more walls of towels. Walls that no one would reach in the next week or so. There, the team could move things around a little more without being noticed. And they could move to other places in the store each night if this area ended up being less secure than expected.

"Thea, trick the cameras in this aisle, please," Jasper ordered. "Holly, Sarena, get down to each end and tell people that the aisle will reopen in a few minutes, we're just cleaning up some broken glass. Everyone else, help me build a door into that empty storage space in the shelving unit between the paper towel display and the next aisle." As Sarena started to walk away, she added, "And maybe leave the hekten over here? I don't think employees are supposed to bring pets to work."

Next to Jasper, Grace's brow furrowed. "Is this the only way into that storage space? That doesn't seem super practical."

Jasper shook her head. "There's a gap at the end of the aisle employees can squeeze in and out of, but judging by how empty the space looks with my x-ray vision, this area doesn't seem to get used much."

"Why don't we just go in that gap then?"

"Other customers are more likely to notice all ten of us sneaking in down there where we can't block the aisle off. Also, this will be more fun."

Within minutes they had an open doorway into a dark, dusty area behind the paper towel wall. Mostly dark. Light poured in in a few places where enough products had been removed from the shelves in the next aisle over, warning that someone walking by might get a glimpse at the team inside the shelving.

She called Holly and Sarena back in, and the others began quickly building the outer paper towel wall back up to keep them all hidden from view. Jasper, meanwhile, began disassembling portions of the rearmost wall to section off their area from other parts of the shelving space, ensuring they stayed hidden from view. Before long, the only light in the space came the smartspheres the team had scattered across the floor, their entire surfaces glowing in flashlight mode, as well as a few beams of light spilling in through gaps near the top of the shelving unit. It was unlikely anyone would be peeking in from that high up, so Jasper didn't worry about those.

"Awesome," Sarena said once the bulk of the work had been completed, her tone making it clear she thought this was anything but. She picked Blitz up off the shelf he'd been sitting on and moved him to her shoulder. "Are we going to spend the rest of the day in a dusty paper towel fortress?"

"Just until the store closes and employees go home," Jasper told her. "Then we can make ourselves more comfortable." She walked over to the paper towel throne she'd put together and collapsed into it. "First, I'd like to make sure we're on the same page about the plans for the next couple days."

"Do we know where Astra is now?" Cutthroat asked.

Thea jumped in. "Not at the moment. But I've put together a tracking system that uses Irosland's cameras and facial recognition to search for him, on top of pulling from any news sources that might be talking about him," she explained quickly. "All I have to do is connect it to the local networks and we'll be good to go."

Jasper yawned and leaned back. "I say we take some time to relax before we go looking for Astra tomorrow."

Cutthroat shot her a surprised glance. "You want the whole day off?"

"Dude, I just broke out of the Shark Tank like a week ago. Then I blew up the labs where I was held prisoner and tortured for over a year. And after that I stole a spaceship from a secret base that used to belong to a resistance I fought in, which ended when everyone but me was killed in a traumatic battle. I think a day off is more than fair."

Cutthroat shrugged. "All right." He rose to his feet. "Hook, Steele, and I are going to see if there's any good bars in the area, then."

"Looking like that?" People might not recognize Cutthroat at a glance if he kept quiet, but sitting in one place for too long in pirate-y clothing was a great way to let people start putting the pieces together.

"We'll grab some plainer clothes on the way out. I'm not interested in being a villain while I'm just getting a drink."

"Well, we should probably stop calling you Cutthroat, then." Jasper folded her arms. "What's your real name?"

Cutthroat's eyes narrowed. "That name died a long time ago. If 'Cutthroat' is too hard a word for you, you can try 'Pirate' or 'Captain.'" He started toward the edge of the inner paper towel fort.

Jasper twisted in her throne to watch them leave. "I'm just trying to be friendly!" she called after Cutthroat as he and his pirates slipped through an opening in the fort, headed for the end of the shelving unit with the gap employees typically used to get in and out of the space. Her gaze flickered to Sarena and Aymes as the sound of the pirates' footsteps faded. "Either of you know anything about him?"

Aymes shrugged. Sarena rolled her eyes and asked, "Who cares?"

"Me. I care about all your names. And your favorite colors, too."

"Well, I don't have one," Sarena said.

"You said in an interview it was orange."

"I just said that to seem relatable!"

"God, you suck."

"My seven Album of the Season trophies beg to differ." Sarena started toward the exit the pirates had taken. "Speaking of which, I have to call my distribution manager and make sure everything is ready for my album release in a few days. I'm supposed to host a live release party on the net, by the way."

Jasper shrugged. "We'll make time for that. You can do it on the ship or something."

"I'm going to find a new tank for Blitz, too." Sarena patted the hekten's head as she walked away.

"Knock yourself out."

Sarena left, and while the others began to get as comfortable as was possible in the storage space, making their own paper towel furniture and unpacking a few belongings, Jasper headed for the bathroom.

After washing her hands, she studied herself in the mirror for a minute. The lingering bruises and scratches from her prison escape were healing nicely. Not as fast as they once would have, but faster than they had when she was dying from the serum.

The growing hope in her chest strengthened. The future was survivable.

When she returned to the storage space, she found that the team had managed to sneak in some blankets and pillows from elsewhere in the store. In the middle of a sort of pillow nest, Thea had Mia's and Chloe's bodies laid out on the ground. Their overall shapes and colors were similar to how Jasper remembered them, but Mia's silver and black body was a bit taller and sleeker. Chloe's gold and black body, meanwhile, had been bulked up quite a bit, and was even taller than Mia's. Jasper estimated it would be close to seven feet once it was standing.

But as excited as she was to see the nearly complete androids...

"Thea, I meant we should all do something relaxing," Jasper said, arms folding. "Not work."

Thea glanced up. "This is relaxing for me."

"It doesn't sound relaxing when you curse at your own code every five minutes," Holly muttered from where she laid on the floor nearby, scrolling on her tablet.

"Trust me on this," Thea said, returning her attention to a control panel in Mia's back. "Besides, I'm closer to being finished than I realized. I was able to fix a coding error in twenty minutes that I thought was going to take hours."

Jasper lowered her arms. "Okay, well, as long as you're having fun." She turned and found Grace and Dax sitting on a paper towel couch, watching some random sitcom on one of their smartspheres. "Hey, Angel, would you want to go check out the park with me in a few hours?"

That would give her some time to curl up in a pile of blankets and take a much-needed nap. She'd enjoyed flying the Comet that morning, but it had been a long time since she flew a spaceship, and getting back into the flow of it had required more mental effort than she'd expected.

Grace flashed her a smile and nodded. "Sounds good."

Chapter Twenty-Eight
Arrivals, Part 2

Jasper expected to be nervous as the time for her and Grace to leave approached. Between the time she'd acknowledged the extent of her feelings for Grace and when she'd been taken to the Shark Tank, she'd always felt some degree of nervousness around her. Hell, even upon returning, being around Grace had made her shaky the first few days.

But instead, when Jasper came back from the depths of sleep and climbed out of the nest she'd made at the edge of the fort, she felt...completely, totally at ease. Excited, sure, but not anxious.

After all they'd been through together, there was nothing to worry about.

Jasper went searching for a fresh change of clothes among the store's selection. She nearly changed into simple black pants and a long-sleeved black shirt, but at the last second decided to swap the shirt for a muted pink one with sleeves that stopped just short of her elbows. She also let her hair fall out of its ponytail and hang down her back.

Part of her felt a little uncomfortable being this exposed, after hiding herself in layers for so long. But she didn't feel frigid and scarred the way she once had, perpetually needing the comfort of her black clothes and dark coat. All she really needed was a little time to adjust.

Grace was waiting for Jasper outside the bathroom. She beamed when she saw Jasper. "You look great," she said softly. "It's nice to see you...like this."

Jasper grinned. "Thank you. It's nice to feel like this." She took a moment to take in Grace's outfit, which wasn't much different from the casual clothes she often wore. Dark blue pants, a brighter blue tank top, and a thick white hooded jacket to help hide her wings.

As they headed for the front of the store, Grace asked, "Where are we headed first?"

"I thought we'd take a path through the mall to the theme park." Jasper ran a hand through her hair. "One of the mall entrances is right on the other side of the MoonCo parking lot."

"Sounds great."

It had been obvious the mall was big when they'd flown over, but it seemed even more humongous walking through it. It held every popular store one could think of, a movie theater, restaurants, laser tag and mini golf, and similar venues invented on other planets: zero-gravity orbitball, blazby arenas, Gemma-whack rings.

"So, is this secretly an opportunity for us to check out Irosland in prep for tomorrow?" Grace asked as they passed through one of several food courts.

"Nope. Though if you do see anything of interest, may as well make note of it." Jasper glanced at Grace. "But I don't want to be thinking about any of that right now." Not that Jasper could entirely help herself. A constant stream of thought at the back of her mind was analyzing the world around her for weapons, escape routes, cameras, potential enemies.

After wandering a few stores, snacking on some frozen moondust cream, and trying out a few games at the arcade—Jasper nailed most of them, though Grace did a surprisingly good job of kicking her ass at a dance pad game—the two moved on to the theme park outside. Jasper scanned them in with some ticket codes she'd persuaded Thea to snag for her earlier.

"Big Astra Entertainment fan?" Jasper asked as Grace's head swung back and forth to take in the rides towering around them.

"Can't say I've seen any of their shows," Grace replied. "You?"

"Me neither. I'd rather just make assumptions about the characters and go off that." She pointed toward someone in the costume of a cartoon alien animal that vaguely resembled a cross between a cow and a bumblebee. "Like, I bet that character's movie is about how they're a time traveler torn between leading the bee revolution against mankind and ruling a town in the Hatuan west as its sheriff."

Grace laughed. "From what I've heard, I think you'd make better movies than Astra's actual directors."

"Damn right I would." Jasper veered toward a line for a coaster with the park's highest drop and several loops. "Roller coasters don't make you nauseous or anything, do they?"

"Never been on one," Grace replied.

"Never?" Jasper paused. "Well, I guess that makes sense." Starr probably hadn't taken her on her on a lot of fun field trips when she was living in the palace.

"But given my flight patterns, I think I'd do just fine," Grace continued. After a moment, she added, "That, and driving with you in the flying car."

Jasper groaned and laughed. "Okay, fair enough."

The two survived several coasters just fine, and Jasper found the quick drops and frantic twists and turns even more fun when she wasn't being chased by people trying to kill her.

"Wanna give the Ferris wheel ago?" she asked Grace as they stumbled off their fifth coaster. "Bet there's a great view at the top." The lights of the park glowing under the now-dark sky, distant cities shining across the iridescent, rocky landscape...

Grace laughed. "We don't really need a Ferris wheel for that."

"Sure, but we also don't usually have time to enjoy the view when we're flying around. And you'll draw less attention without your wings out."

"Fair enough."

Jasper was right about the view being incredible. And there was a bit of thrill that came from being so high up without being enclosed in a vehicle or spaceship. Grace was probably used to that feeling, though.

But speaking of spaceships...

The craft that shot by overhead was fast, but not so fast that Jasper and Grace didn't get a decent look at it. It wasn't a terribly unusual ship, but the attached side engines were much larger than standard for Janus System craft, and Jasper had never seen anything quite like the elaborate patterns of red lines that zig-zagged along its white panels.

Grace frowned. "I don't think I've ever seen a ship like that."

"Me neither." It wasn't as weird as the crescent-shaped ship they'd seen in the footage of Skybreaker arriving in Hatu, but it was still notable.

Before Jasper could decide whether to interrupt her and Grace's date—as brief an interruption as it may have been—with a request for identification, Grace tapped her finger against her comm. "Thea, did you catch that ship that just flew in?"

"Yep. Already working on ID."

Jasper and Grace's seat on the Ferris wheel moved forward and began to drop. Almost time to unload.

"Oh, wow, that's a rare sight," Thea said after a minute. "It's an Interstar Council ship."

Jasper's eyes widened, and she exchanged a surprised look with Grace. The council was finally making an appearance? After so many years of the Starr family's unchecked reign?

"Should we head back to Kronos?" Grace asked. "If Starr has that army he was working on ready to go, he'll just attack them, right?"

"I don't think he'll attack on sight," Jasper replied with a shake of her head. If the council was making moves, the entire alliance was bound to be watching. Rash actions could bring more trouble his way from other star systems. And Starr was careful. Calculating. "They're probably here to conduct an investigation, and I bet Starr will wait for the results of that. If he can get away with continuing on as is without having to start a war, he can save his energy for other ventures."

They didn't even know for sure if Starr's army was ready yet. There had been quite a few cyborgs and weapons at the lab on Reo, but Jasper was skeptical they would win against a large army. Take out a big chunk, maybe, but many of them would be killed in the process too.

"I'll keep an eye on things in the capital," Thea said. "It won't be long until we return to Kronos, anyway, and I'd rather be prepped with AstraSmart code when we get back." She paused. "This council ship is an ambassador ship. No weapons. No reason for Starr to attack. And it looks like it's the only thing that's entered the star system in the past pentasol, according to public radar records, anyway."

Jasper held back the next thought that popped into her head. *Unless they've also got remarkable stealth ships.* Most stealth ships could slip through public radar, but the government's defense satellites would still be able to pick them up. Only the most advanced stealth technology had even a chance of getting through without Starr catching wind.

There was no reason for the council to send any ships of that scope yet, but it was a possibility to consider.

Jasper and Grace grabbed more desserts on their way out of the park and took them back to MoonCo to share with the others. Cutthroat, Hook, Steele, and Sarena came back not long after. And soon after their return, the store closed. The team sent a begrudging Sarena out in a uniform Holly had snatched from storage earlier, and she assured the other employees that she had checked the storage spaces between the shelving units.

After that, Thea put the security cameras on a loop, and the team was free to roam the store. They all claimed various sleeping areas—Jasper in a sleeping bag at the top of a playset, Grace in a hammock nearby, and the others scattered across the tents in the camping area and display beds across the aisle.

Everyone gathered in the camping area to watch television for a while. The sitcom someone put on mainly earned snarky comments from Holly, Sarena, and Cutthroat, with even Rose throwing in a few jabs. But everyone else laughed through most of it, and it was entertaining enough to keep everyone in the area until well after midnight.

It would have been a perfect day, if it hadn't ended with some of the worst nightmares Jasper had ever experienced.

Chapter Twenty-Nine
The Happiest Place in the Star System

Dax wasn't sure if anyone else noticed that something was up with Jasper the morning after they arrived on Iros, but if they did, they didn't say anything. While most of the team chatted over a breakfast of scavenged pastries and meal bars inside the paper towel fort, she was reserved and quiet and kept staring off into the distance with a haunted look in her eyes.

Just as Dax was preparing to ask if she was okay, her air completely shifted. She began smiling and cracking dumb jokes, and by the time Grace returned with the charging cables she'd gone to fetch for Thea, Jasper seemed completely fine. Had she just been tired?

No, even a tired Jasper tended to still be over-the-top in terms of personality. She had to be worried about...something.

Whatever it was, it would have to be worried about later. Jasper clapped her hands together as everyone began shoving the packaging left from their breakfast into trash bags. "All right, today's mostly about winging it, so I'll be speedrunning our intro and getting us out the door ASAP. According to Thea, Astra's going to be leading some investors around Irosland today. She wasn't able to find an agenda for the tour, so the rest of us will be making sure they stay away from the offices while she gets into Astra's systems.

"Holly and Sarena, you'll stay near the offices at the south end of the mall," Jasper continued. "Grace and I will hang out in the middle of the building. Cutthroat, you and your pirates and Rose will stick to the north end."

Cutthroat's eyes narrowed. "Why am I the babysitter?"

"Hey, I'm not a baby!" Rose folded her arms indignantly.

Jasper waved a hand. "Cutthroat, I think you're the most responsible person here, and the least likely to let Rose escape."

Sarena snorted. "Maybe you should put her on one of those toddler leashes." Rose shot her a glare so sharp it made Dax grimace.

"Teams are settled. I don't want to hear any more complaining." One of Jasper's hands moved to rest on her hip. "If we're lucky, this won't take Thea long, and we'll never even have to worry about Astra."

"Well, that's definitely not happening," Holly muttered. "Have you met us? I wouldn't use the word 'lucky.'"

Jasper was already moving on. "Dax, Aymes, you'll hang out at the theme park."

Dax glanced at Aymes, a little surprised at the choice, but he supposed it made sense from Jasper's perspective. Dax had gotten along the best with Aymes while the team was undercover at East Marina High.

Of course, that was before Aymes learned they'd all been lying to him to get intel on Ringmaster.

Jasper continued. "Any questions? No? Good. Everyone get out there! Go team!"

Dax couldn't help but feel a bit awkward—and guilty—as he and Aymes silently walked toward the entrance to the Astra Entertainment park. It was hard to get his mind off Aymes's anger after learning the team had lied to him. Even though they'd all wound up working together after that, he had a hard time believing Aymes could just let all that go. All of the conversations they'd had since he showed up at Jasper's apartment a couple months earlier had been group conversations, spouting ideas about overthrowing Starr, fighting the government, targeting the elite.

Now...

"Sorry again, by the way," Dax found himself stammering after they passed through park security.

Aymes glanced at him, clearly confused. "Huh?"

"Sorry about everything that happened at East Marina. I still feel bad about lying to you." Dax dropped his gaze to the ground. "Must have sucked finding out your new friends were only after information you had."

Aymes sighed. "Yeah, it did suck. But I mean, I get why you guys did it. I was on Ringmaster's side, even though I knew what he was doing was wrong. I hadn't seen him do anything horrible enough to turn against him." Glancing at Dax, he added, "Especially since you guys were technically villains, too."

Dax wasn't entirely sure that should have been past tense—the line between hero and villain had never been more blurred to him. But it was a small point. At any rate, it just wasn't the team's fake high school identities, or the volleyball camaraderie that Aymes learned was a façade, that was bothering Dax right now.

What also bothered him was what Grace had revealed to the team shortly after Aymes's first visit.

Apparently, during their first trip to Iros, Jasper had deduced that Aymes was Ringmaster's son. And Aymes still had no idea. No idea that that was the reason Ringmaster had pursued him as a sidekick. Neither Jasper nor Grace had seen the point in telling him now that Ringmaster was gone, though Grace did feel a bit torn on the matter. He did have a right to know. But would it help him? Or hurt him?

The rest of the team had been equally uncertain. Holly was the first to say she felt they should continue keeping it under wraps for the time being, and Thea had said that was fine by her. It seemed like a good idea to Dax too, at the time, but now he was having a hard time ignoring the secret. As he set his sights back on the park around him, he found himself asking, "Do you miss working with Ringmaster?"

Instead of an immediate rejection of the idea, Aymes hesitated. "I mean, he was a terrible person. I knew he was a villain from the start, obviously, but I didn't really realize how awful he was until everything went down with the warps.

"But he taught me how to use my powers. And this might sound weird, but…" Aymes sighed. "It seems like he genuinely cared about me. More than just as a tool to help him enact his crimes."

Dax was struggling to think up a response to that, so he was relieved when their conversation was interrupted by an urgent message from Thea over comms. "Hey, I need someone to get their hands on Astra."

"Whoa," Jasper cut in. "I thought we didn't need to interact with him."

"And I thought I'd be able to bypass his two-step verification," Thea replied. "But this thing's a brick wall. The only decent piece of AstraSmart code I've seen so far. I could potentially spoof a signal from his device, but I'd need to clone its software to be able to do that, anyway."

"Could we take the time clone his sphere without him noticing and delay the hack until later?"

"In theory, yes. Do you think it's worth waiting that long just to mitigate a little risk?"

After a long moment, Jasper sighed. "Let's just get this done now. Astra and Starr aren't particularly close, outside of the palace tech contract. But still, everyone, please try to be subtle."

"Copy," Thea said. "Cameras are showing Astra and a few investors in the theme park."

Dax tapped his comm to unmute. "We're on it. Where in the park?"

"Headed toward the Ferris wheel, walking just east of the roller coaster with the glow-in-the-dark tracks."

"On our way. Keep us updated." Together, Dax and Aymes switched course and headed for Astra.

Once they had eyes on the CEO and his crew of potential investors, Aymes asked, "Any ideas on how to get his smartsphere?"

Dax's gaze darted around the crowd for a few moments before landing on one of the park's costumed characters, some kind of furry blue alien feline with bright green spots and pink horns shaped like a giraffe's. Two employees in plain park uniforms were escorting the character toward a nearby building. "I've got one," he replied.

He and Aymes followed the character as their handlers guided them through a door marked employees only. With their blasters drawn, cameras stalled courtesy of Thea, and no one else around, it was easy enough for Dax and Aymes to persuade them to hand over the costume and keep quiet. Aymes left them tied up with silver ropes that he assured them would dissipate in twenty minutes.

The two took the costume and found their way into a storage room. "All right, who's putting on the costume?" Dax asked. He hated to force Aymes into it, but it did not look pleasant.

Aymes held out a hand and formed a fake professional camera from his silver energy. "Can you make a camera?"

Dax sighed and put the character's giant round head on over his own.

"Besides, if you get heatstroke, you can heal yourself," Aymes added.

Dax managed a weak laugh at that. "Fair enough."

A minute later, they were outside trailing Astra again. Aymes recreated his fake camera and, once the two were close enough, darted into Astra's path. "Good to see you, sir, how would you and your esteemed guests like a picture?" Aymes gestured to Dax as he struggled to catch up in the awkward and uncomfortably hot costume.

Astra didn't look terribly enthused, but to Dax's surprise, one of the investors lit up like a Christmas tree. "Oh, I love Mimy, she's one of my favorite characters!"

Astra's expression changed dramatically, a wide smile crossing his face. "We'd love to get a picture. Get in here, Mimy."

Dax shuffled into the middle of the group and put his arms around the closest investors. After pretending to take a few photos, Aymes held out a hand toward Astra. "I'll just need your smartsphere for a moment."

Astra's brow furrowed. "What for?"

"To transfer the photos."

Astra sighed. "Did they change the photo sharing system again? I asked them to stop doing that."

Aymes nodded. "My apologies, sir, I just do what my manager tells me."

Astra hesitated, his gaze flicking sideways to the potential investors. Seeming to want to avoid friction in front of them, he said, "No worries, young man, you're doing a great job. Here." He dropped the sphere into Aymes's open palm.

"Quick, press the top of the sphere," Thea instructed.

Aymes pulled back from Astra. His finger moved over the device quickly. "Got it," he muttered, turning away from Astra and pretending to squint at his camera. "I think."

"It worked. I'm onto the next step. Thanks."

While Aymes continued to fiddle with the fake camera and the sphere, Astra took a closer look at Mimy and frowned. "Aren't you supposed to have two handlers with you?"

Dax had no idea if the characters were supposed to talk, or what Mimy sounded like, so he just nodded and gestured vaguely to the crowd nearby. Before Astra could look too hard for character security, Aymes shoved his sphere back into his hand.

"It could take up to an hour for the photos to appear in your gallery," Aymes told Astra. "Contact customer support if you have any issues."

Once they were a short distance away, Aymes and Dax paused to observe Astra and the investors. A small silver songbird darted down from the sky and landed on a low-hanging tree branch behind the group.

"Astra's saying he has to make a quick call…" Aymes's brow furrowed as Astra took a step back from the group and held his smartsphere up to his mouth.

"Oh, damn it," Thea muttered.

"What?" Dax asked.

"There's another verification required from a secondary device. But it's not Astra's, it's a completely different sphere."

"How are we supposed to find it, then?"

"Hang on, let me throw a tracking algorithm at it."

Aymes waved a hand frantically to catch Dax's attention. "Astra was talking to his security team. He's headed back to his office."

"And the investors?" Dax asked.

"Yeah, they're going with. He's still playing up the tour aspect."

"Well, let's follow," Dax decided. "We can intervene if they get too close before Thea finishes."

Aymes agreed, and they set off as fast as they could manage with Dax in the costume. They were only on the move for a few moments when Thea spoke again. "Okay, the other sphere I need is nearby, too. But not in Astra's party."

"Undercover security?" Jasper suggested from wherever she was.

"Seems likely." Clicking came from Thea's end. Then, "I found the device's serial number. It's going to be a sky blue mini model. I'll see if I can narrow its location any further." White was the most common smartsphere color, but others weren't uncommon. Knowing that it was blue would certainly help, though, on top of it being a smaller model.

Dax and Aymes had nearly followed Astra and company to the park's entrance when a brown-furred Hatuan with a wolfish face stepped into their path. At first glance, he looked like any other tourist. But when the man spoke, fangs flashing, he said, "Can I get your names and employee IDs?"

"Thea, can you run facial recognition on this guy?" Dax asked under his breath.

"Just finished. That's Irosland's head of security. Sands Ropeak."

Aymes cleared his throat. "Uh...I'm new, I don't remember my ID number."

Ropeak's hand moved to his side, where the handle of a blaster waited at his belt. "I'm going to need you two to come with me."

"Run?" Aymes asked, glancing at Dax.

Dax nodded in affirmation. "Run."

The two broke into a sprint. Dax tore off Mimy's head and tossed it aside as he ran, earning a few alarmed shrieks from nearby children. It was a dramatic improvement, but the rest of the costume was still keeping him hot. No time to get it off now, though.

It didn't take long for more undercover guards to come out of the crowd, moving into Aymes and Dax's path wherever they tried to run. The two quickly wound up back-to-back as security surrounded them. Once they had nowhere to go, Ropeak reappeared and strolled toward them. "Let's avoid causing a scene, please," he said as he reached them. "I don't want to make things painful for you two. Just come with me and answer a few—"

A buzz came from somewhere in Ropeak's vicinity, interrupting him. With a sigh, he drew a mini blue smartsphere from his pocket and glanced at the message projected from the top. The text was too small for Dax to read from a few feet away.

Ropeak's eyes narrowed. To the other guards, he said, "I'm following Astra. Take care of them." With that, he stepped away and headed for the park's exit.

"Ropeak's got the sphere we need, but Aymes and I are surrounded," Dax muttered into his comm. "He's headed toward the mall's north entrance."

"We'll intercept him," Cutthroat replied.

Dax's head turned, and Aymes met his eye. Aymes's fists went up. "Ready?"

Dax nodded and mirrored the motion. "Ready."

Chapter Thirty
Bounce High, Kid

Rose gleefully ignored Cutthroat calling after her as she darted between racks of clothing. Within minutes of entering the store that had caught her eye, she had her hands on a spiked leather jacket in a deep shade of green and spiked combat boots to match. She kicked off the plain boots she was currently wearing and slid her feet into the new ones.

Cutthroat caught up to her as she shrugged on the jacket. "What is this, a costume? What are you going for here?"

"Thorn," Rose answered plainly.

"Huh?"

Behind him, a spiked red collar hanging on a jewelry shelf captured Rose's attention. She darted past Cutthroat and between the other two pirates to grab it. When she returned to the pirates a moment later, new collar strapped to her neck, Cutthroat was muttering something into his comm. Rose swept her gaze over nearby shelves, scanning for anything else of interest.

"Come on," Cutthroat said, interrupting her search. "We need to intercept Astra's head of security and get his smartsphere."

"Are we hoping to retrieve it without him noticing?" Hook asked.

While they talked, Rose subtly began yanking the price tags off her new clothes.

"That would be ideal, but I'm not sure how good our chances are." Cutthroat folded his arms. "Our top priority is preventing Astra or Ropeak from getting to Thea before she's done. That way, they won't be able to confirm there was a security breach at all."

"But we're allowed to beat him up, right?" Rose asked eagerly.

She didn't get the response she was hoping for. Steele huffed. "I don't understand why we didn't leave the child at the MoonCo." His voice, as usual, had a bit of a rasp to it.

"Me neither." Cutthroat shot her an annoyed glance.

Rose did her best to act like that didn't sting a little. Of course Cutthroat saw her as a child. She technically was one. But if he could just be a little more open-minded… He knew about her weapons, didn't he? Was it really too much of a stretch to perceive her as competent, despite her age?

"Can't we leave her here?" Hook asked. "She seems to be having fun."

Cutthroat shook his head and started toward the store's exit. "Jasper wants her in our sight at all times. Besides, I don't trust her to stay put."

"He's right. And you can't stop me from coming with you." Rose stuck her tongue out at Hook and Steele before running to catch up with Cutthroat. The two pirates brought up the rear. With Thea offering guidance over comms, it didn't take long for them to find Sands Ropeak.

"There he is." Cutthroat's eyes narrowed as they found the man walking briskly through the crowd, talking into his blue smartsphere. "Let's all move in together."

"On it!" Rose broke into a sprint toward the man.

"Rose, wait—!"

Rose's mad dash toward Ropeak wasn't as reckless as it looked. She ran toward him at an angle that would put her in his blind spot, thanks to the help of a large support beam in the middle of the mall corridor. And by the time she was in his field of vision, it was too late. Rose snatched the sphere right out of his hand and kept running. "Tag! You're it!"

It took the stunned Ropeak a moment to give chase. "Hey, kid, get back here!"

"I've got the sphere, Thea. What do I do?" Rose asked as she fumbled with the device. She threw quick glances back every few seconds to check the distance between her and Ropeak.

"Activate the holoscreen," Thea instructed. "There should be a prompt asking if you're trying to log in."

Rose tapped the top of the sphere and groaned at what came up instead. "Hang on, it needs fingerprint verification!" She would have to lure Ropeak into close combat. Getting out of this crowded corridor would help. Rose's eyes landed on a sign up ahead. A wide grin crossed her face. *That'll do.*

"Rose, wait up!" Cutthroat growled into comms. He and his pirates weren't far behind Ropeak.

Relax, pirate, I got this. Rose made a sharp left and cut into the trampoline park.

She blew past the woman working the front desk, who was too distracted by a video on her tablet to even notice. Ropeak had the same luck. Rose paused next to one of the trampolines, giving him the chance to *almost* catch up. Once he'd nearly reached her, she jumped back onto the tramp and launched herself toward him, spinning through the air above him. She extended an arm to grab his wrist and flipped him onto his back as she landed.

Rose nearly had his fingerprint to the scanner—an illuminated spot on the sphere's top—when he broke free, jumped to his feet, and grabbed her arm. Oops. She'd expected him to be strong, but she may have slightly underestimated just how strong. She struggled in vain to break free from his grip. His other hand moved toward the sphere she still held, ready to snatch it away.

Rose hadn't fully gained control of the thrusters in her feet, but she could at least activate and deactivate them on command, and that was good enough for now. All she needed was to go up. It was a shame she'd be blowing a hole in the bottom of her new boots, though.

The thrusters came to life, and Rose shot out of Ropeak's grasp with a little more velocity than she'd expected. Breaking free from Ropeak also sent her shooting away from him at an odd angle. She frantically shut the thrusters off, but not fast enough to keep herself from slamming into one of the trampolines angled against a wall. The next thing she knew, she was sailing uncontrollably through the air.

Ropeak ran toward the spot where she'd be hitting the ground. Rose activated the thrusters again briefly, just enough to change her directory and land about ten feet away instead. She came down hard on another trampoline and immediately went back up. Ropeak darted forward, jumped onto the same trampoline, and lifted a fist as he flew through the air toward her. Rose wildly flung her free arm in hopes of somehow deterring him. His attack missed, and the two went back down.

For the next few moments, Rose and Ropeak bounced up and down on the trampoline, circling each other. Nearby, parents shouted in alarm and grabbed their children. Rose dodged the next swing of Ropeak's arm and twisted in the air. She shoved her foot into his stomach as hard as she could, launching him backwards against one of the wall trampolines. He bounced off it and slammed face-first into a foam pit.

This wasn't working as well as Rose had hoped. Time to get a little distance and make a new plan. She activated her thrusters and shot into the air. Near the ceiling, she turned them back off, grabbed a support beam, and hung on.

Before she had much time to think, she spotted Cutthroat, Hook, and Steele coming in the front entrance. The woman at the front desk was no longer distracted by her tablet, but she was apparently still oblivious to the chaos happening behind her. She waved a hand to stop the pirates. "Sir, this is the children's area. You and your...friends can't be here without a child."

Cutthroat sighed and pointed. "That one's mine. Up there."

The woman glanced up, and her eyes went wide when they found Rose. "Young lady, you can't be up there! How did you even—?"

Rose looked down to see Ropeak climbing out of the foam pit, looking extremely pissed off. *Let him take the sphere back on purpose while he doesn't realize the scanner is active, then once it's unlocked, take it back,* Rose decided. She let go of the beam and used her thrusters to slow her descent.

She hit the ground next to a couple of parents watching their toddler bounce on a mini trampoline. They had seemingly failed to notice the ongoing fight. What really caught Rose's attention, though, was the very delicious looking blended ice cream drink in one of their hands. Rose grabbed it, darted forward to the trampoline as the toddler stumbled off, and used it to launch herself back into the air. Confused exclamations came from below as she flew toward Ropeak.

Ropeak lifted his fists in anticipation of Rose's arrival. She chugged the drink mid-air—she was right, it was delicious—chucked it toward a trash can below, and landed directly in front of him.

It was easy enough pretending to slip up and allow Ropeak to take the sphere, but it came at the unfortunate cost of a blow to the stomach. Rose's jaw clenched as she doubled over. She barely managed to keep her eyes on Ropeak's hands to confirm they touched the fingerprint sensor. A heartbeat later, she used her thrusters to gain extra power and lunged at him, knocking him onto his back. The smartsphere slipped from his grasp and rolled across the floor. Rose went after it.

"Thea, now," she hissed. Her hand found the sphere just as a small holoscreen popped out of the top, displaying the alert that requested secondary verification for security system access. All that was left was to tap the button.

Rose's finger was an inch away from success when a foot slammed into her and knocked her on her back. She watched through spinning vision as Ropeak snatched the sphere out of the air and ran.

Dang it. "Ropeak got the sphere back before I could hit the confirmation!"

"All right, I cancelled the verification so he won't realize what we're doing," Thea said. "And I can resend the fingerprint verification signal now that I've recorded it. But I still need the confirmation taken care of ASAP."

Rose's lungs demanded ragged breaths as she pushed herself up. Cutthroat, Hook, and Steele were coming her way now. Behind them, Ropeak was making a quick escape via trampoline, taking high arcs through the air toward the exit.

"What are you doing? He's getting away?" Rose jumped to her feet and nearly toppled over. Cutthroat's hand moved to steady her.

"Making sure you're okay," he said. "That was an impressive fight."

"But I failed!"

"You got the fingerprint verification recorded. Plus, you delayed his approach to the offices." Cutthroat looked Rose up and down, then let out a heavy sigh. "Not bad, kid."

Rose frowned. "Why do you sound disappointed?"

"I'm not."

"Then what was that sigh?"

Cutthroat straightened up. "I know being a clone shouldn't mean much as far as personality goes, but...it's still surprising how much like her you are."

Something about the statement stirred an unfamiliar emotion in Rose's chest that was borderline uncomfortable. Hoping to distract herself from it, she turned to face the exit as Ropeak ran out. "Well, what are we waiting for? Let's go get that guy!"

Chapter Thirty-One
Ultraviolent Light

It wasn't the plan going south that put Jasper in a bad mood, but rather the group of young teenagers that made the mistake of crossing her path. They'd seemed harmless enough at first as they walked by, though their laughter was annoyingly loud. But Jasper wasn't going to give them a second thought until the Drink Cup Incident occurred.

One of the teens, a pastel pink-skinned girl with long golden hair and two short antennae protruding from her forehead, finished off a neon pink soda with a loud slurp before tossing the empty cup right onto the ground. With absolutely no acknowledgement of what she'd just done—and none from her friends, either—the girl continued talking. "We're so close to a hundred-game win streak. I think if we broke it now, I'd kill who ever beat us."

Jasper, who'd been leaning back against a wall with Grace, unfolded, straightened up and took a step forward. "Hey!" she snapped.

The cup's owner whirled around. "Hey what?" she spat in response. The other teens halted around her and turned their annoyed gazes on Jasper.

Jasper gestured to the nearest trash can. "The trash is ten feet away! Clean up after yourselves, for heaven's sake. What are you, animals?"

The girl's eyes narrowed. "What are you going to do, make me?"

Jasper's hands twitched at her sides. A couple of the teens laughed.

Grace leaned toward Jasper. Voice low, she said, "I agree that they're obnoxious and they should clean up after themselves, but I don't know that now's the best time to make a scene."

She was right, but it still took a long moment for Jasper's shoulders to sag and for a sigh to escape her mouth. "Fine."

Grace moved to pick up the cup. More chuckles came from the teens. Jasper's hands curled into fists again, but she forced herself to keep her response to a sharp glare pointed in the group's direction. If she looked remotely like Van Terra right now, it would have been tempting to whip out the villain persona to scare them. But her colorful, casual clothing was a far cry from the right look, and on top of that, Holly had braided her hair, keeping her from easily throwing it into its usual ponytail.

The urge to come up with some other way to get petty revenge on the teens was strong, but there wasn't time for such a detour. Not long after Thea's request for verification from Astra's sphere came the revelation that she needed a second one, and then there was frantic chatter over comms as the team coordinated to identify and track the head of security.

And then the chase was on.

Jasper and Grace were crossing a large intersection in the center of the mall when they nearly collided with Astra. They jumped out of his path in the nick of time, barely escaping his notice. As soon as he was past them, they moved to follow.

Voice low, Jasper said, "We've got eyes on Astra." The men walking with him must have been the investors.

"Is Ropeak with him?" Thea asked.

"I don't think so." Jasper kept up a casual demeanor as she scanned the crowd around Astra.

"Ropeak just left the trampoline park," Cutthroat said. "He's fallen pretty far behind Astra. But he is still headed for the offices."

"Well, we don't need Astra anymore, right?" Holly asked. "Just Ropeak's sphere."

"But we do need to keep him away from the offices," Jasper replied. "If either of the men make it there, Thea's screwed." Delaying Astra should be manageable, though, even if there were more undercover guards around. And... "Maybe if we grab Astra, we can use him to lure Ropeak to us."

"That'll cause more of a scene than we already have," Holly pointed out.

Thea chimed in. "I think it's worth grabbing Astra anyway. Stop him from getting to the security room, at least. Even if I manage to sneak out without being seen, he could disable everything I've done so far and make it harder for us to try again."

Jasper exchanged a glance with Grace. "You ready?"

Grace gave her a nod. "Sure am. Got a plan?"

"Yep. Follow my lead." Jasper broke into a record-setting speedwalk to cut Astra off. "Excuse me, sir, try some free samples of our lotion—"

"Sorry, I'm busy." Astra tried to sidestep her and walked right into Grace. Grace procured a lotion bottle that she must have snatched off a nearby display, cap already open. One well-aimed squeeze was all it took to blind Astra.

Astra yelped in pain and attempted to wipe the lotion off his face with his sleeve. Jasper grabbed his forearm before it reached his face and began to drag him toward one of the halls shooting off from the main corridor. "I'm so sorry, sir. Here, let me help you to the bathroom to wash that off."

Grace flashed the perplexed investors a smile. "We'll be right back!"

Once Grace had caught up to her, Jasper glanced back. Quietly, she said, "Investors look too confused to do anything, but we should keep an eye out for security—"

Astra started up a sudden struggle, nearly managing to break free of Jasper's grasp. "Let me go! I'm not letting you take me anywhere!"

"Relax, dude, we're not gonna hurt you. Probably." Jasper's grip on his arm tightened. "We just need to borrow you for an hour or two."

Grace's eyes focused on something behind Jasper and widened. "Look out—!"

Jasper ducked in time to avoid the swing of the man's fist, but her grip on Astra loosened enough for him to break free and start running. The security guard that had attacked Jasper turned. "Wait, sir!" he called after Astra. It was no use. Astra was too freaked out to even listen to his security team. Being half-blind probably wasn't helping, either.

While the guard was distracted, Jasper grabbed Grace's hand and ran. The two were fast enough to narrow the gap between them and Astra, but not fast enough to get to him before he found a door. The door was locked, but Astra moved through easily by swiping his badge, though he did fumble with it for a moment. The delay gave Jasper just enough extra time to catch the door before it fell shut.

Jasper let Grace slip through first before following, yanking the door shut with a hard thud before Astra's security guard could follow. He would undoubtedly have a badge, too, so Jasper smashed her right fist against the handle, twisting it out of shape and bending the internal locking mechanism. After that, she and Grace entered a dark hallway in time to catch Astra hurrying through another door. It was closed by the time they reached it, but this one wasn't locked.

The room on the other side had racks occupying two of the walls, holding what appeared to be armored vests attached to blasters. Half the vests had pads scattered across their fabric that gave off a faint blue glow, while the other half's pads were red. There was another door in the third wall, which Astra must have already gone through.

"What is this?" Grace glanced around. "Why are there weapons in a mall?"

Jasper instantly identified the equipment. She couldn't hold back a grin. "That other door must go into the arena. And no one's in here, so there might be a match going."

"Huh?"

Jasper crossed the room to one of the racks. "Arm yourself. We're going in."

Grace was clearly still confused, but she joined Jasper in sliding on a blue vest and picking up the attached weapon. Together, they passed through the other door and stepped into ultraviolet light. The sound of artificial laser blasts and children shouting filled the air. Somewhere nearby, someone was crying.

Jasper's eyes went wide when they returned to Grace. "Whoa, your wings glow like crazy in the UV!"

Grace glanced over her shoulder and stretched out one of the wings that had been relaxing behind her. It was a vibrant white, glowing even brighter than the neon fixtures designed to light up under the UV. "Whoa."

"Well, better keep 'em folded up tight, if you don't want to make yourself a target."

"Am I in danger?" Grace asked as she folded the wings up and adjusted her shirt to hide them better.

"Only in danger of getting owned by children." Jasper froze as familiar laughter echoed through the air. Her eyes narrowed. "And annoying teenagers, it would seem."

"Some would argue that we're annoying teenagers."

"Me, yes." Jasper raised an eyebrow. "I don't think the word 'annoying' could ever apply to you, though."

Grace grinned. "That's sweet. So, are you going to tell me what's going on here?"

Right. "The name of the game is laser tag. These guns shoot out harmless lasers. If you hit someone in their vest, you get points, and they can't shoot for a few seconds."

"Got it."

The two started into the maze of walls filling the laser tag arena. The game had been invented after Jasper had left Earth, so she'd only ever played it here on Kronos. But from what she'd read on the Earthnet, the Janus System had done a pretty good job of recreating the game. The biggest difference was that the arenas out here had sections where gravity was oriented differently, forcing players to adjust to walking on walls and even ceilings in a few places.

At a corner, Jasper slowed and peered around it into a narrow corridor. A few teenagers ran past at the other end of the hall, one of them very familiar-looking. The girl who'd tossed the drink cup on the ground earlier was here, along with her friends.

Jasper glanced back at Grace. "Whaddaya say we kick some teenage butts and catch Astra at the same time?"

Grace lifted her weapon and eyed it skeptically. "I know it's probably similar to aiming a blaster, but I don't know if I'm good enough at that to beat kids who play this regularly."

"Don't worry. I'll do the shooting. You're going to help us nab Astra." Jasper swept her gaze across the arena with x-ray vision to get a better idea of the layout. "Looks like he's trying to hide. He's probably realized these teens are hardcore." The team opposing the teens looked to be a lot younger, and they all seemed pretty upset. Hiding in corners, sitting on the floor with their knees pulled to their chests, and there was more crying on top of what she'd heard when they first entered. The teens definitely weren't going easy on the little kids.

Flipping back to her regular vision, Jasper continued. "It doesn't matter if he's not actually playing. No shot those teens let him go out the exit. Not when they have a chance to bully him, now that their real opponents have given up."

"What's the plan, then?" Grace asked.

"There's an emergency exit in that corner." Jasper pointed. "Astra's switching directions and headed for it. Lure the teens into his path to block him. I'll come in after."

"Will I get there in time?"

Jasper smirked. "You will if you fly."

Grace's wings were back out in an instant. One jump had her in the air, where she soared easily over the maze. She had the teens' attention immediately.

"Hey, who was that?" someone shouted nearby.

"I didn't see them earlier."

"The lights on their vest are blue. Let's go shoot them!"

Jasper grinned and lifted her gun. Back to x-ray vision. *My time to shine.*

While the teens moved loudly across the arena toward the exit, talking with each other and laughing, confident they had the win in the bag, Jasper was a shadow. She moved through the upper levels quietly, staying directly on top of them, jumping between walls and ceilings where gravity allowed.

At the exit, Grace descended to the ground behind a wall and folded up her wings again to vanish easily. The teens gathered in the open space in front of the door. While they looked around, trying to figure out where she'd gone, Astra came stumbling into view.

Grace was momentarily forgotten. All weapons were now pointed at Astra. "Please, I wandered in here by accident." Astra lifted his hands. "I'm not playing, don't shoot me—"

Big mistake. The teens all moved in unison to block the door. The pink-skinned girl, who seemed to be their leader, laughed coldly. "Too bad, old man. If you're in the arena, you play the game."

Astra frowned. "Old?"

"He doesn't have a vest, though," one of the girl's friends pointed out. "We won't get any points."

The girl shrugged. "We've already got way more points than those kids we were fighting. We could do nothing the rest of the round and still win." She took aim. "But shooting lights at this guy's face until he starts crying sounds fun."

Before the girl could fire, Jasper made her move. She dropped to the ground behind the group of teenagers. The lead girl turned and grinned. "Hey, she's got a blue vest. Shoot her."

A smirk turned up the corner of Jasper's mouth.

Despite being outnumbered, Jasper dodged every red beam. Every one of her shots, meanwhile, found their mark. One by one, the teens' vests were disabled. And whenever one came back online, she had them down again in an instant.

No real violence. Jasper didn't lay a single finger on any one of them, though the temptation to gently but firmly knock a few to the ground did arise. But that would be against the spirit of laser tag. And she wanted to obliterate these kids with nothing but pure laser.

Finally, as Jasper shot down the leader for the last time, a loud buzzer signaled the end of the round.

"Winner, blue team!" a voice announced over the speakers.

"No." The pink-skinned girl dropped to her knees. "No, no, no! We worked so hard for this!" She looked up. Tears appeared in the corners of her eyes. "How? How the hell did you do that? Even after years of playing, I've never seen anyone shoot like that."

"Wanna know why I'm so good?" Jasper tapped her gun against the side of her head. "It's because I don't litter."

Grace emerged from the shadows and grabbed Astra by the collar of his jacket. Jasper left the wide-eyed girl and her friends behind and helped Grace drag Astra into the hallway outside the emergency exit. Grace pinned him to the wall. Jasper drew a blaster from her side and placed its muzzle against his forehead.

Astra's eyes darted up to the weapon. "You're threatening me with a fake laser gun?"

"Hm? Oh, no, this is a real blaster." Jasper moved her arm and fired into the wall behind her, leaving a smoking hole. Astra yelped as she returned the weapon to his forehead.

"Please, I don't have time for this." Astra squirmed in Grace's grasp. "I have tickets for an event tonight and I have to leave soon if I'm going to make it!"

Jasper raised an eyebrow. "What event?"

"None of your business."

"Why bring it up then?" Jasper muttered in annoyance. She shoved a hand into the pocket of Astra's jacket and found his smartsphere. Holding it up to his mouth, she growled, "Now, tell Ropeak you need him to come save you."

Chapter Thirty-Two
AstraDumb

The maze that was the AstraSmart Home Store became a blur around Holly as she absentmindedly trailed behind Sarena. Sarena was commenting on just about every appliance and piece of furniture they passed. Most of the comments were negative.

"Terrible color palette on that one, sheesh." "Since when has Hatuan wood been in style?" "That microwave would clash with every kitchen in the star system."

Naturally, Holly tuned her out pretty quickly. She had her own reservations regarding the company's products, but she liked to think hers were a little more...practical.

"AstraCouch smart couch?" she muttered, stopping next to a very wide piece of black furniture that reflected colors like an oil slick. "How can a couch be smart?"

"It's got a computer that adjusts the seat, tells you the weather, plays music, that kinda junk." Sarena folded her arms, scrunching the fabric of her tan overcoat. A wig of straight black hair fell to her shoulders, different from both her natural hair that marked her as South Siren and the wig she wore as Sarena Trench. Sunglasses also helped hide her identity. Well, both identities. "That style is very...last pentasol, though. I'm shocked they'd have something like this out on the floor."

Holly rolled her eyes and moved forward, taking the lead. When would they get a chance to do something other than look at overpriced housewares?

Thea's voice once again echoed over comms, reminding everyone that she was stuck in her progress. "Someone needs to get that sphere from Ropeak, pronto."

If only he'd come through here, Holly thought. *I'd get that sphere out of his hands.*

But she and Sarena were close to the offices, and the goal was to *not* let Ropeak get this close. Still, though, it was looking more and more likely that the others wouldn't be able to stop him before he made it this far.

"Grace and I have Astra," Jasper said. "We're trying to use him to lure Ropeak to us, but we haven't gotten a response."

Thea sighed. "Yeah, it's not working. He's still headed for the offices."

"Smart man," Jasper muttered.

Holly perked up slightly. "Where is Ropeak approaching the offices from?"

"He's coming down the main corridor on the west side of the mall," Thea replied.

Holly glanced at Sarena. "Looks like we're the last ones between Ropeak and the offices."

"Ropeak's got some other guards moving with him, too," Thea warned. "At least five, as far as I can tell."

"We're trying to catch up," Cutthroat said. "But Ropeak's moving fast, and his security team is trailing behind to intercept anyone who tries to attack him."

"We're even farther behind," Dax added. "But still moving."

Holly turned in a slow circle, scanning her surroundings while Sarena moved on to inspecting a reclining chair. "Thea, you've got visuals through the mall cams, I'm guessing?"

"Yep."

"Great. Can you give us directions to the entrance Ropeak is approaching? This place is a bit of a maze."

"Well, since I'm stuck until someone gets that verification done, I guess." Thea sighed. "So, there's a restaurant at the south end of the AstraSmart store that he'll have to pass through to get to the offices. The fastest way to the restaurant is through the store directly, so he's definitely going to be coming through."

"What floor is the restaurant on?" Holly asked.

"Second. Looks like you're three floors up from that, but you're not far from the store's mall entrance, so you should have time to intercept him. Head right and cut through the living room displays."

Holly caught Sarena's attention and gestured for her to follow. Together, they passed through staged rooms. Their reflections joined them briefly in absurdly reflective kitchen appliances. Children bounced up and down on towers of mattresses. Some teens had started building a fort out of boxes, the camera in one of their hands suggesting it was for some sort of net video prank.

"You sure this is the right way?" Holly muttered as she ducked through an awkward hole in the wall that led to the next room. What a strange setup. The gaggles of children running about seemed to enjoy it, though.

"You're on the right track," Thea assured her.

Finally, Holly and Sarena emerged into a more open space. To their right were rows of shelves with decor items. To their left, a railing separated them from the floors below. Escalators moved up and down in the distance, and staging areas surrounded the open space.

"He's walking into the store," Thea warned. "Second floor. That balcony to your left should—"

Holly darted to the balcony and vaulted over the railing without hesitation.

"I didn't mean jump over the balcony! I was just going to tell you to look down and see if you could spot him."

Holly hit the ground a floor down with a thud. "Too late." As she'd noted when they'd entered the store, each floor jutted out a little farther than the one above. Another railing a few feet away from Holly was now the only thing between her and the second floor. After a quick glance up to ensure Sarena was preparing to follow, she went for it.

This drop was a little farther. Holly rolled after landing and sprang to her feet. Movement in her peripheral caught her attention. She whirled and found herself staring into the eyes of a brown-furred Hatuan with a wolfish face. A perfect match for the description of Ropeak the others had given.

Oh, well. They were going to get his attention soon one way or another. Avoiding being seen was pointless. Holly threw a punch.

Ropeak dodged, drew a blaster, and took aim. A solid roundhouse kick knocked the weapon out of his hand before he could fire. He might have been head of security, but with most of his work being at a mall and a theme park, he probably didn't have much experience with true criminals.

"I need backup," Ropeak growled, undoubtedly into a comm of his own. Holly's gaze darted to his jacket pocket, where a faint bulge indicated the likely location of his smartsphere.

"How close is his backup?" Holly asked under her breath.

"They're all seconds from the second floor entrance," Thea replied.

Holly lunged at Ropeak, throwing everything she had at him in order to knock him to the ground. She went down with him. After a few moments of struggling, they rolled apart. Roughly six undercover guards—Holly assumed that's what they were, anyway—burst into the store within seconds of each other.

Holly climbed to her feet, now wearing the form of Ropeak.

Ropeak's jaw clenched as he stood up next to her. The hand holding his blaster went up. "She's a West Kronosian! Shapeshifter! I'm the real Ropeak."

"*I'm* the real one." Holly raised her own blaster, mirroring him.

The other security guards exchanged confused glances. A few reached for their own weapons, but none made any moves to fire.

Sarena dropped to the ground about ten feet away, having hidden away her wig, sunglasses, and the coat she'd been wearing to disguise herself. Her eyes had taken on a white glow. She lifted a hand and moved her fingers into position, preparing to snap.

Ropeak didn't seem to notice her, still focused on the standoff with Holly and his team. "Can you prove it?" He reached a free hand into his jacket. "I've got my smartsphere." He held it up for the rest of his team to see.

Holly exchanged a quick glance with Sarena. Sarena smirked. Her fingers snapped. The shockwave sent the sphere flying out of Ropeak's hand.

In the same moment, Holly fired her blaster at the floor to send the security team scrambling backwards. As soon as she fired, she began running after the sphere. Her outstretched hand barely caught it. Clutching it tight, still sprinting, she glanced back.

Sarena was on Ropeak before he could catch up. While the two exchanged a few blows, Holly slowed, her eyes searching for escape routes. "I've got the sphere, Thea."

"Heard. Give me just a second while I resend the verification message."

The guards all quickly came to the conclusion that Holly was the fake. They surged toward her. She let herself fall back into her usual human form and picked up the pace, circling back toward Sarena.

"Launch me up!" Holly shouted at her as she approached. She jumped into the air.

Sarena blocked a swing from Ropeak before glancing Holly's way. "Oh, sure, whatever you say. No trouble at all." Despite the sarcasm, Sarena did put her power into her voice. The wave of energy sent Holly flying just high enough to grab the balcony railing of the third floor.

Holly slid the sphere into her jacket and pulled herself up. That should put enough distance between her and Ropeak for her to confirm the verification without any trouble—

Something shot up into the air at her right. Metal hooks latched onto the railing. Cursing, Holly scrambled the rest of the way over the railing and started running. "Ropeak has a grappling hook!" she exclaimed. A glance back showed that he was already over the railing, too.

"Oh, seriously?" Jasper exclaimed. "What model is it? I kind of want to take it—"

"We have bigger things to worry about, Jasper!" Holly slowed and elbowed Ropeak in the face as he caught up. His head snapped back, but despite the blood trickling from his nose, he didn't take long to get moving again. Holly pushed herself to move even faster.

"Thea?" Holly tried. "How close are you?"

"Sorry, I'm waiting for my system to reconnect. Another twenty seconds or so."

Damn it. She needed just a little more energy. She reached down into that little bit of tension that always resided in her chest and...let it go.

Holly felt the shift roll through her body's cells as she vaulted over a couch. Peachy skin turned green, ears became pointy, and her hair became annoyingly poofier, though the braid she had it in helped mitigate that. As she flew over it, she snatched a remote off a coffee table staged in front of one of the thinnest TV's she'd ever seen. She veered left, then sent the remote spinning toward Ropeak's head. A satisfying thwack told her it made contact, buying her a few more seconds.

Holly brushed a hand against the sphere in her jacket to ensure it was still there. "And you said I don't need his fingerprint again, right?"

"Correct," Thea replied. "I just need a tap when the confirmation screen comes up."

Well, that offered some small relief. Holly threw another glance back at Ropeak. "Sarena, where you at?"

"Knocked down the rest of security. Trying to catch up."

Holly spent a few moments trying to navigate a maze of couches before giving up and going over them. On the other side, she found herself in a wide-open space packed with staged kitchens. Wait, no, not fake kitchens, but a real cafeteria. Wait, they sold food *inside* the AstraSmart home store? Who spent that much time buying furniture? Just pick any old bed and get the hell out.

Then again, matching patterns and color schemes and finding the best electronic specs had never been something she cared about.

It would be hard to dodge Ropeak in this space, so Holly took a page out of Jasper's book and stole a bowl of pasta and meatcubes from a man as she ran by. One well-timed throw later, and the bowl was clattering to the floor, leaving a smattering of noodles and meat and sauce dripping down Ropeak's front. He was forced to slow in order to wipe the food off his face and clear his vision.

One last section of living room furniture stood between Holly and the end of the store, where a sign marked the entrance of the restaurant Thea had mentioned earlier. The last barrier between them and the AstraSmart offices.

"Thea?" Holly tried again.

"Ten more seconds."

Holly leapt over a couch and slid under a coffee table on the other side. As she came up, she grabbed the closest edge and flipped it, putting up a wall between her and Ropeak.

Ropeak grabbed a taser from his belt and pointed it at her. "Hand over my sphere. I've got a few questions that you're going to answer—"

Sarena slid between them and swung a lamp at Ropeak's head. It knocked him flat on his back, hard enough that he gasped and didn't immediately move to get back up.

"Nice timing." Holly had to admit, Sarena was a surprisingly good combat partner.

"On my part, sure. You could use a little work with your foot movements."

Holly's jaw clenched. *Never mind.*

"Okay, the verification signal just went through," Thea said.

Holly held up the sphere and tapped the confirmation button on the holoscreen that had opened. "You got that, Thea?"

"Got it."

Ropeak sprang to his feet and lunged for the sphere, taking both Holly and Sarena by surprise. Holly yelped as he snatched the device from her hand and broke into a sprint. Holly cursed. "He's running for the offices," she warned Thea as she began to run after him. He disappeared quickly into the restaurant ahead.

She swore she heard the faint crack of Thea's knuckles over comms. "Then I guess it's my turn."

Chapter Thirty-Three
Mechanatee's Marina

Almost done. Almost done. Thea's fingers moved with precision as they popped wires into place, flipped switches, sent technopathic pulses into the bodies of the androids in front of her. The tall, stocky, black-and-gold form that would house Chloe's A.I. The smaller, sleeker, silver-and-gold figure that would be Mia.

"So, you got all the verification you need, right?" Jasper asked her. "Are you downloading the database now?"

"Yeah, I'm on it," Thea said absentmindedly. And despite her current focus on the android bodies, she *was* on it.

She sat in an empty room that was technically part of the building's offices, allowing her access to their servers. But there was a reason it was currently unoccupied. A pipe had burst a few days back, leaving a hole in the wall that had a very flimsy temporary patch. It likely wouldn't be the first place Ropeak went looking for an intruder, but he was still sure to find her here sooner rather than later.

The chaos of your average Mechanatee's Marina restaurant was audible just beyond the door. Small children running free, hopped up on cheese-drenched food and drinks overloaded with sugar. Despite the fact that both the dining tables and a play area of twisting tunnels and ball pits on multiple levels stood between the office and the stage, Thea could hear the faint music played by the animatronics that were the restaurant's mascots.

"Ropeak's somewhere in the restaurant," Holly warned. "He must be getting close to you, Thea. You don't have much time."

Thea glanced at the bar on her laptop screen indicating how much longer the download had. Roughly five minutes. "Guess I'm bringing in backup," she muttered. It wouldn't take Holly and Sarena—and hopefully the others—long to catch up, but she needed every second she could get.

Thea gingerly snapped Mia and Chloe's back panels into place, then rose to her feet. Stretched her arms. Cracked her neck. Then, with a snap of her fingers that was purely for fun, she brought Mia and Chloe to life. Well, brought them online would be a better way of putting it.

While the androids climbed to their feet, Thea picked up her mini tablet from off the desk and turned on the screen. She scrolled through the list of connections the tablet had established. Security cameras, local networks, phones, computers, and...well, that was new. Thea lifted an eyebrow. "Wirelessly controlled, eh? Well, thank you for the extra minions."

Another tap of a button brought up a control interface. That was pretty easy to figure out. In fact, after a few moments of study, Thea was able to tap into the network mentally and take control with her powers, rather than manually hitting buttons and adjusting systems.

In the distance, the music stopped. A few children screamed in confused alarm. Thea grinned.

"Chloe," Thea said, gaze flicking to the android that had moved to stand at her right. "Stay here and guard the download on the laptop. If you get overwhelmed, call for backup." Her attention moved to the left, where Mia stood. "Mia, we're intercepting security."

As she and Mia left the office, Thea checked cams on her tablet. Ropeak was still leading the way, but the other guards she'd identified were with him now, forming a group that was fairly obvious. They stood near the restaurant's dining area, apparently having never approached the offices from this side, judging by the confusion in their expressions. The chaos of Mechanatee's would keep them at bay for a few more moments.

Thea rushed past packed dining tables and towering play structures to confront them, distancing herself a little from Mia. Even in the chaos, Mia drew attention, and Ropeak's eyes settled on her quickly. He didn't notice Thea until she was practically on top of him.

Ropeak tried to circle around Thea to get to Mia, but she stepped sideways into his path again. His expression darkened. If he'd had any doubts before, they were gone now. Thea was an enemy. "Step aside, please," he said. "Or my team will have to detain you."

Thea lifted an eyebrow. "You think you can?"

"You're outnumbered."

"Not quite." Thea smirked. Ropeak's lips parted. Before he could get another word out, an animatronic manatee tackled him to the ground.

It wasn't a particularly accurate manatee. There were legs where a tail should have been, enabling it to walk, and it was dressed in steampunk-style clothes, its outfit completed with a top hat and monocle. "Hiya kids, I'm Mechanatee!" the animatronic bellowed gleefully as it slapped Ropeak with one of its flippers. While Thea could take control and manipulate the programming that controlled the animatronics' actions, she couldn't help the fact that their voice boxes only had a few pre-recorded phrases.

The rest of the animatronic band members joined in to help their leader fight the other security guards. They fought with serviceable skill, but they were limited by Thea's ability to give them all commands at once, trying to match their opponents in the moment. Mia, on the other hand, was pre-programmed with combat ability. The android moved with blinding speed, delivering precisely timed blows aimed at where her opponents were about to be, not where they were, perfectly calculating trajectories with her 360-degree view of the world around her.

Ropeak grunted as he managed to roll out of the brawl. He put a hand to the comm into his ear. "Code Viridian. All available security personnel to the main office—"

The seabird animatronic kicked Ropeak in the face, knocking the comm out of his ear, but the damage was done. More security would be en route, many undoubtedly already close to the offices.

In fact, a few had apparently already been stationed in the restaurant. Well, if there was a place for heightened security, it was a free-for-all of children right by the main offices. The undercover guards around the space might have slipped past Thea without notice, if they hadn't all stepped away from the walls and corners in the same moment. She mentally ordered Mia to go after them. But while Mia could fight multiple people at once, capturing all six might be beyond her. It would be easy enough for even one to slip past while she tried to get the others restrained.

The brawl, meanwhile, was winding down, and Ropeak was pinned to the ground by an anthropomorphic crustacean robot. Holly and Sarena ran over, both breathing hard. Holly was in her green-skinned West Kronosian form, to Thea's surprise. She decided against mentioning it.

"Can you manage these guards?" Thea asked the two with a gesture. "A few more got away. I'm going after them."

Holly nodded. Sarena turned and gave one of the men attempting to get up a hard kick in the side.

As Thea ran toward the offices, she checked in on the download progress, linked to her tablet. Still a couple more minutes left. Chloe should be able to keep multiple guards at bay, but it would only take one reaching the computer to shut down the data transfer. Plus, if guards made it that far, then Astra would know for certain someone had gotten into his system.

As Thea cursed under her breath, wondering whether she'd be able to catch up fast enough, a blur shot past her. "Don't worry, Jolt." The voice from the blur was faint, but it echoed louder in Thea's comms. "I got 'em."

Thea slowed, giving herself a moment to catch her breath for springing back into action. "Cool. Thanks Rose."

"Nope. Right now, I'm Thorn."

Rose's response made Thea lift an eyebrow. She'd picked out a...code name for herself? Thea wasn't sure whether the girl fancied herself a hero or a villain, but right now, it didn't matter. Thea went right back to sprinting.

"Rats," Rose exclaimed. "The two guys I'm after are splitting."

"Hang on, I'm almost there," Jasper replied.

Jasper? "If you're running, I'm not sure you'll be able to catch up," Thea told her.

"I'm not on foot."

Before Thea could ask Jasper what she meant by that, she got her answer in the form of a shopping cart shooting into the restaurant, powered by a fire extinguisher. Jasper was perched on top of the cart, aiming the makeshift engine behind her. Judging by the strength and duration of the foam shooting out of the canister—and the fact that flickering violet flames occasionally peaked through the white cloud—she had made some chemical modifications to the extinguisher.

Thea shook her head. How was she still surprised by Jasper's antics after so long? At least Jasper was dressed in random clothes to blend in. Hopefully, no one would recognize her. "Chloe, how are things in the office?" she asked.

"No security has arrived, yet."

That was a relief. Thea barely dodged a racing child and circled around a wall separating a section of dining tables. On the other side, she caught a glimpse of a man with his back pressed to a support pillar, one hand inside his jacket. His eyes were on two other slightly more obvious undercover guards as they were plowed down by Jasper's shopping cart.

Thea used his distraction as an opportunity to lunge forward and deliver a blow to his jaw. He cried out in pain as he crumpled to the floor, drawing stares from nearby parents.

"Nothing to worry about," Thea assured them. "Just some security...practice drills." She grabbed the man by the arm and dragged him back to where Holly and Sarena guarded the others.

While Holly moved to tie the man up, Ropeak rolled onto his back and shot Thea a glare. "What do you want, Jolt?" he spat.

Thea smiled. "You recognize me? I didn't realize I was *that* prolific."

"I do my best to keep villains that pose a special threat to us at the back of my mind. Technos included. Now, care to tell me why you're all here?" He shot a sideways glance at Holly and Sarena, likely having recognized them as Red Holly and South Siren.

Thea folded her arms and lifted an eyebrow. "What makes you think you're getting answers? Did you forget we have you tied up?"

Ropeak huffed. "You might have our security outnumbered, but police will show up eventually. And Iros only employs the best and brightest officers. Astra pays them well and gives them good weapons."

"We'll be long gone by then." Still, there was one concern lingering at the back of Thea's mind: the aftermath of all this. If Starr caught wind that people associated with Van Terra were involved in an attack on AstraSmart, he was certainly going to pay close attention. And it wouldn't be impossible for him to piece together the team's plan, if it was obvious what code Thea had downloaded.

A plan for damage control came together in Thea's mind. In order to distract Astra's security team from realizing what she'd taken, she would leave something behind.

She pulled out her tablet and walked away, typing quickly. Then, with the press of a few buttons, a second progress bar appeared next to the download box synced to the laptop, signaling that an upload had begun.

Chapter Thirty-Four
Child's Play

Jasper launched herself off the shopping cart just as the fire extinguisher began to run out of steam. She nearly landed right on top of the guard she was chasing—a plain-looking, gray-skinned Hatuan man—but he darted out of her path in the nick of time. Ahead of them, a children's play structure spanning several stories towered over the surrounding dining area. It was also the main obstacle between them and the offices.

Rather than go around the structure, the guard ran straight for it. Jasper went after him, cursing as he dove into a tunnel and disappeared into shadow. It may have been possible to shorten the distance to the offices by going through the structure, but navigating the tight spaces and turns would probably increase the time it took him to get to the other side instead.

It was, however, a great way to distract Jasper while other guards tried to get to the offices first. But Rose insisted she had this guy's partner covered, and Thea had just announced the rest of them were securely tied up.

So, Jasper tailed her target to ensure he didn't make it to Thea's workspace.

Rather than following him directly into the tunnel he'd chosen, Jasper gracefully scaled the towering play area and dropped down onto a platform near the structure's center. She scanned the clusters of children moving around her.

"Hey, kids," she said to a nearby group waiting for their turn on a slide. "Spread the word. There's a grownup running around the play area. Gray skin, dark blue shirt, black pants. It's important that he doesn't escape. Anyone who helps will get some, uh—" Her hands moved frantically between her pockets. "—some of these bad boys." She drew out a few pouches of sour candy.

The boy in front eyed the candy skeptically. "There's free candy like that in the vending machines."

Jasper frowned. "The candy in the vending machines isn't free."

"It is if you hit it hard enough."

As much as that endeared Jasper to the small child, she didn't have much time to win him over. "Fine. How about some money." She pulled a stack of jano bills from another pocket. A very thick stack.

The boy grinned. "*Now* we're talking! With that kind of money, I could buy enough rare cards to finally beat Gordox at the Star Conquerors card game."

"Yeah, whatever, just try to spare a little for your fellow chaos-makers." Jasper tossed him the money and dug out a few more stacks for his friends. "Now, children, go out into the world and do my will."

The kids scattered quickly, and Jasper could only hope their love of antagonizing adults would lead them to do as she requested. She, meanwhile, flipped to heat vision and scanned the structure until she spotted a form much larger than the kids around him. The guard, just a couple levels down from her.

Jasper dove headfirst into a slide that spiraled down a few levels, to a platform just beneath the one the guard stood on. She tumbled out at the bottom and sprang to her feet. A short sprint and a hard jump launched her over a railing and out of the tower she'd been in. She grabbed one of the poles supporting it and swung up onto the next level.

Jasper stumbled onto the platform just as the guard started up a ladder on the other side. Her gaze moved up, and she realized he was headed for a slide that would drop him much closer to the other side of the play structure.

A few kids waiting in lines for slides and a rock wall at the platform's other openings stared at the two adults that had entered their space. Jasper noted a couple of jano bills poking out of some of the kids' pockets.

She pointed to the guard. "Uh, stop that guy!"

The children glanced at each other, whispered back and forth for a moment, then linked arms in front of the slide entrance, forming a wall to block the guard's escape. "We're playing Redshift Rover!" one screamed gleefully.

"My mom says I'm not allowed to play that game—" another child started as he was dragged into the formation of a second line on the other side of the baffled guard. His protest was lost in the cheers and whoops of the kids around him.

"We launch—Norvo!" a boy in the first line proclaimed. He and another girl swung their arms and unlinked them from the boy standing between them, sending the tall, blue-furred boy flying forward. His large triangular ears twitched with glee as he barreled toward the security guard.

"Wait—" the guard said, lifting his hands. Too late. The child slammed into him with surprising force, knocking him back off his feet. He landed with a grunt of pain.

Jasper grabbed the guard and flung him over the railing and onto a massive net stretched across a space in the middle of the play structure. As he bounced, she hopped down to join him, drawing a small dagger as she did.

The plan was to free a few ropes from the net and tie the man up, but as Jasper made her way across the net toward him, he lifted a taser and aimed it toward her. She froze. It wouldn't hurt her as much as intended, but there was a high chance it would screw with her systems a bit. And it would certainly be unpleasant.

The man took advantage of her hesitation to roll to the edge of the net and drop onto the top of a tunnel connecting two platforms. Cursing under her breath, Jasper scrambled after him. She chased him across the top of the tunnel and onto the platform at its end. As Jasper jumped down, she drew a throwing star from inside her coat and sent it spinning at the guard's hand, knocking the taser from his grasp and slicing open his palm. The star clattered to the ground, where Jasper was able to snatch it back up. The taser, meanwhile, sailed onto the plastic roof of a lower structure.

Hopefully no kids find a way to get their hands on that. The last thing she wanted was to accidentally start a game of taser tag. She'd have to come back for it later.

Hissing in pain, the guard grabbed his bleeding hand and dove into the tunnel they'd just crossed. Jasper followed. She had to grab his ankle to stop him from escaping out the other side. She yanked him back to the middle and swung her fist at his face. He barely dodged the punch.

The two exchanged a few more blows in the tight tunnel. Jasper managed a strike that made the man collapse onto his stomach. The structure trembled around them. Jasper's next blow missed as the man twisted away. Her fist slammed into the tunnel wall.

The tunnel broke open, dropping the two of them into a ball pit.

"That thing can't possibly be up to safety standards," Jasper muttered as she sat up. At least the fall to the pit wasn't too far. A child that fell from there probably wouldn't face more than some light bruising. Still, she'd have to send someone to block off the tunnel once she was done dealing with the guard.

The guard scrambled out of the pit, Jasper close behind. A well-aimed blow to his upper back with her still-startling strength knocked him back to the ground.

"I'm back in the office," Thea announced. "Download's done. I'm clearing out."

"Cool," Jasper replied. "Let's meet back by the restaurant entrance." She grabbed the guard by the collar of his jacket and tossed him back into the ball pit. "Hey kids, that guy's got a ton of candy in his pockets! Go take it from him, it'll be fun!"

Leaving the man to drown in a pool of plastic balls, sticky children, and a few mystery liquids, Jasper strolled to where the others waited. Holly and Sarena stood guard over the pile of tied-up security officers, Ropeak included, shooting glares at any civilians who gave them too much attention. Jasper freed her hair from its braid to further disrupt her already casual look, hoping to reduce the chances of her villain persona being recognized.

"Not sure how much longer we can stand here with these guys," Holly said. "If Jolt's in the clear, we should—"

One of the guards sprang into motion. The man had sliced his hands free from his ropes with a razor blade he must have had in his pocket. Still clutching the blade, he lunged at Jasper.

Mia sprang into Jasper's path to deflect the blow. Chloe, meanwhile, grabbed the man from behind and slammed him to the floor. Thea joined the group, having been following just a few feet behind the androids.

Jasper grinned. "Nice work on the androids, Jolt." Hands moving to her hips, she added, "We couldn't have done it without Mighty Mia and Cosmic Chloe."

Holly groaned. "Oh, god, don't give them hero names—or villain, whatever—"

"Too late."

Behind Holly, Rose came flying over to the group, thrusters blazing. She clutched the guard she'd been pursuing by his jacket, leaving him to swing wildly as she came to a sudden stop. She tossed the guard to the floor and dropped to the ground next to him, a wide grin on her face, her hair a wild mess. "That was fun!"

The guard groaned and mumbled something about needing to throw up.

Jasper tapped her comm. "All right, Angel, go ahead and free Astra and meet us at the base. Same goes for everyone else."

The rest of the team confirmed they'd heard. Jasper, Holly, Sarena, Rose, Thea and the androids left the pile of security behind and headed for the exit. They passed the restaurant's animatronics, which Thea had left standing motionless after the brawl with security had finished.

"Hey, we should take one of those home," Jasper said, pausing to examine the seabird clutching a saxophone. "It'd make a fun decoration in the apartment."

She got an enthusiastic exclamation of agreement from Rose, but the others weren't so keen. Though she was genuinely tempted to bring the singing robot along, Jasper conceded it wasn't quite worth the effort and moved on.

She grabbed an abandoned piece of pizza off a nearby table, earning disgusted looks from the others. Hey, it didn't have any bites out of it. It was probably as good as new. As she chewed, she said, "Well, that whole operation was less subtle than I'd hoped. We drew quite a bit of attention."

"I think we'll still be okay. I threw a virus into the system before I left," Thea explained. "It'll start slowly eating their files. Very slowly. I'm sure their tech team will have it destroyed within the hour. But I left behind a message with it, some nonsense about how this is only the beginning and I'll send a worse one, next time, if they don't meet my demands. That should provide a believable reason for all this. Believable enough that Astra won't admit to Starr that his security was breached so easily, hopefully."

"And what, exactly, are your demands?" Jasper asked.

"Dark mode for their appliance screens."

Sarena lifted an eyebrow. "That's something I can buy Van Terra doing, but it seems a little dramatic for Jolt."

Thea shrugged. "Jolt can be petty. And the lack of a dark mode setting did drive me up the wall while I was picking apart their machines, especially late at night. I'm shocked it hasn't been implemented already. I mean, if you're going to get something from your fridge in the middle of the night, you don't want its built-in screen blinding you..."

Thea continued talking about appliance settings pretty much up until they left the mall. Grace joined them at the exit, and Jasper shot her a glance. "Astra?"

"Left him by that laser tag place," Grace replied with a shrug. "Guess he'll be glad he gets to make whatever his plans are for the night."

Jasper frowned as she recalled what Astra had said earlier. "Right. Wonder what that's about."

"Astra's plans for the night?" Thea asked. "I can take a look at what I downloaded and see if there's anything about it in his files. I grabbed a few other random things besides the network code."

"It's probably not important." Jasper shrugged. Maybe he was headed to a movie premiere or a dumb play or a fancy orchestra concert. Rich people stuff. Ready to forget the matter entirely, she led the way toward MoonCo.

Ten minutes later, they were sneaking into the store's back entrance, which Thea had hacked the night before to find its security code. After that, they split up and slipped into the shelving fort one at a time.

Jasper was the last to arrive, having been distracted by the free food samples available around the store. When she entered the fort, Thea was deep in the stolen files, glancing between her tablet and her laptop.

"I think I've got something," she said as Jasper approached.

Jasper folded her arms. "What?"

"I did find what appears to be tickets for something in Astra's messages, but they're encrypted. I'm working on cracking it, but it's strange that the encryption is so tough in the first place. Must be for something...secret."

"Illegal?" Jasper lifted an eyebrow. Maybe they could run a smear campaign on Astra. She wasn't sure how that would help them specifically, but the dude sucked, so there was that.

"Maybe. Oh, hang on, the output is finally loading..." Thea leaned forward. Her brow furrowed. "It is a ticket. For something called...the Lion's Den?"

Jasper's heart turned to ice and crumbled in her chest.

Chapter Thirty-Five
Shades of Light

The motorcycle didn't look any different than it had before, but then again, it hadn't really appeared damaged in the first place. Jasper moved her gaze over it slowly, searching for…nothing, really. But she couldn't help herself.

"As far as I can tell, it's running just fine now," Thea was saying. "I reset a few of the systems and buffed some circuits—"

Jasper barely heard her as she laid out the repairs she'd made to the motorcycle in more detail. Finally, she trailed off, and Jasper glanced up at her.

"You feeling okay?" Thea asked after a moment, her tone hesitant.

Jasper sighed. "Not really. The Lion's Den brings back some of my worst memories." She returned her gaze to the motorcycle. "But I think after I blow off some steam, I'll be ready to start planning."

Despite the others' concerns, she'd decided to put everything else on hold to focus on stopping what was happening at the Lion's Den. After her escape all those years ago, she'd tried to forget the place existed. Even if she had felt the occasional flare of desire to go back and *really* burn it down, to try to rescue the other prisoners, she'd never had the resources. Never had the strength.

But now, with her team bigger and stronger than ever, she had a chance.

"Thanks, Thea." Jasper grabbed the handlebars and wheeled the motorcycle toward the edge of the roof. Thea nodded and returned to the assortment of chairs the others had rounded up and brought up here, hoping to enjoy some fresh air.

Jasper had tried to explain the Lion's Den, her capture, her time there as matter-of-factly as possible, but it had been impossible to hide her trauma. Hopefully, a quick ride really would make her feel better. She adjusted her grip on the handlebars and prepared to start the engine. The action was interrupted by a voice from behind her.

"Can I join you?"

Jasper glanced over her shoulder at Grace and felt part of the weight in her chest lift. "Sure." She grabbed her helmet from where it hung on the handlebars and held it out to Grace.

Grace shook her head. "I'm gonna fly."

Jasper grinned and lifted an eyebrow. "Think you can keep up?"

"Guess we'll find out." Grace returned the smile.

Laughing, Jasper revved her engine. She shot forward across the roof, feeling the evening air rush over her with a whoop of joy. A shadow—Grace's shadow—passed over her as she reached the edge and dropped.

Bold move, for a test run. For all she knew, Thea could have completely screwed up the vehicle's glide system, and it would plummet to the Earth and shatter into irreparable scrap. But Thea didn't make mistakes like that.

Sure enough, with the flip of a switch, the bike's wings emerged, and Jasper slipped from free fall into a glide toward the roof of a nearby market. More jumps and drops—and a few bursts from the anti-gravity mechanism—took her onto the streets just outside the Irosland theme park. Under the setting sun that made the crystal landscape beyond the city shimmer, she raced past food trucks and artist's booths and shacks peddling souvenirs. Palm trees had been planted along the sides of the street, likely brought in from somewhere like Sa Ren, given the lack of plant life that was native to Iros. A lot of water had to be funneled to this part of the moon, too, to manage all these water fountains. *Great use of the moon's limited resources.*

Grace kept pace in the air above, keeping about fifty feet from the ground. As Jasper neared the end of Main Street, Grace spoke over comms. "That all you got? This isn't much of a challenge."

Jasper laughed in response. "Just warming up."

The gates to the theme park loomed ahead, still packed with people trying to get in before the end of the night. The roar of the engine sent them scattering as Jasper approached. She raced past startled security guards into the park. Grace easily soared over the security checkpoint. Guards followed, of course, but they had no hope of catching up.

Lights blinked on around them as the sky dimmed. Roller coasters and towering rides and the Ferris wheel began to glow neon. Jasper set her sights on a sign warning that the roller coaster behind it was currently shut down.

Perfect. She raced past the sign, jumped the gate, and landed in the yard under the coaster track.

Another jump brought her onto the track itself at its lowest point. Despite the fact that the ride wasn't running, the neon pink, blue, and green lights along the track were on, casting a glow over Jasper as she raced up an incline. Grace caught up at her right, wings spread wide.

Jasper's mind briefly went back to the other time she'd been on a track like this, during one of Ringmaster's races on Sa Ren. The stunt had been painful, but it had earned her first place. Now, without a roller coaster to worry about, villains to compete against, and with Grace by her side, she was having a lot more fun.

She eased to a stop at the top of the incline, which turned out to be the highest point of the ride. Grace landed next to her. "There appear to be security vehicles coming out way," Grace noted, pointing to the flashing lights below that marked the small hovercarts racing toward them.

"Took 'em long enough." Jasper glanced down at the steep hill before her. "Should have time for this, though."

"Seriously?" Grace joined her in looking down. "That must be terrifying on a motorcycle."

"I've done worse."

"Are you going to use anti-gravity?"

"Nope." Jasper rolled forward. "Race you to the bottom!" Her stomach lurched as she went over the edge.

Grace let out a shriek of surprise, though it sounded more thrilled than scared. A moment later, she was diving through the air at Jasper's side, wings folded in.

The curve of the track caught Jasper at the bottom, sending her flying up the next hill. She swerved to fly off the track and extended the vehicle's wings again. Grace kept up, not losing an inch despite the rapid change in direction.

Jasper led them away from the approaching security vehicles, though lights warned that there were more squads coming at them from other directions. Jasper drew a blaster and blew the lock off a gate in the coaster yard fence. The gate swung open, allowing her to glide through.

As they neared the edge of the park, Grace suddenly veered away from Jasper, headed back toward the park's center. "Where are you going?" Jasper called after her, though Grace would hear her much better over comms than through the air at this distance.

"Be right back!" was Grace's only response.

With a shrug, Jasper continued on to the much bigger fence around the park itself. With no gate in sight, she had no choice but to blast open a hole in the fence itself with her weapon. She moved into a parking lot. Past shuttles waiting to transport tourists to hotels. People shot her surprised looks as she flew by, but she couldn't have been much more than a blur to them, and they were gone in an instant.

Jasper came to a halt at the edge of the lot, in an empty, darker area beneath a lamppost with a burnt-out light. Security's sirens were only a faint echo in the distance. Less than a minute later, Grace came down from the sky and landed next to her, clutching something. She held it out to Jasper.

A plush toy, snatched from one of the carnival game stands. It depicted the saxophone-playing seabird that existed in animatronic form back at Mechanatee's.

Grace watched Jasper take it with what seemed to be a hint of hesitation in her gaze. "Not quite the same as a full-sized singing robot, but..."

Jasper laughed as she took the plush. "I love it. Thank you." She twisted and swung her legs off the motorcycle, then stood, bringing her face close to Grace's.

Jasper kissed her.

As she pulled back, Grace's worried mouth relaxed into a smile. Though, some of her hesitation returned as she asked, "You ready to head back?"

Jasper glanced down at her motorcycle's handlebars. "Well, everything seems to be in perfect condition, so I'd call this test run a success."

"That's good, but I meant more...emotionally."

Oh. Jasper swallowed and nodded. Glancing back up, she said, "Yeah, I... I think I'm ready."

Still, she took her time on the ride back. Grace joined her on the motorcycle this time.

On Main Street, dancers with glowing jewelry and torch jugglers had stolen much of the attention. Jasper slowed down even further to take in the view. "I hate to enjoy something run by a guy like Astra, knowing what kind of shady practices happen behind the scenes, but this is a fun place."

She felt Grace's shoulders shrug behind her. "At least we did some damage. Stole some stuff."

Jasper chuckled, but she still couldn't help but feel like it wasn't enough. Like nothing they did would ever be enough in such a big universe. Countless more Starrs, Astras, people cutting corners however they could just to get a little more money...

Well, if they couldn't change things everywhere, at least they could make a difference for some people. And hopefully, there were people trying to do the same in other parts of the galaxy.

Back at the MoonCo, which was closed by the time Jasper and Grace returned, Jasper interrupted some TV watching, snacking, and a card game to force everyone to gather around a fake display campfire. Most of the team filled a display couch someone had dragged over, sitting on its arm and spilling onto the floor, while Cutthroat and his pirates dragged over stools from other areas to sit on. Jasper stood on top of the grilling rack set up over the fire, hands clasped behind her back, the coat she'd thrown over her clothes on the way in swaying when she moved.

"Lion's Den is going to be a tough egg to crack," she began.

Immediately, Dax's hand went up. "Uh, aren't eggs easy to crack?"

"Yeah, pretty sure the expression is 'tough nut to crack,'" Thea added.

Sarena shot them both an incredulous look. "What are you all talking about? The expression is 'tough moonrock to crack.'"

Cutthroat rubbed his forehead. Aymes grimaced.

"Okay, okay, it'll be a tough Nova Cora bottle to shatter." Jasper turned. "The place will be crawling with security guards, probably even more than when I was last there. But they shouldn't have anything crazy in terms of weapons."

"Can we do what we did at Sky Labs and use a fake villain race to help us?" Grace suggested.

Jasper shook her head. "I had that thought too, but I just don't see it working, logistically. This thing is way farther underground, and I remember some of the tunnels being pretty damn narrow. Most vehicles won't fit." After a moment's thought, she added, "And even if we could get enough racers down there, there will be a bottleneck much worse than any of the choke points at Sky Labs, so the guards will have an easier time taking out the villains."

"And where is this place, anyway?" Sarena asked.

Jasper sighed. "That's our other main issue. I don't...remember, exactly. It's been a long time." She turned her gaze to a wall, vision blurring. "And everything right after my escape is a little hazy, too."

Sarena huffed. "How are we going to find it then?

"Simple. We ask the people who know." Okay, maybe simple wasn't the *best* word, but most elite had probably been to a Lion's Den match at some point in their lives. Jasper had seen the Starrs themselves visiting the arena.

All the team had to do was figure out how to get the information out of said elite.

"Are we sure we want to take this detour right now?" Cutthroat asked. As the room's eyes turned to him, he added, "I'm not opposed to helping you with this, Jasper, but we can't exactly waste time when it comes to dealing with Starr. He's building that army. The more time he has to prepare those weapons and cyborgs, the harder it will be to bring him down."

"Well, last I heard, Thea still hadn't turned anything up on where he's keeping those weapons and cyborgs." Jasper shot a quick glance at Thea, who nodded.

"I'm still running every possible scan and analyzing every piece of data from around the star system I can get my hands on," she said. "Nothing unusual yet."

Jasper shifted her attention back to Cutthroat. "You're right that we can't just ignore him. But I think the best place to keep working on the issue is Kros, anyway. And I don't think the Lion's Den will take us long. We can multitask."

"Destroying the place will certainly draw attention," Cutthroat warned. "Do we want that?"

Jasper's jaw clenched. "Yes. We're bringing this fight to a head. We already destroyed Sky Labs, which was one of Starr's biggest assets. He won't let us keep hiding forever." She took a deep breath and closed her eyes. "How about this: let's get back to Kronos tomorrow. We can all be thinking of ideas for dealing with the Den, but we'll worry about concrete details once we have its location." Eyes opening, she added, "Any questions?"

"Yeah, I have a question," Sarena said, arms folding. "Anyone think it's weird we haven't heard from Skybreaker in a while? The last villain she killed was like, three pentasols ago."

"Uh, I meant about the Lion's Den."

"But she was trying to kill us! She was chasing us around the star system!"

Holly raised an eyebrow. "She has a point."

"Well, yeah, it is a little weird," Jasper conceded. "But I don't see a reason to worry any more about her than usual."

"She may be planning something," Cutthroat said in a low voice.

Jasper pinched the bridge of her nose and sighed. "Thank you. Very reassuring, everyone." As if they didn't have enough to stress over already. "How about we all go to bed, and we can worry about my evil clone in the morning?"

"If she doesn't kill us in our sleep," Sarena muttered.

While the others moved off in different directions, Grace approached Jasper. Jasper hopped off the table and found herself even closer to Grace than she'd expected. Despite the flutter that put in her stomach, she grinned. "What's up?"

Grace shrugged. "I still have some energy. I might go flying again."

Jasper glanced in the direction of the parking lot and smiled, her mind going to the Comet hidden nearby. "How would you like to learn a different kind of flying?"

IV. THE LION'S DEN

217

Chapter Thirty-Six
Falling Stars

Janus accompanied Governor Starr and Captain Cora to the meeting with the Interstar Council's ambassadors. Deep in the heart of the Governor's Palace, where Starr had all the advantages. The council ship may have hovered over the building, but it wouldn't be able to do much to save the ambassadors if Starr ordered them killed.

In her previous call with Janus, Meg had suggested Starr might attack immediately. But if she really thought that, she'd overestimated his impulsiveness. Starr, as Janus had expected, would meet with the council and let them begin their investigation. He had all the advantages. Time was on his side.

There wasn't much reason to pay attention—not yet, anyway—so Janus let her mind wander. It was impossible not to feel a little apprehension around the council's arrival. She hated Starr, but if the council attacked, his forces would take a heavy blow. He seemed confident he'd win, and maybe he would, but it was vital to Janus's plans that the army remained as large as possible when Meg made her move.

The fate of the star system depended on it.

As they approached the conference room, Janus had to resist the urge to send a message to Grim Machine, to check up on his progress. The other thing demanding space at the front of her mind. But it wasn't worth the risk of Starr noticing she was up to something, even if he seemed rather occupied with his own thoughts at the moment. And Meg had recommended Janus only send private messages in her apartment, where the techs had more control over any spying equipment, or outside the palace entirely.

She'd sent Grim Machine to the ruins of Sky Labs to search for the schematics she wanted. It might be stupid to hope there was enough of the server tech intact for him to locate the data, but the search would be more than worth it if he found the designs. The final touch that would truly make her into the perfect weapon. Something that would guarantee her victory over Jasper Van Terra.

The council members sent to look into Starr's rule over the Janus System already waited in the conference room. Starr took an empty chair at the head of the table, and Janus silently moved to stand behind him. Captain Cora, meanwhile, stood at his left.

"Let's begin." The council member who spoke appeared to be originally from the Janus System. Was that intentional? He was a bald, blue-skinned Sa Renian with slitted pupils in his lavender eyes. "Governor Syrus Starr, did you receive the communication transmitted to your palace earlier this pentasol?"

"I did," Starr replied coolly.

Janus swept her gaze over the other council members. A handful of others from the Janus System; a human—thought stars knew if they were raised on Earth or elsewhere; a pair from the Ra System with cow-like horns and dark patches on their nearly white skin; and a single white-feathered, black-beaked humanoid from the Aquila System. Eight in total.

The lead council member nodded. "Very well, then. You may call me Merf. I'll be leading the investigation. You've been told why we're here, but I'm required to give you a brief overview of why the investigation has been initiated and our first steps before we move forward.

"Now, the Interstar Council was founded to establish a network of star systems where leaders could be trusted to value the lives of their citizens in equal or greater to that of their own wellbeing—"

Janus fought to avoid rolling her eyes as Merf launched into a long-winded explanation of the council's founding. Everyone knew this. Well, everyone in the room. For most outside the government, the existence of the council was a distant concept. Especially for those it had failed to do any good for.

Merf was still going "—as we feel it is cruel to make great advancements, particularly to medical technology, while withholding them from those who cannot pay, or pouring government money into extravagances for the elite while people starve on the streets." His gaze wandered the conference room as he spoke.

Starr raised an eyebrow. "Surely you know many extravagances already in place in the upper district have been here since long before I took the position of governor."

"Certainly. But our initial scans revealed many empty rooms. Surely, those would make fine homes for those in your city who lack shelter? Give them space to recover and get back on their feet?"

Starr pressed his lips into a thin line. He offered no response.

"I would hope you've read the codes, at least," Merf continued. "The council's expectations for those star systems are part of the alliance and enjoy its trade benefits."

"I'm very familiar with the alliance's rules," Starr told Merf. "A thorough check of my government's accounting will reveal we've committed no crimes with our budgets or laws."

"I believe that. But we've caught wind that there may be transactions happening outside the books that would violate your promises to the alliance."

"Caught wind from who?" Starr's tone became more demanding. "Do you have spies on Kronos? Or are these unsubstantiated rumors you're acting on?"

"The council does not employ spies. We simply keep our ears open."

The council does not employ spies. A technicality, likely. Janus refused to believe they weren't obtaining secret intel by some means or another, even if it meant going through a middleman to avoid putting the spies directly on their payroll. Hell, spies gathering intel might not even know what they learned was going to the council.

"There is one other matter, however, that we are here to investigate," Merf continued. "And the council has voted to place a classified status on this one, meaning we do not have to tell you what it is we're looking for."

The labs. The weapons. The secret army. That had to be it. Starr would undoubtedly assume that's what they were after, too. Would he take additional steps to hide his work? Or hope that it was already hidden well enough? Even Janus hadn't figured out where he'd moved the cyborgs and the rest of the weapons after Reo, though she hadn't been able to ask Meg for help on that matter. She wasn't sure if the council would be able to do any better in their search.

Janus had taken some time to read the alliance's codes and guidelines. If the council voted to remove Starr, they would put one of their own in control long enough to host a new election. An election that another upper district politician would undoubtedly win. So even if the council did manage to rid the Janus System of Syrus Starr, another of those damn elite would take his place. The Starr dynasty would end and another one just as awful would replace it.

She needed something more destructive. A fire to burn out the top levels of Kronos. Something dangerous, something that could make the world even worse if she didn't play her cards right.

But it was the Janus System's only hope.

"Anything else to share with me before you begin your investigation?" Starr asked.

Merf shook his head and rose to his feet. "We will demand full access to your palace and records."

"I wouldn't expect any less."

"And if anything should happen to us, the Interstar Council's army will come at you in full force."

Starr's lips pressed into a thin smile. "Understood." He nodded to one of the security guards waiting by the door. "Show the council members around. Give them whatever they ask for."

The council members followed the guard out into the hall. Once they were gone, Starr rose to his feet and walked to the door. Without a word, Janus and Captain Cora moved to follow.

At the end of the hallway, Starr halted and waved his hand. "You two are dismissed for the night."

"Are you sure, Governor?" Captain Cora asked. "I could tail those council members and keep an eye on them."

"Security can handle those accountants themselves. Not much you can do, for now." Starr turned toward a hallway branching to the left. "If you really want something to do, go patrol the streets."

"Yes, sir." Captain Cora saluted. This time, Janus did roll her eyes, though neither of the other two noticed.

Captain Cora left quickly. Before Starr could turn to leave, Janus quietly asked, "Think they'll go looking for the labs?"

"Probably. But you have nothing to worry about. I already have plans to handle them, should they vote to move against me." He turned and met Janus's eyes with a cold intensity. "Assuming I can count on you."

"Of course." Janus said the words with quick confidence. A somewhat real confidence. She did need his armies to succeed. Just...not for the reasons he thought.

Starr nodded, seemingly satisfied. "Good. Now go get some rest. The next few days will be busy."

Free from Starr's watch as she headed back down the hall they came, Janus opened her mind's message center. *Grim Machine. Status.*

All recoverable data has been transmitted to your online server, came Grim Machine's quick response. *Upload should be done any second now.*

Thank you. Janus backed out of her communications with Grim Machine and found a new message from Meg waiting.

Meet at the top of Prism Tower. 20:00.

Two hours from now. Good. That would let Janus take her time slipping out of the palace. She'd feign going to bed as Starr had instructed.

Once in her room, it didn't take long to use the program Meg had installed in her mind's systems to fake her tracker location and loop the camera feed. Then, she changed into plain dark clothes, hid her hair under a simple cap, put on a black face mask, and moved to the window. Guards patrolled the grounds below, and many of the balconies had a pair of guards stationed on them, as well.

Janus stepped up onto her railing. If those schematics were in the data Grim Machine recovered, if Meg's team could figure out how to replicate them...sneaking out would become much easier.

In the meantime, though, her usual methods would do just fine.

Her room was near the top of the palace, a subtle move on Starr's part to put more distance between her and the exits, while pretending the sole reasoning had been to give her one of the nicest rooms possible. But in doing so, he'd made an alternative method of escape a little easier. She jumped up from balcony to balcony—as Merf had pointed out, many of the ones on the upper levels were empty and led to dark, unused rooms—until her hands found the edge of the domed roof.

She scrambled to the top of the dome, took a deep breath, and flung herself forward, sliding down the other side. It gave her enough speed to launch herself forward when she hit the bottom and just barely manage a landing on a skyscraper below. Just before her boots hit the roof, she drew a blaster and fired it downward. The force slowed her descent just enough to make the landing bearable.

Another ten minutes of bounding over rooftops brought her to Prism Tower. As Janus expected, it wasn't Meg that met her on the tower, but one of Meg's lackeys. A small man with goat horns and legs, purple eyes with goat-like pupils, and pastel yellow fur. Black hooves poked out of the bottom of his purple pants. Janus nodded a greeting to him.

"It's a pleasure to meet you, Skybreaker." The man held a black duffel bag out to Janus. "Meg asked me to give you this."

As Janus accepted the bag, the man pulled a small black box—some sort of radio communicator—from his pocket and held it up. Meg's voice came from the speaker.

"Sky, how are ya?"

"Uh, good," Janus told her as she studied the bag's exterior. Nothing of note. "Has your team taken a look at the data Grim Machine sent?"

Meg chuckled. "Yeah, we did. Took some digging, but we found those schematics you were lookin' for."

Janus glanced up, her heart quickening its pace.

"Team's workin' on them right now," Meg continued. "While we're on that, though, I've got somethin' I need you to work on."

"I assume it involves whatever's in here?" Janus resisted the urge to open the bag. She could take a closer look once she was back in her room.

"Sure does. Fun new weapon for you to try out," Meg told her. "There's a list tucked in there, too. List of targets. I want you to use that weapon on them, nothing else. Got that, dear?"

"Uh, sure thing." What the hell had Meg given her?

"We'll call again soon so you can tell me how things go with that weapon ya got there. Have a good night, Sky."

Before Janus could get her thoughts together and offer a 'good night' in response—or ask any further questions—the man pressed a button on the communicator and returned it to his pocket. He nodded to Janus as a sleek, flying limo slid into the air behind him. Without another word, he turned around, crossed the roof, and climbed into the vehicle.

Twenty minutes later, Janus was back in her room at the palace, partially thanks to the help of a grappling hook. She locked the door, brought up the hall cameras on her tablet so she'd have warning if anyone approached, then moved to her bed to open the bag.

The weapon inside looked like a massive blaster, closer in size to a shotgun than a handgun. Beneath it was a tiny data chip. Janus left the chip out on the bed, but returned the weapon to the bag and stashed it where she kept everything else she had to hide from Starr: a hidden compartment in the wall, behind a panel that only opened when a lengthy code was typed into the microwave in her personal kitchen. Meg had sent a fake construction crew into the palace to install it. An impressive feat.

Once the weapon was safely stashed, Janus popped open one of her sphere's data ports and inserted the chip. The holoscreen came on, revealing a short list of names.

Janus was surprised to find Captain Cora's name on the list.

Chapter Thirty-Seven
Treason's Greetings

Coming down from the atmosphere to the streets of Kronos had given Grace plenty of practice flying the Comet. She'd found herself a bit flustered at first—Jasper made it hard to focus, standing behind Grace with a hand on her shoulder, close enough for Grace to feel the heat off her skin—but she was getting the hang of it. Enough to park them in a roof lot near a Bibi's without too many complaints of a rough landing. Most of the ones she did get were from Sarena.

From there, it didn't take the team long to find trouble. Or, rather, for trouble to find them. Grace was the first one to spot the rapidly growing crowd outside the window of the Bibi's. While she squinted at the people outside on the sidewalk, trying to figure out what was happening, she was vaguely aware of a cashier calling an order number, of Jasper walking to the counter to collect.

The rest of the group had crowded around a single table. There was only room for Rose, Cutthroat, Sarena, and Aymes to actually sit. Dax was behind Aymes, studying the menu, Holly was a few feet away reading something on her tablet, and Thea stood between the two with folded arms. Hook and Steele had remained behind on the Astronomer.

As Jasper rejoined the group with the drink she'd ordered, Thea asked, "Have you considered maybe you should stop drinking Nova Cora?"

"Hey, I've cut back quite a bit—" Jasper started defensively.

"No, not for your health—though, that's a good reason, too. But I meant because of Captain Cora."

"Oh, you think it's morally irresponsible to buy drinks from the company sponsoring that guy?"

"Exactly."

Jasper shrugged. "Good thing I steal most of the ones I drink." She took a sip through her straw.

Holly chimed in. "Yeah, but people might see you drinking it and think you endorse Captain Cora."

"What sane person would think that I of all people—?"

"Uh, guys?" Grace finally found her voice and turned from the window. "Something's happening outside."

All eyes went to the window. To the crowd that swept through the street outside, seemingly picking up passersby as it moved, growing denser by the second. And as the rest of the team moved closer, pressing in around Grace, it became apparent that many of the people in the crowd were carrying signs.

ENFORCE LAWS AT STORMTIDE FACTORY

Stormtide Policy Unfair!

Employees dropping DEAD on the job

A few of the signs even pleaded for help from the Interstar Council rather than the Kronosian Government. *Interstar Council S.O.S.*

"Well, a big riot meant to draw the government's attention seems like our cue to make like a leave and tree." Jasper turned to face the counter and shouted at the employees, "Ay yo, y'all got a back exit we can use?"

"Uh, some of those signs have pictures of Grace on them," Dax noted.

Aymes lifted an eyebrow. "And a few people are in Superangel costumes, too."

Grace immediately started moving toward Jasper. "I second Jasper. Let's get out of here."

"That neon idiot is out there!" Rose exclaimed.

"Captain Cora?" Jasper asked, lifting an eyebrow as she whirled around. Grace inwardly groaned, knowing their chances of leaving just dropped to zero.

"How did you know that's who she was talking about?" Sarena asked.

"Who else could she possibly be referring to?" Jasper turned. "Grace, can you Superangel up?"

Grace grimaced. "Right now?"

Jasper's brow furrowed. "What's wrong? I thought you liked being Superangel now."

"I do! It's just—" Grace sighed, her gaze flicking to the window. "That out there is different. That's not saving people from a car crash or a bank robbery. They're using me as some kind of...revolutionary symbol!"

"We can use that."

Grace's hesitation must have shown on her face, because Jasper's expression instantly softened. "All right, I get it. If you want to slip out the back and head home, I wouldn't blame you. Taking the lead of a protest... It's totally okay if you're not ready for that."

Grace closed her eyes and forced herself to breathe. *Ready?* Would she ever really be ready for something like that?

Not if she avoided it, she realized.

"Maybe..." Grace still couldn't entirely shake her hesitation, but another part of her was fighting against it now. "Maybe I can do something."

"Really, Angel, there's no pressure—"

Bruce Wright was out there, Grace reminded herself, flashes of that day he'd arrested her popping in her mind like fireworks. He was a danger to those people. Enforcing laws meant to keep them down, undoubtedly ready to use violence if he felt they were out of line.

"I have to protect them from Wright," Grace said. "Or Captain Cora. Bruce. Whatever he is now, I doubt he's here to play nice with those people."

Jasper nodded solemnly. "You're probably right about that."

One more deep breath. Grace lifted her chin. "My costume's in my bag on the Comet."

"Getting over to that roof lot without getting trampled might be tricky."

"I'll fly over," Grace replied. "I'll just have to go around the block and stay high so no one notices me until I'm in costume."

"I could distract them," Sarena offered.

Jasper shot her a suspicious glance. "Distract them *how*?"

"Singing. Duh. It's one of my main talents, or did you forget?"

A heavy sigh came from Cutthroat's direction. Aymes cocked his head. Thea lifted an eyebrow. "What are you going to sing?" Thea asked.

"The hit single from my upcoming album, obviously. 'Revolution.'"

"Oh, yes, a song called 'Revolution' by a rich, privileged pop star actress who lives in a massive penthouse." Jasper folded her arms. "Fitting."

"Hey, I wasn't always rich! Don't forget I grew up in the Tide District. The song is about fighting back when I was a kid living down there."

"Even if you have a point, you can't sing that."

"Why not?"

"It's corny."

"Corny?" Sarena sounded incredulous.

"I've heard the song, Sarena. It's a dance song they're blasting in clubs all over the upper districts. No one associates it with social justice."

Grace leaned toward Dax as the argument continued. "I'm gonna go grab my costume. Have 'em let me know over comms once there's a plan." With all the chaos outside, she was beginning to think she didn't really need a distraction to get back to the Comet.

Dax nodded. "Sure thing."

Moments later, Grace was out in the night air, wings spread wide. Once she'd circled the bulk of the protesting crowd, she touched down on the roof lot where the Comet waited and darted into the ship. Voices rang out in the night air behind her, patches of unified chants mixing with individual screams and shouts.

Mia and Chloe were sitting inside the ship, and Grace was surprised to find they were chatting with each other when she walked in.

"—which is why I suspect those betting on the Sand Serpents players will win the most money." Mia's head turned. "Oh, hello Grace. You look startled."

"I, uh, sorry," Grace stammered as she started toward where her bag lay on the ship's floor. "I guess I thought you two would just be sitting in silence."

"Thea wanted us to develop our conversational algorithms," Chloe explained.

"Uh, cool. What are you talking about?"

"Fantasy Sandsurfing teams. Thea won't allow us to actually sign up and play, but we're making predictions for the season anyway."

The two androids got back to chatting. Grace quickly changed and hurried back out of the Comet. Still no word from the others, but they seemed to have come to some sort of agreement about what they'd be doing to help the protestors. On a skywalk passing over the Bibi's across the street, Sarena was attempting to garner as much attention as possible. But rather than revealing herself as the famous pop star, she wore sunglasses and a short wig of curly pink hair. Grace wasn't sure what the point of that was.

Thea sat at Sarena's side, looking reluctant to be helping at all, but still doing a remarkable job of taking control of every speaker in the vicinity: store speakers that usually played background music for shoppers, rarely used speakers on street posts meant for government announcements, the music players in parked vehicles. It all added to the volume of Thea's drones that hovered above. But with all the chaos, it was barely enough to carry Sarena's voice to the street below.

Bruce stood on a ledge jutting out from a building a couple of storefronts down from the Bibi's. He'd apparently had taken on a few new sponsors, indicating that plenty of big companies found him to be a suitable advertising board. The majority of his suit was still Nova Cora-branded, but a few patches had been slapped on the arms and chest. Kappa-Omega, Mota Mart, a chip brand, a flying car company…

As Grace expected, Bruce was not here for the people's benefit. He spoke into a microphone that had also been connected to speakers all over the area. But Starr had sent out far more drones than Thea, and he must have had a tech team on the sidelines, because some of the street post speakers were jumping back to Bruce's control as well. His voice overwhelmed Sarena's.

And, Grace realized with a start, his drones were armed with small blasters.

"—return to your homes," Bruce was saying. "If you are unhappy with your working conditions, contact your lawmakers. Bathing the streets in blood and broken property is the wrong way to make change."

Amidst the outraged shouting, one voice near Grace managed to just be heard above the chaos. "Our district leaders have no power! The upper districts veto all the help they try to give us!"

"It is up to you to persuade your employers to treat you fairly," Bruce continued. "If you don't like how they treat you, find a new job."

Grace's eyes rolled. Did Bruce realize the absurdity of what he was saying? Or did he truly believe it? These people's employers wouldn't make changes they deemed unprofitable if their hands weren't forced by the law—and even that might not be enough, if they weren't properly punished for breaking it.

Most of the employers in these districts would be treating their workers the same across the board, anyway, as long as they could get away with it. Switching jobs wasn't likely to do anyone much good.

On the streets below, police officers under Bruce's command forced their way into the crowds, waving blasters liberally. A few blaster beams lit up the night. The shouts and screams that followed spurred Grace into action. Her wings flung out, and she was off like a shot.

"Captain Cora," Grace exclaimed as she touched down on the roof near him. She drew her sword and pointed it at him. "Don't you dare position yourself as a defender of the people. You are only here to defend the elite from their anger. Their *justified* anger at how they are treated."

"Superangel?" Bruce sounded more amused than surprised as he turned to face her. His helmet was on, but his visor was up, letting his gaze meet hers. "Well, well, well. You claim to be a hero, and yet you run on the wrong side of the law."

"The laws are wrong, then," Grace snapped back. She took a step forward, making a conscious effort to hide her shaking. She wasn't scared, but adrenaline overwhelmed her. Adrenaline and rage.

"You're naive, Superangel. Starr's rule over the Janus System brings order where there would otherwise be chaos."

"What's the point of order when all these people are hurting?" Another step forward. Grace wasn't really trying to argue with Bruce—he was too far entrenched in elite propaganda to win over in a simple debate—but she wanted the people below to know their cause was just. That they should keep up their fight. And that they weren't alone.

Before Bruce could respond, Grace lunged. Her wings beat against the air to push her hard and fast at the cyborg cop. Her sword hit his armor—

—and bounced right off. Grace was knocked to the roof flat on her back. As she sat up, groaning, Bruce lifted his arm. His armor transformed, pieces rising up and clicking together to form a blaster cannon.

Grace rolled as the weapon fired. She dodged the blast, but she wasn't in the clear. It hadn't looked like a particularly powerful energy beam, but it was strong enough to break open the roof, sending her tumbling into the space below. She hit the floor of a dim room, only illuminated by city light spilling in from the gaping hole above. It appeared to be a kitchen for a closed restaurant.

Jasper cursed over comms. "He's got one of those super weapons powered with warp energy. Angel, you gotta get out of there."

"And let him use it on the people?" Grace climbed to her feet.

"We don't know that he'll do that."

"I doubt he came out here just to talk. Police are already firing their blasters. I don't see why Bruce wouldn't fire his as a show of force. He's here to scare people."

Jasper sighed. "I guess we do have him outnumbered. Just don't let any of his blasts hit you," she said. "Let's get as many people as possible on Bruce."

Grace spread her wings and pushed off the ground. "Where are you, Jasper?"

"Smashing up police cruisers. But I'll head toward Bruce. Got any plans of attack?"

"He's vulnerable when his weapons come out. It leaves gaps in his armor." Grace grabbed the edge of the roof with her free hand as she reached the gap and propelled herself into the open air. Her other hand tightened around her weapon's handle.

Bruce, who'd moved away from the gap, whirled around. Before Grace could plan her next move, however, something behind him caught her attention. Dax climbing up onto the roof.

"I can hit him without worrying about armor," Dax said through comms. "I'll keep out of range. If you keep him distracted, I've got some injuries I can throw at him."

"You got it." Grace brandished her sword and charged, eyes on the spot on Bruce's arm where the blaster would emerge. Sure enough, as she approached, the metal components began sliding and rearranging. Grace flipped her blade through the air at the last moment, preventing Bruce from realizing where she was aiming until it was too late to move his arm.

The blade slipped between the cracks and found Bruce's flesh. He yelped in pain and swung wildly, knocking Grace free. She kept her hold on her sword and landed on her feet.

Bruce aimed his blaster at her, jaw clenched against his pain. Grace readied herself to dodge. She didn't have to. Bruce suddenly doubled over, letting out another cry of pain. He still hadn't noticed Dax on the other side of the roof, eyes narrowed in concentration.

While Bruce straightened up and tried to get his bearings through the pain—Grace suspected it was a broken rib Dax had healed at the Iros hospital they'd stopped at before leaving the moon—a new attack came in the form of a silver bird swooping at him from above.

A single blast sent the bird disintegrating into silver wisps of energy. Bruce's eyes darted up to where Aymes hovered on a silver platform overhead. "The Apprentice?" Gaze shifting back to Grace, he added, "You claim to be a hero, but you're working with a villain?"

"People change. The Apprentice cares just as much about the people of Kronos as I do," Grace replied with a shrug before swinging her sword again. It was more of another distraction than a real effort to get at his arm again. Someone else had joined the fight: Cutthroat. He came running at Bruce from behind, blaster aimed.

Bruce pulled down his visor and turned to face Cutthroat, ignoring Grace's sword as it once again bounced off his armor. Cutthroat squeezed his trigger, and the blast from his weapon cracked Bruce's visor.

Bruce muttered something Grace couldn't hear. Comms, likely. Was he calling for backup?

She sliced at Bruce's arm again, preventing him from firing and getting in another cut. It was impossible to see the damage, but his gasp and a few staggering steps sideways told her she'd been fairly successful. She took the opportunity to ram the hilt of her sword into his already compromised visor, putting more cracks in it.

Bruce yelped again and dropped to one knee. While he fought off whatever new pain Dax had inflicted on him, Aymes formed another bird from his energy and sent it to peck at the gaps in Bruce's armor.

Flashing red and yellow lights lit up the rooftop. A hovering police cruiser descended toward the brawl. Rather than sending out more officers to help Bruce—ordinary police wouldn't have lasted long against Grace and the others, anyway—they dropped a ladder from a hatch that opened on the cruiser's bottom.

Jasper and Holly finally joined them on the roof. As they sprinted toward Grace and Bruce, Bruce pointed his blaster toward Grace, deterring her from making any moves as he took steps toward the ladder. Jasper drew a blaster and took aim but hesitated. Grace nodded at her to fire as she backed away from Bruce, ready to dodge any shots.

Jasper's blast took Bruce right in the visor, shattering it completely. He managed to grab the ladder as he stumbled. A moment later, his other hand grabbed one of the rungs—made of thin metal chains—and he started his ascent.

Blaster shots from officers in the cruiser deterred Aymes's flock of tiny birds. The cruiser moved up about twenty feet in a quick burst, preventing anyone else from grabbing on to the ladder. Grace spread her wings, ready to fly after Bruce, but he aimed his superpowered blaster at her again. She froze.

"You can't fight him alone, Angel," Jasper said as she caught up. She rested a hand on Grace's shoulder. "Good fight, though. Roughed him up enough to send him running."

Still, Grace muttered a few curses as Bruce disappeared into the cruiser. In the blink of an eye, it was shooting off into the night. Other police cruisers remained in the area, a few still dispatching officers onto the streets, but their numbers were minuscule compared to that of the protesting citizens.

Jasper gave her a reassuring smile. "You good?"

Grace nodded. "Yeah. I'm good."

"Anything else you want to say to the people?"

Not really, but Grace supposed she should come up with something. She crossed the roof to the edge and peered down at the packed street.

"Bruce disconnected from those drones," Thea said. "I'll patch your comm to them so the people can hear you better, Grace."

"Hey, what about me?" Sarena protested.

"You can keep singing your cringy revolution anthem when she's done," Jasper replied. "Why do you even care? You didn't bother to reveal yourself as the real Sarena Trench." Quieter, she added a bitter, "Coward."

If Sarena had a response to that, Grace didn't hear it. There was a soft beep in her ear, and then a louder one echoing from the drones. Grace lifted her chin.

"Keep fighting!" she shouted to the people. "Change is coming, and I will help you bring it. But it's up to you to refuse the poor treatment, the low wages, the long hours. The elite can't survive without you holding them up. But you won't survive if you don't stand together."

Cheers and shouts came in response, no single voice discernable, no particular words or chants decipherable to Grace's ears. But the general tone seemed positive.

Unsure what else to say, what else she could do, she flew off into the night.

"You coming back to the Comet, Angel?" Jasper asked.

Grace slowed her ascent and glanced down at the city. "I'll meet you guys back at the apartment," she decided.

"How about you meet on the street outside instead, and we get you some more flying lessons in?"

Grace shook out her hands. Something to take her mind off things, something to focus on...that did sound nice. "Sure thing," she replied.

Chapter Thirty-Eight
Fast in my Spaceship

Grace dropped onto the sidewalk next to the Comet. Jasper leaned against ship, arms folded. "Ready?"

"To trade one stressful situation for another? I guess." Grace walked up to stand next to her.

Jasper laughed and started toward the door. "You did great."

"I mean, I know what all the controls do now. I think." Grace followed Jasper into the ship. "My landing didn't exactly earn any applause."

"Only weirdos clap when spaceships land, anyway."

"If you say so." Grace entered the cockpit behind Jasper and slid into the pilot's seat while Jasper took the seat to her right

While Grace started up the engine, Jasper clasped her hands behind her head and leaned back in her chair. "I think we should do a supply run."

"Supply run? Apartment's pretty stacked on snacks."

"I was thinking the explode-y kind of supplies."

"Oooh. Gotcha." Grace pushed a lever forward, and the Comet lifted up off the street. "Last I checked, there were a lot of grenades and ammo in the hall closet, too."

"Yeah, I'd say what we have is plenty, ordinarily. But...something big is coming. I don't know exactly how it's going to play out, but I'd rather be overprepared than the alternative."

Grace shrugged. "Sounds good to me. Where do we go to get these supplies?"

"I'll give you directions. Just head toward the ocean for now. Veer a few degrees south." Jasper studied the evening sky ahead of them. After a few minutes, she said, "I haven't picked up more ammo from this place since before you joined us, I think."

"I remember you bringing home some boxes of grenades one time, right after we got back from fighting Ringmaster on Iros."

"Oh, yeah, you're right. That was my last supply run," Jasper said. "It's not just grenades I get here. Smoke bombs, gun ammo, uh, also one of the guys that works there makes this really good lunberry jam that they throw in for free if you buy enough stuff."

Grace laughed. "Has he considered doing jam full-time instead of crime?"

"Apparently he's very good at both."

Jasper guided Grace to a warehouse near some docks. The sunlight had faded from the world by the time they landed. Grace brough the ship down in a small mostly empty lot, only occupied by a few beat-up wheeled vehicles.

"Are these people...dangerous?" Grace asked as she shut off the Comet.

Jasper rose to her feet and stretched. Yawned. "Nah. Not to us. I've been a loyal customer for starcycles."

Still, as she led the way off the ship, Grace couldn't shake the sudden feeling in the pit of her stomach that something about this place wasn't right.

A massive rolling door was open a few feet in the side of the warehouse, offering a glimpse at stacks of boxes inside and dozens of workers milling about when Grace crouched to peek. A few workers stood outside, too, chatting with each other.

Jasper waved a hand as she and Grace drew closer, catching the attention of one of the workers. "Hey, Evi, right? I need some stuff."

A woman with bright pink fur and large ears turned around. "Oh, Van Terra. You—you want your usual restocking order?" She seemed nervous as she stammered out the words. One of her ears twitched a few times.

Jasper frowned. "Double my usual. And throw in a box of drones." Those would be for Thea, presumably. "Everything all right?"

The woman nodded quickly. Then hesitated. "We just...had a management shift recently. But I can get your order fulfilled. I'll be right back, if you want to go ahead and transfer the money."

Jasper looked a little skeptical, but she pulled out her smartsphere and opened a banking app. "Same account numbers as before?"

"Yep!" the woman squeaked as she hurried over to the warehouse door. She ducked underneath it and disappeared inside. Jasper glanced at the other workers, who quickly returned to their hushed conversation, avoiding eye contact.

"Is this normal?" Grace whispered.

"Not really. Some of the workers have always been skittish, but Evi usually isn't. Makes me wonder if I need to be worried about this new management."

Grace shot a glance back at the Comet. "Want me to turn the engine back on?" They might need a quick escape.

"Not yet. No need to make everyone even more nervous. But be ready to run."

A few minutes later, there was a grinding noise, and the warehouse door lifted a few feet higher into the air. Evi and a few other workers came out with boxes. They practically ran them over to the Comet, where Jasper opened the door for them. Then, she and Grace stood by and watched them load the goods.

"Should we help them?" Grace asked after the workers left to grab another load.

Jasper shook her head. "They don't like outsiders going into the warehouse."

The workers brought out two more rounds of boxes before things got quiet for a few minutes. Finally, Grace frowned and asked, "Is that everything?"

"No way." Jasper glanced into the ship. "That's maybe half of it."

There was movement at the door again a moment later. Evi and the others brought more boxes out, but instead of bringing them all the way over to the ship, they set them in front of the door. A couple more minutes passed, then the workers disappeared again.

"That looks like the rest of it," Jasper said, nodding toward the boxes. "Not sure why they're leaving them over there though." She took a step forward, starting toward the rest of the supplies, when more people emerged from the warehouse. Jasper stopped in her tracks.

The five men all wore outfits of white leather, gold jewelry, and matching gold belts flashing in the glow from the lightposts around the parking lot. Blasters hung at their sides.

"Slicers?" Jasper exclaimed. "Since when do they operate over here?"

The man leading the group of gang members must have heard her, because he shouted back, "Since we felt like it, Van Terra. Which means you're not welcome here anymore!" He glanced back and gestured to the chatting workers. "Take those boxes back in."

"What the hell? I already paid for that!" Jasper drew a blaster of her own. Took aim and a step forward. "Give me today's order, and I'll never come back. How's that?"

"Sorry. Our business, our rules." The lead Slicer drew his own blaster, and his friends followed suit. "I'd suggest you leave, but I also really want to shoot you."

Jasper's eyes narrowed. Her calculating expression shifted into place.

"Ah, what the hell," the Slicer said. "Let's shoot her anyway."

Him and his men began firing.

Grace lunged forward and flung out her wings to shield her and Jasper. Jasper ducked but didn't make a move toward the ship hatch.

"Jasper!" Grace hissed. "We need to go!"

Jasper cursed under her breath but hurried into the ship. Grace followed, grimacing as she felt some of the blaster beams bounce off her wings, the reverberation echoing through her bones. She and Jasper raced into the cockpit, where Jasper slammed the button to close the hatch. To Grace's surprise—and mild horror—Jasper then slid into the same seat she'd sat in on the way here.

"Uh, maybe you should fly us out of here," Grace said.

"You've taken it easy so far. Time for you to learn to fly fast."

"Wouldn't it be better to learn that when I'm not actually under pressure?" Grace exclaimed.

"Relax. Those blasters won't do anything to the Comet, and I don't think these guys are actually prepared to do much more than shoot at us while we fly off."

Right. Slicers were far from the scariest enemy they'd faced. Grace could get them out of here. She took a deep breath and dropped into the pilot's seat. "If you say so."

Start the engines. Get into the air. Hit the throttle. The ship shot forward with startling velocity, a little harder than she'd intended. Cupboards in the open space behind the cockpit swung open, and something large and person-shaped flew out of one of them, crashing into the floor with a loud yelp.

Jasper glanced back, but Grace didn't dare take her gaze away from the window for than a split second. "Rose?" Jasper yelped. "How? I saw you walk into the apartment with everyone else!"

"I ran back while you were talking to Grace," Rose replied. The statement was accompanied by a shuffling sound that suggested she was getting up off the floor.

"And no one noticed you run off?"

"Sarena did, but she just shrugged."

Grace risked another glance away from the windshield as they shot up into the sky. Rose hurried into the cockpit with them. "So, what's up?" she asked. "I heard blasters."

"We got scammed." Jasper's expression darkened. Then, she studied Rose for a moment. "Hey, Angel. I have an idea."

Grace sighed. "Am I going to like it?"

"That depends. Do you like flying really fast and dodging obstacles?"

"Not in a spaceship."

"Well, you'll learn to love it. Rose, I need you to sit here and push a button when I tell you to." Jasper stood up and gestured for Rose to take her place in the chair.

"All I'm doing is pushing a button? Lame." Still, Rose settled into the seat.

"It's a weapon. Sort of. Does that make you feel better?"

Rose grinned. "Weapon? Hell yeah!"

Jasper lifted an eyebrow. Instead of commenting on Rose's language, though, she pointed to a dark green button concealed by a transparent case. "Lift that case and press the button when I tell you to."

Rose nodded. "Got it. Is it gonna fire a big laser?"

"You'll see." With that, Jasper walked out of the cockpit to the door. "Angel, crack the door about a foot, please!"

Grace scanned the buttons and sliders, taking a moment to remember which one controlled the door settings. She adjusted a slider, pushed a button, and the door in the slide of the ship slid open.

"Turn on stealth mode, too!" Jasper called. "Then take us back down to the warehouse. I'm getting what I paid for."

Grace activated stealth mode, then moved her hands to the wheel, where they tightened until her knuckles went white. "You holding onto something, Jasper?"

"Yep!"

Grace glanced at Rose. "Seat belt?" Rose huffed but grabbed the chair's belt straps and clicked them into place. Then, Grace pushed the wheel forward, and they dove.

As they flew back toward the warehouse, Jasper shouted some tips at Grace on how not to crash into the ground. She also explained that Grace should fly as close to the remaining supply boxes as she dared. Hopefully, most of them would still be there.

"And then what?" Grace called.

"Then Rose will push the button!"

"And then what?"

Jasper's head turned, and she grinned. "You'll see."

Grace's heart fluttered, and she smiled back, even as she shook her head. "So dramatic!"

Moments later, they were close enough to the warehouse to make out the individual workers. One was picking up boxes from outside the door, but it looked like most of the pile was still there.

At the ship door, Jasper began firing her blaster, scaring workers away from the goods. The ground came closer. Grace somehow managed to tighten her grip on the wheel even further, preparing to yank them up and away from the asphalt.

Just as her hands moved to adjust the wheel, Jasper shouted, "Rose! Button!" Rose flipped up the glass case eagerly and slammed her fist against the button beneath.

The parking lot beneath the ship lit up with a pale glow. Grace caught the briefest glimpse of the boxes lifting off the ground and flying toward the ship before she had them pointed upward again.

Rose leaned forward, trying to figure out what was happening through the windshield but struggling with the angle. "What did that do?"

Jasper stumbled into the cockpit and hit the button to close the door. "Tractor beam. Sucked up all of the boxes. They'll be hanging onto the bottom of the ship now."

"That's not a weapon!" Rose exclaimed.

Jasper shrugged. "Depends on your definition of 'weapon.'"

Rose rolled her eyes, but after a moment said, "I guess that's kind of cool."

Jasper took a step forward and rested hand on the back of Grace's chair. "Good job, Angel."

"Thanks. Glad I didn't kill us all."

"This ship was built for battle. Even a crash straight into the ground at full speed has a decent shot at survival. Assuming you're wearing a seat belt." After a moment, her grip on the chair tightened. "I didn't think we'd be running into Slicers any time soon. They didn't seem like a super serious gang last time we fought them."

Grace glanced at her briefly. "Think we need to worry about Omic Attom?"

"No idea. I thought he was just a greedy editor who started up a gang for some extra security, but maybe he's getting involved with bigger stuff." Jasper moved forward into the space between Grace and Rose's seats and settled onto the floor cross-legged. That made Grace's body tense, her focus on the sky ahead sharpen. However well-built the ship was, she didn't want to find out how survivable an accident was the hard way, especially unbuckled.

After a moment, Jasper asked, "Anyone want to get a snack?"

Ten minutes later, they hovered at the ordering window for a Bibi's. Jasper moved to the door as Grace opened it and climbed onto the wing to place their order. Just as she was handing over the janos to pay, everyone's comms echoed with the sound of Thea's voice.

"I found something."

Jasper whirled around, clutching the bag of food the employee had handed her. "About the Lion's den?"

"Yeah," Thea replied. "I've been scanning encrypted transactions across the net, searching for any with the same encryption that Astra's ticket had. And I found a few matches. Some of the tickets are for tomorrow night."

"Are we going to try to get its location from the people the tickets belong to?" Grace asked.

"Seems a good place to start," Jasper replied. She tossed the bag of food to Rose to catch, then turned around to grab a few drinks from the employee. "Where can we find them, Thea?"

"A few of them will be together tomorrow, actually." Thea paused. Then, sounding slightly amused, she asked, "Anyone up for a round of kronospar?"

Chapter Thirty-Nine
Kronospar-ty

Kronospar was basically golf. Mini golf, specifically. But the course was an elaborate journey across Kronosian rooftops, down fire escapes, under overpasses, and through buildings whose spaces had been rented by the Diamond District Kronospar Club.

Jasper adjusted her cap with the club's logo. She held a hot pink golf club—sorry, *kronospar* club—over her shoulder. At her right, Dax held a similar club in pastel blue. The two had stolen outfits with the kronospar club's logo on them as well, allowing them to blend in with the rich elite who'd come out to play the game this morning.

Holly and Grace's job today wasn't too difficult. They'd be chatting with people across the various districts to get a feel for the general consensus on Captain Cora and Superangel. Thea, meanwhile, would be trying to dig up more info on the Lion's Den on her own. She was also chasing a rumor that had Jasper a little unsettled: Grim Machine had apparently been spotted in the lower districts recently.

She was pretty sure she'd left him completely unable to function in the jungle on Reo when they'd last fought. Maybe even beyond repair. But that apparently wasn't the case. The question was, who had gone through the trouble of finding him and fixing him up?

Jasper shook off her concerns about the robot. There was nothing she could do about them right now. She focused her attention on a large hovercart as it landed on the balcony where she and Dax waited with the other kronospar players. Club employees hoped out and ushered the players into the cart.

As they settled into their seats, an East Kronosian man in the next row up glanced back and shot Jasper a suspicious look. "Haven't seen you before. You new?"

"It's been a while," Jasper replied coolly as the hovercart lifted back into the air.

"I don't see humans here much." *Translation: This is a place for the city's elite.* Humans weren't out of the ordinary in the Janus System, but they were typically found in the middle or lower districts. But there were exceptions...

"My father was ambassador," Jasper told the man. "Used to work at the Governor's Palace. He's retired now, but he gave me a nice sum of cash as a birthday gift. Thought I'd pop in for a round or two."

The man nodded, seemingly accepting her story. He glanced at Dax. "And who's your friend?"

"My cousin." Jasper leaned forward and lowered her voice. "His parents don't let him go out much, so I thought I'd do him a favor. Forgive him if he doesn't do too well."

Jasper wasn't sure whether Dax heard her, but he would probably be grateful for the excuse. Given how well he'd done in volleyball while the team was at East Marina High, Jasper doubted he'd do much better here. She'd brought him along because Holly and Grace were the best at politely interrogating people, Thea was preoccupied with her work, and neither Cutthroat nor Sarena were interested.

Aymes *had* actually offered to come as well, but Jasper didn't want to draw even more attention by bringing along three humans. Rose had tried to tag along too, of course, but Jasper was able to distract her with a new, delightfully violent TV show. Hey, at least it was animated.

A few minutes after taking off in the hovercart, they arrived at the first tee box. Jasper found herself at the front of the line. With a shrug, she dropped the glowing pink kronospar ball she'd selected earlier onto the ground, moved into position, and swung her club.

The ball went sailing over the edge of the roof and into a gutter. It rolled down, came out an opening a story down, and bounced onto a fire escape. After tumbling down a few stairs, it fell off the metal structure and landed in a parked car via its sunroof. The Diamond District Kronospar Club's logo was plastered on the vehicle's side.

Right on target. Having a computer in her brain really helped.

The man who'd spoken to her on the hovercart let out a low whistle. "That'll be hard to follow."

As the next kronosparer moved up to tee, Jasper walked to the man and found a spot at his left. "So, any fun plans for the night?" she asked. "I'll be in the city a couple more days and I need more things to do."

The man chuckled. "I don't think you'd be interested in where I'm going."

"Why's that?" Jasper lifted an eyebrow.

"It's not as...*innocent* a sport, let's just say. And I'll be watching, not playing."

That sounded promising. Jasper leaned toward him. Lowered her voice. "You'd be surprised. You ever hear of the alkura fights they do out on Hatu?"

The man shook his head. "Sounds like a good time."

"It is. I ran a circuit myself, for a while. Now I'm looking for a new venture. I've got some tough humans who'd like a chance to show off. And I've heard rumors..."

It was the man's turn. He gave Jasper a nod, a look that suggested the conversation would continue once he'd swung.

His hit wasn't bad. His ball landed on the fire escape just above the vehicle they were aiming for. While the next player moved up to take his place, the East Kronosian returned to Jasper's side. "Even if you would enjoy my plans for the night, the place I'm headed is hard to get into. I certainly don't have the power to get you there."

"Really? You seem pretty powerful."

The man laughed. "I'm flattered, but surely you don't actually believe that."

Behind him, it was now Dax's turn. With a surprisingly hard but unsurprisingly unsteady swing, Dax sent the ball sailing toward traffic. One of the employees hurriedly tapped the screen of the tablet they were holding, and a device on top of the hovercart let out a beam—tractor beam, Jasper realized—that locked onto the ball and pulled it back in the blink of an eye.

Dax shot Jasper an anxious look. "Maybe I should just watch."

"Sure, if you'd rather," Jasper replied with a shrug. It's not like they'd actually paid for their game.

The hovercart took them to the fire escape next so those who hadn't gotten a hole-in-one could get their balls into the vehicle. Then, after retrieving their balls, the group flew to a nearby roof. Here, they walked the rest of the way to the second tee box, passing through a massive pipe suspended by a crane. One end of the pipe hung at the edge of the roof. The other led onto a platform where the group gathered and found themselves overlooking an abandoned construction yard.

Jasper landed another hole-in-one—through some pipes, down some ramps of wooden boards, and into a bucket held in the air by another crane—then approached the East Kronosian again. "So, if you're not powerful enough to grant me access to this event, who do I have to go to?" she asked him.

"It won't be easy, even if I give you names," he said. "Not just anyone can be hearing about this place. They'll want to vet you."

"Can you at least point me in the right direction?" Jasper asked.

"Well, you'll have to get in good with the Fayes."

The Fayes? "They...run the place?" It hadn't occurred to her that the Den would be run by a single elite family, but she supposed it made sense.

A pale North Kronosian woman on the man's other side, apparently within earshot of him and Jasper, let out a chuckle. "You know, I heard one of the Fayes was supposed to be coming out with us today," she said to the two.

The man glanced her way and raised an eyebrow. "Why didn't they, then?"

The woman nodded toward another man nearby—another East Kronosian, with skin an even deeper shade of red than Jasper's new friend. "Ask your cousin over there. The Altairs have made some vague threats to the Fayes recently. Rumor has it the Fayes were planning to run in their district's next election."

Jasper smirked. Those rumors were mostly the result of her team's work. Maybe the Fayes would actually go after other districts eventually, after losing theirs to Merama Tidewater in the last mayoral election, but she'd expected they'd go after less threatening prey first. So, she'd ensured that the most powerful upper district families—primarily the Altairs and the Vegas—feared that the Fayes would come after them instead.

A yelp of pain made Jasper whirl around. The other club members turned, too, finding that one of the players had apparently sliced his hand open on something. A sharp nail protruding from a splintered railing. It was on the other side of some fluorescent yellow tape warning that the area beyond wasn't confirmed to be safe, but that hadn't stopped the man from getting too close.

An employee darted over to the bleeding man. He had pale blue skin with a metallic sheen to it. Straight black hair flopped around his face as he ran. Jasper wasn't sure exactly what species he was, though she'd seen people like him before. One of the Reon races, maybe?

Within seconds, that line of questioning was wiped from Jasper's mind. She and Dax watched with wide eyes as the man's hands emitted a blue glow that healed the wound within seconds.

Jasper nudged Dax with her elbow. "Uh, you wanna talk to that guy?"

Dax blinked. "You don't think it's a coincidence?"

"Sure. Could be some big cosmic coincidence. Or, maybe the fact that this guy not only has the same power as you but also manifests it in the exact same way *might* signal some connection."

Dax sighed. "Yeah, okay, but what am I supposed to do? Just walk up and talk to him?"

"That's exactly what you should do!" Jasper grabbed Dax's shoulder and gave him a gentle shove toward the employee as he moved back to where the hovercart waited. Not wanting to leave him completely on his own, she followed at a slower pace and hovered nearby as Dax attempted to start a conversation with the employee.

Dax led with a very compelling, "Uh, hi."

The employee—who looked to be about high school age, maybe a little older—lifted an eyebrow. "Hi?"

With a sigh, Jasper swooped in to help Dax out. "Sorry to bother you, but we were curious about that healing power of yours…" Her gaze darted to the nametag on his club shirt. "Wix."

Wix shrugged. "It's uncommon, but IT runs in some family lines where I'm from."

"And that would be…?"

"Uh, I'm from one of the Reon clans," Wix said, confirming that Jasper's initial guess had been correct.

"Reo," she mused. She rested a hand on Dax's shoulder. "My friend here's got that same healing ability. Blue glow and everything. We've been trying to figure out where he got it."

Wix glanced at Dax. "What's your name?"

"Dax."

Surprise flashed across Wix's face. "That's my great uncle's name. Well, Daxxer, but most of 'em use the same nickname."

"Is it a common name in your clan?" Jasper asked, before they could get carried away with coincidences.

"Somewhat. But I only mention it because he ran off to Earth."

Dax frowned. "Why'd he do that?"

"Dunno," Wix replied with a shrug. "Didn't know him that well." He leaned toward the hovercart's control console and started the engine as kronosparers wandered back over, ready to move on to the next spot.

Jasper exchanged a glance with Dax as they climbed onto the cart. "You ever meet your grandfather?"

"Not on my mom's side," he replied. "But I do know I was named after him."

"Guess you're an alien, then. Congrats." Jasper clapped him on the back. "Hey, you and Holly could start a club."

"Well, I'm only a quarter alien. If my grandfather really was from Reo, anyway." Dax's brow furrowed. "Shouldn't it have been more obvious that my mom was only half human, though?"

"If he ran off to Earth, he probably had a way to disguise himself," Jasper told him. "Could've just been makeup, but maybe he had tech that altered his skin color. Temporary dyes that are injected into the skin, super thin jumpsuits that reflect light to match the color you want, et cetera."

The hovercart lifted into the air. Dax nodded slowly. He hadn't expressed incredible shock at the possibility was an alien, but he was definitely still processing the idea.

"Your mother could have used whatever your grandpa had to disguise herself, too, if she thought it was necessary," Jasper added. "And by the time the genes got to you…" She shrugged. "Hybrid genetics can be unpredictable, and a quarter breed showing no signs of their lesser ancestry isn't unusual. Plus, you were raised on Earth. Epigenetics could've played a role, encouraging your human characteristics to show over any others."

"You think I'd show some Reon traits if I'd been raised there?" Dax asked.

"It's possible." After a moment's hesitation, Jasper added, "You good?"

"Yeah, I guess. I mean, it doesn't change anything, really." Quieter, he added, "Though, it does make me wish I could talk to my mom. Ask her about Grandpa."

Jasper was quiet for a long moment. "She…disappeared before you went through the warp, right?"

Dax nodded.

Jasper didn't know much about the Reon species, and she knew even less about how their genes mixed with humans—hell, she hadn't even realized they were genetically compatible in the first place. Did they have longer lifespans? Age at different rates? Was there any possibility Dax's mother was still alive?

She sighed as she stepped up to the tee box at their next stop. Her questions around Dax's heritage faded from her mind, replaced by numbers and calculations offered up by her cybernetic brain implants, responding to her desire to hit the kronospar ball into the tiny basket hanging from a lightpost a few stories down from the roof they stood on.

A bounce off an awning, a roll down a gutter, and some ping-ponging between parked vehicles, and Jasper had yet another hole-in-one.

Chapter Forty
Holly Jolly

Holly was just about ready to knock the next Nova Cora can she saw out of its owner's hand. The mid-to-upper districts had always been full of people who got on her last nerve, but this new Captain Cora fervor was really pushing her limits. She would have preferred that she and Grace stuck to the lower districts today, but Jasper was insistent they conduct a thorough survey of public opinion.

Down in the lower districts, responses had been about what they'd expected. People were inspired by Superangel's fight during the protest, and seeing the defeat of Captain Cora—however temporary—had stoked the growing flames of revolution. More protests were coming. Tensions were building. And if the government—or the Interstar Council—didn't do something big soon, the people were going to take matters into their own hands.

But in the higher levels of the city, where people were at least comfortable in their lives, if not filthy rich, the citizens were afraid of change. Even people who wouldn't be hurt by changes to the system, people who might even have something to *gain*, were standing by Cora. Standing by the governor. Standing by the law.

Holly shook her head as she and Grace walked away from a group they'd chatted with outside a cafe. They were more toward the center of the city at the moment, rather than in the true upper districts, which made people's love for Captain Cora and Starr even more baffling. "Do these people not realize that they're more likely to wake up poor and be forced to move to the lower districts than they are to make enough money to become one of the elite?"

Grace shrugged. "Guess not. But I'm not surprised. It's easier to imagine themselves as part of the upper city than the lower."

She was right. Unfortunately.

Holly glanced around as the two took a turn and crossed a long skywalk stretching between buildings. Captain Cora merch was abundant. Mostly T-shirts, but a few people were sporting pins, water bottles, hats, and even jackets that resembled his costume.

"Excuse me!" Grace waved a hand at a couple of young adults walking by. They weren't wearing any obvious Captain Cora merchandise, so there was no reason to assume their opinions right off the bat. Still, Holly knew the chances were high that they liked him.

The group paused, and Grace quickly rattled off their spiel about conducting a survey for some citizens' group they'd made up. Despite speaking fast, her tone boasted confidence, not nervousness. She'd come a long way from that terrified young woman Holly had helped break out of prison all those months ago.

"—Cora's just a glorified cop," one of the women was saying. "We were rooting for Superangel."

That snapped Holly from her thoughts. "You were?"

The others nodded alongside the women who'd spoken. One of them unzipped her jacket to reveal a shirt with an image of Superangel, wings spread, printed huge across the front. A man in the group chimed in, gesturing to his friend's shirt. "Yeah, she's a symbol of revolution."

Holly swept her gaze over their nice clothes, their luxury brand bags, and yes, even a Nova Cora bottle poking out of one of their purses. *Yeah. Revolution against you.*

Okay, that wasn't entirely fair. These people weren't filthy rich, just making enough to afford a few luxuries here and there. They were essentially middle management. Not enacting the laws that kept the elite at the top, but not doing anything to stop them, either. The glue that kept the whole system together rather than the engineers or mechanics that made sure it ran.

But still. If they would just use their brains and think for more than two seconds about politics...

"Where'd you get that shirt?" Grace asked, sounding a little dumbfounded.

"Mota Mart, believe it or not. You can find similar ones in pretty much any store." The woman zipped her jacket up.

One of her friends chimed in. "Actually, the Kappa-Omegas up here are selling Captain Cora merch instead. We've decided to boycott them, though."

Sure. Easy enough when you could buy your Nova Coras somewhere else instead. "Pretty sure the same company owns both Mota Mart and Kappa-Omega," Holly muttered under her breath. Play both sides, and you'll always profit. And it wasn't surprising that a big corporation like Mota Mart would take the chance to profit off Grace, even if she was rallying against their business practices. This woman must not have given the purchase that much thought.

Well, there was one thing Holly could do to test how much they actually cared. "So, you would be willing to join the lower districts in a protest, then?"

That changed the group's attitude. They all shifted uncomfortably, suddenly glancing everywhere but at Holly and Grace.

"I mean, it's...not really something everyone can do—" one finally stammered.

"Yeah, I've got work most nights—"

"I don't have transportation—"

Holly waved off their protests with a dismissive hand. "Thanks for answering our questions."

Grace spoke in a low voice as they walked away. "That was smart, asking them about joining the protests." She threw a quick glance back. "I mean, how many of these people think that buying a shirt with my face is doing anything to improve the city?"

"Too many, I'm sure."

"Should we be more aggressive with people like that? Tell them that buying merch isn't good enough if they actually care?"

Holly hesitated. "We could drive them to turn against the lower districts, if we push too hard. As much as I wanted to rip into those people for buying revolution merch at Mota Mart and not caring enough to do anything of actual value, I don't think it would do much good."

They talked to a few more people before Jasper contacted them over comms with new information. Apparently, the Lion's Den was owned by none other than Holly's own family. Great.

Holly sighed. "Want me to poke around and see if I can find the place?"

"If you're not up to it, we can try Thea first—" Jasper started.

"No, I want to do this." Holly lifted her chin. "Let's take everything they have and burn it to the ground."

"Well, I don't know if we're going to use fire to destroy the place, necessarily. I had some other ideas we could try—"

"It's a metaphor, Jasper." Holly cracked her neck. Then her knuckles.

"Oh. Right."

Holly muted her comm and glanced at Grace. "Well, guess I've got a new mission. You okay talking to people in the upper districts by yourself?"

Grace nodded. "You going to be okay talking to your family?"

"When I get to wear someone else's face and scam them?" Holly smirked. "Hell yeah."

The two split, and Holly made her way to the Prism Spire, the iridescent skyscraper that housed the Faye Penthouse. From a nearby roof, it was easy enough to steal the form of a passing security guard as he did his rounds outside the Faye home. Once he moved around the corner on the balcony, Holly mimicked his body, made her way over via a skywalk and a short drop, and slipped inside.

She recalled what Jasper had told her about being caught by a gang and handed over to the Den. The Thunder Serpents might not be around anymore, but maybe the Fayes had another gang looking for fighters. Or, hell, maybe all the gangs in the area knew they could get a decent payout if they sold someone to the family.

Regardless, she hoped she could use that intel to get something useful out of them. She decided to go straight to the top and track down Vixor, who acted as the head of the family. He may have lost the last election for district leader, but that just meant he would be searching for other ways to gain the family money and power.

It didn't take long for Holly to bump into a real guard. Not the one whose face she'd stolen, thankfully. The man she did bump into frowned, though. "Ax? What's up? I thought you were outside."

"Just rotated," Holly replied. "But I have some info Vixor needs to hear."

The guard raised an eyebrow. "Hope it's not bad news." He thumbed over his shoulder. "I just got done standing outside his office. He should still be in there."

Holly nodded in thanks and hurried past him. A few turns later, she reached a door of deep red wood covered in elaborate carvings. With a polite nod directed at the current guards, she knocked.

There was a sigh, then a mildly annoyed, "Come in." Holly recognized Vixor's voice. She turned the handle and slipped inside.

"Just got some intel from the streets, sir," she said. "Someone heard a few gang members talking about sneaking into the Den and stealing whatever they can find. They think they deserve royalties for a fighter they sold us, rather than just a flat payment."

Victor turned in his chair to look her way, brow furrowing. "Which gang?"

Holly took a chance. "Slicers. Not sure if they represent the whole gang's interest, or if they'd be going rogue with this plan."

"Well, they won't make it through security," Vixor said with a dismissive wave of his hand. "But I suppose we could send them a warning."

"I could go in person, if you'd prefer to avoid any potential...communication issues," Holly told him. "Den's not too far from here, right?"

Vixor shot Holly a glance that bordered on suspicious. "You've never been?"

"I have, a few times. It's just...been a while, and my sense of direction isn't great."

"Well, it is a hassle to get the encryptions set up on the usual lines." Vixor sighed. "I'll send some guards to accompany you. Maxy knows the way. It's practically a straight shot down."

Well, that was fine. At least Holly would still get the place's location. Of course, giving Den security a false warning for potential robbery might make whatever Jasper had planned harder. And attacking the guards or randomly fleeing could raise alarms, too.

A few different ideas on how to handle things stirred in Holly's mind as Vixor called for a few guards to come to his office. The men arrived quickly, were given a brief rundown, and then they were all sent on their way.

As they neared the ground-level streets, Holly interrupted the small talk between the other guards to say, "Y'all wanna keep watch at the entrance while I explain the matter to security?"

The other three men exchanged glances, small shrugs, then finally, nods of agreement. Holly held back a smirk. Once again, people's desire to do as little work as possible was going to make her job a piece of cake.

Chapter Forty-One
The Birth of a Revolutionary

"What are you doing in my house?"

Jasper barely heard Sarena's borderline shrieking as she opened the fridge. "Sar, do you have anything healthy we can mix into these smoothies for your guests?"

Sarena marched over and pushed the door shut. "My chefs are handling meals for them! You don't need to be here! How did you even get in?"

"You left the balcony door open." Jasper straightened up and internally couldn't help but smirk a little at the height she had on Sarena.

"Okay, *why* are you here?"

Jasper could almost hear Sarena's teeth grinding. She shrugged. "We tried calling like fifty times. We're trying to have a team meeting. You know, for the Lion's Den stuff?"

Sarena's gaze moved down a little, and she finally noticed the small can of energy drink Jasper had slipped out of the fridge. "Give me that!" She yanked it out of Jasper's hand. "I'm busy with my god damn album release, asshole. Remember?"

"No. Why would I remember that?"

"How could you forget? I had billboards put up all over the city!"

Jasper's brow furrowed. "Is that really the best use of your money?"

"Considering I've already made the marketing budget back in sales, yes."

"Well, your fans are rabid, and I did see that you released ten version of the thing, for some reason, so I guess that makes sense."

Sarena hissed. "So you did know it came out today!"

"I know everything, Sarena." Jasper strolled past her and back into the living room. There was a faint splashing sound as Blitz moved to the edge of his tank and pulled himself up onto its glass wall, seemingly eyeing Jasper up. "I also know that people think the album sucks."

"No they don't!" Sarena followed Jasper into the room. Then, a bit more hesitantly, she added, "Not all of them."

"Sure." Jasper turned to face her and folded her arms. "Sarena, who are you? The revolutionary who sings about breaking down palaces and overthrowing dictators through poorly written metaphors? Or the pop star who bought a third yacht two seasons ago?" Brow lifting, she added, "Or, are you the supervillain who smashes up the upper districts for jewelry, but never really attacks anyone in power? Claiming to fight a system without ever doing anything that could actually break it?"

Sarena scoffed. "Poorly written metaphors?"

"That's your takeaway? Good heavens. Sarena, do you want us to beat Starr?"

"I want you to beat Skybreaker so I can go back to being South Siren!"

"Okay. That's something." Jasper reached into her coat pocket, pulled out a second energy drink can she'd snuck out of the fridge earlier, and cracked it open. After taking a sip under Sarena's murderous gaze, she added, "Would you be upset if Starr went down?"

"Of course not! I do hate the guy. But I'm not going to be the one to put my neck on the line to try to get him removed." Sarena hesitated a moment, then added, "I will fight him as South Siren. It's a good way to blow off steam. But I'm not risking Sarena Trench."

"Some revolutionary you are." Jasper lifted an eyebrow.

Sarena rolled her eyes. "I'm still willing to fight for the Tide District. I helped get Merama into a higher district so that she'd have more power over their laws!"

"Yeah, and then you cranked this album out so that people would forget you got involved in politics in the first place." Jasper took another sip. "You're welcome for our help with that, by the way. Did you have any plans on how to help them if we hadn't come along?"

Sarena pursed her lips. "I do donate to the hospitals and stuff down there."

"And you always turn it into a PR day."

"Is that so bad? That people see me doing it? There's usually a spike in donations after I visit a place. And it encourages other celebrities to do similar stuff."

Jasper pointed a finger at her. "You're not wrong. You have had a positive impact on the world, in some cases. But are you doing it because you care, or for the positive attention?"

Sarena was quiet for a long moment. Then, she said, "Don't you think it can be a mix of both? Don't act like none of the good stuff you've accomplished didn't come from selfish motives."

Despite the accuracy of the dig, Jasper smirked. "You're not wrong there, either. I'm having a hard time figuring out if you're selfish in a mentally deranged detached-from-reality kind of way, or in a normal person way. You've been famous since you were a teenager. That doesn't exactly lend itself to healthy emotional development."

"But I lived in the Tide District before that!" Sarena protested. "I still understand what it's like to be a normal person."

"Well, first of all, the lyrics on your last few albums beg to differ. I think I recall a song dedicated to just listing off how much all your jewelry costs?" Jasper put a hand on her hip. "Second, Sarena, I did a little digging. You grew up in the Tide District because your dad *owned* a factory down there. You were wealthier than most people around you. And you had a better outcome than the other mutants because he took you to an upper district hospital."

Sarena's hands tightened into fists at her side. "It still wasn't as glamorous as life in the upper districts."

"Oh, I'm sorry, I didn't realize it was a competition."

Sarena hesitated. Then asked, "Why are you interrogating me about this? I already told you I'm willing to keep helping. Why do you care what my motives are?"

"I'm trying to get you all in on this. Part of me thinks you genuinely aren't capable of actually doing anything that could shatter the life you have right now."

"Are you calling me a coward?"

"Yes."

"But I've been helping you morons!"

"Begrudgingly. But you won't let us use your full potential. And I'm pretty sure you only hang around us because you're still afraid of Skybreaker."

Sarena's eyes narrowed. "What do you mean by 'full potential?'"

"If you'd revealed yourself as Sarena Trench at that protest instead of pretending to be some rando singing her music, it would have been a lot more inspiring for those people."

"Yeah, and Starr could've had me arrested for escalating a protest."

"That's the cost of making things better. If you aren't willing to put your status on the line, you're never going to make any real change for the Tide District."

Sarena rolled her eyes. "Uh huh. Got any other brilliant ideas on living up to my full potential?"

"If you were more vocal about taking action against the upper districts, it wouldn't be you standing alone. The other elite might not side with you, but you have a rabid fanbase that includes young people in the upper districts who haven't completely fallen in line with their parents' way of life."

Sarena lifted an eyebrow. "You think those whackos can actually be useful?"

"They've gotten people fired, for starters. Editors who said critical things about you, even wealthy ones at big publishing companies with a lot of status," Jasper pointed out. "Granted, most of them were just moved away from front-facing positions, but still. And that was all without any direct command from you." After taking another sip of her drink, she added, "Imagine if you straight up told your fans to, say, boycott the big chain stores until they increase employee wages. Or to vote for the people running against the incumbent families. Or to harass politicians until they pass laws increasing health care budgets for the lower districts!"

Jasper sort of hated the idea that so many people would only take steps to make change if their favorite pop star they'd convinced themselves would be their best friend given the chance told them to, but she had to work with what tools she had.

"Hell," she continued. "You could probably incite a riot if you really wanted."

Sarena turned her head, her gaze settling on Blitz in his tank.

"So, the question still stands. Are you a villain? Are you a pop star? Or are you a revolutionary like you claim?" Jasper folded her arms. "Or are you just whatever's trending?"

"I'm whatever's *fun*." Sarena looked at Jasper again. "I like being a performer. And I like being a villain."

"Well then, why don't you take a break from reading mean reviews about your album and come help us smash some stuff?"

Chapter Forty-Two
Deals With Devils

Under a glittering night sky—overshadowed by much brighter and shinier city lights—Janus hefted the weapon Meg had given her over her shoulder. It was apparently called a W-F7. Rather uncreative, in her opinion, so she'd decided to name it Starfeller.

Now, it was time to find out what the thing actually did.

Janus took a step forward, bringing herself to the edge of the roof, and peered down into the many layers of Kronos. Many of these people would die in the coming months. But if all went according to plan, those who survived would find themselves in a world run by Skybreaker. An absolute power who would tear down the elite and force order upon a chaotic system. The people wouldn't save themselves, so she'd save them instead.

Assuming she could win this war. Or, more accurately, if she could lead all of the forces looming over the Janus System to lose. Starr's army, the Interstar Council, and...*her.*

Speaking of *her*, Janus had a job to do. She cracked her neck and brought the list of names Meg had given her into a visual overlay. The name on the list that she now found most surprising was a man named Omic Attom. Head editor of a "news" site called Starchatter. Well, former head editor. He'd been forced to step down last season to avoid a boycotting of the company by enraged Sarena Trench fans after an article attacking her had been posted under his name.

But he hadn't truly faced any punishment. While his name could no longer be found anywhere on Starchatter's net page, he played just as much a role in their publications as he had before. In fact, he'd technically been promoted behind the scenes. Pay raise and everything. *Elite bastard.* Even when they screwed up, they got richer and more powerful. Not that she really considered writing a mean article about Sarena Trench worthy of punishment, but it was the principle of the thing.

Sarena Trench's name was also on the list, along with Captain Cora of course, and a few prominent gang members. Meg, like Janus, must have figured out that Sarena Trench was South Siren.

Starfeller still on her shoulder, Janus stepped over the edge of the roof and dropped onto a hovering billboard. As it dipped slightly from the force of her landing, she changed the overlay on her mind's screen to a camera feed. She flipped through tapped security cameras from around the upper districts, focusing on popular elite party spots.

While she searched, she hopped from the billboard to a skywalk and traversed the railing for a minute, ignoring odd looks from people crossing the walkway correctly. As she reached a corner and jumped from the railing to a lower rooftop, she finally spotted Attom in one of the camera feeds. He sat at a bar, chatting with a few other people in suits.

The feed was attached to a club called Moonbrews, roughly a ten-minute walk from where Janus stood now. Ten minutes at her pace, anyway. Ten minutes of darting between buildings, across skywalks and billboards and the occasional piece of construction equipment, sometimes even hopping across the roofs of vehicles hovering in traffic.

As she neared the club, she snagged a jacket with "Security" written in bold white letters on the back. The guard she took it from didn't even notice his jacket disappearing from the back of his chair in the bar he lounged in. Janus also found a pair of baggy black pants in a clothing store to throw on.

With both articles of clothing on top of her suit, the Skybreaker look that many people in the city would recognize was broken. Now, she was just a security guard with a motorcycle helmet and an unusually large blaster.

A few more minutes of walking brought Moonbrews into view. The glamorous club was shoved into a skyscraper between two other glamorous clubs. Janus wondered how the elite decided which fancy box of flashing lights and blasting music they would choose to buy overpriced drinks at on any given night.

She jumped down onto one of the building's balconies, startling a few drunk elites searching for a new bar to hang out at, and strolled up to the club's entrance. She nodded to the bouncer as she passed him. He nodded in return and continued assessing people in line. No alarms raised. Not a second glance given.

Attom still sat in the bar seat he'd been in when Janus first spotted him on cams. Rather than approaching him, she moved to a nearby wall in a dimmer section of the club. There, she stood unnoticed, practically a statue monitoring the party in near perfect stillness.

She watched Attom chat with other elites, a couple of whom she identified as fellow Starchatter executives. Boring. Thankfully, things got a little more interesting when that crowd left and Atttom remained behind. New people took over the empty seats. People who looked a little out of place in the upper district club. Rather than suits or dresses—or the casual, shimmery, but still clearly expensive clothing that younger elites tended to wear—the newcomers were dressed in white leathers. Some had gold accents in the form of jewelry and belts. The outfits were plain enough to not draw too much attention, but it was clear they weren't the typical upper district crowd.

On top of that, they only spoke to Attom for a few minutes before leaving the club. Janus lifted an eyebrow under her helmet as they walked out, wondering what the conversation had entailed. The men looked like they could have been gang members. Were they threatening Attom?

Whatever the reason for their visit, Attom didn't stick around for long after they left. Janus stepped away from the wall as he headed out of the bar and trailed him to the door.

Elites, of course, were above walking to get around. A sleek black hover vehicle picked Attom up outside, forcing Janus to come up with another way to follow him. Thankfully, there was a lot of traffic in the area, making it possible for her to trail the vehicle from rooftops and skywalks.

Attom was dropped off on a balcony circling Chroma Tower. He entered the building and made his way to an apartment door. It locked behind him, as Janus discovered when she reached it moments later. After glancing down the hall in both directions to check that no one was nearby, she lifted her cybernetic leg and kicked the door with as much force as she could muster. The lock cracked and the door swung open, slamming into the wall with a resounding thud.

Attom, who stood in the kitchen on the other side of the large couch and holoscreen projector that occupied the living space, whirled around in alarm, a drink in his hand. Janus used another kick to close the door again—though it didn't exactly sit right in its frame anymore—and took a step toward the man.

He wasn't alone in the apartment. Figures emerged from darkened doorways around the room and quickly surrounded Janus. Gang members. White leathers and gold jewelry. The various daggers and knives in their hands had golden handles, and that was enough for Janus to finally identify them.

"Slicers." Janus lifted an eyebrow. "They follow your orders?" The conversation at the bar hadn't been a threat, then. Maybe a status report or update of some sort.

"I own them," Attom said in a low growl. He took a sip of his drink, a dark blue liquid that Janus guessed was some sort of wine.

"Own them? Interesting phrasing." Janus slid Starfeller off her shoulder and let it fall into her other hand. Some of the Slicers moved closer, others lifted their weapons higher. A couple of blasters came out.

Attom ignored Janus's statement. "Who sent you?" he asked. "I wasn't aware anyone wanted me dead, at the moment. The Altairs have been satisfied with my prices, haven't they?"

On another night, Janus might have enjoyed dragging the conversation out, toying with him, but she was almost as much in the dark as he was. She had no idea why Meg wanted him dead—or if he was just a random target to test the weapon—and she had no idea if the Slicers were relevant to the job.

Janus shrugged. "Guess you're not as smart as you thought." She aimed the weapon. More blasters came out, along with a few demands for her to freeze. Several Slicers moved in front of Attom to block Janus's line of sight. Well, they were surprisingly loyal, she had to admit.

Her mind raced. If she fired at Attom and everyone fired at her, she'd only have a split second to dodge. She could do it. But she wanted to be able to focus on Attom, on the weapon and how it worked. The aftermath. So, deal with the Slicers first? At least, the biggest threats. Only seven of the roughly fifteen gang members had blasters out. She'd still have to move fast to ensure Attom didn't get away. But she could do it.

Janus slowly lowered Starfeller to the ground. Attom frowned. "Are you...surrendering?"

Her hand slipped into the stolen security jacket, to the pocket where she'd stashed a few throwing stars. A grin spread across her face under her helmet.

She sprang into action. Her smile still lingered as the throwing stars lodged themselves into arms and sliced open hands. Cries of pain echoed through the apartment. Janus went to another pocket, where she retrieved a few throwing knives and used them to knock the remaining few blasters from Slicer hands.

Maybe she could still have fun with her prey. Even if carrying out Meg's tasks was just a means to an end, a way to gain trust. The world was better off without Attom and these Slicers, anyway. No reason to feel bad that *some* of her goals just happened to align with...that woman's.

While the Slicers that she'd yet to hit scrambled for blasters, Janus snatched Starfeller back up and took aim at Attom. Slicers still attempted to shield him from her, and she only had a split second to make a decision. She fired, thinking that worst-case scenario, if the Slicers took the blow instead, she'd have time to fire a few more shots—

There was no need to fire again. No need at all. After she squeezed the trigger, there was a flash of iridescent light, a beam that completely swallowed Attom and two Slicers and threw pale shades of every color across the room.

When the light faded, Attom was gone. The Slicers had vanished with him. For a moment, all Janus could do was stare at the spot where they'd stood, stunned. Had that vaporized them entirely?

The floor and surrounding furnishings were untouched. The blast was incredibly well-tuned to only impact the target bodies. Did it only affect organic matter? Well, their clothes had gone with them, so maybe common clothing materials were included? Was that possible?

Janus was out of time for analysis. The other Slicers got over their momentary shock at Attom's disappearance and swarmed toward Janus. Damn. She'd hoped they might scatter if their leader was...killed? Apparently not.

Janus turned the weapon on the Slicers and began firing. Starfeller had more of a cooldown than she'd been expecting, but the nearly ten seconds she had to wait to fire again made sense, given the amount of power it had to be using for those blasts. She drew a small blaster from her side to deter Slicers from getting too close while she waited to be able to fire again.

Expecting that Starfeller would scare them off sooner rather than later, she attempted to catch as many as possible with each beam. Her second attack caught two, and the following three. After that, the rest of the gang members finally scattered. Some went out the window, others ran deeper into the apartment searching for other escape routes, and one even dove into a laundry chute. Janus pulled Starfeller's trigger a final time, and one last Slicer was caught in the beam before he could escape into a hallway. The beam also grazed an overhead light in a kitchen and made the bulb shatter.

That had been the only source of light on in the apartment. The weapon's iridescent light faded, and Janus was left alone in darkness and quiet.

Eight Slicers plus Omic Attom, all gone without a trace. She glanced down at the weapon in her hands, her night vision taking over. Was this similar to the tech Starr had been developing? Powered by energy from the spacetime warps? Or was there more to it?

Feeling uneasy for a reason she couldn't quite place, Janus hefted Starfeller back onto her shoulder and strolled to the window. One of the Slicers had left it open in their escape. Janus stepped out and hopped down onto a fire escape.

Starr. Meg. The council. Jasper Van Terra. People who all had their ideas about how things should be run. People who would not stop until they won or died.

Janus had only one path to take to ensure she took power, to ensure she could force the pieces of this broken system into order. But some pieces didn't belong. Some would have to be discarded.

One by one, she would strike her enemies down, until she was the most powerful person left standing. Until the world had no choice but to bow to her. Until the Janus System was ruled by the woman who'd taken its name as her own.

Chapter Forty-Three
Remember That Guy?

Jasper scribbled away on the holoscreen. The team was gathered around her in the living room, watching as she noted potential routes to the Lion's Den on the map of the city's various underground tunnels. Tunnels surrounding the spot where Holly had marked the Den's entrance.

"We should do some more recon in the area around it. Identify all the possible exits from this sublevel of the city." Jasper took a step back and assessed the work she'd done so far. "Thea, can you grab some more maps and see if there are any lower or higher tunnels intersecting this zone that don't appear here?" When a few moments passed without a response, she glanced toward Thea.

"Hm? Oh, yeah, maps, I'll grab those." Thea glanced up from her laptop. "I was just reading the news—you remember Omic Attom?"

Jasper's brow furrowed. "Yeah, from Starchatter?"

Sarena let out a hiss of disgust. "I hate that guy! He wrote a really mean article about me for last season."

"Actually, Jasper wrote—" Holly started.

"What happened to Attom?" Jasper cut her off.

"He's missing. Possibly been killed." The reflection of Thea's laptop screen scrolled in the window behind her. "Happened a couple hours ago, around midnight."

It was already two hours past midnight? The realization seemed to draw out the exhaustion Jasper had been subconsciously keeping at bay. After Holly had returned with the Lion's Den's location, all everyone had wanted to focus on was finalizing the details of their plan. Well, except maybe Sarena. But at least she was participating mostly without complaint.

"Witnesses say there was a commotion in his apartment and some flashes of bright light," Thea continued, still scrolling. "Then some people came out his windows. I've got security footage from his apartment complex loading…"

While the footage loaded, Thea connected her laptop to the smartsphere on the coffee table, temporarily replacing the holoscreen Jasper had been scribbling on. Moments later, video began playing. People came flying out of the windows of what was apparently Attom's apartment. People in white and gold, armed with daggers and blasters. One of them turned and fired a blast directly at the camera watching him, ending the clip.

"Looks like Slicers. Attom's gang." Jasper folded her arms. "Well, they won't talk to the police. If we want to know what happened, we'll have to ask them directly."

"Do we really care enough to look into this?" Cutthroat asked.

"Yeah," Sarena added, collapsing onto her back on the couch. "Let's just say 'good riddance' and move on."

"Attom may own a gang, but it still seems weird that he'd be killed so abruptly. Why now?" Jasper began to pace in front of the screen. "You said he was missing. Only possibly dead. They didn't find his body?"

Thea shook her head. "Nothing in the apartment but a little blood. And none of it was even identified as his, so it was probably from the Slicers, or maybe his attacker. He had security cameras in his apartment, but something disrupted their recording, allegedly." Her gaze darted to the final frame of the video displayed on the holoscreen. "No nearby cameras captured him leaving the rea, though."

"But we know he was inside the apartment when this happened?"

"He was seen on camera entering the apartment just minutes before the incident."

Jasper processed all of that for a few more moments before stopping and turning to face the rest of the team. "I want to investigate. At least try to talk to a few of those Slicers."

"You think you can get them to talk?" Grace asked skeptically.

"Yeah, I doubt they're big fans of yours," Holly added under her breath.

Jasper flung out her arms. "Seriously? Do you guys even know me? I get people who don't like me to talk all the time!"

"I still think it's a waste of time," Cutthroat said.

"Noted." Jasper rubbed her forehead. "I promise I won't take long. Once I get back, we can focus on the Den again. How about we break for the night and start fresh tomorrow afternoon?"

There were some grumbles of agreement—and snoring from Sarena, who'd dozed off on the couch. As the team began to disperse, Jasper realized Dax had also fallen asleep, huddled in a pile of blankets on the floor. Holly and Thea noticed, too, and moved to scoop him up off the floor.

Cutthroat glanced at them. "You going to grab Sarena too?

Jasper shrugged. "She'll be fine there."

Cutthroat grunted, a noise that sounded like agreement, and trudged off down the hall. Holly and Thea went next, carrying Dax.

Jasper glanced at Grace as they started down the hall behind the others. Grace's guest room now hosted Sarena, Cutthroat, and the handful of sirens and pirates that were staying here tonight instead of back on the Astronomer. Sarena had expressed annoyance at sharing the space but still accepted the arrangement surprisingly quickly. Jasper had expected her to return to her penthouse to sleep, but she was apparently more worried about Skybreaker killing her than she was about maintaining luxury.

The night before, after returning from the big show-off with Bruce, everyone had passed out on various pieces of furniture, with few having the energy to drag themselves to beds. Jasper could have gone to her room, but she'd stayed out in the living room, finding comfort in having everyone so close. Tonight, though, despite the hour being even later, they were all—well, almost all—moving into the actual bedrooms. Which meant she and Grace had to make a decision.

"I understand if you want space," Grace said, pausing before they could reach the door to Jasper's bedroom. "I don't mind going back out to the living room—"

"I'd rather not be alone," Jasper cut her off. She couldn't help but wince at herself. Quieter, she added, "I know I said that before, I'm just...still not quite over it."

Grace blinked at her. "Over it? Jasper, you were in prison! Not to mention everything else that happened to you. No one expects you to be over it."

Jasper nodded. Then, she grabbed her door, pushed it open, and slipped into the darkness. Grace pulled a smartsphere for light from her pocket as she followed. The door clicked shut behind her. In the far corner of the room, Rose was already snoring away in the smaller bed Jasper had ordered for her.

"Thank you," Jasper said quietly in response to Grace's statement as she settled onto the edge of her bed. Truth be told, even if they didn't have guests, she would have searched for the courage to ask Grace to keep staying in her room. She'd found the first night, when the entire team had stayed with her, more reassuring than she cared to admit.

But she didn't want to pressure them all into joining her. And despite the fact that her emotions felt like frayed rope—or maybe because of that—it was probably for the best that she try to make time to focus on things between her and Grace.

Grace circled the bed to the other side from Jasper and collapsed onto her back, wings extending slightly. She set the sphere on the nightstand, switched off its light, and moved her hand to her stomach. Her eyes drifted shut. With so many late nights, the team had picked up the habit of just crashing in their clothes, then changing and showering the following morning.

Jasper fell onto her own back. It was nice that the exhaustion would take her into sleep before her mind could wander into the worst of her memories, but her dreams weren't likely to be much better. At least this time she wouldn't be alone when she inevitably jolted awake.

"You mentioned you wanted me to practice more with the Comet tomorrow morning," Grace said, eyes still closed. "Should we put that off so you can try talking to Slicers?"

"We can do both," Jasper replied. "I'll have you fly me around to look for them. And possibly act as my getaway driver." Some of the tension eased from her muscles. Talking about mission stuff relaxed her slightly.

"You think they'll attack you?"

Jasper shrugged, though Grace couldn't see it. "Hopefully not. It'll definitely take some convincing to get them to talk, but if I can corner just a couple who were at Attom's apartment that night, the odds will be in my favor."

They didn't say anything else after that. Judging by the change in her breathing, Grace fell asleep almost immediately after. It didn't take Jasper long to follow.

She slept through the night and was startled to find sunlight on her face when her eyes next opened. She had no recollection of what she'd dreamed, only a vague sense of lingering anxiety. That faded quickly when she turned her head to find Grace looking at her.

"Feeling okay?" Grace asked.

Jasper nodded, a small smile finding its way onto her lips.

She gave Grace a quick kiss, despite knowing it was going to throw her body's nervous and circulatory systems out of whack for the next five or so minutes. Worth it. Grace went into the bathroom to change and quickly rinse off, and Jasper took her turn after.

They ventured out to the kitchen about half an hour later, Jasper dressed in a suit rather than the plainer black clothes she usually wore, with a very nice white coat on top. With Grace's help, she'd managed a braid that was almost as good as the ones Holly did.

Cutthroat was the only other person out in the living area, besides a still-sleeping Sarena on the couch. "Still going to investigate this Attom business?" he grumbled from behind his mug of coffee as Grace opened the fridge to search for a quick breakfast.

"I won't take long. Pinky prommy." Jasper held up her pinkie finger. Cutthroat's expression didn't change, and she wasn't sure if he simply didn't care, or if he was trying to mask befuddlement at the expression. The latter idea was more entertaining, so she went with that.

She and Grace gathered a few containers of fruit and energy bars before leaving the apartment and walking to the parking garage where the Comet waited, safely locked up and defended by its outer shell. Other flying craft were parked here, albeit much rougher looking, but at least the small ship didn't stand out too much.

Grace hopped in the pilot's seat, and Jasper settled in at her right. As she tore open an energy bar, she said, "Alrighty, take us to Starchatter. We'll start there."

"You think the employees will know something?" Grace asked as she started the engine.

"Probably not, but there might be Slicers hanging around."

Grace guided them out of the garage without hitting anything. Once they were in the sky, she kept to the edges of the city's air traffic, giving herself some leeway to take wider turns and move at a slower pace as she continued to adjust to the ship's controls. Still, she was doing pretty good for someone who had never driven or flown anything until a few days ago.

Finally, she slowed to a stop in front of the building that housed the Starchatter offices. "Should I park us somewhere nearby?"

Jasper shook her head and rose to her feet. "Stay in the area and practice flying. Try and get comfortable moving at faster speeds in tighter areas."

Grace nodded. "You'll call if you need help?"

"Of course." Jasper hopped out of the ship, crossed the balcony into the building, and made her way to Starchatter's reception desk.

As she approached the desk, the blue-furred man on the other side—with tall ears that resembled a rabbit's—glanced up. Jasper also noticed a few "security guards" leaning against a wall close by, not looking terribly professional. They wore white shirts and pants under their black jackets, and had an above-average amount of gold jewelry on their hands, fingers, ears, necks...

Jasper shoved her hands into the pocket of her coat and leaned down toward the receptionist. "Hi, I had a meeting with Mr. Attom scheduled, though I understand he's...no longer around. Is there someone else I can speak to?"

Brow furrowing, the man began typing on his keyboard. The holoscreen in front of him scrolled slowly. "Hmm. What was the meeting about? I don't see anything on the schedule for today. He was supposed to be over at the Crystal District office to handle some business there."

Jasper lowered her voice but still kept it loud enough for the guards to overhear. "It was of a more...sensitive nature, regarding another business of his. My apologies, you might not be the right person to talk to. Is the head of security around?"

The receptionist let his gaze dart to the guards behind Jasper. The sound of footsteps followed a moment later. She turned as one of the Slicers reached her side.

"I'm part of Attom's security team," the man said. He looked like he had a fair amount of East Kronosian in him, with a strong red tinge to his light skin and curls of pale hair falling to his shoulders. His eyes were mostly black, too, though they were interrupted by green irises. "Can I help you with something?"

So, they were still monitoring Starchatter after Attom's disappearance and possible death. Did they believe he wasn't dead? Or was someone else paying to keep them around now? There were plenty of vultures in the upper districts who wouldn't let a dead man's business go to waste.

Jasper picked one of the potential lies she'd come up with on the flight over. "I was, uh, gathering some information for Attom. Seems I was too late."

"Maybe it can still help us figure out what happened."

Jasper turned her body to fully face him. "I can share what I know. Though, I'd like to know exactly what happened to Attom. I might be able to piece together who was behind this. Is there anyone who was with him that night that I can talk to?"

The man didn't even hesitate. "Yeah, you can talk to some of the guys. Let's talk at Attom's apartment."

Jasper's brow furrowed. That easy? The Slicers must have been desperate for information. Though, they'd never struck her as the most cunning of the gangs. Without a leader, they'd likely become disorganized, and maybe even a little panicked. Still, something didn't feel quite right as she followed the Slicers out of Starchatter's offices. But there were only three men accompanying her. Easy fight, if it came to that.

They led her to a flying car parked in a nearby lot. As she circled around to climb in the back, she muttered into her comm, "Angel, I'm sending my location. Follow at a distance."

Chapter Forty-Four
Shut Up and Fly

The Slicers flew Jasper to Chroma Tower, where a short walk on a balcony brought them to Attom's apartment. "Any police still crawling around?" Jasper asked as one of the Slicers procured a key card and swiped it.

"Nah, we convinced them to wrap up their investigation early this morning," another replied as the door swung open. The group entered. A Slicer on Jasper's right tapped a button on the wall as he passed it, turning on a handful of the overhead lights.

"Now, before we get too far, why don't you start telling us whatever it was you were supposed to report to Attom?" The curly-haired man who'd initially approached Jasper stopped in the middle of the entry space and turned to face her.

"I'm a private investigator of sorts, you could say," Jasper told him. "Attom thought someone might be planning to either abduct or kill him, so he asked me to look into it."

The man folded his arms. Lifted an eyebrow. "Uh huh."

Jasper got the feeling he didn't believe her. She opened her mouth to continue, but before she could get another word out, the faintest sound reached her ears. The brushing of a boot against floor, maybe. Whatever it was, it made Jasper instinctively switch to x-ray vision and scan the space.

Just as she processed the sight of a dozen more bodies hidden behind doors and around corners, down hallways and behind distant furniture, they began to move. Jasper let her vision return to normal as Slicers poured into the living room. Behind her, the front door opened again. She glanced back and watched a few more men come in to block off her exit.

A trap.

Jasper turned again, cursing under her breath as she counted the men. She wouldn't have been too worried a few months ago, but her strength had noticeably faded since taking ThetaEight. She still had more strength than an ordinary human, her cybernetic brain components, and a couple of enhanced limbs, but it was hard to remember sometimes that she didn't quite have the same odds in a fight that she used to.

Of course, her enemies didn't know that. Not yet, anyway.

"Van Terra," the apparent leader said, a smug smile touching his lips. "It's exciting to meet you. I believe some of the men here were present during the fight you started at Starchatter offices a little while back."

Jasper shot him a glare. "How did you know it was me? I'm in disguise!"

"We've been looking for you. The whole gang's on high alert."

Damn. "Guess this was a bad day to skip makeup."

The leader chuckled and gestured toward one of the Slicers standing behind him. "One of my friends here has an x-ray vision chip implant, and he's got the best software in intelligent skeletal identification. Knows your bone structure pretty well."

"Creep," Jasper muttered. She'd have to think up a way to combat that, in case she had reason to worry about others with the ability in the future. A realistic face mask with metal hidden inside, maybe? She folded her arms, eyes narrowing as she lifted her chin. "Wait, so you figured out who I was and let me do my whole spiel anyway? Seriously?"

The leader shrugged. "We had to lure you here. We've got some questions, Van Terra." He folded his arms. "My friend with the x-ray vision? He was here with Attom when he was attacked. And while the attacker was wearing a helmet, underneath, she apparently looked identical to you."

"Ah, I see." Jasper lifted her hands. "There's been a bit of a misunderstanding. That was probably my evil clone."

"You expect us to believe that?"

"It's true! The governor cloned me in a secret lab!"

"Now you're just being ridiculous."

Jasper groaned. "Listen, dude, I have no reason to lie to you. I came looking because I was curious about what happened to Attom. Why would I come to you guys if I were the one who'd attacked him?"

The leader glanced at the Slicer he'd gestured to earlier. X-ray Guy. "What do you think?"

X-ray Guy shrugged. "Van Terra's motives usually don't make sense, from what I've heard."

"If you tell me what happened, I can help you guys track down the real attacker. I've been trying to take her down for a while." Jasper kept her hands up, not wanting the Slicers to think she was reaching for weapons.

"Let's take her to the holding room, for now," Leader Guy said. "I'll call Jupitrell and see what he wants us to do." He glanced at Jasper. "Why don't you give us some more info about this supposed evil clone of yours, and if we find proof she exists, we'll consider working with you."

Jupitrell? The name sounded a little familiar, but Jasper couldn't place it. She let her hands drop to her sides and rolled her eyes as some of the Slicers moved into the kitchen. "I'm very busy, you know. I don't have time to sit around all day while you make a futile attempt to find her."

"This isn't a request, Van Terra," Leader Guy said. "You're in our custody."

"Is that a polite way of saying you're taking me hostage?"

Leader Guy didn't respond. Instead, he glanced toward the kitchen. One of the Slicers opened a cupboard and twisted a knob inside. A thud came from behind the fridge, and as a Slicer woman pulled the appliance forward, a hidden door slid open in the wall.

Jasper raised an eyebrow as Slicers surrounded her and guided her toward the dark opening. The Slicer's base, maybe? Hidden among luxury elite apartments? Bold choice, for a gang. Especially a smaller, newer one.

Jasper probably should have felt more concern at being taken captive, but she was still relatively close to escape routes, had weapons hidden in her coat, and wasn't too awfully outnumbered. And she was still determined to get one of the gang members to tell her what they'd witnessed.

Had Skybreaker really been the one to attack Attom? Why? And if she had killed him, what had she done with the body?

Jasper was led into a room made up of concrete walls and floors. Cold white lights glowed overhead. A desk and chair were set up in one corner, with a few filing cabinets standing nearby. The Slicers guided her to a different corner and plopped her down in a metal folding chair.

Leader Guy, meanwhile, flipped a switch next to the room's opening, and the wall slid back into place. Then, he pulled a smartsphere from his jacket and moved to the other side of the room to talk to someone quietly.

Jasper waved a hand, catching the attention of X-ray Guy. "Hey, dude, could you please tell me what happened last night? Anything you saw might help me find the real attacker."

X-ray Guy folded his arms and shook his head. "Not until I get the go-ahead."

Other Slicers spread out around them, none seeming particularly interested in listening to what Jasper was saying, though they had blasters at the ready if she caused trouble. She leaned toward X-ray Guy and lowered her voice. "You have to get permission just to tell me what you saw?"

The man's eyes narrowed.

Jasper leaned back and shrugged. "Some command structure you've got there."

"You're not going to bait me, Van Terra," X-ray Guy said. "I have no interest in telling you what happened unless I'm ordered to."

"I'll tell you and you alone about my clone. *You'll* be the one who pried information out of *me*."

She saw it. The briefest flash of hesitation in his gaze. She decided to offer a little more bait to sweeten the deal.

"Did you pay close attention to what she was wearing?" Jasper asked. "She may have been in disguise, but I assure you you've heard of her. Skybreaker."

That piqued his interest. "Your clone is Skybreaker?"

Jasper nodded. "If you tell me a little more about what happened, I can tell you for sure whether it was her."

X-ray Guy glanced at one of his nearby colleagues. The other man shot Leader Guy—who was still deep in conversation—a glance, then returned his gaze to X-ray Guy and shrugged.

X-ray Guy let out a resigned sigh. "There's...not much to tell, anyway. A person with a skeleton and face that I recall being identical to yours came crashing through the front door while Attom was in the kitchen."

Jasper raised an eyebrow. "Do you spend all your time in x-ray mode?"

"Decent amount." The man shrugged before continuing. "Now that I think about it, she was wearing a security guard's uniform, but that helmet she was wearing—yeah, I guess it could have been Skybreaker. Anyway, all of the posted guards came out to defend Attom. The attacker had this massive blaster. And when she fired it, the beam was...huge. And...shimmery?" A hint of fear had crept into the Slicer's voice. "Everyone caught in the beam just...vanished. Nothing left behind."

"Like they were vaporized?"

"I guess." The man grew visibly more uncomfortable. "I don't know."

Another warp energy-powered weapon, maybe? Something the team hadn't seen yet? Brow furrowing, Jasper said, "News said that apartment security footage was blank during the time of the attack."

"We wiped it ourselves," the man admitted. "Can't have word of Attom's connection to the Slicers getting out."

Jasper had guessed as much. She yawned and leaned back in her chair. "Well, all I can tell you is that the same lab that made my cybernetics cloned me and unleashed her on the world. She's been trying to kill me for some time now. Not sure where she got this new weapon or why she'd go after Attom, though."

"And she's Skybreaker?" X-ray Guy asked.

Jasper nodded slowly. Then, abruptly, she jumped to her feet. Slicers jumped into action, but she didn't even give them a chance to take aim. As she raced through the room, dodging when her internal computer warned of blasts that were coming a little too close, she shouted, "Thanks for the chat!"

A few Slicers waited by the door, of course, thinking they'd be able to deter her. She got in close before any had a chance to fire. A flip of the switch made the door start opening again. A dagger slipped from her jacket into her hand, and then she was swiping with blinding speed.

It took longer than it once would have for her to drop all of the Slicers around the door. By the time they were down, the next wave had almost reached her. She darted out into Attom's apartment and raced toward the exit. Footsteps warned that the Slicers were pursuing. Jasper tapped her comm as she ran. "I need extraction. I'm headed for the west side of the Chroma Tower."

"On the way," Grace said. "Uh, what level are you coming out of?"

"A few down from the top. I'll be on a balcony."

She'd lost some of the speed she'd once had, too, but she was still fast enough to just keep ahead of the gang. Her main concern was blaster beams coming at her from behind. She relied on her audio detectors to warn her when she needed to dodge. As more and more weapons fired, the world around her slowed. She slowed, too, but it let her think about how she was going to react, let her focus on how to get out of each beam's path without running into another.

She made it to the edge of the building and turned the balcony's corner. "Angel? Just hit the northwest corner—"

The Comet came soaring up from below and jerked to a painfully abrupt halt next to the balcony. Jasper climbed up onto the railing. As she jumped onto the ship's wing, its door slid open. More blasters fired behind her. She dove in.

Jasper slammed into the floor with a painful thud and a groan.

"Jasper!" Grace exclaimed, glancing back from the pilot's seat. "You okay?"

"Fine," Jasper replied as she climbed to her feet. Her breaths came hard and fast as she staggered into the cockpit.

"What happened?" Grace pushed one of the levers, guiding the ship away from the building and toward air traffic.

"Well, I was able to hear from a Slicer what happened. After a bunch of them took me hostage." Jasper settled into the other chair. "But hey, at least I know where a Slicer base is, now." Might be too much to hope the space connected to the apartment was their main headquarters, but there could be information leading to their HQ somewhere in there. A problem for another day, maybe.

They'd barely reached the end of the block when the roar of a new engine joined the sound of traffic. Jasper craned her neck to glance out toward the rear of the ship. A white ship with gold accents, similar in size to the Comet, had emerged from a parking bay in Chroma Tower.

"The Slicers have a ship?" Jasper exclaimed as the craft started toward them.

Grace's eyes went wide with panic. She kept them moving forward in a straight line, and they weren't moving anywhere close to the ship's top speed.

"Angel..." Jasper said, a warning in her tone as she brought up the Comet's rear-view camera for a better look at their pursuers.

"They're chasing us! What do I do?"

"Fly!"

Grace's hands squeezed the wheel. Jaw clenched, she said, "No shit! Where do I go?"

There was something weirdly satisfying about hearing Grace curse so aggressively. Jasper grinned. "Well, I guess this is as good a time as any to teach you evasive maneuvers."

"Some less dangerous practice first would be nice! Why don't you take control?"

"You got this!" Jasper rested a hand on Grace's shoulder. "The key here is going to be frequent, sharp turns. If you can get around enough buildings fast enough, you'll eventually lose them. And go faster!"

Grace pushed the throttle to its limit. They shot forward. Jasper yelped.

"You said faster!" Grace protested as Jasper's grip on her shoulder tightened.

"Yeah, no, this is great!" Jasper's voice rose with her reply as Grace took a sharp turn. The shift sent Jasper knocking against her. As soon as she was able to get herself upright again, Jasper pulled herself all the way back into her seat and yanked her seatbelt on.

Grace immediately took a turn in the opposite direction. Jasper caught another glimpse of the Slicer ship in the rear camera as the Comet moved behind another building.

"Good start," Jasper said. "Just keep making maneuvers like that, as fast as you can."

Another sharp right seemed to put them even further ahead of the other ship. A slow smile spread across Grace's face. "I think I'm getting the hang of this!"

Another corner. And then they were nearly colliding with air traffic crossing in front of them. Grace yelped and pulled up. Jasper wasn't sure if she'd intended to pull on the control wheel as hard as she had, but it sent them veering straight up for only a moment, and then backwards, nearly upside down.

Jasper opened her mouth to give Grace more advice, but Grace pulled another maneuver before she could get a single word out. The ship twisted in mid-air, righting itself, and made another sharp turn, narrowly missing the side of a glittering gold skyscraper.

"You've got good reflexes," Jasper said with a grin. She gave Grace's shoulder a reassuring squeeze.

"Thanks." Grace shot her a brief look to return the smile before returning her gaze out the front window. "You'd do better, though." She sent them soaring upward again. Below them, the Slicer ship came flying out from the street below and went tumbling into the traffic stream Grace had narrowly avoided. Vehicles honked and swerved to avoid collision.

"Well, in my defense, I have a computer in my brain," Jasper replied as she watched the Slicer ship struggle to right itself. "This kind of thing came naturally to me."

"Ah, so you cheated?" Grace twisted the wheel.

Jasper smirked. "Getting a good hand isn't cheating." Especially when the guy who gave you said hand sliced your palm up in the process. And broke your wrist. And rubbed salt in your wounds, for good measure.

"Fair enough." Grace glanced at the rear camera screen, which revealed the Slicer ship was coming their way again. She turned left, then made another immediate left. When their pursuers came down the same street, they'd be forced to guess which direction Grace had gone after.

Unfortunately, they chose correctly. Grace cursed.

"You're doing great!" Jasper tried to assure her.

"I'm clearly doing a bad job, if they're still on us!"

"You're fine. These guys are pretty good pilots." Jasper leaned forward. "It's time we brought out the Comet's secret weapon."

"Which is?"

"A weapon." Jasper slid open a panel, revealing a keypad. She punched in a string of numbers, hoping she'd recalled them correctly. To her relief, the light above the keys flashed green, and a nearby panel slid aside to reveal a new set of controls.

While the massive blaster emerged from the ship's roof, Jasper checked the cams. "They're getting too close. If I hit them at full blast, the shrapnel could hit us." She shot Grace a quick glance. "I need you to swerve up when I tell you. Too soon, and they'll follow our trajectory. Too late, and, well—"

"We die?"

"No, not die. Probably. Just risk injury. And ruining the Comet."

"You sound more worried about the ship than the 'potential injury' part."

"Nah…" Jasper leaned forward and lined the Slicer ship up in her sights on the blaster's control screen. "Though as far as my concerns go, I'd say it's a pretty close second." She threw another glance at Grace. "To my safety, anyway. Yours is far above any dumb ol' ship."

"Stop being sappy and shoot them already." Grace seemed to be trying to hide the grin creeping onto her face.

Jasper laughed. "All right. Pull up in three…two…"

Grace's hands tightened on the wheel.

"One!"

Jasper pressed the fire button, and the ship jerked upward. Behind them, the sound of blaster fire was followed by an explosion. Jasper had hit something important. Maybe a few somethings.

As the smoke faded on the camera screen, she spotted a few parachutes popping into view. The Slicers had decided to abandon ship and escape with their lives. The remains of the ship careened onto a nearby rooftop, coming to a smoking halt. Jasper breathed a small sigh of relief, grateful they wouldn't have to run interference on a ship crashing through the city.

Grace let out a shaky breath. Her shoulders sagged. "We in the clear?"

"Yup." Jasper hit the button that would retract the blaster back into the ship.

"I did okay?"

"You did amazing." Jasper leaned back in her seat and sighed. "Side quest complete."

Chapter Forty-Five
Mistlefoe

Grace anxiously paced in the living room while the others finished getting ready. Sliding on coats, packing up bags, speculating on how the night would go.

She wasn't nervous about the attack on the Lion's Den. In fact, she wished that's what they were doing tonight. But that would take place tomorrow. Tonight was all about her. Well, Superangel. She was far less nervous than she had been when she'd first started using her superhero persona, but all this talk of revolution and uprising in the streets had her second-guessing herself.

Tonight's not about fighting, she reminded herself. *It's about helping people.*

The others were loading up bags with food, not weapons. The food they'd gathered was mostly canned or packaged goods with a long shelf life. Things packed with nutrients, though they may not have exactly been on the tasty side. Hopefully, if the upcoming turmoil hurt food production or otherwise stressed the supply chain, this would help. It was all stuff stolen from upper district emergency storage, so it came with the double purpose of taking away the safety net the elite could fall back on if their workers began striking.

Grace wore her Superangel costume. Jasper wore a Santa costume, and she'd convinced most of the others to wear elf costumes. The exception was Rose, who also insisted on wearing a Santa costume. She and Jasper had matching red-and-white outfits and fake white beards. Even if it was a bit silly-looking, it at least lowered the chances anyone would recognize Jasper.

Grace still didn't understand the whole Santa thing. From what Jasper had told her, many people on Earth convinced their children that the powerful being traveled the world delivering gifts, only to then have to tell them once they were older that it was all a lie and the gifts came from the parents. Why not just give your children gifts? Jasper was insistent it was about the "Magic of Christmas," but Grace still didn't quite get it.

Sarena entered the room with Blitz on her shoulder, her outfit not quite as elf-ish as the rest, but she'd at least committed to lots of red and green and a pair of pointed shoes with bells on them. A fluorescent pink crustacean slipped from the Blitz's tentacle into his mouth as the two passed through the doorway.

Jasper, meanwhile, set down the bag she'd been packing with canned meat and walked over to Grace. Her brow furrowed as she approached. "Are you still...nervous being Superangel?"

Grace shook her head. "It's not that really. Just...what if..." She sucked in a sharp breath. "What if I inspire these people to revolt and they all get killed? Their blood will be on my hands!"

Part of her expected immediate reassurance from Jasper, but Jasper hesitated. "I don't know what will happen. Taking to the streets to fight against Starr—it is dangerous. People likely will die. But with all the suffering happening in the lower districts, with or without us, this revolution will happen eventually. We're just giving them our help. And a little inspiration."

"I guess." Grace sighed. "But...I still don't know if I can handle being the person they look to."

"We aren't forcing people to fight," Jasper said softly. "Everyone who joins the battle will have made that choice. Many of them will choose it over the slow and persistent suffering they already face, in hopes there's something better on the other side. You can only push people so far before they break." A distance crept into her gaze.

Grace nodded, all the horrible news stories from the past few months rolling through her mind. When you'd lost your home, your job, any hope of a future under the current system, what were your choices? Accept suffering and death?

Or fight. Fight until you died or won something better. If your life was misery anyway, why not at least try?

Jasper shook her head, as if she were shaking off old memories, and lifted her chin. Loud enough for the whole room to hear, she asked, "Everyone about ready? Sun's already going down."

Well, one sun was down. Gemma, the star closest to Kronos right now. The Janus system's other sun, Myni, was a distant spot in the dark sky, an extraordinarily bright star. Grace cast it a quick glance as she followed the group out of the apartment. As the team strolled to where the Comet waited, Jasper gave them some reminders.

"In the lower districts, our focus is telling them something big is coming. A movement against Starr. Real action, not just words and protests that lead to nothing," she said. "In the middle districts, we need to convince them they should side with the lower city, not the upper. The elite have convinced them their lives will be better if they stay in line, and things are decent enough for them that they don't face the same pressure to revolt. But things *could* be better for them, too.

"We need to find every weakness in the system—increasing bills, worsening job market, less help with medical care—and convince the people that those things can be fixed," Jasper continued. "Show them that the middle districts are edging closer to becoming like the lower districts than the upper."

Grace studied Christmas decorations as they walked. She'd seen far more extravagant lights and trees and odd statues—nutcrackers, Jasper had called them?—in the upper districts, but there was a lot of effort being put in down here, too. With just about a week left until the holiday, festivities had ramped up to a maximum.

For the first hour or so, they split into groups, delivering smaller family-sized bags of food to apartment complexes. Grace flew around while the others walked, save for Jasper, who flew in the Comet while Rose tossed packages out the hatch onto porches.

In slightly more social parts of the city, the team regrouped and found public parties to distribute food at. Cafes, restaurants, bars, and other gathering places hosted public parties with music, games, and whatever small amounts of food and drink they felt they could let go for free.

Around here, when the team began spreading whispers of looming revolution, the people were willing to listen. Some hesitant, some eager, but all willing.

As they moved up through the city, though, trying to talk to people got trickier. Their fear of losing what they had outweighed their desire to earn more. Sure, change could bring them higher wages, a better support system, improve the nearby transport lines and medical care. But they weren't starving *yet*, weren't dying of curable illnesses *yet*, weren't unable to afford small luxuries *yet*.

The team moved on to a beach-themed restaurant—with Santa hats on cardboard cutouts of marine animals and string lights wrapped around fake palm trees—and began passing out bags as they had earlier, offering similar words of advice. *Prepare yourselves. Revolution is coming.*

Once Grace had unloaded the duffel bag she'd brought from the most recent trip to the Comet for supplies, she joined Jasper at the edge of the restaurant's main dining space. Jasper observed the crowd, waiting for the right moment to jump in.

Grace's gaze flitted upward, and she frowned. "What's that?"

"Huh?" Jasper noticed where she was looking and followed. A sly grin crossed her lips. "You've never seen mistletoe?"

Grace shook her head. "Why would they hang leaves from the ceiling in a random spot?"

Jasper opened her mouth to reply, but they were cut off by Holly's voice over comms. "Hey, Jasper, we ready to talk to these people? They're not gonna hang around forever."

Jasper turned to where Thea stood nearby and said, loud enough to send a hush through the crowd, "Thea, I believe you had some notes you wanted to share?"

Thea set a smartsphere on one of the tables. One tap of a button lowered the volume of the holiday music playing throughout the restaurant. The next tap brought up a massive holoscreen with a graph. The speech she'd repeated so many times that night already began again. "This starcycle, each of the wealthiest four elite families made more individually than everyone in the middle and lower districts combined. A few families below them come pretty close. And Syrus Starr's salary by itself tops the chart."

"The median income of this area is far closer to that of the lower districts," Thea continued as she pointed to a section of the graph, "than anywhere near the lowest-earning families in the upper districts."

Grace glanced around. Some people gathered near the table still looked skeptical—one guy in a Captain Cora jacket even looked annoyed—but many were nodding slowly.

"Think about it," Thea went on. "You could help the elite beat down the lower districts, or you could help the lower districts demand better wages and fairer laws that would improve your own lives more than you'd expect.

"But media made by the upper districts focuses your attention on the lower. Things are so much worse down there, it makes you feel great by comparison. On top of that, you're convinced that if you work hard enough, you could become one of the elite—"

Gasps and shouts came from the direction of the door, cutting Thea off. Grace turned with the rest of the team, alarm coursing through her.

Captain Cora stood in the doorway, a sack over his shoulder and surprise on his face.

Chapter Forty-Six
Someone's Halls Are Getting Decked

Jasper's instinct was to lunge at Bruce, but she held herself back. This was Grace's fight. Though, the thought of footage of Captain Cora fighting Santa spreading across the net was pretty funny…

Grace sprang into action. Sword drawn, wings spread, she launched herself at Bruce. A few people in the room chanted Captain Cora's name, but they were quickly drowned out by people cheering for Superangel. Civilians moved into cramped clusters against the walls, but many weren't too scared to lift spheres and tablets and begin recording.

Bruce tossed aside the sack he'd been carrying. It hit the floor, and bottles of expensive drinks spilled out and rolled across the tile. He'd had a very different idea in mind for gifts to bring to the people. Not a bad gesture, necessarily, but not nearly as practical for people going through hard times. His instinct was still to reach for his blaster, but Grace got in close too fast for it to do him any good. He was able to use it to block a few swings of her sword, but he soon tossed it aside and drew a new weapon. A baton.

It didn't matter much that he clearly wasn't used to close combat with a skilled opponent. His armor withstood the blows from Grace's sword with nothing more than a few scratches. Enough force and time might let her get through eventually, but she'd likely need to switch tactics soon.

Jasper drew a blaster of her own and took aim, waiting for a chance to disable Bruce so that Grace could end the fight. Her mind was already contemplating what they might do after. Take Bruce prisoner? They'd have to ensure he had no weapons or armor, no chance of escaping, if they were going to keep him alive…

A nearby window exploded, and a figure hit the ground, rolled, then sprang to their feet. As the figure rose to their full height, Jasper cursed, overcome by a mix of surprise and fear. What the hell was Skybreaker doing here?

Bruce pointed his arm blaster at her. "Skybreaker. I thought we might meet eventually, but you've been so quiet lately."

Skybreaker raised a weapon of her own, a massive blaster completely unlike anything Jasper had never seen before. It didn't even resemble the high-powered blasters Starr's engineers had designed to run on warp energy. Grace's eyes went wide, and she stumbled backwards away from Bruce.

Skybreaker pulled the trigger. Blinding white light flooded the room. Jasper squeezed her eyes shut against it, and shimmering iridescence danced in her otherwise dark vision.

When her eyes opened, Bruce Wright was gone.

Jasper turned her attention on Skybreaker, trying to mask her surprise. And the dread creeping in. Something about that weapon's blast...

She shook off her discomfort and forced a grin. "Sky, where the hell have you been? I was starting to worry about you."

Skybreaker's expression was unreadable under that helmet. She hefted the weapon onto her shoulder and sighed. "Grim, take it from here."

Another crash came Jasper's right, making her turn as Grim Machine tore through the wall between the restaurant and the shop next door. Grimbots poured into the room behind him. Grim Machine and Skybreaker? Working together? When had that happened?

The other members of the team emerged from the crowd and gathered behind Jasper. Grace hurried over, too, keeping an eye on Grim Machine as he shook off rubble.

Cutthroat drew a blaster from his coat. His attention was on Skybreaker, who watched the team with a cocked head, seemingly waiting for them to make a move. "What the hell happened to Captain Cora?"

"Thea? You got anything?" Jasper threw a quick glance back.

"I can review camera footage later," Thea replied. "But I'm not sure I'll be able to pick up anything useful."

Grim Machine moved suddenly, lumbering toward the team. Skybreaker turned and sprinted toward the front of the restaurant. Jasper cursed and ran after her. Grim Machine was a distraction. One the team could handle.

"Jasper, wait!"

The alarm in Grace's voice made Jasper stop in her tracks and whirl around. Her gaze first went to the team, then to Grim Machine. Surprise made her eyes go wide.

Grim Machine's grimbots were jumping onto him, grabbing at his shoulders and back. And as they latched on, pieces of the robots' outer armor shifted and moved, rapidly taking on a single, new form. A much larger form.

Grim Machine had fused with his smaller minions.

"Good luck with that one, J!"

Jasper turned in time to see Skybreaker salute before stepping backward off the balcony railing out front, massive weapon still resting on her shoulder. Jasper cursed and ran back toward the team. Going after Skybreaker now would be stupid. She wasn't an immediate threat, and the team would need all the help they could get with Grim Machine's new form.

Still, even as Jasper began firing at Grim Machine, assessing what level his strength was at now, noting the slower speed at which he moved, Skybreaker occupied the thoughts at the back of her mind. She hadn't turned that terrifying weapon on Jasper and the others. Did that mean she didn't want them dead? Or was the weapon only capable of firing once? Maybe it needed to be charged. That *had* been an insanely powerful burst of energy.

"His armor's not even denting under our blasts," Cutthroat warned quietly. Grace flitted through the air around Grim Machine's head, distracting him while the others tried to fire. Sarena let out a few sonic shouts. They were powerful enough to make the robot stumble but didn't seem to do much damage otherwise.

The only person not fighting was Thea, who was crouched under a table typing frantically on a laptop. If they couldn't destroy Grim Machine, maybe she'd be able to hack his systems and shut him down.

"He has to have vulnerabilities," Jasper muttered. "The gaps at his joints."

Nearby, Holly replied, "You're not wrong, but they're narrow. It's hard to aim a blast in there."

Jasper glanced up at Grace, who narrowly dodged a swing of Grim Machine's hand. "It'd probably be easier to jam a blade in."

"We'd need quite a few to get him to stop fighting."

Jasper returned her blaster to the holster at her side and drew the short sword she'd brought along. "We'll see about that." As she charged forward, she shouted, "Angel! You and I are going in. Everyone else, distract him!"

Grace kept up her efforts around Grim Machine's upper body while Jasper darted around his legs. She swiped at the gaps in his armor, easy to spot by the neon blue light glowing within. Often, her blade only swiped through air, but she sometimes felt the weapon break wires or scrape components that were hopefully important.

Just as Grim Machine was starting to slow and stumble, a grimbot broke off from his body. Then another. And another. Blades popped out of their arms as they emerged. Jasper staggered backward, sword at the ready to block.

Grace landed next to her, also driven away by the armed grimbots. While a few of the bots continued to swipe and lunge at her and Jasper, the rest scooped Grim Machine up and carried him away.

"Don't let them get away!" Jasper shouted.

"What are we supposed to do?" Sarena shot back. "We can't get through his armor!"

"Grace and I were making progress! That's why they're fleeing! We can't let them—" Jasper cut off as one of the robot's blades swung dangerously close to her face.

Something moved through the restaurant on the other side of the retreating bots. Thea darted between tables, dodged a few blades tossed her way, then dove to the ground and slid toward Grim Machine. More Grimbots moved to attack, but the rest of the team moved faster to intercept, allowing Thea to freely pass underneath Grim Machine's body.

She sprang to her feet a moment later and waved an open hand. "Let's get out of here!" Her other hand seemed to be holding something, but it was impossible to be certain with her fist clenched.

Jasper glanced at Cutthroat, who nodded. "Maybe we can take him," the pirate said. "But this was unexpected, and we're surrounded by civilians who could get caught in the crossfire."

Jasper sighed. Right. It would be better to catch Grim Machine somewhere else in the city, where they weren't surrounded by random people. And maybe they could brainstorm some faster ways to get through that armor of his.

"Clear out!" she shouted to the team, turning to evacuate the restaurant in the opposite direction as the robots had gone. After a moment, she added, "Remedy, check for any injured before going. Superangel, give him a hand if he needs it!"

Dax and Grace nodded. While they began sweeping the room, calling out for anyone who needed healing to make themselves known, Jasper hopped through the shattered window that faced the city. Cool night air nipped at her as she landed on the balcony outside that wrapped the building.

No sign of Skybreaker.

And no sign of Bruce Wright.

What did that weapon do to him?

The rest of the team gathered around her. It didn't take long for Dax and Grace to join them, to Jasper's relief. No one must have been severely hurt.

As they walked away from the restaurant, Thea fell into pace at Jasper's side and held something up. A piece of Grim Machine's armor, with some wires hanging off the back. "This has computer components in it. I might be able to learn something useful about his programming. Maybe even figure out who built him."

Jasper lifted an eyebrow. "How'd you pull that off him?"

"I was able to disable some of the locks holding his armor together," Thea said. Seeing the question on Jasper's face, she quickly added, "I'm not sure how easily I could do it again. His systems were vulnerable while they were carrying him off—you guys must have triggered something while swiping at him—but I couldn't access his software for most of the fight."

Jasper shrugged. "Well, it's something." After some hesitation, she said, "And that weapon Skybreaker had?"

Thea's expression darkened. Her hand tightened around the electronics she'd stolen. "I'll look into it."

Chapter Forty-Seven
Signals

The apartment had seen its fair share of pacing, especially from Jasper, but the past couple of weeks must have set some kind of record. As Jasper moved from one side of the room to the other, she listened to the others discuss the fight that had occurred just hours earlier.

"—must be the same thing she used on Attom, based on what Jasper said," Holly was saying. "But why is she vaporizing people?"

"I want to know where she got a weapon like that," Cutthroat muttered. He took a sip from a mug that Jasper was pretty sure only held hot chocolate. Rose had been running back and forth between the living room they occupied and the kitchen, filling mugs and handing them out.

"It's advanced tech, but it doesn't resemble what we saw on Reo," Thea said, nodding in agreement. "I don't think Starr's people made this."

"Well, maybe we could let her take out a few more of our enemies before we worry about stopping her." Sarena leaned back against the couch, hands resting at the back of her head, eyes drifting shut.

"Are you an idiot?" Holly hissed. "There's a decent chance that we're next on her list of targets!"

Jasper came to a stop in front of the holoscreen she'd been scribbling on a few minutes earlier and shook her head. "There's something bigger going on here. I assumed Skybreaker was working solo, but maybe someone gave her that weapon. And that could explain how she's been able to prevent Starr from figuring out she's Skybreaker. I'd be shocked if he didn't have cameras and a tracker on her."

"You really don't think Starr had this new weapon developed in one of his labs, too?" Sarena asked.

"If that were the case, she wouldn't have killed Cora with it." Jasper folded her arms. "He wouldn't order his new hero killed, and Skybreaker wouldn't risk him finding out she did it."

She glanced at the screen again. Some of the notes were plans for the Lion's Den, while the rest revolved around the Governor's Palace. She'd made lists of the work the team had done while she was in prison: what Thea believed she was capable of in terms of hacking AstraSmart, floor plans for the palace, and even intel Holly had discovered while shapeshifting and sneaking in. She hadn't dared go anywhere too secure, but she'd learned some useful things about the guard situation, camera placements, and general layouts.

The Lion's Den was more pressing—Jasper wanted to handle that before storming the palace—but she couldn't stop working through how they would get to Starr. She knew when she wanted to strike.

"We'll worry about whatever Skybreaker's doing later," Jasper said, turning to face the team. "We need to get our hands on that weapon, but it'll be easier once we've taken the palace. Especially since she's apparently still relying on her position with Starr.

"Now, there's going to be a massive party at the palace on Christmas Eve," she continued. "I say we crash it. Thea can give us a boost by screwing up as many systems as possible. Then we can bring—"

"Whoa!" Thea sat up suddenly, pushing aside the laptop she'd been working on to stare at something that had just popped up on her sphere's holoscreen.

"Uh, got something you wanna share with the class?"

"Yeah, this is weird. Check out these communication logs." Thea leaned forward and pointed at a dot amidst a sea of more dots that were beyond comprehension to Jasper.

"You were able to get communication logs from the armor you pulled from Grim Machine?" Jasper asked, brow furrowing.

Thea nodded excitedly. "I went for the piece that I sensed the most data chips in. I doubt all of his data and logs are here, but there's a pretty good chunk. Anyway, check this out. The most recent messages have been exchanged within the Janus system, but a few of these signals...wow." She scrolled down the screen. "These were sent to the edge of the star system, apparently to long-distance comm warps. But the warp points aren't matching with any public databases."

"Secret long-distance warps? Those exist?" Grace asked from nearby.

"Oh sure, there's plenty," Jasper answered, eyes still on Thea's screen. "The underground space warps meant for people to go through are a bit dangerous, but the worst-case scenario with an off-the-record comm warp is that your message doesn't go through."

"Well, he was getting responses, so this warp was well-built." Thea lifted an eyebrow. "I can ping the warp and see if I can get any info, but I doubt I'll turn up much."

Cutthroat's eyes narrowed. "Who the hell could Grim Machine be talking to outside the Janus System?"

No one had any theories to offer. Jasper had a few ideas, but nothing worth presenting without solid evidence. Could he be working with a government from one of the other star systems in the alliance? Or an independent organization?

"I'll look more into the code behind these long-distance comms," Thea continued after a moment. "And the wavelengths used. Maybe I can find a way to intercept any others that get sent into the system."

"Okay, great. That something you can do in the background?" Jasper asked.

Thea nodded.

"Cool. Then let's take a look at our plans—"

Rose came darting into the room with another mug of hot chocolate, this one for herself. Fluorescent marshmallows in various geometric shapes were piled on top. She settled onto the couch next to Grace, who was studying Jasper's holoscreen carefully.

Grace lifted an eyebrow. "Got our attack on the palace all sorted out?"

"Almost," Jasper replied. "But first, we have the Lion's Den to deal with." She swiped her hand across the holoscreen to dismiss some of the notes, shifting the screen's focus to the Den.

"But you were just talking about attacking on Christmas Eve!" Sarena protested. "You didn't finish explaining the plan before Thea started talking about those long-distance signal thingies."

Jasper waved a hand dismissively. "We'll go over it tomorrow. I was mainly talking out loud to get my thoughts organized. This is what I want to focus on right now." She turned. "Tomorrow, we attend the Lion's Den with fake tickets that Thea will obtain for us."

That was the truth—her mind was scattered, and it was time to focus on the Den. Part of her wanted to do nothing else until it was a pile of ash. Another part was terrified of going anywhere near it.

Focus on your rage. Not your pain.

Jasper brought up a map of the Den that Thea had put together using a combination of city plans and imaging drones. Jasper had filled in the rest with memory. She pointed out a few spots. "These are the exits. All heavily guarded. The only spot visitors are actually allowed to enter is here." Her finger moved to a point near the bottom. "Everything else is emergency exit only. From what we've gathered, guard patrols are far more intense than they were when I broke out."

"Okay, so why don't we just burn it to the ground?" Sarena asked. "Won't matter how many guards there are with a big enough fire."

"They've got plenty of anti-fire equipment in place, it seems." They'd probably beefed those systems up after Jasper's escape. "No chance a fire we start lasts long enough to ruin the place. And I considered bombing them, but the problem with that is that this isn't just about destroying the Den. We have prisoners to rescue." Her chest squeezed at the thought of the people being held captive underground, forced to fight to the death day after day. "Obviously, we did pull something similar off at Sky Labs, but that wouldn't have worked without the villain race, and I already explained why that won't work here.

"So," she forced herself to continue. "The first part of the plan focuses on clearing a path between the prisoner quarters and this exit." She pointed out a corner of the Den on the map. "If we set a fire, with their new safety measures, we won't get much time. So, we're going an alternative route to distract the guards and viewers." She reached into her coat and drew out a vial of bright blue liquid.

Grace's eyes widened slightly. "What is that? Where'd you get it?"

"This?" Jasper gave the vial a shake and laughed. "Dyed water. Completely harmless. But we're going to use it to make people at the Den think someone hit them with a biohazardous material. It'll actually be Dax making people sick, so no one we don't want targeted will be in any actual danger."

"Guess that means I have a lot of healing to do before tomorrow night?" Dax added.

"Yep. You'll be hitting up hospitals tomorrow. Don't worry about how deadly the stuff you heal is. The people attending Lion's Den fights are rich enough to afford the best care." And the world would be better off if most of them died, anyway.

"Wait, what's the point of the vial, exactly?" Sarena asked.

"We'll walk around not-so-subtly pouring these in drinks. Once people start getting sick, the connection should be made quickly. And by spilling a large puddle in the area we need to ourselves, we'll get it blocked out of the evacuation. Den security will focus on getting their patrons out safely before investigating, and we can focus on getting out the prisoners."

"And then we destroy the place?" Rose asked. A hot chocolate mustache clung to her upper lip.

Jasper grinned. "And then we destroy the place," she agreed.

Chapter Forty-Eight
Butterfly Effect

The line into the Lion's Den wasn't long, but it did move slowly. Security checked everyone who passed through thoroughly. Signs warned that large bags weren't allowed, nor were weapons or outside alcohol.

Grace leaned to the side to peer around the people ahead and glimpsed the bar beyond the security check. Drinks were sold in very small amounts at a time. Something to do with a previous incident, apparently.

While she, Thea, Holly, Dax, and Rose had entered the line, Cutthroat and Sarena had split off behind them. They'd be hanging out by the team's target exit, ready to move in to fight security and get prisoners out when the action started.

Thea's fake tickets and quick manipulation of the x-ray scanners got them in, and on the other side, the group split again. Holly would circle the entire stadium, shifting forms and making a show of pouring the blue dye in drinks. Dax would be a few minutes behind her, slowly infecting people with various illnesses he'd cured earlier. Thea, already in the closed-circuit camera system now that they'd entered the Den, headed off to spill the extra dyed water in the exit corridor.

And Jasper, well... Jasper had another way in.

For now, Grace was charged with keeping an eye on Rose, which left her feeling more nervous than she likely would have. No one was keen on bringing Rose along, but she'd proved herself capable on the previous couple of missions, and likely would have found a way to tag along anyway. Better to keep her where they knew what she was up to.

Once everyone was ready, she and Aymes would head to the prisoner barracks to free them, while Jasper would be grabbing the prisoners being kept in the wings by the arena.

Grace, Rose, and Aymes navigated the walkway at the front of a seating section. Grace's right hand grazed the railing separating them from the arena far below. Massive metal sheets had been drilled into the walls surrounding the arena's dirt floor, covering up what had apparently once been wood.

The team had been among the last visitors to enter. Grace and the others were still walking when an announcer's voice boomed through the speakers in place around the Den.

"Looks like we're ready to send out tonight's opening act!" the man bellowed. "While everyone finishes buying drinks and finding their seats, we'll be treated to a fight between new Den fighter Bobclaw and a Hatuan white wolfoid!

The gate at one end of the arena lifted with a metallic whine. Grace winced at the sight of a young boy being shoved out of the shadows. The copper-skinned Si Heran had dark hair that had been cut close to his scalp. His wide, serpentine eyes shone under the arena lights.

Then, the arena's opposite gate opened.

As soon as it had enough room, the white-furred creature charged into the light, growling a two-toned sound from its massive jaws. As its two voice boxes quieted, it skidded to a halt and lifted onto its hind legs. Two tails swished behind it.

Grace didn't think the Si Heran boy could have looked any more terrified, but she was proven wrong when the wolfoid dropped back onto all fours and padded across the dirt toward him.

"We should save him," Grace whispered.

Aymes looked like he felt the same way. But despite the pain in his eyes, he replied, "The others aren't ready yet. If we expose ourselves too early—"

"I know." Grace's fists clenched at her sides.

The boy—Bobclaw, according to the announcer—lifted one of his shaking hands, revealing the small dagger he'd been given to fight the beast. At Grace's side, Rose let out a low hiss. "Are we going to do anything?"

Grace rested a hand on her shoulder and squeezed. "If we act now, we'll ruin the plan."

Rose glanced up at not Grace, but Aymes. "Can't you do something? Just to save him?"

Aymes hesitated, then set his jaw and nodded. "I'll see what I can do. But I can't do anything the crowd will see."

Grace caught a flash of something silver moving through the air. Then, her attention was drawn to the arena below, where the wolfoid was charging

Bobclaw. Bobclaw yelped and scrambled toward one of the arena walls. The wolfoid was nearly on him when something made it pivot. Its jaws snapped at a point in the air that Grace swore she saw shimmer.

Behind the wolfoid, Bobclaw glanced at his dagger. Something new settled into his frightened gaze. Grace wasn't sure if it was determination or pure survival instinct, but something drove him to lunge and drive his weapon into the wolfoid's side.

Piercing shrieks of pain reverberated from the wolfoid's throat. It twisted and swiped at Bobclaw with wide paws. Bobclaw barely dodged. While the wolfoid tried to get its bearings, Bobclaw moved in again with the dagger. He left a deep gash running from its ribcage to its hip.

The wolfoid let out another growl and whirled on the boy. Grace grimaced. The wolfoid was huge. Even if Bobclaw had plenty of time to slash at it, it would take a while to go down. "He needs to go for the throat," she said.

"Yeah," Aymes agreed. "He's probably too scared to get that close to its face." His hand twitched at his side. "Maybe I can…"

He trailed off as Bobclaw went running away from the wolfoid. The wolfoid charged after him, and it was far faster. In fact, if *something* unseen didn't cause it to trip and stumble, it would've had Bobclaw pinned fast.

"Should we really be letting Rose watch this?" Holly asked over comms.

Grace glanced at Rose, who had her wide eyes fixed on the arena. She'd thought for sure they'd be questioned for bringing someone so young in, but to her surprise, there were plenty of other children in the crowd, many even younger. The wealthy elites apparently thought watching Den matches was a great pastime for their kids.

"I don't think she'd like the idea of being forced to stop," Jasper said. "But you have a point. Though she's already seen a lot of violence. And we don't really know the full extent of what she went through at the labs…"

"I'll pull her away if things get really bad," Grace said, quietly enough that Rose didn't hear. "But I think things are under control."

In the arena below, Bobclaw reached one of the walls. The wolfoid was just getting back on its feet. In the blink of an eye, it was charging again. Bobclaw flung out his dagger in desperation, making no move to dodge or rush toward the animal. Grace began to reach toward Rose.

Another flash of something caught the wolfoid's eye, making it turn abruptly just a few feet from Bobclaw. Bobclaw sprang into action, once again aiming for the wolfoid's side. Grace wanted to shout help at him, but she bit her lip.

Aymes's hand twitched again. The wolfoid made another sharp turn, its jaws snapping at something overhead. It was almost on top of Bobclaw now. Bobclaw began swinging, not seeming to be aiming for any spot in particular. The wolfoid lunged at something in the air just above him.

The swinging blade sliced open its throat.

The animal collapsed in a heartbeat, and Grace suddenly felt a surge of guilt. Poor animal. It was as innocent as Bobclaw in all this. But an animal couldn't be reasoned with.

Something darted through the air at the railing and came toward her, Aymes, and Rose. A silver butterfly landed on Aymes's hand. Its wings flapped slowly for a long moment before it evaporated into silver energy, then vanished.

"Why would it go after a butterfly instead of the fighter?" Rose asked skeptically.

"I've been experimenting with emitting sound from my energy formations using internal vibrations," Aymes explained, his hand dropping back to his side. "The butterfly was letting out a sound that would have been highly irritating to the wolfoid but wouldn't be picked up by anyone else's ears."

The announcer declared the end of the fight while Grace let out a sigh of relief. No one seemed to have noticed Aymes's distraction. A shaking, bloodied Bobclaw was escorted out of the arena. Grace caught a glimpse of one of the guards locking chains onto his wrists as they entered the shadows.

The announcer continued. "And now, for our first big match of the night, we have a new free agent who made quite the entrance demanding a fight tonight. Their opponent will be Pyre, who's got a long win streak under his belt."

Opposite the arena from Grace, a figure walked up to the railing and vaulted it over it. His black cloak fluttered as he dropped into the dirt. His hood fell back as he landed, revealing the maroon-skinned face of an East Kronosian. Black waves of hair fell to his shoulders. He straightened to his full height and turned to face the center of the arena.

The gate that Bobclaw had used opened once again. Another cloaked figure emerged from under the gate, this one's black cloak laced with neon pink designs at the edges. A large, wide-bladed sword rested on their shoulder, glowing a soft pink as well.

"Now, time to meet our newcomer," the announcer said. "Please welcome to the Den the one and only Upriser."

Chapter Forty-Nine
Echoes

Screams and shouts rose from the crowd with their anticipation as Jasper and Pyre circled each other. Pyre tore off his cloak, revealing elaborate circuitry built into his shirt and pants, all wired to a large weapon on his back that almost looked like a blaster. Almost.

Jasper raised her sword. It was a show of strength, but it doubled as a signal to the others to move forward with the next step of the plan. The sword raise earned a few cheers of "Upriser" from near the railings, but most of those cheering in the crowd were rooting for the already established fighter. Pyre had been in the Den long enough to earn quite a few fans.

Pyre grabbed the weapon from his back and took aim. Even separated from its holster, there were still several thin tubes running from the weapon to the equipment on his back. It wouldn't be as simple as dodging a blaster beam. When he squeezed the trigger, fir burst from the end of the weapon. Anyone attempting to dodge an ordinary blaster, not knowing what to expect, would still be burned by the flames.

Jasper, anticipating the attack, dropped flat to the ground. Flames shot by overhead while she rolled and finally jumped to her feet out of range. Pyre attempted to swing the weapon to bring the flames onto her, but he couldn't move the bulky weapon quite as fast as she could run. She moved around him in an increasingly tight circle, closing the distance between them while just staying out of reach of the heat.

She had to disable the flamethrower as quickly as possible if she wanted to win this fight. Pyre had a few other tricks up his sleeves—hopefully nothing he hadn't displayed in previous fights she'd studied from the Den's archive footage in the minutes before the match, courtesy of Thea—but the flamethrower was his biggest advantage.

Jasper readied her blade. Pyre, anticipating her attack by how close she'd gotten, turned off the flamethrower and slid it back onto its holster on his back. Jasper pulled up short and dropped into a defensive stance, sword at the ready.

Pyre lunged at her, one of his hands moving to something at his side. Another weapon, but which one? Jasper ducked to the right and swung, missing Pyre's body entirely and instead slicing through one of the tubes running into the flamethrower. Fuel sprayed into the air and splattered on the dirt.

Jasper quickly backed away from Pyre, getting out of range—hopefully— of whatever he was pulling out next. She cursed as she slowed, beginning to feel out of breath. This fight would have been much easier not long ago.

You'd be dead if you hadn't reversed the serum, she reminded herself. Dead, or close to it. This fight could be going much worse.

Pyre attacked again, this time swinging a blade. The sword was nearly as long as Jasper's, though only about half the width. And it was on fire. Jasper jumped back, narrowly dodging the first swing. She threw her own blade up to block the second. She winced at the sight of the weapons clashing. Her blade could stop bullets, but high heat for an extended period of time could weaken the metal.

Jasper took a deep breath and moved in, summoning all the strength she had and forcing the world to slow as much as she could manage. She knocked Pyre's blade aside with a hard swing, then began a barrage. She swiped at his legs, his hands, his chest, driving him backwards, nearly making him stumble once or twice. His face twisted in fear in slow motion, but Jasper barely noticed it.

Finally, breathing hard, Jasper lowered her blade and straightened up. The world moved back into motion, and her limbs responded at full speed again. For a moment, Pyre only swayed, glancing down in disbelief at the tears in his clothing, at the gashes bleeding underneath.

Then, he collapsed. Jasper threw back the hood of her cloak and grinned.

"And it seems that Upriser takes the win—oh, hang on, what was—?"

The announcer cut off abruptly. Cameras around the arena, meant to show a zoomed-in view of what was happening in the fights for those farther away, reflected Jasper's face to the audience. Then, courtesy of Thea, wanted posters of Jasper Van Terra popped up alongside the live images of her. She grinned.

At that moment, the announcer began to speak, apparently not yet realizing that Van Terra was standing in the arena below. "Esteemed guests, we've just received word that there may have been a potential biohazard introduced to the facility. We're going to begin an evacuation. Please identify the nearest security guard and follow them in an orderly fashion—"

It quickly became difficult to hear the announcer's voice over the panic in the crowd.

"—We will be avoiding the northwest portion of the Den—"

Security guards came pouring out of the tunnels toward Jasper.

"—medical attention will be available once you are out of the facility—"

Jasper cracked her neck, moved past where Pyre lay groaning in pain on the ground, and began spinning her sword in her hand as the distance between her and the guards closed.

They were easy to plow through.

"Think the crowd's more panicked about the biohazard, or me?" Jasper asked into the comms as she sent the last guard flying back with a hard kick from her cybernetic leg.

"The people starting to get sick are way more worried about the biohazard," Dax replied. "But a lot of people are talking about you, too."

Jasper smirked. "Good."

"How does that help the plan?" Sarena asked.

"It doesn't. I just like being a menace."

Jasper barreled into the tunnel ahead in time to see the last of the waiting prisoners being unlocked from the wall. Others were being led away in chains farther down the corridor.

The guards here went down just as fast as the others had. Jasper was losing steam, but she wasn't done fighting, yet. As long as she avoided running unless it was absolutely necessary, she had a few more bouts in her.

Once she'd taken care of the guards, Jasper turned to address the prisoners. She couldn't help but notice Bobclaw standing at the back of the group, shaking and still splattered with wolfoid blood.

"Uh, hi there," Jasper said. "How about we get you all out of here?"

Most of the prisoners didn't say a word in response, but they all followed Jasper when she started down the hall. Good enough. Hopefully, once the team got them back to Sarena's penthouse with the people they'd rescued from Sky Labs, they would start to make progress toward recovery. Some of the former lab prisoners had begun doing well enough for the team to start looking into getting them into other living arrangements.

Jasper glanced back at her followers frequently, scanning the hall behind them for guards. "Where are you taking us?" one girl finally asked. Her voice was hoarse. Timid.

"Somewhere safe," Jasper promised.

The fastest route to the planned exit took them through the weapons room. Their reflections followed them in blades on the wall. Jasper was halfway through the room when she stopped dead in her tracks.

The floor below her still bore a faint bloodstain. Before she could fully process what she was doing, Jasper dropped to one knee and brushed her fingers against the cold ground. In her mind, she could see Mars's body beneath her.

"Um, are we going the right way?" Bobclaw asked quietly.

Jasper shook herself and jumped back to her feet. "Yeah. Sorry. This way, keep it moving." She forced herself forward again.

Grace's voice came through the comms. "We've got the prisoners out of the barracks. En route to the exit."

"Good. We're almost there, too." As Jasper said the words, she stepped out of the weapons room and into the final hallway between them and the exit. The section ahead, where the blue puddle lay, had been hastily taped off with caution tape. But besides that, the hallway was empty. Jasper continued forward.

"Uh, is that safe?" one of the prisoners behind her asked as she ripped aside some of the tape.

"It's just water," Jasper replied in a low voice, in case any Den employees happened to be nearby. "Perfectly safe." To prove it, she strolled through the puddle, her black boots splashing through the blue. The others followed tentatively, a few at first, one by one, then the rest in a nervous shuffle.

"Hey! Stop right there!"

Jasper cursed and whirled around. Instead of lifting the sword, she drew a blaster from under her cloak and aimed it toward the three security guards coming down the hall toward them.

"Keep going!" she ordered the prisoners as she moved between them and the guards. "There's help waiting just around the corner."

She heard footsteps but didn't have time to make sure everyone was moving. The guards began firing their blasters. Jasper fired back, but she was mostly focused on getting her sword up to deflect the beams away from the prisoners.

Finally, one arm swinging, she refocused the blaster and pulled the trigger. The middle guard went down. The other two ducked into the weapons room for cover. They began to fire more sporadically after that, ducking out one at a time to get a few shots in.

After blocking a few more shots from their blasters, Jasper let out a dramatic sigh. "You're just wasting everyone's time. You're not going to take me down like that!"

No response. Ugh. Jasper glanced back over her shoulder at the now empty hallway. At the corner at the end. She could hear voices in the distance, barely audible. Into her comm, she asked, "Did the prisoners I was with make it to the exit all right?"

"Yeah, looks like they're all here," Cutthroat replied.

"Great." Jasper moved backwards toward the exit, keeping her eyes on the door up ahead. But it had been nearly a minute now since either of the guards had tried to shoot. Her mind went to the map of the Den, tracing possible routes they could be taking to get to her.

She glanced at a doorway to her right. That hall wrapped around the weapons room and connected to the corridor on the other side. She sheathed her sword, readied her blaster, moved to the door, and pressed her ear against it.

It was quiet for a long moment, and Jasper nearly moved away and headed for the exit. Then, a shout cut through the air and made her heart skip a beat. A fight? But who...?

Jasper kicked the door open and charged before she'd processed the scene ahead. As she approached the figures struggling in the narrow hallway, she realized there were three. The two guards and—

Bobclaw.

He was swiping wildly at the guards with a dagger. Bigger than the one he'd had in the arena, which would have been taken from him after his match anyway. He must have grabbed it while they were walking through the weapons room, then. Smart kid.

He was fighting pretty well, too. By keeping himself between the guards at such close range, he'd prevented them from firing their blasters. But they'd switched to throwing fists, and judging by how much worse Bobclaw's face looked than it already had, they'd landed a few hits.

Still moving at full speed, Jasper swapped her blaster for a dagger and went into the fight with her blade spinning. A slice to one guard's neck, a stab to the second's abdomen. While the first collapsed quickly, the second staggered for a moment. He would likely go down fast, too, but Jasper wasn't taking any chances. She drove the dagger deeper into his stomach, yanked the blade free, and knocked him to the ground with a swift kick.

Breathing hard, she turned to Bobclaw and looked him over, making sure he had no serious wounds. "Looks like you held up all right, especially considering it was two against one."

Bobclaw nodded, wide-eyed.

Jasper straightened up and sheathed her dagger. "Not bad. It was smart to think they'd come around another way."

Bobclaw glanced at the dagger still his hand. "Thanks."

"Ready to get out of here?" Jasper clapped one hand gently against his shoulder, and they walked to the exit together. They were nearly there when Jasper, more quietly now, said to him, "My first fight was against an alkura."

Bobclaw shot her a surprised look. "You—but they said you were a free agent?"

"Tonight I was. But the whole reason I came here to save you all..." Jasper's jaw tightened. "I was in here for a long time. And it was a long time ago. But...I won't lie, it stays with you."

Bobclaw's mouth opened, then closed. He nodded. Past the bruises and weariness, there was a determination burning low in his gaze.

He'd be okay. Eventually.

At the exit, they found a crowd gathering in the massive cistern beyond the Den's doors. Walkways passed over the few feet of water currently occupying the room, though there was space for the water to rise after a good storm. Grace, Aymes, and Rose had brought the rest of the prisoners. Sarena and Cutthroat were examining the bodies of security guards that must have turned up over here, and Holly, Dax, and Thea were keeping watch nearby.

"Everyone's out?" Jasper called.

Thea turned, revealing the tablet she held in her hands. "No heat signatures anywhere in the Den," she confirmed.

Jasper reached into her coat and drew out the detonator. As with Sky Labs, they'd had to be careful about where they placed explosives. Even more so here, where they were even deeper underground. They couldn't do too much damage without risking collapse of structures higher up. But, with what they had planted in strategic locations a level up from the Lion's Den before coming in, they'd be able to cave in the entrances. No one would be able to get back into the Den any time soon.

"Start walking," Jasper ordered everyone. "I'll blow 'em once we hit the exit on the other side of the cistern."

At said exit, Jasper was the first to stop and turn around. She could see some of the others turning in her peripheral, but her focus was on the open doorway ahead. The Den exit they'd passed through. She lifted the detonator. Her thumb found the button.

The ground trembled like she'd set off a mild earthquake, and then stone was tumbling down from the ceiling in a square area in front of the doorway. More booms echoed in the distance, signaling more collapses both at the other exits and inside the Den itself.

"If my life were a TV show, how many episodes do you think would end with me dramatically blowing something up?" Jasper asked as she watched the last of the rubble rain down.

"Too many," Holly muttered.

"Not enough," Rose countered loudly. "We should blow some more stuff up!"

Holly shot her an exasperated look. "You haven't even been with us that long!"

Laughing, Jasper turned around. She looked over her team, and then the rescued Den fighters. Some had already experienced the horrors she had, perhaps even seen worse than she'd personally been through in the Den, but they were safe.

Maybe not entirely free from what they'd experienced, but safe.

Chapter Fifty
The Sky in Skybreaker

Janus hovered at the doorway to Starr's office, listening to him demand more sweeps from the police search teams. Demand that more camera footage be recovered and painstakingly searched through. No rest until his precious superhero Captain Cora was found.

Quietly, she crept away from the office. He hadn't seemed interested in involving her in the search, which was a relief. And if he kept himself occupied late into the night looking for the missing man, all the better.

She'd already feigned not feeling well after dinner earlier, which should help keep Starr off her back for at least part of the day tomorrow, but her advanced healing would make it suspicious if she stayed down too long. Hopefully, he'd be too distracted looking for Captain Cora to notice. If she was still struggling by the time Starr needed her for something, she'd have to come up with another excuse.

For now, though, she focused on slipping out of the palace. The only way to make this work was to leave now. The process was going to take hours, and that didn't take into account how long it would take her to be able to walk again afterward.

Once she was out of the building, her focus was on the race through the city. On leaping from rooftop to balcony to stairwell. No motorcycle tonight— she wouldn't be able to drive it home. She was relying on whatever plan Meg had cooked up to get her back into her room at the palace without discovery. Part of her was terrified of that reliance, but she didn't think Meg would betray her tonight. Probably never, as long as Janus had her convinced she would still be useful.

Maybe another version of Janus could serve Meg forever. Be her right hand instead of Starr's. But this version of her wasn't wired for that.

Janus arrived at the meeting point and found herself in front of a door into what seemed to be a restaurant kitchen. She punched in the code Meg had sent her earlier. The door unlocked, and when Janus stepped inside, instead of a kitchen, she found an operating room. She would have called it a makeshift operating room, but the tech Meg's team had dragged in looked as advanced as anything one would find in an upper district hospital. Maybe even better.

The yellow-furred, horned man with black hooves that had given Janus Skyfeller greeted her as she stepped in. "Are you ready, Skybreaker?"

Janus nodded. "Let's do this."

The others in the room, all wearing medical scrubs, flitted about while the horned man led her to a side room and handed her a hospital gown. Janus changed quickly and made a beeline for the operating table once she was done. Just moments later, one of the doctors was pressing a mask to her face.

Janus's hands tightened around the edges of the table as she began breathing the anesthesia. The skittish, anxious, untrustworthy part of her screamed in protest at letting people she secretly considered enemies put her to sleep. But if they followed through...this was worth the risk. *Worth the risk,* Janus repeated to herself as the world faded into nothing.

She came to what felt like moments later. Slowly, groggily, her mental alarms screaming at how difficult it was to move or think.

But she was in her bed at the Governor's Palace. She was alive. And...

Janus summoned the strength to push herself upright. Yes, they'd done it. Meg's team had pulled through. And they'd managed it faster than Sky Labs ever had, according to the files Grim Machine had recovered.

It was still dark outside, and when Janus checked her clock, she was relieved to see how early it was. It was unlikely she'd have missed anything important from Starr.

To her surprise though, when she checked her messages, she did have one from him. Thankfully, it had only arrived a few minutes earlier. *I have news. Call me when you see this—don't worry about what time it is.*

Janus stretched her arms, testing the aches across her upper body. Oof. Her healing was doing work, but that didn't mean much right after a major operation. Still, she felt good enough to carry on a conversation, so she started a call to Starr's line.

"Eighteen," he answered quickly. "How are you feeling?"

It was a status check on one of his most valuable assets, not true concern for her wellbeing. "About the same as after dinner. Not sure I'll be up and about until later today."

"Sorry to hear that." Wow. The words almost sounded genuine. "It must be a bit serious, if your healing hasn't handled it already."

"We'll see. What's your news?"

"The Lion's Den was destroyed. Van Terra's work."

Good. Though, Janus's jaw clenched at the thought of how reckless whatever Jasper must have pulled off had been. Just one more pentasol, and Janus could have massacred everyone in charge and freed those people herself.

But that wasn't the response Starr was expecting. "Do we know how she found it?" Janus asked.

"No. Probably a leak on the Fayes' side. They aren't nearly as careful as I am. I don't care much about the Den, but it's still a victory for Van Terra I'd have preferred to avoid. Do you have any new ideas on taking care of her?"

Janus wished she did. But as much as she hated Van Terra, Starr and Meg had been much bigger issues in her mind. Van Terra was a bug she could squash later.

"I think I'm narrowing in on where she's hiding out in the lower districts, based on recent sightings. I'll keep working on that as soon as I can."

"Good. I'd like her dead by...what's that party we're throwing for next pentasol? Christmas?"

"The palace party? It's Christmas Eve."

"Well, I'd like her dead by then."

Janus's hands tightened into fists in her lap. "I'll see what I can do."

V. THE GOVERNOR'S PALACE

Chapter Fifty-One
My Mind Palace is a Bouncy House

The morning of Christmas Eve seemed to sneak up on the crew. Despite most of their conversations in the days prior revolving around their plans for the day, it still felt a bit surreal waking up that morning.

Thea was the first person out to the kitchen. As she sat at the counter, her mind worked on multiple puzzles at once.

Her main project, at the moment, was the studying tech she'd stolen from Grim Machine. And tracking those mysterious long-distance signals he'd been picking up messages on. Her main project was *supposed* to be finalizing her work with the AstraSmart network at the Governor's Place, and she was working on that, too. But the signals were too compelling to ignore.

Somewhere in the back of her mind, other trains of thought raced about, slipping in and out of her conscious attention. Final touches to Dax's energy-focusing suit. Potential improvements to Mia and Chloe's bodies. Buffing up the anti-hack software she'd implemented to the team's devices. Some vague idea on recovering memories lost in the warp...something triggered by her work trying to recover hidden data from one of the chips in Grim Machine's armor...

One by one, Holly, Dax, and Grace joined Thea in the kitchen. Just as Grace was settling down at the dining table, the door to the apartment swung open. Sarena strolled in, wearing a fluffy coat, a wig of short black hair, and sunglasses. She sighed as she lifted Blitz out of her purse and set him on the counter. Then, she began taking off her disguise. "How much longer is my penthouse going to be used as a shelter for people we break out of underground prisons?"

"Just buy another one," Thea suggested. "You've got the money."

Sarena huffed. "I was saving up for a sea cruiser."

"Don't you already have one of those?" Holly asked from where she lay upside down on the couch, legs hanging over the back. She didn't even glance up from her tablet.

"A better one," Sarena replied through clenched teeth.

Thea sighed. "I've got a program actively hunting down public shelters we can take them to," she told Sarena. "Unfortunately, most of them are already packed to the brim. If you donated some of your money to public services instead of buying fancy boats, maybe there'd be more places we could take them."

Behind Sarena, the door flew open again, this time with much more gusto. Jasper strolled in with Rose behind her, a sack over her shoulder.

"What's that?" Sarena asked, turning.

Cutthroat followed the two in and pulled the door closed behind him. "I just went to check on my crew and make sure they're ready for the day," he said. "I don't know why these two tagged along."

"To get Christmas Eve breakfast. Duh." Jasper emptied the sack onto the counter, sending packages of pastries and canned drinks everywhere. A few rolled up to Thea's laptop.

Dax and Grace approached the counter. Dax furrowed his brow. "Uh, I don't think we're going to be able to eat all of this."

"And I'm not blown away by the nutritional value here, either," Sarena added as she picked up a neon blue roll that had some kind of cream oozing into its plastic wrapping.

"We're going to use it to sneak the signaling devices Thea needs into the palace. Holly will disguise herself as catering when she heads in."

Holly surveyed the pastries. "I assume Thea will need them to not actually get eaten?"

Thea shrugged. "As long as they're intact, they could transmit signals from someone's stomach for an hour or so before the stomach acid wears through the protective casing. The devices are meant to endure pretty tough conditions."

"Okay, well, assuming we don't want what we're doing to be *discovered*," Holly said sternly, "I'll have to hide the food after I sneak it in."

"Are we sure this is up to the palace's standards?" Grace prodded a box of "fruit" squares that likely didn't have an ounce of real fruit in them. "The stuff I ate when I lived there was pretty fancy."

"We'll just doctor this all up. Plating can work wonders for perception." Jasper opened a cupboard and dug out a box of serving platters that Thea vaguely remembered her bringing home the day before.

While Jasper brought the platters to the counter, Rose grabbed a solnut butter roll off the top of the food pile, tore off its wrapper, and eagerly began devouring it. Grace and Dax grabbed some of the platters of the stack and began arranging food on them. Holly set to work unwrapping the food.

"Thea," Jasper said as she worked. "Have you sent out the recording I made yet? Spread around a little more money as motivation?"

"I told you three times I took care of that already," Thea told her.

"Just double checking."

"Quadruple checking," Thea corrected.

Before Jasper could make any comments back, Grace held up one of the fruit bars and asked, "Uh, is this mold?"

"Probably." Jasper shrugged. "We'll just whip up some frosting and cover it. Remember, no one's actually going to be eating these."

As she spoke, Rose grabbed another package from the pile and began unwrapping.

"Most of this won't be eaten," Jasper corrected as she picked up her finished platter and carried it over to the dining table.

Once the team had assembled a few more doctored-up platters, Holly loaded them onto a small cart Jasper had procured from somewhere. While Holly finished her preparations, Thea switched her focus to a program trying to dig up deleted files from the data downloaded off the piece of Grim Machine. She studied the code, mind working. Deleting data from a device usually didn't *actually* delete it. Not right away, at least. Often, it was just hidden away until it needed to be overwritten.

Thea glanced up at Dax, who was tentatively tasting one of the canned drinks that had rolled out of the bag. It wasn't a perfect metaphor, but brains were often compared to computers. But was a change in the way data was stored something that the body perceived as needing healing?

With a heavy sigh, Holly finally grabbed the catering cart and wheeled it toward the door. "All right, I'm headed out." She paused and shot a glance at Cutthroat, who nodded.

"I'll be right behind you," he said.

"You've got your camera?" Thea asked.

Holly held up a button-shaped device for her to see before returning it to her pocket and continuing to push the cart forward.

Jasper grabbed Holly's arm, stopping her just before she reached door. "Be careful, all right? I know you're smart, but this is the belly of the beast we're talking about."

Holly turned, lifting an eyebrow. "This is going to be dangerous for all of us."

"I know. This is just...you sure you can handle this part of the plan?"

Thea glanced up, feeling a bit of apprehension creep in herself. This part of the plan was important, but part of her wondered if it really would have been so bad if she hadn't caught wind of this meeting Holly was going to interrupt. There was no telling for sure was Starr's reaction was going to be. How dangerous this would really turn out.

"You wouldn't have asked me if you didn't think I could." After a long moment, Holly's expression softened ever-so-slightly. "I'll be fine, Jasper."

Holly reached for the door handle and was interrupted again by an alert from Thea's laptop. Thea perked up as a box popped up on screen. A message found on the long-distance signal she'd been tracking. She scrambled to get the computer into her lap and start typing, ignoring confused glances from the others.

Finally, Jasper cleared her throat. "Got something you'd like to share with the class, Thea?"

"Hang on." Just a few more lines of code...

The full message opened up, and Thea sighed. Encrypted. Of course. And it was something she hadn't seen before. It was going to take her algorithms some time to get anything useful from this. "I found a message on that long-distance signal Grim Machine was using, but it's encrypted," she explained to the others. "Not sure how long it will take me to crack it open."

"Great," Jasper said. Her arms folded. "And how's AstraSmart coming?"

Thea gestured to the cart as Holly rolled it out the door. "Pretty much ready to go. Just need those signaling devices to get into the palace network."

"Fair enough." Jasper tore a piece off the cookie Rose had just opened, ignoring Rose's protests. Jasper chewed and made a face. "Geez, is that just colored sugar?"

Well, if Jasper thought it was gross, then it had to be pretty awful. Any lingering urge Thea had to give the food a try vaporized instantly.

Jasper brushed cookie crumbs off her hands and addressed the team. "Okay, while the rest of us have time to kill, let's get to work on those weapon modifications. We didn't quite get finished yesterday."

While Thea continued typing, Jasper dumped a bag of grenades, knives, crowbars, throwing stars, and other assorted weapons onto the floor. Then, she added a bag of Christmas decorations to the pile. And a few cans of paint. The rest of the team dove into the piles and began working.

With her signaling devices en route to the palace, Thea figured she may as well finish prep on her AstraSmart hacking program and make sure everything was ready to go. But before opening it, she found herself turning her attention back to the encrypted message. Just because it had been sent on the same long-distance signal didn't mean it had gone directly to or from Grim Machine. She was still working on cracking his already downloaded correspondence, and this encryption seemed a little different.

But there still had to be some sort of connection. And Grim Machine was somehow connected to Skybreaker. Following this trail could get the team answers about Starr's plans, about Skybreaker's mysterious new weapon, and about any other surprises lurking in the shadows.

Chapter Fifty-Two
Bouts of Holly

Holly adjusted the jacket of her catering uniform, ensuring the button camera was secure, and double-checked her reflection in the shiny metal surface of the dessert cart. On the landing pad around her, carrier vehicles dropped off teams of workers and countless party supplies. Up ahead, she could see plenty of other catering teams making their way toward one of the palace's service doors. Including the bakery she'd stolen her uniform from. Holly approached them with her cart and eased into place at the back of the crowd of bakers and their many other carts of food.

A moment later, the service door opened, and a man in a palace security uniform waved for the group Holly had joined to enter. They were led into the lower halls of the palace, up an elevator, and through a collection of kitchens already packed with chefs and bakers preparing for the party. In a prep room next to one of the kitchens, the caterers were left to begin unpacking and plating their goods.

Holly wheeled her cart to a corner behind a large cooler and began removing plates from the cart. She unmuted her comm as she did and, after glancing back to make sure no one was watching her too closely, said, "Thea, you there?"

"Yup."

"Picking up a strong enough signal yet?" Holly bent down to slide one of the plates underneath the cooler.

"Connection did just get a big boost. If you could get at least a few devices a little deeper into the palace, that would help."

"Got it." Holly slid a few pastries into her jacket pocket, hid the rest of the trays in places she didn't think anyone would check before the end of the party, and slipped out of the prep area.

"Heading up," she informed Thea, and anyone else on the team tuned in to the mission. Everyone was likely paying attention to at least some degree. "You got a visual on any council members yet?"

"Leader's already in the council room, along with the Aquila System rep." Thea paused for a moment, the empty space filled with a couple of clicks. "The two from Ra are eating...oh, looks like the human is headed for a bathroom."

Holly's heart quickened. That would be perfect, if she could make it in time. "How far from me?"

"I think you can make it. There's gonna be an elevator on your left up ahead. Hop inside."

Thea guided Holly up several floors and down several hallways. At this point, her catering costume wasn't going to be enough to keep her out of trouble if she ran into security. She flipped the jacket inside out as she walked, hiding the company logo, and changed her appearance to that of a North Kronosian. Her skin turned near white, her hair shortened to her shoulders and went black, her eyes took on a pale opalescence. She added half a foot to her height, too, for good measure.

Finally, the entrance to the restrooms appeared up ahead. The door was just falling shut as Holly turned the corner. Her pace quickened with her pulse. "That them?" she whispered.

"Yep. Erio Moonring."

"Human, right? That doesn't sound like an Earth name."

"No, seems he was raised on a space station near the Aquila System."

Holly eased open the bathroom door and was relieved to find it empty, besides Erio, who occupied a stall at the far end. Holly tossed the pastries into a trash bin while she waited for him to emerge.

When Erio stepped out of the stall, he looked surprised to see Holly. "Sorry, this one's usually empty—is it all right that I'm in here?"

He thinks I'm palace security, Holly realized. "It's fine," she told him as she strolled toward him. "I was just sent to make sure you were on your way to the meeting."

Erio's brow furrowed. "Yeah, I was headed there after this—"

Holly already had the syringe out of her jacket and in her hand. She darted forward and jammed it into Erio's neck. "Sorry," she told him as she injected the pale liquid into his veins. "But you'll be fine in a couple of hours." She caught him before he could collapse to the tile, doing her best to avoid hurting him any more than necessary. The council members didn't seem to be bad people, even if they'd been pretty much useless in dealing with Starr.

Holly dragged him back into the far stall and propped him up as best she could. Once she felt she had him positioned so that he wouldn't fall to the ground, she studied his face for a long moment, then changed her form to match his. Then, she swapped their jackets.

"Cutthroat," she said as she straightened up. "What's your status?"

"I'm in position. The Ra System members haven't shown up yet."

Holly headed for the bathroom door. "Great. Thea, directions?"

"Take a left out of the bathroom…"

Five minutes later, Holly was standing at the entrance to a conference room. She sucked in a deep breath and stepped in.

Ten palace security guards stood around the room, backs to the walls. At the table itself were two members of the Interstar Council: the apparent leader, Merf, a blue-skinned Sa Renian whose bald head reflected the room's lights. Sitting at his right was a humanoid alien with a black beak for a mouth and white feathers all over the rest of their body. Probably from the Aquila system.

"Erio," Merf greeted Holly as she approached the table. "Ready to begin?"

Holly nodded and settled into a chair across from him. She was saved from having to engage in further conversation by the arrival of two other council members, the two Ra System aliens with black patches on their white skin and horns growing from their heads. One of them asked Merf, "Are we the last?"

Merf nodded. "The others returned to the ship to finish the final report." He glanced at one of the nearby security guards as the two took their seats. "Will Governor Starr be ready soon?"

The guard nodded toward another standing at the end of the room. The second guard stepped forward and set a smartsphere on the table. With a tap, he brought up a holoscreen showing Syrus Starr's face. Wherever Starr was, he sat in a chair behind a desk, his gaze focused on a partially visible holoscreen.

Merf's eyes narrowed. "I believe we requested that he appear in person."

"I'm afraid the governor's schedule for this week has been set since before your arrival on Kronos," the head security guard replied. "You're fortunate he was able to make time where he is to call."

Starr spoke next. "Will this be an issue, or should we reschedule?"

"It's fine," Merf said, still sounding displeased. "We'll be live streaming this meeting to the council station, as well." His gaze darted to a smartsphere on the table in front of him. A faint red glow on the top indicated it was recording the space around it. Tone becoming slightly threatening, Merf added, "As well as other council ships in the area."

Holly resisted the urge to raise an eyebrow.

"Let's begin, then." Merf rose to his feet. "During our time here on Kronos, we've uncovered evidence of secret properties under Starr's employ. These include a lab here on Kronos, a facility on Reo, and space stations around the star system operating outside of public record."

Voice rising, thickening the tension in the room, Merf continued. "We also found a broadcast released by an anonymous party earlier this season to be true, despite efforts by your government to disprove the claims and evidence it presented. You were working with the villain Ringmaster on some of these secret projects. And we even found strong evidence indicating you have been directing a gang called the Red Blades to operate in ways that benefit you.

"Additionally, our assessment of your legal and economic systems indicates a massive power imbalance between Kronos's upper and lower classes." Merf took a deep breath and locked eyes with the projection of Governor Starr—whose face revealed no reaction to this speech, no hint of emotion at what the council leader was saying. "All of this information, including very detailed reports from our field agents and hard evidence, is in the file we sent to your office.

"Unless you can submit adequate proof that these projects were carried out without your knowledge," Merf continued. "And that you are taking active steps towards improving the conditions in Kronos's lower districts, we will be removing you from your position as governor."

Starr let Merf's words hang in the air a long moment before speaking. Expression calm, voice cool, he said, "It seems you put a lot of work into your investigation. Unfortunately, the Janus System will be withdrawing from the Interstar Alliance. You have no authority to take my power away from me."

Merf barked out a cold laugh. "The Alliance does not allow peaceful withdrawal during an active investigation. We are prepared to use force against your government if we deem people to be in active danger due to actions taken by you."

"Well, I'm afraid our little game has come to an end. You win." Starr rose to his feet, the top of his head leaving the screen, cutting him off at the neck. "And this is the part where I flip the table."

The call with Starr ended with a click. The security guards, in unison, drew their blasters. Holly only had a split second to react, though a small part of her had feared this might be Starr's response, as insane as it was. She dove out of her chair as the first round of blasts rang out.

Mixed with the cries of confusion—and pain—from the council members was the surprised shout of a guard. One who'd been shot through the chest. Holly only took a moment to watch the guard collapse, to watch his blood begin pooling on the floor, before sweeping her gaze over the other council members.

Merf was on his back, a wound in his neck spilling blood, his eyes staring lifelessly up at the ceiling. One of the Ra representatives appeared to be dead or close to it as well, but the other crouched next to them apparently unharmed. The Aquila member clutched a bleeding leg where they'd fallen to the ground a few feet from Merf.

Holly rose to her feet, drew her own blaster, and locked eyes with the one guard who hadn't drawn a palace-standard blaster. The one who'd fired on another guard instead of the council. Silver eyes met hers.

Cutthroat sprang into action, swinging the butt of his weapon into the side of the nearest guard's head. Holly fired in rapid succession, taking down two others. The remaining guards fired another round, aiming to kill the council members they'd failed to get on their first try. Holly rolled across the ground away from the clustered council, dodging the blasts aimed at her.

The remaining survivors both collapsed. More blood gathered on the floor.

Holly rolled, sprang to her feet directly in front of a guard, and drew a dagger. A quick slice across his neck dropped him. From there, she managed slice up those standing near him, only getting grazed once in the arm by a blaster beam in return. The other guards hesitated to keep firing for fear of hitting their colleagues. And then Cutthroat was cutting them down with his own dagger. It took less than a minute for him and Holly to take down the remaining guards.

"Shit!" Holly cursed as the last guard dropped. "He really—I didn't think Starr would actually have them killed in here."

She and Cutthroat raced to the room's exit together. More security would be on the way quickly. Even if there weren't cameras being actively monitored in that room, someone was bound to have heard the commotion.

As they approached an intersection, Holly shot Cutthroat a sideways glance. "Meet you at the southwest lounge window." Their pre-planned exit location.

Cutthroat nodded and split from her, veering down a hall branching to the right. While Cutthroat went to prepare their ride, Holly sprinted toward the bathroom she'd left the human council member in.

Erio was still unconscious, but all it took was a dose from another syringe to wake him. And a couple light slaps. As he came to, his eyes went wide, and panic coursed through his expression. "Why do you look like me?"

Right. Holly switched back to her human form, though that only seemed to startle him more.

"Who are you?" he demanded. "And why are you—?"

"No time," Holly cut him off. "I'm getting you out of here. If palace security gets their hands on you, they'll kill you."

"What? What about the meeting with Starr...?" Erio trailed off, realization dawning on him. "I've been unconscious. What happened at the meeting? Is Merf—?"

"Dead." Holly didn't see the point in sugarcoating it. "So are the others. Starr ordered it."

"Our army will attack the palace."

"He's got his own army. Something I don't think you found in your investigations." Holly straightened up and yanked Erio to his feet. "You have to get off Kronos, get back to the council, and warn them. Whatever army you have, Starr's prepared for it. And he's got something bigger. You guys need to come at him with everything you have."

Chapter Fifty-Three
Last Call

Tension in the apartment had been building all morning. Everyone was breathing a little easier now that they knew Holly and Cutthroat had made it out of the palace safely, but there was still an uneasiness hanging in the air.

Thea, however, tended to not notice when she was completely absorbed in her work. A few final taps, and her latest task was complete.

"Video's up," she announced. Thea had pulled everything she needed form the camera Holly had worn into the palace. And posted it on the net for the whole Janus System to see.

Jasper, who sat on the counter near Thea, crossed one leg over the other and took another sip of her smoothie. "Sweet. That should do quite a bit, on top of all the other work we've done encouraging people to protest today." Her expression darkened as she added, "With the council no longer around to save them, maybe they'll realize they have to save themselves. Fight back."

Thea nodded, scrolling through the initial reactions as they rolled in. "There's the weirdos defending Starr, of course, but most people are rightfully appalled and want to take some kind of action."

The apartment door opened, and Holly strolled in, Cutthroat close behind. "How are things outside?" Jasper asked, shooting them a glance.

"Protests are already starting," Holly said. "And I wandered through some shops and whatnot on my way back. Those who aren't already out are talking about it."

Jasper nodded. "We should have a pretty considerable force by tonight, then."

Thea began responding to a few online comments here and there. *We outnumber them.* If all the people of Kronos came together, there was nothing Starr could do. Even if he had firepower, he couldn't run the planet without a workforce. People simply refusing to work even without violent action would put a halt to the operations the elite were dependent on for their luxuries.

Of course, if Starr was confident he could defeat the council, he had to have quite the force lurking somewhere. The people as a whole might be able to stand up to him, but that would only work if they weren't intimidated into going about business as usual.

Thea glanced across the room to the table where Grace and Dax sat, also scrolling through social sites and news forums. They'd expressed hesitation over putting ordinary people in danger by riling them up, but at the end of the day, people still got to choose whether they stepped outside and took a stand. And the alternative was living in a system trying to wring as much work out of them as possible. Giving them scraps in return. Even if Jasper's plans hadn't led the team to incite a rebellion today, it was still going to happen. Protests had been popping up for a long time now.

"Every empire falls eventually," Thea muttered. She knew enough about history to know that much. And it seemed to hold true across the galaxy. A power imbalance was unstable at its core.

A new comment popped up in response to one she'd left. *He can only rule us if we let him.*

Jaw setting with determination, Thea kept scrolling. Boosting photos of protests as they moved upward toward the upper districts. As expected, police were mobilizing to block people's way up.

"Getting people into the upper districts is going to be tricky," Thea said as she watched one of the videos. "Every one of their police precincts are mobilizing. Probably bringing forces up from the lower districts, too. They won't let a single out-of-place rioter get into the elite neighborhoods if they can help it."

Jasper leaned over to peer at the screen. Her eyes narrowed. "If they think they can go on and throw their party without interruption, they're in for a surprise."

Grace glanced up from her own screen. "What do the other elite think of all this?"

Sarena, who laid on the couch in the next room, held up her tablet and waved it for the others to see. "You're in luck. Every group chat I'm in is blowing up with talk about the protests and the party."

Jasper raised an eyebrow. "You're in group chats with elite families?"

"Obviously." Sarena's eyes rolled. "A lot of them want to lock themselves up in their penthouses until this blows over."

"Bold of them to assume it's just going to blow over," Jasper muttered.

Sarena let out a cold laugh. "It's worked for them so far. Anyway, Starr sent out a message to some of the families, and one of their dumbass teenagers leaked it here." She tapped her screen, sending the image to a spare smartsphere on the dining table in the form of a holoscreen projection.

Dax leaned forward to study the message. "There is nothing to worry about," he read. "All available security and police in the city will ensure we have a safe and comfortable night at the palace. And you won't want to miss what we have planned."

Thea shrugged. "Even the police will be outnumbered if we can muster enough people. And we can probably handle a lot of the security forces ourselves."

Jasper twisted and craned her neck, peering at Thea's screen for a long moment. Finally, Thea asked, "Can I help you?"

"Any signs of...well, anything?" Jasper took another sip of her smoothie before continuing. "If Starr's army is big enough to handle the council's, it has to be making some kind of mark...somewhere."

Thea shook her head. "Nothing on radar in the Janus System. No unusual signals. Nothing on any of my scans. There does seem to be some activity just outside the system, but there's not much equipment out there I can access to get more accurate readings."

"You think that's the council?"

"Seems likely."

"Is it possible their forces will be enough?" Grace asked.

Jasper sighed. "I have a feeling Starr wouldn't make a move like this if he wasn't certain of the answer." With that terrifying sentiment, she took another sip of her smoothie and hit the bottom of the cup, filling the apartment with a lovely slurping noise.

An alert popped up on Thea's laptop screen, notifying her that her decoding software had run into a problem with the long-distance message she'd found. She brought it up and frowned at the screen.

"Are we sure we should still move forward with storming the palace, then?" Dax asked.

"If there's no army yet, yes," Jasper replied. "If we can overwhelm Starr on the ground and keep him distracted, that might be enough for the council to win when they get here.

"Plus, as long as Thea can still get into AstraSmart," she continued. "The palace itself shouldn't be much of a challenge—"

At that moment, only half-paying attention to what Jasper was saying, Thea cursed and began typing more aggressively on her laptop's keyboard.

Jasper frowned. "Uh, is AstraSmart really giving you that much trouble?"

Thea shook her head. "No, I've got that running in the background right now. I'm still trying to decode this new signal."

A few words unscrambled. Not much, but what did appear made Thea's eyes widen. She closed her eyes and focused on the code with her power. Not the message itself, but the file containing it.

Her brow furrowed as she noticed something she hadn't picked up on before. Despite being broadcast on the signal Grim Machine had been using to communicate with...whoever he was communicating with, this message didn't seem to have been meant for him. The other messages stored in his system had been tagged with an ID number that this one didn't have. And its source coordinates were different, too. And...

"Thea Smith," she muttered as another piece of text from the message unscrambled. Her algorithm seemed to have finally cracked the encryption and was decoding the text much faster now.

Jasper's brow furrowed. "What was that?"

"This message...seems to be directed at me." Thea opened another program and set it running with a tap on the side of the laptop. In a way, she was contributing power from her mind—her technopathy—to the process, offering a nuance to the program's A.I. that could help it find some clue in the code it wouldn't have detected otherwise.

Holly folded her arms. "Maybe we should make some last-minute moves against the elite families. If they finally go to war with each other, it could be enough of a distraction to buy us more time to prepare for Starr's army."

"Hm." Jasper rubbed her chin. "I'm not sure what we can do before the party. They've all been looking forward to that."

"They'll all be together in one place at the party. It would be the perfect place to start a war."

Cutthroat joined the conversation, his tone skeptical. "Seems a little last-minute."

Holly shrugged. "It could still be useful. And we know everyone already thinks the Fayes are after their district. We can work with that."

"I agree, but elite wars tend to be focused on politics, not violence," Jasper pointed out. "I'm not sure how much good it would do us."

"I don't know, Starr did have the Red Blades working for him," Grace chimed in. "And the Fayes were running the Lion's Den. They might be more into straight up attacking each other than we thought. It wouldn't be surprising if other families have gang connections, too."

Holly nodded. "And now that we've taken away some of those other avenues, they're under even more pressure than before. I could make some time before things ramp up to fuel the flames."

Jasper nodded slowly. "Yeah, I suppose you guys have a point. Let's go ahead with that, then. May as well." After a moment of thinking, she added, "Speaking of gangs, we should also find out what the Slicers are up to, now that Attom is...out of the picture. Maybe we can get them involved in the fight."

Thea straightened up in surprise, nearly falling off her stool. "This message *is* for me!"

Jasper shot her a startled glance. "I thought that was on Grim Machine's signal?"

"It was sent on the same signal, but it was coded a different way and came from someone else. They must have known that I'd gain access to the signal, somehow."

"Is it from the council?" Grace asked.

"No, I don't think so, they have their own signal they use that's completely different. And I've tried communicating with them on that before." Thea glanced up at the team. "Whoever this is, they want to meet up."

"They didn't say who they are?"

Thea's gaze flicked over the short message. "It says my name, then, 'We're an organization also trying to get justice for what Starr has done. We think our chances will be better if we work together.'

"They also gave me another code to crack that will let me access a local signal," Thea continued. "And asked if we could meet somewhere in Kronos."

"Could be tricky, fitting that into our schedule," Jasper noted.

Holly folded her arms. "And, uh, it could be a trap? I'm a little more worried about that part."

"Could be," Thea agreed.

Everyone glanced at Jasper. After a long moment, a grin crept onto Jasper's face. "What the hell. Let's see what the deal with these guys is. I'm in."

Chapter Fifty-Four
Does It Count As A Family Reunion If You've Never Met Before?

Grace stood on a rooftop at the city's edge, alongside the rest of the team. Ahead of them, the waves of Kronos's ocean crashed against rocky shoreline. The building beneath their feet was a warehouse meant to store imports brought by ships from scattered mining rigs across the water.

At her right, Jasper stood with one hand clutching Grace's and the other on a blaster. Cutthroat had brought the pirates Hook and Steele, and Sarena had brought a couple of sirens as well: a bald, orange-skinned woman named Carcinia, and a yellow-skinned woman with a pair of antennae, completely red eyes, and braided fiery orange hair named Hyva. Thea was watching for signals on her tablet, while Dax and Holly stood on either side of her, gazes jumping between the screen and the sea. Aymes stood with a ring of silver energy clutched in his grasp, his gaze locked on the rough waters.

Rose had been left in the Comet parked nearby, with the promise that she could fly the ship over to rescue them if things went wrong. Grace assumed that meant Jasper was confident things *wouldn't* go wrong, given that Rose didn't exactly have much by way of flying skills, but the distant anxiety in Jasper's gaze combatted that assumption.

Finally, something appeared on the horizon. The small spacecraft approached with remarkable speed, though Grace suspected the Comet would be just able to beat it if necessary. This ship was a dark metallic color and a fair amount smaller than the Comet, though much wider proportionally. It also had a flattened appearance. Judging by the size of the small domed cockpit poking out of the top, the craft could probably only fit two people. Maybe three could squeeze in, max.

The ship flew over their heads and landed on the opposite end of the roof behind them. The team turned around as the engines died down. The dome on top of the ship lifted, allowing the pilot to scramble out onto the ship's nose and slide off it. She dropped to the roof with a thud and straightened up, giving everyone the chance to look her over.

The girl was young-looking, around the age of Grace and the others in Jasper's original team. She was a human with dark brown skin and short curls that had been dyed purple, though a small section at the roots showed the hair's original black color. She wore black tactical gear.

Thea strolled forward without hesitation, her brow furrowed. "You're the one who sent me that message? How did you know it would get to me?"

The girl nodded as Thea came to a stop a few feet from her. "I found footage of your team fighting Grim Machine and saw that you'd taken some of his guts. I hoped that meant you'd be able to crack the same long-distance signal I had," she explained. "I threw together an encryption that only someone like you would be able to get into in any reasonable amount of time and, well, here we are."

Thea lifted an eyebrow. "You must be a good hacker, then."

The girl shrugged. "I don't have your technopathy, so it takes me a lot longer to crack stuff like that. But yeah, I got in a while back."

"All right, all right, let's get some basic information before too much geeking out happens." Jasper took a step forward, waving a hand. She'd returned her blaster to her side, apparently deciding there was no need for it for the time being. Grace let Jasper's hand slip from hers so she could approach Thea and the stranger.

"Who are you?" Jasper continued, her question directed at the stranger. "And why did you contact us?"

The girl swallowed and glanced at Thea. "My name's Zoe Smith. I'm Thea's great-niece."

The words left Thea wide-eyed, jaw dropping slightly. "How—how did you find me?" she finally managed to ask.

Jasper's mouth opened to add something, but she seemingly changed her mind and closed it, allowing the two to finish their conversation. Grace took a tentative step forward to bring herself back to Jasper's side.

Zoe folded her arms. "I started looking into your disappearance a few years back, after I got recruited to Earthguard. With their resources, I found the Earth records on you regarding that incident that gave you your powers. And then I found signs that you'd wound up here in the Janus System, un-aged since your disappearance." Hesitantly, she added, "I don't have anything close to the full story. All I knew is that Jolt was probably you."

Thea let out a sound somewhere between a surprised laugh and a sigh. "Yeah. It's…a long story."

"I'll have to hear it later, then," Zoe replied. Her gaze moved past Thea to the rest of the team, and she addressed everyone when she spoke next. "Like I said, I'm with Earthguard, and my superiors were taking a huge chance sending me to meet you. They didn't think it was a good idea, but it looks like you're all fighting Governor Starr, from what I've gathered. So, I was hoping I could persuade you to work with us."

"Earthguard, eh?" Jasper sounded skeptical as she repeated the organization's name. "What the hell have you all been up to? I haven't heard a thing from you since your agent failed to rescue Grace from the palace."

Grace winced.

"I'm sorry," Zoe said. "Kara knew going into that mission that it was a long shot. We knew Starr was about to kill Grace anyway, so we risked it. And she was able to at least get Grace out—"

"And right into jail," Jasper cut Zoe off, hands moving to her hips. "If I hadn't saved her, she'd be dead."

Grace's brow furrowed. Sure, Jasper cared about her. Of course she'd be upset about Earthguard's failure. But Grace wouldn't have survived without Kara getting her as far as she had before getting killed. There had to be more.

"Kara did get me away from the bodyguard sent to kill me," Grace pointed out quietly. "I'd be dead without her, too."

Jasper's expression softened, and she let out a heavy sigh. Her hands dropped to her sides. "*I'm* from Earth, and I never got any help. Neither did any of the other abducted kids that got turned into slaves or fighters or lab experiments."

Zoe bowed her head. "We got a bit away from our original mission, I think. Earthguard was founded to protect humans who wound up off of Earth, for whatever reason. But we stumbled across the Starr family's inter-star system smuggling operation, and then got a bit sidetracked by his other plans…" She cleared her throat. Chin lifting again, she continued. "Anyway, we're trying to fry some bigger fish now. But if we succeed at this, big power systems will topple, and it'll make stopping the smuggling much easier."

"All right," Jasper conceded after a moment. Her arms folded, and some of her usual confidence crept back into her voice. "One last question. How did you know about Grim Machine's signal in the first place? That doesn't seem to have anything to do with Starr, as far as I can tell."

"Oh, we've got quite the file on Grim Machine," Zoe said. "We've been investigating him ever since we caught wind that he might have come from the Ra System."

"And you care about the Ra System because…?" Jasper lifted an eyebrow.

Zoe shrugged. "The higher-ups haven't told me much. I don't think even they know what's going on, just that there's something fishy happening over there," she said. "Anyway, we are pretty focused on Starr right this second. And after what happened with the council earlier today, all available Earthguard forces have been summoned to Kronos."

"Great," Jasper said, a hint of sarcasm in her tone. "But if you don't have a full army, I don't think you're going to be much help."

"Uh, Jasper?" Dax said quietly. "We don't exactly have an army, either."

"I know that!" Jasper rolled her eyes. "I just think between us, the people we're gathering, and what the council does have at their disposal, a small team of spies isn't going to do much good at this point."

"We're more than just spies. We can fight." Zoe folded her arms and lifted her chin.

Jasper sighed. "You wanna fight Starr? Great, have at it. But if you wanna team up with us, then you work for me. I'm in charge of tonight's Operation Lead A Revolution To Starr's Christmas Eve Party, and everything's pretty much in place for that already."

"That's nice. But what intel do you have on Starr's army?"

Jasper's eyes narrowed. "You know about Starr's army?"

A sly smile touched Zoe's lips. "We may not have been able to get anyone into the palace or labs since Kara, but we have been able to find our way into some secret weapon factories around the system," she said. "We've been keeping as low a profile as possible, but we have been around."

Jasper still looked skeptical. "So, where is Starr's army, then? I thought we'd have seen it by now, what with the council's army being on their way."

"Well, last I heard, he was assembling all the pieces separately across the Janus System. New labs for the cyborg soldiers, secret factories for ship parts. All powered by spacetime warp energy." Zoe paused. "You know about those?"

"Believe me, I'm painfully familiar with what Starr's been doing with spacetime warps." Jasper nodded for Zoe to go on.

Zoe nodded. "Anyway, production died down a few weeks back. We assume Starr started shipping his soldiers and equipment here to Kronos, but our spies weren't able to get details on when or how. Technically, we aren't certain anything's been moved."

"So, you've got nothing."

"We've got details on the cyborg soldiers' physical limitations, the types of weapons they're armed with, and specs for the ships they'll be flying in."

"Alright, fine, you've got slightly more than nothing," Jasper conceded. "Still doesn't do us much good if we don't know their current positions." She glanced at Thea, then back at Zoe. "I don't suppose we're lucky enough for Starr to be using AstraSmart in his army ships and bases?"

Zoe shook her head. "It's all been built custom by his own engineers and programmers." Looking to Thea, she added, "No one at Earthguard has cracked any of it. I don't know if you'd have any more luck."

Thea nodded slowly, considering. "Sounds like the kind of thing that would take me a month to get into, at best. By the time I found a way in, they'd have spotted me and found a way to kick me out."

"So, we gave up on that side of things, and we hit a bit of a dead end." Zoe shoved her hands into the pockets of her jacket. Her head turned so she could glance back at her ship. "Is Starr really still moving forward with that party tonight?"

"Yep," Jasper confirmed. "Sent out a message to the elite promising they'd be safe, despite the protests. And the fact that he killed several council members." She threw a glance over her shoulder. "Any updates on that front, Sarena?"

Sarena huffed and pulled out her smartsphere. Messages scrolled across the small projected holoscreen. "Lots of people are confirming that they're still going."

"They really trust Starr that much?" Cutthroat scratched at his beard.

"Starr, sure, though that trust may be waning. But it sounds like they'll give him a chance to prove himself as their leader tonight," Jasper said. It was clear from her expression the gears in her mind were turning. "But just because they all trust him doesn't mean they trust each other. He's kept them under control even with what we've thrown at them the past few weeks, but they are close to snapping."

"So, now what?" Sarena asked, a bit louder than necessary. "And can we consider moving this meeting to somewhere more comfortable?"

Jasper ignored her. "We also have a wild card to worry about. Skybreaker. I don't know if she'll fall on Starr's side when the actual battle starts, but I doubt she'll be on ours."

"We should have a plan to deal with her just in case," Grace said. There was an implication in her voice, a hint of an idea the team had discussed before.

Jasper nodded.

"So," Zoe said. "Do you want to meet up with the rest of the Earthguard members that are already here and see what we're working with?"

"Yeah, sure, fine, whatever." Jasper's hands slid into her coat pockets.

While Zoe began to explain where they would be heading, Grace slipped one of her hands into Jasper's closest pocket. Her hand brushed against Jasper's, and Jasper moved to intertwine her fingers with Grace's.

Chapter Fifty-Five
Fleet

At the back of the Comet, Grace settled into a seat next to Thea. Dax took the seat on her other side, and Holly grabbed a handle on the wall and stood next to the group. Jasper piloted, keeping them close to Zoe's ship as they soared over the ocean.

Holly was the first to speak. "You doing okay, Thea?" she asked, her voice low.

Thea glanced up, surprise flashing in her expression. "Huh?"

Holly nodded toward the front of the ship, toward the open door to the cockpit where Zoe's ship was visible out the front window. "I mean, having a relative pop up out of nowhere must be…a lot to process."

After a moment, Thea nodded and let out a slow breath. "It's weird. I think I…haven't let myself think about Earth in a long time. Or my family."

"Me neither," Dax added quietly.

Grace swallowed and glanced at the window. Once, she would have thought she could relate to this conversation. But she'd never really left behind a family in the first place. There were people out there who'd lost a girl named Grace Alvarez, but Grace wasn't her. Just a clone. An echo.

With the others having spent so much time in the warp, and Grace being cloned so long after the original Grace's abduction, there didn't seem to be much left for any of them on Earth. Even Jasper had long outlived her life there. But still, Jasper had expressed interest in escaping to Earth…

Thea and Dax exchanged a glance. "I have a million questions I want to ask her about my family," Thea said quietly. "But I'm also terrified of asking them. If my parents are still alive, they'd be nearly a hundred."

"Same with my dad," Dax said. "But hopefully my younger sister is still alive, at least."

Grace glanced at Holly, who was watching the two with a genuinely pained expression. Grace swallowed. "I don't know much about sending messages across star systems, but is there no way you can try contacting them to see if they're still alive?"

Thea shrugged. "Believe me, I've thought about it. The biggest issue is that even if I send a long-distance message through a warp that will take it to Earth, they have no way of picking it up. Earth's technology is nowhere close to what we have here. The only way to find them is to actually go to Earth."

"And even though we can access the Earthnet, finding information on whether a couple of random people are still alive wouldn't be easy," Holly added. "Plus, while accessing data on their net is easy enough, it's not really set up to interface with other star system networks. Assuming we could even find an account that belongs to them, doesn't mean we could send a message."

Dax folded his arms. "Maybe Earthguard can help? They said they're trying to help people who were abducted, and they're all from Earth, so they probably run their operations from there."

Holly's expression darkened. "They haven't exactly accomplished much so far. But yeah, maybe they can do something."

The group fell quiet after that. Ten minutes later, the Comet slowed, and they were touching down on what Grace guessed was a small island, from what she could see through the window.

The team filed out, Rose included, though Cutthroat was keeping a careful eye on her as they disembarked. Outside the ship was a rocky shoreline wrapping around a forest of towering trees, each with curling needles in varying shades of green. The forest itself was only the size of a few city blocks, and the thin stretch of shoreline wrapping around it appeared to be the island's only other feature.

Nearby, Zoe climbed out of her ship and gestured for the team to follow. "Our temporary base isn't far."

They walked through the shadows of the trees for about five minutes before emerging in a large clearing. Grace was a bit startled to realize the clearing itself was taking up most of the island, and that the forest was only a layer wrapping around the outside. Spacecraft were parked all across the open space, many of them several times bigger than the comet and armed with various weapons.

"How do you know that Starr doesn't know you're here?" Jasper asked, turning in a slow circle to study the tree line behind them.

"There aren't any shipping routes anywhere near here, we've never picked up any probe signals, and nothing's ever come close on radar." Zoe shrugged. "Maybe we missed something, but we're fairly confident no one has seen us come or go. There's nothing of value to the Kronos government on or near this island, so they have no reason to monitor the area very closely. Getting the ships into the system without drawing attention was the biggest challenge."

Jasper moved to inspect a nearby ship, and Grace trailed behind, more focused on the island itself. The ground beneath them was entirely reddish dirt, not becoming grass until it reached the shade of the trees.

Zoe removed a communicator from her pocket and spoke into it. A minute later, a few other Earthguard agents emerged from one of the ships. The team regrouped around them.

"Well," Jasper spoke first, shoving her hands in her coat pockets. "Your ships look pretty nice, I'll give you that. Should be able to handle themselves in a battle, even against Starr's advanced weapons." She glanced at Zoe. "But there's not much here by way of numbers. If we unite with the council, maybe we'll be okay, but Starr must have a lot of confidence in his army, doing what he did."

One of the other Earthguard agents—a woman with shoulder-length straight black hair and brown skin—replied. "We do have the advantage of knowing what Starr's soldiers and weapons look like, even if we don't know how many he's made."

Jasper nodded. "I'd like to see those specs."

The agent who'd spoken nodded and led Jasper's team into one of the ships. As they walked, she introduced herself as Agent Singh and explained that she was the leader of the Earthguard unit here on Kronos. Once inside, she gestured for them all to gather around a table. A smaller-than-average silver smartsphere sat in the table's center.

Thea took the seat closest to the sphere, launched its holoscreen, and began browsing the files within. There were 3D models of rectangular carrier ships, of people with cybernetic skeletons, of weapons.

Jasper sat next to her, and the two studied the models with an intensity that was beyond Grace. She wasn't sure exactly what details they were looking at, but whatever they were, it apparently made far more sense to them than it did her.

"Well, these carriers will be full of superpowered soldiers and weapons," Jasper said eventually, straightening up. "But I think the ships themselves will go down pretty easy. If we can get them out over the ocean, your ships and even the Astronomer should be able to take them out without collateral damage." Glancing toward Agent Singh, who'd moved to stand in a nearby corner with her arms folded, she added, "Would be a lot better if we could coordinate with the council too, though."

Thea glanced up. "You guys don't have any communication with the council?"

Singh shook her head. "We tried sending them messages in hopes we could work together, but we never got a response."

"Probably deem it a violation of their stupid laws to work with a group like yours," Jasper muttered. "At any rate, we're running low on time, so we'll have to work with what we've got." She rose to her feet and began to pace.

"Your ships will be useful in a fight, but I think there's something else you can help us with," she continued. "The Governor's Palace is full of servants kidnapped from other worlds. I planned to come up with a way to help them after all this, but you guys could get in there and start pulling them out while we distract Starr with massive protests."

"Surely Starr will be able to defend his palace against protestors who don't have any heavy artillery," Singh replied, frowning.

"We'll be helping them out. But we don't want him to realize what a threat the rebellion is until they're right at his door, because yes, he could put up more defenses." Jasper turned and met Singh's gaze. "Which is why we have another distraction planned. Speaking of, Thea, you were able to confirm that once you're in the AstraSmart network at the palace, you'll be able to get in to other devices all over the city, right?"

Thea glanced up from the holoscreen she was still studying and cleared her throat. "Right, uh, small update on that. AstraSmart decided to implement my demand."

Jasper's brow furrowed. "Huh?"

"They added a dark mode option." When Jasper still had nothing to offer but a blank stare, Thea continued, "Which affects the code—look, I can still get in, I just have to add a few more protocols to make sure my hack affects devices using the new setting."

"How does a visual settings change affect their security?"

"All the code is intricately connected!" Quickly, Thea added, "Don't worry, though, I'll still able to get in. And the palace tech will be the hardest part. Once I'm into that, yes, any other smart appliances in the city will be easy."

Jasper nodded. "Good." Turning back to Singh, she said, "How about I lay out the rest of what we have planned so far, and we see where we can fit you in?"

Singh nodded and started toward a door near the front of the ship. "Follow me." All of the other agents—save for Zoe—joined her.

While Jasper went to explain the plan to the other Earthguard agents, Zoe moved to the table where the rest of the team was gathered. She grabbed an empty chair as she approached and set it down next to Thea.

"Back when Earthguard found out that the Fayes had taken in a couple of human kids—well, I didn't get my hopes up at the time, but then we confirmed the names." Zoe sat down in the chair and glanced at Thea. "Your siblings always hoped I'd find you."

Thea looked up, surprise flashing across her face, immediately overtaken by something more like apprehension. "Are they...?"

"My last trip to earth was a couple months ago. Your sister just moved into a nursing home, but she's doing pretty well. We made sure she's at a high-quality place. It's got great reviews. And your brother's living with his kids—my parents."

While Thea nodded slowly, processing what Grace was sure must be a torrent of mixed emotions, Dax spoke up. "Do you have a way of going through Earth records and checking if my family's...?"

"We already looked you up," Zoe replied with a nod. "You've got a younger sister living in Oregon. We checked in on her once we learned about you. She's in a pretty good retirement home. We sent some money her way, too."

Dax exchanged a look with Thea. There was too much emotion in both of their expressions to really read what they were thinking, but Grace got the feeling that there was some fresh hope there.

Holly folded her arms. The gaze she fixed on Zoe was a bit cold as she spoke. "You guys know anything about that Laika Academy that recruited all of us and got us thrown in a spacetime warp? I think they owe these two some apologies. And they should be the ones taking care of their families."

Zoe's brow furrowed. "We did hear about Laika while trying to figure out how Thea and Dax wound up in another star system. But that trail turned into a dead end. We couldn't find a trace of them."

"I'm sure Jasper would love to poke around," Grace said softly. "If anyone can find them, it's her."

The hint of a smirk touched the corner of Holly's mouth. "Damn right."

"We could get you to Earth," Zoe told them. "We have our own transportation networks, so you wouldn't need to worry about dodging the government or paying a sketchy underground transport team."

"We need to see this through first." Thea glanced at Dax, who nodded. "Then, we'll do everything we can to prevent this from happening to anyone else."

Chapter Fifty-Six
Show Time

The woman Grace saw in the mirror was strangely unfamiliar. For the first time in a long time, she forced herself to really study her reflection. The hard look in her eyes, the wings lifted high behind her with confidence, the muscles in her arms that were more defined than they had been when she'd first fled the Governor's Palace.

And, of course, the Superangel uniform.

"You can do this," she whispered to herself. There was no more time for second guessing. For doubting herself. The city was going to break, the people were going to revolt, and all she could do was try her best to keep them safe while they did.

She stepped out of the bathroom and headed for the living room. Her eyes went to the windows as she entered the space. The sky was darkening. Late afternoon already. The day had felt like a blur, even with the detour to meet Earthguard and check out their ships.

The others were prepping weapons, checking the news, and shoving down some last-minute food. Amid the chaos, Grace's eyes found Jasper's. Jasper grinned, and Grace's smile came easily, despite her anxiety.

Jasper hurried over to her. "You ready?"

Grace nodded. "Sounds like things are getting intense in the lower districts."

"Yeah. The sooner you get out there, the better," Jasper said. She quickly added, "As long as you still want to do this."

"I do."

There must have been enough confidence in her lifted chin and hardened expression, because Jasper didn't press her further. Instead, she smirked and said, "Then get out there, Superangel." She grabbed one of Grace's hands and gave it a quick squeeze.

Grace leaned forward to kiss her. "I'll see you soon," she said quietly after pulling away.

"You'd better." Jasper let out a soft laugh, but there was a hint of apprehension hiding behind her eyes. This was the most dangerous plan they'd ever put into action. And they still had no idea what to expect from Starr.

Grace said quick goodbyes to the rest of the team before leaving the apartment. Once outside, she immediately spread her wings and took to the air. The usual sounds of the city—the traffic, the music drifting out of clubs and restaurants, the casual chatter of people on the streets—were joined by the sounds and shouts of protest that had grown familiar in the past few weeks. Grace circled several blocks, noting the crowds of varying size that congregated across the lower districts.

She picked one of the smaller crowds to be her first to address. She soared over them from behind and glided toward the street ahead. Her wings folded in, and she dropped. A thump shook her body as her boots met asphalt.

There was no sign of vehicle traffic on this street, though a few cars had been abandoned along the sidewalks. It seemed people in the area had given up on navigating the growing crowds by car. Most vehicles down here were typically delivery or company vehicles, anyway. Everyone else walked or took public transit—sketchy as it could be—to save themselves the cost of even the cheapest vehicles.

Regardless, the only movement was the crowd ahead marching toward her. As people began to take notice of her, the pace slowed and the shouting quieted. A few people chanted her name, but when Grace lifted her sword into the air, they fell silent and allowed her to speak.

"I am leading the way to the palace," she announced. "Some of my friends will be joining us. With your numbers and our power, we will remind the governor and the elite that the city does not function without you. Their wealth is built on your labor, and it's about time we stopped letting them take advantage of us.

"While you starve and struggle and work long hours, they are throwing an extravagant party at this very moment," Grace continued. Sword lowering, eyes narrowing, she added, "And with Starr's ordered killing of the Interstar Council members who came to investigate him, it's clear that laws will not change things. We must put on a show of force. It will not be easy. It will not be safe. But it is the only alternative to continued suffering. If you are willing to join me, I'll do everything I can to defend you."

The silence that followed her words was quickly broken by cheers and chants. Grace swallowed a sudden bout of fresh anxiety that threatened to wash over her. *We're doing this. We're committed. And they're committed. They don't want to live this way anymore.*

Grace glanced toward a bar at her right. Through the window, she could see that the screens inside were playing the video Thea had leaked. Most people had to have seen it already, or at least heard of it. Any attempts Starr's administration had made to bury Thea's broadcast of the video had failed. The video of Merf listing Starr's crimes, everything the council had found in their investigation. The video of Starr's guards turning on them. Killing them.

Any hopes the citizens of Kronos had had that someone would step in, that the council would save them, had been shattered, even if they did claim to be sending an army to remove Starr. Any lingering belief that Starr wasn't as bad as he seemed, that the elite were anything other than selfish...it was all gone, and it had been replaced with burning rage. With a fire that would not be easily extinguished.

The upper district propaganda machine was hard at work, but it clearly wasn't enough. "Then we march on the palace!" Grace's final shout mixed with the crowd's chants and screams. While they pressed forward, she returned to the air and sought out another group to speak to. She wouldn't have time to meet with all of them, especially if she wanted to beat them all to the palace. But she could give them some direction and motivation to keep going, and spread the word that she was fighting, too.

Grace forced herself to address larger and larger crowds, and her nerves eased gradually. The people were glad to see her and often cheered her on, even if she was just passing by overhead.

Don't they get I'm just a person like them? Grace's confidence had grown, but she still didn't think she'd ever perceive herself as strong as they did, as heroic. They saw a leader where she saw someone following Jasper's plan.

But she did trust in herself, now.

After another one of her speeches, Grace decided to head straight up a few levels to catch up to the very front of the marching protesters. She adjusted her wings, pushed hard, and soared. All around her, people were taking every possible route to the upper districts. Piling into elevators and exterior lifts, filling escalators, marching up stairs and fire escapes. A few passing cars looked full, too. It seemed anyone lucky enough to own a vehicle with flying capabilities had invited as many as possible to join them.

The protestors who'd gone the farthest were beginning to reach the higher points in the middle districts, the perimeter of Starr's security forces. Grace had expected the officers and guards strolling the walkways bordering the middle and upper districts, but she was surprised by the number of cruisers flying around, too. And as she took notice of them, she also began to notice many were pursuing the protesters' vehicles.

One cruiser shot past Grace with its sirens blaring and fell into pace next to a battered flying vehicle that Grace wasn't sure she'd have dared to ride in herself. She adjusted her angle and raced through the air toward the two vehicles as they slowed. She caught up within seconds and slammed her boots against the cruiser's backend, sending it spinning away. "Go!" she shouted to the driver of the protestors' vehicle. They sped away without further urging.

The police cruiser's engines roared, and the vehicle reoriented itself. The officer in the driver's seat turned it to face Grace. Her eyes narrowed as she met his gaze through the window. She shook her head at him—though she doubted that would deter him from continuing to follow orders—before shooting upwards through the city toward the more intense conflict.

Grace's reflection raced her in passing windows. Neon lights brightened as the sky faded. People shouted her name from walkways and balconies as she passed.

Superangel.

Her heart beat faster with every skyscraper story she passed, with every cry and shout from the people. *Be strong for them. Be strong for the team.*

Be strong for Jasper.

Grace finally broke the skyline and burst into the open space of Kronos's lower atmosphere. She sucked in a deep breath and tipped her head back. Her wings stretched out wide to each side. The wind whipped stray pieces of her hair in a frenzy around her face.

It took a moment for her head to clear. The speed at which she'd come up here had been near dizzying. Easily one of the fastest flights she'd ever performed. Once she felt her heart rate begin to steady, she forced herself to look down.

There it was, gleaming in the last dying rays of sunlight and reflecting the multitude of colors from the city below. The Governor's Palace.

In addition to the sun's near disappearance, heavy gray clouds were rolling in fast, reflecting the city lights back down on it. Judging by the chill in the air that even Grace could feel, it would be snow that fell from them. She hoped everyone on the streets had dressed appropriately.

Beating her wings just hard enough to keep herself hovering in the air, she tapped the comm in her ear. "The first waves of protestors are trying to enter the upper districts."

"Roger that," Jasper replied. "I'll be there in a minute. The others are making their way up to help. Thea, you ready to flip the switch?"

"Just give the word, and we're good to go," Thea affirmed.

Grace touched down on a rooftop nearly as high as the palace and dropped into a crouch.

"I think we're ready for our last surprise, too," Jasper said. "Let's send that final broadcast out. Let our contestants know it's time."

"On it."

Grace could almost hear the smirk in Thea's voice. She felt a grin break out on her own lips. Another way to distract Starr and even deal some blows to palace security, hopefully.

Shifting her weight slightly, Grace let out a small sigh. Her breath clouded the air in front of her, but the air wasn't quite frigid enough to make her uncomfortable.

"All right," she murmured, more to herself than anyone else. "It's show time."

Still, Jasper gave a response that promised a wicked grin. "Damn right, Angel."

Grace rose to her full height, took a step forward off the roof, and dropped from the sky.

Chapter Fifty-Seven
Blackout

Jasper was the last member of the team to walk to the front door, a few more weapons than usual strapped to her body. She'd be the last to leave, but she wasn't leaving the apartment empty. Rose sat on the couch in the living room, glaring at the holoscreen that Thea had locked on a broadcast of some cartoon.

Jasper paused and watched her young clone as she held a finger to the comm in her ear to check in on the others. "All right, Angel, how are things on the streets?"

"Good. If they can start breaking through the security lines, the first waves of protestors should be about another twenty or so minutes from the palace."

It was a tight window of time, but Jasper could make it work. She nodded—more to herself than anything else—and moved on. "Sarena, you're already inside, right?"

"Yep."

"Great. I'm going to check in with you again in a few minutes. I want to know what the elite are up to. Holly and Dax, you're with the crowds?"

"A little ahead of them," Holly replied. "Trying to get some officers out of the way."

"But we're good, so far," Dax added.

Jasper's hand moved to the handle. Rose glanced her way. Ignoring the annoyed look in the girl's gaze, Jasper said, "All right. And your prep, Thea?"

"Everything's ready."

"You've still got your line open with Zoe?"

"Yep." The sound of clicking keys on Thea's end just made it through with her voice.

"Perfect. I'll swing by to check on you in a few." That left two. "Aymes, ready for me in the Comet?"

"Aye aye, captain." Aymes's voice walked a fine line between sarcastic and monotone.

"And Cutthroat?"

"Astronomer's in the sky in what seems to be a safe area," Cutthroat replied. "Still no sign of this army we've been worrying about."

"Let's not get our hopes up," Jasper muttered. She turned the door handle.

"I can help!" Rose jumped to her feet, the pout on her face that had been lingering for hours now giving way to something more energetic. "I've helped on missions before! What makes this any different?"

Jasper shook her head. "You are good on missions. But this is different. This is a war."

"But—"

"No buts. You're staying safe." The door gave way to Jasper's push, and she stepped out into the apartment hallway. The door clicked shut behind her. Silence followed.

Jasper let out a soft sigh. Short of locking Rose up, she wasn't sure she *could* stop her from coming out and trying to help. And even then, the girl could probably pick a lock. *Please don't do anything stupid,* Jasper thought toward her as she set off down the hall.

Outside the apartment building, a few flakes of snow found their way into Jasper's hair and onto her coat. She wiped a few more off her cheeks as she set off toward where Aymes waited with the Comet. As promised, she would check in on a few members of the team before making her dramatic entrance.

"All right, Sarena, you got a minute to send me your camera feed?" Jasper asked as she started up a fire escape.

Sarena wearing a hidden camera pinned to her dress probably wasn't super necessary for the plan, but Jasper was dying to see the faces of the elite as their party—and their city—fell apart in front of them.

"Sending it now," Sarena replied, her voice low. "There's a lot of whispering. Families are starting to separate from each other. Any trust they have left for each other is hanging by a thread."

"And their trust for Starr?"

"I don't think it's much better, but they don't seem to be worried about him taking their power the way they fear the other families will. They know

Starr already has what he needs, in terms of territory. And he needs the elite to manage the upper districts for him so he can focus on other things."

An alert popped up in the corner of Jasper's vision, notifying her that someone wanted to transmit a video feed. She accepted. Above her, Aymes brought the Comet down level with the platform she was stepping onto.

Jasper hopped onto the Comet's wing and hurried in through its hatch. "Take us to the Skyway E entrance on Opal Boulevard."

"On it," Aymes replied.

While they lifted into the sky, Jasper put her focus on the camera feed, letting it take over her entire field of vision. She was given a view of a massive ballroom with walls that glittered in various pastels, carved from some kind of opal or quartz. It was even more dazzling than the election party had been. Silent and nearly invisible drones drifted around near the ceiling, trailing streamers and strings of lights. What a use of stealth technology. *Sheesh.*

Jasper was also annoyed by how little the palace seemed to care about the Christmas theme. The trees scattered throughout the room were every variety *but* coniferous. And they were decorated with...feathers? And gemstones? On top of that, there was hardly any red or green to be seen. The color scheme was the upper district standard "pale iridescence." It was pretty, sure, but for every party? Really? The lower district parties may not have been nearly as extravagant, but at least they'd been accurate.

Jasper's gaze flickered to the massive sack sitting on the floor of the Comet in the corner. "Sarena, how are they responding to you and the other non-family celebrities?" she asked as the camera turned, offering a view of a spectacular banquet.

"They've been friendly, but seem cautious," Sarena answered. "I've been doing more observing than talking, so far."

"Well, let's see it."

Sarena headed toward a group of Altairs clustered near the dining area. Some of the tables were full of either elite families or other celebrities chatting quietly, while others had moved to socialize on the dance floor.

"Where's Starr?" Jasper asked.

Sarena glanced back, showing that Starr stood on an elevated section at the opposite end of the ballroom. There were about a dozen security guards gathered around him, in addition to the many other guards posted around the ballroom. Most kept to the walls and corners, trying to avoid drawing attention, but it was impossible to ignore the tension their presence brought.

Skybreaker—in a plain gray and white suit and a long gray jacket, with her white hair in its usual ponytail—also stood at Starr's side. There was no sign of that massive vaporizing weapon she'd been running around with before.

"Trying to avoid drawing his attention, obviously," Sarena muttered. "Given that I openly supported Merama and Superangel. But with everything else going on, I don't think I'm too high on anyone's list of priorities."

The camera view returned to the group of Altairs as Sarena continued toward them. Jasper scanned the faces of the East Kronosians but couldn't identify any in particular by name. Sarena seemed to know them fairly well, though.

"Sedna," Sarena said in greeting to a woman, the tallest in the group. Then, she nodded to the other two. "And Eris and Orcus. It's been a few seasons, hasn't it?"

While the reception wasn't exactly as warm as it would be coming from friends, the group did seem pleased to see Sarena. There was some small talk before Sarena began steering the conversation. With a glance toward Starr, she lowered her voice and said, "I almost didn't come, to be honest. Especially with all the drama between the big families."

"It's a little more than drama," Sedna muttered. Her red skin was a few shades darker than the other two in her party, a stark contrast to her shiny white hair that sat in a pile of intricate curls on top of her head. "More and more of those Fayes have been lurking in our district, talking to our voters. It's obvious what they're trying to do, with our election being the next one up."

"Yeah. And they don't shapeshift well enough to hide what they're doing," the man to her right added.

The third looked off camera toward where Jasper knew Starr was standing. "I'm a little surprised Starr hasn't intervened."

Jasper grinned. This was the line of discussion they wanted.

Sure enough, Sarena jumped on the comment. "Well, why would he? It's technically legal and, more importantly, it benefits him."

Sedna raised a white eyebrow. "Benefits him?"

Sarena shrugged. "As long as the elite families all have to keep an eye on each other and defend their own power, no one can focus on moving up and encroaching on what Starr has. Or try to take his place."

The discussion continued, but Jasper only half-listened as the Comet slowed to a halt, coming to rest on a rooftop near the palace. The door slid open again, and she grabbed the sack from the corner and hopped out. Aymes followed.

"You ready?" Jasper asked him as he strolled to the edge of the roof.

Aymes stared down the palace for a moment before nodding. "Yeah. I am. Should I start?"

"One minute. Let's make sure our big distraction is ready." Jasper turned and strolled toward the figure hunched over near an adjacent corner of the roof, hood over their head. She recognized the black leather jacket over the hoodie—it was the one with a bright yellow lightning bolt plastered over the front.

As she walked toward Thea, she tuned back in to Sarena's feed in time to watch one of the Altairs asked a question. "Didn't you endorse Merama? The woman who took over the Fayes' District?

Sarena sighed and offered the excuse the team had helped her come up with. "It was my manager's idea. I try not to play politics—it doesn't sell as many tickets. But my team thought it would appeal to my primary demographic."

Sarena's deflection seemed to work. Jasper put the feed in the background of her consciousness again as she reached Thea's side. She set down the sack, then sank to the sleek, polished black rooftop that reflected neon lights dancing nearby.

"Ready?" Jasper asked her.

Thea looked up, knocking her hood back off her head. "Just as ready as I was the last time you asked." Jasper shot her a look with a raised eyebrow, and Thea met it with a skeptical expression of her own. After a moment, they both broke out into a grin.

"Thanks for putting up with me, Jolt." Jasper tipped her head back to watch the faint stars appearing in the still-darkening sky.

Thea laughed. "Thank *you* for putting up with *me*. I'm not always a hundred percent here."

"That's all right." Jasper checked her feed yet again. It was starting to feel like she was juggling knives. Flaming knives. Flaming knives that could explode at any moment.

Sarena seemed to be wrapping up her conversation with the Altairs. "I do think this might be the last chance for the elite families to make a move, if they disagree with how Starr handled matters with the council or the last election," she said. "If he can keep everyone in line tonight, I think the status quo will stick and he'll maintain his position."

Another man nodded. Then said, "Jupitrell was saying something like that earlier."

As Sarena walked off, the Altairs began to whisper. Loud enough for her mic to pick up, but not loud enough to make out anything in particular. Jasper, meanwhile, frowned. Jupitrell. That's how she knew the name. He was an Altair. So, were the Slicers…?

A brief glance back from Sarena then showed the Altairs separating to talk to other members of the family scattered nearby. And there were glances from groups of other elite families, more whispers. Sarena approached a cluster of Vegas and began speaking to them.

Jasper leaned back on her hands, listening to the distant chants of protestors and wailing sirens. What would the city look like come morning?

She gave it another minute before looking at Thea again. "All right, sounds like the elite are about as on edge as they're going to get. Start phase one."

Thea pressed a few buttons, a wide smile spreading on her face as she did. "Piece of cake."

"Can you get me the ballroom cameras?"

Thea nodded, and within seconds, the single camera feed from Sarena was replaced with a wall of various angles from around the ballroom, as well as the adjacent kitchen where chefs were preparing fresh food to bring out to the banquet.

"Dumbasses," Thea said. "Why does a toaster need to connect to the internet? Now I've hacked half the palace through your toaster!"

There were indeed several toasters lining one of the countertops. But while an AstraToast may have been the vehicle to get Thea in, it was far from the biggest contributor to the chaos. Ovens and stoves shut off, putting a halt to the food prep and sending chefs into a panic. Fridges shut down, too. Other items, meanwhile, turned on at random. Blenders, mixers, timers. The collective sound was loud enough to leak into the ballroom.

Meanwhile, out in the ballroom, the drones lost power one by one and plummeted to the floor, sending people scrambling. With the lights they'd been dragging around extinguished, it became much harder to see in the room. The speakers playing music let out bursts of static before falling silent, emphasizing the chaos in the nearby kitchen.

A whoosh in the air above caught Jasper's attention. As she climbed back to her feet, Grace folded her wings in and dropped to the ground a few feet behind her and Thea.

"Just knocked a barricade of cruisers out of the sky," Grace said as Jasper turned to face her. "They were empty, but at least the officers that were using them will have a hard time getting around."

"Excellent. I wish you could see what I'm seeing," Jasper replied, her smile wide. "Starr's party has turned to an absolute mess in a matter of seconds."

Grace grinned back. "Sounds delightful. Maybe we should crash the party?"

"Soon," Jasper promised. Glancing at Thea, she asked, "Were you able to get into AstraSmart networks outside the palace?"

"Yep. I've found devices in just about every room across the upper districts. And most of them are on the same networks as everything else in those homes and businesses." Thea looked up from her laptop screen. "Want me to go ahead and...?"

"Get your finger on the button. Pull the trigger when I say," Jasper told her. Then, louder, she said, "Aymes, time for you to do your thing."

Aymes, who'd still been staring at the palace, nodded. His hands lifted, and his face twisted in concentration.

He claimed to have practiced this dozens of times by this point, even pulling off a few full-scale test runs out at sea on a boat borrowed from Sarena. Jasper had faith in his ability to make the constructs successfully. She just hoped she was right about them being indestructible, too. It seemed impossible to make something that even the high-powered blasters wouldn't be able to destroy, but Aymes could apparently concentrate enough energy to make it so. The tradeoff, of course, being that his creations would be temporary.

One by one, narrow walkways with railings formed at the edges of the skyways that passed closest to the palace. They began as projections of silver light before hardening into something that resembled metal as they stretched toward the place balconies, creating a path for people to approach the formerly inaccessible building.

As soon as the walkways were complete, Aymes let out a deep breath and took a few staggering steps backward.

"You okay?" Jasper asked, hurrying to his side.

He nodded. "Should be fine in just a minute." He reached into his pocket and pulled out a meal bar. "This will help."

"Good." Jasper rested a hand on her hip as Grace came to stand next to her. "And those will really last all night?"

Aymes nodded. "Well into tomorrow morning. They'll start dissolving slowly from one end, so anyone still on them will have plenty of warning to get off."

"Fantastic. Thea will put word out to be off them by sunrise, anyway. Just in case. But thank you." Speaking of Thea, Jasper threw a glance her way. "All right, Thea. Do it!"

Side by side, she and Grace stared out at the city. Nearby, Thea announced, "All right, I'm overloading every circuit I can."

The lights in the upper levels of skyscrapers began to go out in patches. The city skyline darkened in every direction, and the wave of darkness traveled downward as well, until it hit the upper limits of the middle districts.

Jasper's hand slid into Grace's.

Because the government had been so insistent on keeping upper, middle, and lower electrical grids separate—mostly to prevent anyone from trying to convince them to funnel electricity down to the poorly-maintained lower systems when they inevitably failed from time to time—there was no way anyone to fix the problem but to wait for Thea to lose access so that the systems could reboot and come back online. Emergency generators at places like hospitals would be left to function, but everyone else was in the dark.

Thea also redirected power to keep a few lights on in the Governor's Palace. The outer rooms went dark, but the cameras in Jasper's vision told her there was still some light in the ballroom. Perfect.

Aymes crumpled the wrapper of his meal bar and shoved it in his pocket. "Got anything specific for me to do yet, Jasper?" he asked.

Jasper shook her head. "Keep an eye on the fight from above. Step in to help where you can."

Aymes nodded and hopped onto a silver platform as it materialized next to the roof. His Apprentice costume—they really needed to decide on a new name for him—whipped in the wind as he shot off into the sky.

Jasper returned to where Thea sat and picked up the sack she'd brought from the Comet. She slung it over her shoulder. "Now if you'll all excuse me, I've got a party to crash." She grinned. "And some holiday spirit to spread."

Chapter Fifty-Eight
In The Trenches

It had been a while since Sarena had attended a big upper district party. She'd been avoiding them the past season or so, ever since she'd stupidly let herself get involved with Van Terra and Superangel. She still couldn't believe she'd let them talk her into getting her pop star identity involved in such dangerous politics.

Sarena sighed as she surveyed the clusters of elite families, absentmindedly petting Blitz's head as she did. There *had* been good reasons to agree to all this. It had helped Merama, for starters, who still had all that passion for improving the Tide District. Sarena tried not to think much about the streets she'd grown up on these days, beyond mentioning it in interviews to garner sympathy, but most of her sirens were still pretty invested in improving the place.

Still, it all had made her appearance tonight somewhat dangerous. She *had* been formally invited, and Starr had yet to approach her. Even if he simply hadn't noticed she'd made it onto the guest list with the other big celebrities, his security team would have been alerted if she'd been considered a threat to the government. So, her public support of Merama Tidewater and Superangel apparently hadn't been enough to get her legitimately blacklisted.

Starr must have decided that making any statements against her wasn't worth dealing with her rabid fanbase. She hadn't technically done anything illegal, and publicly denouncing a celebrity for supporting rivals to the status quo would look bad for a man who wanted to claim to rule a democratic system.

Sarena slipped into conversation with a few members of the Vega family. Distant relatives of Starr's, though they had about as much power as any of the other big elite families. A woman with pale North Kronosian skin but an odd red tint to her hair—Sarena vaguely recognized her as being the daughter of a Faye woman who'd married into a Vega family—was speaking quietly, her anxious gaze occasionally darting to the nearest pair of security guards. "I think my husband's right. If we don't act soon, another family will get the drop on us."

"But you really think the governor will allow that?" another woman asked.

"He doesn't care if we fight as long as no one goes after him," the first woman insisted. "I'm telling you, if we don't make a move first, someone else will."

"Well." The man standing next to her folded his arms. "If that's the case, are you with us, your in-laws, or with your true Faye family?"

"I'm a Vega to my core," she hissed back. "Those Fayes are traitors, anyway. Shapeshifting spies, too. Can't be trusted—"

Sarena shifted her focus from the family members to the other guests, trying to distinguish the most important members of the various families from others of the same species. Just about everyone in the upper districts was North, West, or East Kronosian, or some mix, but celebrities and other wealthy partygoers tended to dress a bit differently than those involved in politics. But there were some she couldn't place in either category. People dressed a bit more plainly, people hanging around elite families despite clearly not being a member. Many of them were even lower district species, oddly enough…

"What about you, Trench?"

Sarena started. "Huh?"

"Whose family will you side with, if war breaks out?" It was the man who'd questioned the half-Faye's loyalty.

Sarena lifted an eyebrow. "I wasn't aware I had to pick a side."

"Maybe not, if this was the type of battle fought through politics and money. But I get the feeling things might get a bit more…physical." His gaze darkened.

Before Sarena could respond, a commotion behind her made her turn. All nearby eyes moved to the source, and as conversations fell silent, the rest of the room became aware of what was happening, too.

A Faye—Vixor Faye, Sarena realized—was glaring furiously at a North Kronosian man. Another Vega. The Vega lifted his fists. "Well, don't stop after simply shoving me. Come on!"

Vixor brushed off the dark green fabric of his silky suit jacket. "I think that was a perfectly appropriate response to your accusations."

Sarena tapped the comm in her ear to unmute herself. "A fight's breaking out," she whispered. "Vixor Faye and one of the Vegas."

"Really?" Jasper sounded way too excited.

"It's not just an accusation, Vixor," Vega hissed. "We've got security footage of you Fayes snooping around our political headquarters."

"We've sent no one to anyone's headquarters! Whoever it is, they're acting on their own, not on our orders."

A nearby Altair chimed in. "You really expect us to believe that after you lost your district, you're going to sit around and do nothing? It's obvious you've decided to steal on our territory instead!"

Sarena shot a brief glance toward Starr. He was watching the argument unfold silently, his expression unreadable. One of his arms was held out in front of a security guard, apparently to stop them from intervening. At his side, Skybreaker—though everyone in the room would think of her as Subject Eighteen, Sarena reminded herself—had an equally calm expression on her face.

"We've hurt no one and done nothing illegal. Which is less than I can say for the rest of you!" Vixor turned, sweeping his burning gaze across the staring crowd. "Do you think we destroyed the Lion's Den, too? *Someone* attacked us!"

Holy hell. "He just mentioned the Den!" Sarena hissed, struggling to keep her voice down. Sure, this wasn't exactly a public setting, but she'd never heard such explicit mentions of the Den's existence. In fact, she'd thought it was only rumors until Jasper informed the team of her time there.

"That was Van Terra, obviously!" the Vega fired back. "She made that pretty clear."

"She must have been working with someone to have located it! It would have been impossible to find otherwise!"

Around the room, clear lines were being drawn. People moved to reunite with their families, forming large groups. Those left in smaller clusters or even completely alone quickly scrambled to make themselves less obvious. A few singers and actors gathered together while others slipped into place near elite families they apparently felt comfortable aligning with.

The Vegas who'd been standing around Sarena dispersed to join the rest of their family, leaving Sarena as one of the few standing alone. Blitz shifted his position on her shoulder, subtly preparing to fire his laser on her command.

Vixor was still ranting. "And you can't seriously expect us to believe that Merama won that election legitimately!" He took a step toward the Vega and jabbed a pale green finger at the man's chest. "I don't know which family planted her and is directing her, but I'm certain it was someone in this room. We aren't the ones you should be worried about stealing your district."

At the far end of the room, Starr seemed to decide that was enough. He waved a hand in a gesture that Skybreaker apparently understood as a command. She reached behind her back, drew a long, narrow sword, and began walking.

Sarena frowned as she watched Skybreaker stroll toward the arguing men. While she was dressed in stiff gray clothes similar to what she usually wore when parading around with Starr, there was something off about the jacket she wore. It was unusually thick and a bit oversized, looking a bit awkward on her body.

"I think something's off with Skybreaker," Sarena muttered into her comm, her voice fitting in with the other murmurs echoing around the room. "She's wearing this new jacket—"

"Maybe she finally got some taste," Jasper interrupted.

Sarena rolled her eyes. "And she's moving a little awkwardly, too. Still terrifying, just looks like maybe she got injured recently or something."

"We can only hope."

Vixor whirled around at the sound of approaching footsteps. His eyes narrowed and his gaze moved past Skybreaker to Starr. "What's this, Governor? I haven't done anything wrong!"

"Now's a time for unity, not disruptions," came Starr's cool reply.

"I didn't start this!" Vixor glanced toward where a few other Fayes stood nearby. "Well? Are we just going to take this?"

Another Faye, a woman, laughed. "I've had it up to here with these other families. And if Starr's not going to defend us against their antics, then I've had it with him, too." She shot a meaningful glance at a man standing nearby.

The man, one of the plainer guests Sarena had noticed earlier, one who wasn't recognizable as a celebrity or as a core elite family member, reached into his jacket and drew a blaster. That set off a wave of chaos through the room. Some of the random guests who'd gathered with various families drew weapons of their own. Blades, blasters, and some ordinary guns here and there.

The next weapons to appear were those in the hands of palace security guards around the room. In the process, a few lifted jacket sleeves offered glimpses of all-too-familiar tattoos. Blades dripping blood. And then, somehow more startling than the sudden appearance of weapons, a group that had been hiding behind the Altairs moved forward and began peeling off their jackets, revealing white shirts and layers of gold chains around their necks.

Wow. That was a bold move.

"Looks like the Slicers are working for the Altairs," Sarena said. "And it seems a few lingering Blades have taken up positions as palace guards, too."

"Any other gangs present?" Jasper asked.

"None that I recognize, but it wouldn't surprise me if some of these personal guards the elite brought along are involved in smaller gangs. Or otherwise tied to the criminal underworld." Sarena surveyed the glinting weapons and uneasy glances exchanged between the rival families and palace security. "At any rate, we're in a huge multi-way stand-off."

"Well, you're about to get one more violent party guest," Jasper said. "I'm right outside."

Chapter Fifty-Nine
Ding Dong

Snow came down in scattered flurries around Jasper as she fell from the sky.

Her grappling hook caught on a balcony and sent her into a swinging arc toward the Governor's Palace. Her other hand squeezed the strap keeping the massive bag secured to her back.

Below her, crowds of protestors were making their way onto the city's uppermost levels and surging toward the palace. Security and police officers tried to form walls to stop them, but they were simply outnumbered. City forces had weapons, of course, but many of the protestors had brought weapons and makeshift shields to defend themselves. And word had been going around that many of the officers' blasters were experiencing strange malfunctions.

"Thea, you handling yourself okay?" Jasper asked as she neared the end of her swing.

"I'm good," Thea replied. "Ready to head in?"

"Just about." Jasper squeezed the trigger to release and retract the hook. She dropped a short distance onto one of the palace's largest balconies. A line of guards stood between her and the front doors.

Jasper reached into the sack and drew out a lengthy metal bar nearly as tall as her, curved into a hook at one end like a crowbar. And painted with white and red stripes. As the guards drew their blasters and started toward her, one of them frowned. "Is that a candy—?"

"Merry Christmas, losers." Jasper swung.

She didn't have the strength she once had, but her mind's computer was as powerful as ever. The world moved in slow motion. She dodged blaster beams and swung again and again, the metal cane cracking against skulls and bones. One by one, the guards went down.

Jasper leaned the cane up against the wall by the door. "Ready, Thea," she said into her comm.

"Sending the unlock signal to the door."

Moments after Thea had spoken, there was a whirring sound, and then a click. Jasper lifted her cybernetic leg and gave one of the front doors a solid kick. It swung open.

As she walked through the palace corridors, she reached into the sack behind her and yanked out decorations from inside at random. Ornaments rolled across the floor. Strings of lights and tinsel snagged on hanging art and light fixtures and trailed across the floor behind Jasper until they reached their ends.

A second sack lay in the bottom of the bigger one, which Jasper ignored for now. That one containing some more...*interesting* decorations.

Distant shouting reached Jasper's ears before long, guiding her the rest of the way to the ballroom. She dug out the last of the remaining ordinary Christmas decorations and kicked the doors in front of her open.

All eyes were on her in an instant. She grinned and scattered the bundle of tinsel and stray ornaments across the floor in front of her. "What's up, nerds?"

Elite families and celebrities and security guards alike stared at her with expressions that ranged from annoyed to shocked. Jasper's gaze briefly locked with Sarena's, whose mouth quirked up in a slight smirk.

"Van Terra." Governor Starr's voice echoed across the otherwise quiet space, stealing Jasper's attention. "How did you get in?"

Jasper shrugged. "That smart door of yours opened right up. Doesn't seem very smart to me." Still smiling, she added, "I expected more guards between here and the entrance, but apparently they were otherwise occupied."

Starr's eyes narrowed. "And now you're surrounded and outnumbered."

"Well, you're about to have much bigger problems." Jasper tapped her comm. "Space pirate, go ahead."

"And we're completely sure that these heat drone scans are accurate?" Cutthroat asked. "Not that I'd be too broken up about accidentally hitting most of the people in there, but—"

"They're accurate," Thea cut in, her voice sharp.

"Roger that. Firing."

Starr let out a soft chuckle, oblivious to the conversation taking place in Jasper's ear. "Is something supposed to be happening?"

A massive cannonball ripped through the ceiling and smashed into the crystal floor.

Jasper's brain slowed the world on instinct, and her limbs suddenly felt as if they were moving through water as she forced herself to take a step back. Glittering, iridescent shards danced through the air. Eyes widened in panic. Partygoers turned in slow motion to dive for cover. Laughter bubbled in Jasper's chest, her mouth inching open to let it out.

As the last of the crystal shards clattered against the floor, the world resumed at full speed. Jasper's attention was immediately on the security guards charging toward her. She hefted the smaller sack she'd brought into the room with her and drew out what appeared to be an ordinary string of lights. She threw that over her shoulder, for now, and reached back in to pull out a couple of ornaments that appeared perfectly innocent as well.

She tossed the first ornament toward the closest guard. It exploded on impact with the ground, throwing the man backward. The other approaching guards slowed, apprehension in their eyes and hesitation in their steps.

Jasper glanced toward Starr. The cloud of debris thrown in the air by the cannonball was clearing, offering a view of him squeezing a smartsphere. "Raise the turrets," he hissed into its mic. "Find the villain Cutthroat's ship and fire on it! It's close—"

Another guard dared to lunge at Jasper, moving in too close for her to use the next grenade on him. Quick as lightning, she grabbed the light string draped over her shoulder and snapped it at him. The light bulbs exploded on contact with his arm, sending glass shards flying into his neck and face. He yelped and staggered away, his attack put to an abrupt halt.

Jasper turned and chucked the other ornament she held to deter another approaching group of guards. "Those turrets we were worried about are coming out," she muttered as the heat from the small explosion washed over her. "They should be focusing on the Astronomer. If they try to fire on the protestors, Cutthroat will move in close and force them back on him."

"Got it," Grace replied. "We'll push forward and let people start swarming the palace."

Many of the guards were regrouping far from Jasper and taking quietly each other, strategizing. One brave soul, however, drew his blaster and sprinted at her. The weapon went up and pointed her way.

Jasper sighed. "Really, dude? You're going to try to shoot me on Christmas Eve?" She lifted the hand holding the light string and snapped it in warning. The guard squeezed the trigger. She dodged to the right.

Jasper's arm darted out, sending the light whip arcing through the air. The light bulbs shattering hadn't ended the whip's functionality. It had only exposed the weapon's second component. As the string wrapped around the guard's wrist, the exposed wiring that had been hidden beneath the bulbs came to life and sent a pulse of electricity into the body it was touching. The man yelped and collapsed in a heap on the floor. Jasper let the whip fall with him and turned.

Her gaze darted to Skybreaker, who stood stiffly next to Starr as he continued to issue orders into his sphere. Jasper's eyes narrowed. Why wasn't she attacking? Why wasn't Starr *ordering* her to attack? Maybe he was only concerned with his own safety, saving his bodyguard for if Jasper got too close.

Whatever the reason, it didn't stop Starr from shooting a glare at his wide-eyed security guards. "What are you waiting for? Everyone attack her at once!"

One nearby shot the governor a hesitant glance. "But...she's Van Terra."

"She's one person," Starr hissed through clenched teeth. There was a dangerous look in his eyes, more emotion than Jasper had ever seen in the man's face. In any Starr's face. It sent a chill down her spine.

It must have been terrifying to his guards, too, because they sprang into action. Jasper reached behind her back and drew her favorite weapon of the night as they approached. She lifted an eyebrow. "Could I get some help, Siren?"

Rolling her eyes, Sarena started toward her. "I know you hate my music, but do you really have to put so much effort into tanking my career?"

Jasper laughed. "I think you did that yourself with your last album. Oh, and that final episode of Star Conquerors! Don't think I didn't know about that."

Sarena's eyes widened. "What?" she shrieked. "That episode's not out yet!"

"Thea stole me a screener copy from the studio servers."

"She did not! They're still editing it!"

Jasper shrugged. "If you say so. I just think that making your character turn evil out of nowhere was a weird writing choice. No build-up, no foreshadowing—"

The closest guards began firing. Sarena screamed, and the shockwave disrupted the beams of light, making them scatter uselessly. Blitz lifted some of his suckered arms and fired off a few white laser beams, further disrupting the guards' attack.

Starr's eyes widened at the reveal of Sarena's power. He held a hand to his ear and growled something Jasper couldn't hear.

Jasper yanked the sword she'd pulled out of the bag from its scabbard, revealing its vibrant red glow. It was longer and narrower than her favorite, but it was more on theme. And she wasn't one to turn up to a party with a weapon that clashed with the theme.

The guards swarmed her and Sarena after that, apparently deciding that facing them was better than dealing with their boss's wrath.

"Thea, get us some music, please." Jasper lunged into action, dodging blasts and slicing at bodies. "And dim the lights a little? I want my sword to stand out more."

"If that's where your priorities are," Thea muttered. Moments later, the lights went down, and something appropriately Christmas-y came on. It sounded like an alien remix rather than anything actually made on Earth, but Jasper could pick out a familiar tune and words.

Between Sarena's shockwaves, Blitz's lasers, and Jasper's sword, they made quick work of the wave of guards. Jasper couldn't help but notice many of those behind the first wave backing off, slinking away to hide among the elite and their gang members. If Starr noticed the retreating guards, he didn't call them out this time.

Jasper sent the final attacker to the ground with a blow from her sword's hilt and turned to face the governor.

"This is disappointing, Starr." Jasper twirled her sword. "I thought you'd have something better for us than run-of-the-mill security guards."

Starr's eyes narrowed. "Believe me," he said. "I have more."

Chapter Sixty
Dax Frost

There were all kinds of pain in the people around Dax. Bruises and scrapes, wounds from scuffles with security officers, and—infuriatingly—the occasional blaster burn or gunshot.

The most widespread, though, was the cold. The hypothermia. The frostbite.

Before things had begun ramping up the past few months, he'd always healed people one at a time. Even if he jumped quickly from person to person, he'd still only been manipulating one person's body at a time. Now that he had a better understanding of his ability, though, he really could push his power onto multiple people at once. Discovering the reverse aspect had helped. It felt like an exchange of energy now, rather than a one-way transfer—filling people with energy that caused their body to heal rapidly while taking in a different energy that could do the reverse.

The suit Thea had made for him was helping. She'd taken the data she'd gathered before Jasper's return and used it to rearrange the circuits within the suit, pinpointing areas where she could amplify his natural bioenergy and make the transfer smoother, reducing energy loss in the process.

With the suit on, he was staying energized longer. Helping more people at once.

Hurting more people at once.

Dax glanced up from the sprained ankle he was working on and surveyed the crowd around him. The snowfall had been coming and going over the course of the past hour, sometimes barely noticeable, sometimes limiting visibility so much they were forced to slow their progress. Right now, though, the flakes falling around them weren't much of an issue.

They were close to their goal. They'd made it all the way to one of the skyways that cut through the air in front of the palace, and it was strange to see a road that was usually packed with traffic so empty. While the roads in the lower districts had emptied as a result of people joining the upward march, the upper districts had emptied as people hid indoors. So far, the only people Dax and the other protesters had seen had been officers attempting to stop their migration.

Despite how many cruisers they'd destroyed, and the amount of security they'd plowed through, enemies were still coming. As Dax finished healing and rose to his feet, a particularly large cruiser came flying out from behind the skyscraper beneath the palace and soared toward the crowd on the skyway.

Aymes dropped to the asphalt in front of Dax and flung out his arms. A silver translucent sphere enveloped the police cruiser. Then, with a sweeping motion, Aymes sent it crashing through the window of a nearby office building.

Aymes straightened up and adjusted the hat that completed his outfit, the very same one he'd worn as the Apprentice when he worked with Ringmaster. He turned around and found Dax. "Are we ready to cross to the palace?" he asked.

"Almost. Just waiting on the word from Jasper." Dax nodded to where the palace gleamed in the night behind Aymes. "Turrets have been firing occasionally, but they've all been directed at the Astronomer, so far. Cutthroat's mostly been firing back as a distraction, but he was able to take a couple out."

In the air above the palace, the dark form of the Astronomer hovered. Occasionally, it dipped lower, prompting a narrow tower to rise up from the palace's roof and fire off a shot. But the Astronomer was faster than it looked, and the turrets were thankfully a bit slow to fire, requiring a few seconds to move into position. Plus, the Astronomer's shielding was good enough to prevent much damage from shots that did come close.

Aymes threw a glance toward the turrets. "Thea can't disable them remotely?"

"She probably could if that's all she was trying to do, but with everything else she's juggling, another distraction might get her kicked out of the palace's AstraSmart network," Dax explained. "And she's trying to disable as many blasters as she can on top of that, which is the bigger risk to us right now."

A whoosh of air above them made the two look up. A familiar figure was descending from amidst the snow flurries.

Grace landed next to Dax. "I'm going to address the crowd again. I think after that, Jasper is ready for us to make our approach."

Dax sighed. "Okay."

"Something wrong?" Grace's brow furrowed with concern.

"I just wish I could get everyone healed up faster." Dax glanced over his shoulder. "Most people are doing okay, but so many have had to take shelter from the cold. If I could heal them, they'd be able to keep going to the palace, but I won't be able to get to them all that fast." Even with his expanded range, he still had limits. "It could make a huge difference in numbers, though."

Grace didn't get a chance to respond. Holly came sprinting toward them, shouting and waving a hand. "There's a whole fleet of private security officers coming this way," she exclaimed as she reached them. "We've got maybe five minutes."

Dax sighed again. He'd been inflicting wounds on officers nearly as fast as he'd been healing protestors. He didn't have enough negative bioenergy stored up to deal with an entire fleet. Sure, he was far from the only person fighting, but he felt like he should be able to do more.

Grace nodded at Holly. "All right." Her wings spread, and she moved up into the air above the crowd. A hush fell in the vicinity, everyone eager to hear what Superangel had to say.

"I am Superangel," Grace began.

Thea's drones circled overhead, recording and amplifying her voice. Snow clung to her brown hair. As she spoke, she drew her sword from her side and held it out.

"And I am Grace Alvarez, the girl who lived in the palace for years. When I was new to this city, I saved Governor Starr's life, and he betrayed me." She lifted her chin. "As a leader, he has betrayed all of us."

The quiet crowd began to murmur.

"My friends and I have infiltrated the palace already. All we need is numbers. If you're with us, then help us charge the palace!"

A roar of solidarity exploded from the crowds at that, with some chanting of Grace's name—her hero name and her real name—mixed in.

"You've got more backup coming in," Thea said.

"We do?" Grace's brow furrowed, her head turning, wings beating steadily behind her.

"Yep. A patch I installed earlier finally finished."

Patch? Dax mentally cycled through Thea's various projects, wondering which one she was referring to.

The whirring sound of drone rotors cut through the shouting of the crowd. Dax glanced up as two figures passed into the air above them, each being supported by multiple drones. Once they two had reached the open space where Dax, Grace, Holly, and Aymes stood, the drones released the figures, and they dropped.

The smaller silver-and-black android lifted her fists as she thudded against the ground. "The Mighty Mia!"

At Mia's side, the taller and stockier gold-and-black android threw up a peace sign. "And Cosmic Chloe!"

Thea spoke again. "It looks like more police units are mobilizing in the area. Mia and Chloe are armed with light blasters and will do good in hand-to-hand combat. They're going to be focused on protecting civilians."

"Great," Grace said, folding her arms as she descended to the ground. "We ready to go, then?"

"I want to try something real quick," Dax said, that desperate feeling that he needed to be doing more taking charge. "If you want to start getting people to the palace, go ahead."

"We've still got a couple of minutes before any police get close," Holly replied. "We'll wait as long as we can."

After nodding in acknowledgment, Dax raced to the edge of the skyway. He hopped up onto the wall lining the road and peered through the window of one of the skyscrapers looming over him. This was one of the places where those too sick or injured to continue had moved to hide.

Dax held out his arms, though he wasn't sure it was necessary, and sucked in a deep breath. "Here goes nothing," he said under his breath.

Instead of giving in to the urge to latch onto the first person he sensed and give them his energy, Dax forced his senses to expand. One by one, he felt other people pop into his awareness, their ailments pressing against his mind. His power thrummed within, eager to reach out and heal. To transfer energy. The circuits in his clothing began to hum.

Dax finally let the power out.

A blue glow burst from his hands and washed over the window, pouring into the building. A few cries of surprise—and some shouts that sounded excited—just reached his ears. While the healing energy did its work, Dax glanced around. The patients had been shuffled into the building through a door around the corner. He could hurry over there to guide them back to the rest of the protests, but that would take a few minutes—

Aymes descended on a silver platform and came to hover next to the window. A silver barrier formed inside the window, then with a sweep of Aymes's hand, the window shattered—outwards, so that none of the shards were in danger of hitting anyone inside. Dax nodded his thanks to Aymes as some of the protestors moved to the window and carefully began climbing out onto the skywalk.

"Everyone healed, you can join the crowd marching on the palace!" Dax shouted to them, pointing toward the protestors beginning to gather around the walkways to the palace that Aymes had created. "If I missed anyone, I'll come back for you as soon as you can, but in the meantime, follow the orders from the volunteer doctors in there."

"Dax!" Holly shouted. "Incoming!"

Dax whirled around as three small vans dropped onto the skyway not far from him. Each vehicle had "Prism Security" plastered on the side in glowing letters. Security officers poured out of the vans, and Dax quickly reached for the new energies mixing within. As with the healing process, it took some effort to focus his power on more than one person at a time. He didn't bother trying to assign a specific ailment to any individual officer, though he suspected he could if he had the time to focus. Or maybe some more practice.

Regardless, he let his power run free to manipulate the cells in the bodies racing toward him. Officers doubled over in pain and shock. Limbs paled, the very tips of fingers rapidly went red, then dark purple as the process of frostbite was sped up by the energy from Dax's power.

Dax looked away, feeling his stomach churn a bit. While the officers collapsed in various states of pain and distress in his peripheral, Grace, Holly, and Aymes gathered around him. Mia and Chloe were close behind.

Dax lowered his hands and forced himself to lift his chin. "The good news is, I've still got a lot more where that came from."

"Not bad, Remedy." Holly patted a hand against his shoulder.

"Crowd's already starting onto the walkways to the palace," Aymes said. "We should try to stick to the front. I'll take the androids ahead to start clearing out any palace security waiting at the other end."

Dax nodded while the others confirmed their agreement. Aymes summoned silver platforms for himself and the androids. The three shot up into the air and moved toward the front of the crowd.

Grace tensed and spread her wings, ready to follow from the air. A message over comms made her and the others pause.

"Guys, I've picked up a sudden surge in readings just off the coast, not far from the palace," Thea warned.

"What do you mean by readings?" Holly asked, frowning.

"Electrical signals, heat signatures, radio waves…"

"Aymes!" Grace exclaimed into her comm. "Can you come back and help us take a look at what's happening over the water?"

"Sure. I'll leave Mia and Chloe to help the frontlines."

Moments later, Aymes's platform was passing by over their heads. A platform materialized beneath Dax and lifted him into the air, forming a pole for him to grab on to as well. Holly flew up at his right, and Grace's wings carried her with them toward the coast.

When the four reached the edge of the city's buildings, they began a rapid drop into the lower districts. Dax's stomach jumped into his throat and stayed there until the platform carrying him finally began to slow.

"What's happening out there?" Jasper asked as the four landed on the roof of a warehouse overlooking the water.

Dax's brow furrowed as he surveyed the waves below. No sign of…anything, really. He hadn't spent much time by the ocean, but he was pretty sure this was how it usually looked.

"We're not seeing anything," Grace said. "Thea, are you sure—?"

The building trembled beneath them, cutting her off. Then the waves in the distance were getting bigger fast. "Something's happening," Holly warned, one hand moving to her blaster as if she intended to shoot whatever was shaking the sea.

"Readings are spiking," Thea replied, tone frantic. "I'm trying to get drones over there for visuals."

The first object broke the surface. Gleaming black metal. Vaguely rectangular. Easily the size of a one-room apartment.

A ship.

Then came another, and another, and another. One at a time, at first, then they were coming by the tens. By the dozens. All Dax could do was stare, wide-eyed, as what had to be nearly a hundred ships poured out of the ocean and rose into the air above Kronos.

"Guys, what happened?" Jasper's voice cut through the stunned silence.

"Well," Holly said. "We seem to have figured out where Starr was hiding his army."

Chapter Sixty-One
The Enemy of My Enemy is Also My Enemy

Jasper didn't have to ask Thea to send her a feed of what was happening outside. With a wave of his hand, Starr brought up a massive holoscreen behind him. A camera feed from the edge of the city showed the army of ships emerging from the ocean and filling the sky.

While the room stared in shock at the display, Starr spoke into his communicator. "Can we fire on the protestors yet?"

This time, with the rest of the room having been stunned into silence, Jasper's heightened audio sensors were able to pick up the response. "The moment we reposition the guns, that damned pirate starts firing again."

"It's taking all of our turrets to fend him off?" Starr demanded.

"He's got a lot of cannons. And that ship is faster than it looks."

Jasper's relief at that aspect of the plan working was drowned out by the sight of the army. *Hidden right beneath our noses this whole time.*

"What is this?" Vixor Faye shouted at Starr. "What do you need an army this big for?"

"And why weren't we told about it?" added one of the Altairs.

More questions and cries rang out. Some of the palace guards took threatening steps toward the offending elite, but the elites' own bodyguards were clearly not impressed by what remained after the fight with Jasper and Sarena.

Starr sighed. "Enough of this. Blades, Eighteen, prepare your weapons."

The Blades revealed themselves by drawing weapons, many of their tattoos flashing with the motion. Jasper studied them, eyes narrowing. There weren't many, but that worried her more than a small army would have. Starr knew she could handle quite a few Blades.

Starr didn't signal for them to attack, though. And Skybreaker didn't move beyond reached a hand behind her back. Starr's mouth opened, and he launched into what sounded suspiciously like a villainous monologue.

"Elite of Kronos," he began. "We are entering a new era. And in order for Kronos to stand strong against what's to come, I need to know where your loyalties lie."

Blaster fire sounded in the distance. Probably in the halls not far from the ballroom.

"You're going to fight the Interstar Council, aren't you?" It was Vixor again. "Why wouldn't you consult with your mayors before doing this?"

"I don't need to consult with any of you," Starr replied coolly. "Now, Eighteen, let's take out the trash so we can discuss the next steps our mayors should be taking." His gaze shifted toward Jasper and Sarena.

Skybreaker's expression held no emotion as she drew a blaster with a long barrel from beneath her stiff jacket—a long-distance weapon, at first glance. Until she snapped off the outer shell, revealing the staff she used publicly in her Skybreaker persona.

Staff in hand, she lunged at Governor Starr.

Starr staggered backward from the first blow, face twisted in a grimace of pain as green lightning arced through the air around him, brushing his skin wherever it could. Skybreaker stalked forward and raised her staff to swing again.

One of the Red Blades collided with her. The two tumbled to the floor in a blur of gray and black and neon green.

Jasper's eyes widened. The Blade was fast. Unnaturally fast. She gave the ones circling her a second glance, reassessing her ability to handle them quickly. This time, she also noted the blank look in their gazes. What had happened to them since Grace had destroyed their headquarters and gotten them arrested?

"Skybreaker," Starr said as he climbed to his feet and brushed himself off, confirming that he'd realized his right hand's villainous alter ego. "How did you manage to pull that off, Eighteen?"

Skybreaker stood as well. The Blade who'd attacked her writhed in pain, but as the lightning dancing around him began to die out, he started pushing himself off the ground. Skybreaker took a few steps away from him, twirling her staff.

"If you knew, you'd be terrified," Skybreaker told the governor. She then held up the communicator he'd been barking orders into. In a growl that might fool whoever was on the other side into thinking she was Starr in the heat of the moment, she said, "Destroy anything that enters the atmosphere. Ignore the protestors for now."

Then, she dropped the communicator and stomped on it. A crack echoed around the barlloom.

"I suppose this means you could tell me what exactly you did to Captain Cora?" Starr asked, eyes narrowing.

"I could." Skybreaker shrugged. "But I won't."

Jasper's brow furrowed. Something in Skybreaker's mannerisms...did she even know what the weapon she'd been wielding did?

"Very well." Starr made a gesture with his right hand. The Blades began drawing small blasters that Jasper recognized as the warp energy-powered superweapons. She'd need to be sure to dodge any blasts that came out of those.

She did note, though, that some of the Blades weren't drawing weapons. They were simply shrugging off their jackets instead, revealing more than just Red Blade tattoos.

Unlike with Jasper, not much effort had been put into hiding which limbs had been replaced with cybernetic ones. Maybe it was a work-in-progress. Or maybe a trick to convince the enemy they could find the cyborgs' weak points. Jasper couldn't let herself make any assumptions.

Sarena yanked her brown wig off and tossed it aside, freeing her white hair. Her brown irises drowned in the bright light that overtook her eyes.

"Don't attack quite yet," Jasper muttered to her. Then, raising her voice, she glanced at Starr. "You keep making cyborg super soldiers, Starr. Why haven't you turned yourself into one yet?"

Starr actually laughed at that, a cold and bitter sound. "You should know better than anyone how nasty the side effects can be. We've had some promising results, but the process is still imperfect. I'll wait until we've worked out the kinks before I make myself invincible." Gesturing to the Blades that were now closing in on Jasper, Skybreaker, and Sarena, he added, "Besides, my obedient army will do whatever I ask of them."

The Blades didn't display any negative reaction to the statement. They clearly weren't in their right minds. Some kind of brainwashing? Drugs?

"I assume you tried this with all of the arrested Blades. These are just the survivors." Jasper scanned the faces of the Blades, vaguely recognizing a few from past fights.

"No major loss. We can clone the successes." Starr cast Skybreaker a meaningful glance. "Though we'll be a bit more discretionary about who we clone going forward. DNA compatibility isn't all that matters, it would seem."

Then, abruptly, he snapped his fingers, and the Blades sprang into action.

Jasper and Sarena darted in different directions. While Sarena kept some of the Blades at bay with her shouts and Blitz's lasers, Jasper fended off attackers coming from the other side with her sword. About thirty seconds into the fight, as she backed away from an approaching cluster of Blades, Jasper bumped into something. Someone. She was now back-to-back with Skybreaker.

There was no time to deal with her, and she wasn't an immediate threat, so Jasper kept her attention on the Blades ahead. Her sword sliced through limbs, occasionally exposing wires and circuitry instead of blood. She was forced to dodge the occasional blaster beam, frequently saved by her brain's extra components kicking into high gear to give her more time to react.

One beam nearly hit her right arm, and it was only stopped by Skybreaker sticking out her staff in front of Jasper's face and unleashing a powerful burst of lightning that disrupted the beam. Jasper was surprised it worked. She was even more surprised that Skybreaker had attempted it in the first place.

"Thanks," she said, her tone a bit uncertain.

"Don't forget, you're also on my list of people who have to go." Skybreaker spat the words out, but they lacked her usual menace.

"I'm flattered." Jasper stabbed out with her weapon, narrowly missing a Blade. But her attempted strike distracted him long enough for Skybreaker to send a throwing star into his neck. As he crumpled to the floor, Jasper asked, "What was that weapon you used on Bruce Wright and Omic Attom?"

The two were fully in sync with each other now. But Jasper couldn't help but notice that some of Skybreaker's movements were a bit clumsy. Her stance bordered on awkward, too. What *was* up with her? Did she have another big weapon stashed awkwardly under the jacket?

Jasper squinted at the thick, long gray jacket Skybreaker wore. But she didn't have time to study it closely. She swung her sword to block a blow from a Blade—the weapon only sank a few millimeters into his cybernetic arm—and sent him flying back with a kick.

"You get enough sleep?" Jasper asked. "You seem a little off."

"I'm fine," Skybreaker hissed. She swung her staff in a wide arc, channeling bolts of green lightning into a few Blades that had gotten way too close.

Jasper shrugged. "Whatever you say, Sky."

"Don't call me that!"

Jasper couldn't help but smirk. That last exclamation had held way more vitriol than anything Skybreaker had said prior.

After knocking out another Blade, Jasper had a moment to catch her breath and study the rest of the ballroom. She lifted an eyebrow when she noticed the other fights breaking out. Gangs and bodyguards were battling it out, and even a few of the elite family members were in rather pathetic-looking fistfights with each other.

"Sarena, try to inflame those fights between the elite," Jasper said. "As long as they stay at each other's throats, Starr can't mobilize them or their forces against the people."

A moment later, after Sarena had confirmed she'd heard the order, Skybreaker spoke. "You seem off, too, by the way," she said.

Jasper grimaced. Skybreaker hadn't seen much of her since she'd taken ThetaEight. Not sure how to respond, she simply lifted her sword and braced herself for the next wave of Blades.

Skybreaker wasn't done. "The elite war would be a pretty good idea, ordinarily. But tonight, it's just going to make things worse."

Jasper glanced back at her. "What makes you say that?"

"You have no idea what you're up against. What's out there. I waited this long to attack Starr because I needed his army. If the elite weren't so on edge, I could have used their private forces, too."

Before Jasper could ask her to elaborate—though she doubted Skybreaker would have told her anything more, anyway—a palace servant sprinted into the ballroom, breathing hard. "Governor Starr! Communication systems are glitching. The turret commander sent me to tell you—"

The rest of the servant's words were lost as Thea spoke in Jasper's ear. "Ships are approaching the atmosphere. They look like council ships."

"I'd say that's good news," Jasper muttered. "But I can't imagine they'll do much against those ships Starr pulled out of the ocean."

"I'm not sure they're going to do much at all," Thea said. "They aren't attacking yet."

Jasper's brow furrowed. "Well, what are they doing?"

"Just...sitting there."

Starr held up a hand, and the Blades all fell still, arms dropping to their sides. From what Jasper had picked up, the servant had been sent to deliver him the same news. Once the servant was done speaking, they held a new communicator device out to Starr. He accepted it.

"Hold fire," he said into the communicator. "Let the council watch, if that's what they want. Only attack if they start firing."

"He's going to deal with the people and elite first, then worry about the council," Jasper told the others quietly. "We can't give him room to breathe. We need to get the council to attack. Anything they can do is better than nothing."

"Earthguard's gone radio silent," Thea added. "Last I heard, they were able to get some people out of the servant's quarters to a larger carrier ship waiting in the atmosphere, but I'm not sure what's happened since. I'm sending out regular messages, but who knows when or if we'll get a response."

"Lovely," Jasper muttered. Her hand tightened around her sword's handle. Her gaze flickered to Skybreaker, who was still breathing hard from the fight. Jasper's eyes narrowed.

Whose side are you on, Sky?

Chapter Sixty-Two
It's All Coming Together

Starr's momentary distraction issuing battle plans triggered another round of elite skirmishes through the ballroom. Jasper and the others were ignored by the Blades in the meantime—they apparently only responded to direct commands from Starr.

It didn't take long for the fights to settle into two main battles: the Vegas versus the Fayes, and the Altairs against some of Starr's closer cousins. Other elite who didn't have the power to hold their own in a fight had either taken sides with bigger families or scattered against the walls to avoid drawing attention.

Starr finally glanced up from his communicator and watched the battling gangs and security through narrowed eyes. Jasper muttered into her comm, quiet enough that even Skybreaker couldn't hear. "Cutthroat. We need to start a fight between Starr's army and the council ships."

"Already working on it," Cutthroat replied.

A blaster knocked out of a Slicer's hand skidded across the floor and came to a rest at one of the Blade's feet. The man didn't move an inch.

Sarena leaned toward Jasper. After shooting Skybreaker—who was also observing the ongoing battles—an apprehensive glance, she said, "So, uh, what's the plan from here?"

Jasper was saved from thinking up a response by the sound of Starr's voice resounding through the ballroom, bringing the skirmishes around them to a halt. Jasper realized that one of the members of the extended Starr family, their personal security force rapidly losing to the Faye's gang of thugs, had approached Starr. Maybe to ask him to stop the fight?

If that was what their request had been, they must have been disappointed to hear Starr's answer. "It's time that things changed in Kronos's upper districts," Starr said. "In order to stand against our enemies, only the strongest can be allowed to indulge in our luxuries."

With that, he'd all but encouraged the fights to continue. The winners would be his new favorites, and the losers would fall in rank. Or worse.

Jasper's gaze flicked around the battlefield. In the fighting's momentary pause, she could see that the Altairs' Slicers had managed to subdue the Starrs and had many of them tied up. The Starrs had apparently been dependent on the palace's security force to protect them, but the governor had not allowed them to aid his less powerful relatives.

The Fayes' personal bodyguards, meanwhile, had left the Vegas' security team scattered unconscious across the floor. Hell, at least a few were likely dead.

"Being at the top won't be just about politics anymore," Starr continued. "It will also require power."

"Cutthroat? Status?" One of Jasper's fists clenched and unclenched at her side. They were so close to everything colliding. And it was probably about time she got herself out of the palace. Starr's attention was being pulled in multiple directions, but he'd been after her for a long time. Once his attention was fully on her, getting out would be no easy feat.

"Cutthroat's a little busy at the moment," Thea said. "I'm lining him up for a good shot."

A small camera feed popped up in the corner of Jasper's vision. She expanded it, leaving just enough space to keep an eye on the ballroom. The sight of pastel pinks and oranges momentarily surprised her. It was still not long after midnight, but Kronos's current position meant that the more distant sun's light was already washing over the city. The cold temperatures would remain for another couple of months, but the darkest part of Kronos's winter was over. What looked like early morning skies would linger for hours before true sunrise.

One of the city's various security cameras, pointed up toward the ships gathered in the lightening sky, was in the perfect position to display the massive blaster beam that erupted from somewhere in the atmosphere and pierced one of Starr's black carriers through its front window.

It could have been from any of the council ships, but Jasper had seen that same shade of purple fire from the Astronomer before. She wasn't sure exactly where Cutthroat had hidden himself behind the council's frontlines, but that only made it more convincing that the council had been the ones to attack. It helped that Cutthroat had only been using cannonballs to attack the palace previously.

Jasper felt some relief at how easily the carrier was damaged by the beam—it immediately dropped from its position in the sky and spiraled back toward the sea below. But they'd known the carriers wouldn't be unreasonably difficult to destroy. The real challenge was the army inside.

Starr whirled around and watched the ship fall on the holoscreen showing the view outside the palace. Moments later, his communicator beeped. "Governor, the Interstar Council has started firing on us."

"Fire back," Starr replied curtly, eyes not leaving the screen.

Jasper's jaw clenched as she listened to Thea say something about Cutthroat dropping closer to the palace to continue guarding the protestors while they broke in. If the council couldn't hold up to Starr's forces, the entire army they'd brought could be wiped out, and Starr would be free to keep ruling as he pleased.

Jasper couldn't help but feel resentment toward them at the same time. *It's their responsibility to deal with him. The people of Kronos shouldn't have to fight.*

"Council's holding up to the initial round of fire better than I thought they would," Thea noted. "Their ships must be pretty damn strong."

"Starr's carriers are firing with warp-powered weapons, I assume?" Jasper asked quietly. The Altairs and Fayes were eyeing each other up, some of their bodyguards starting to circle each other.

"Looks like it," Thea answered.

"Still no word from Earthguard?"

"Nothing yet."

Damn it. What had happened to them? Some part of Jasper felt concern, especially for Zoe, but it was hard to focus on that through all the building frustration. It was the standing around, she realized. She needed to get back out there and make sure the rest of the plan was working. Though, they'd pretty much reached the end of the actual planning part. From here on out, the vibe was more "hope for the best."

There was just one last piece that needed to come into play.

"Thea, how long until our...other team gets here?" Jasper asked.

On the ballroom's holoscreen, the carriers were approaching council ships. Rather than the continuing to fire, though, soldiers—those new high-tech cyborgs armed with what might be the most powerful handheld weapons in the galaxy—disembarked the carriers and jumped onto council ships via grappling hooks, landing on any surface they could manage. They quickly began shattering windows and blasting open doors to make their way inside.

On the ballroom floor, the Fayes' security team attacked first. There were more of them left standing, and they made surprisingly quick work of the Altairs' forces. A minute later, the Fayes were left as the winning family. For now, at least. Jasper noted that members of the other families were typing messages on communicators or muttering quietly into smartspheres.

Starr turned away from the holoscreen, and it seemed he was ready to turn his attention back to Jasper and Skybreaker. Skybreaker, seemingly having the same thought, lifted her staff and pointed it toward the nearest Blades, who still stood as still as statues.

Jasper shot a quick glance toward Sarena, who stood nearby with her chin lifted and Blitz scanning the space behind her, bracing herself for a fresh wave of attackers. Then Jasper's attention shifted back to Starr, and their gazes briefly met. There was no emotion in his eyes. He waved a hand, and then the Blades were moving again.

Jasper swung her sword. The first Blade went down quickly, but the next three weren't so easy. She quickly found herself prioritizing defense over offense, and it was all she could do to keep the three at bay. *Damn it.*

Finally, one of her jabs went deep into one Blade's abdomen, and he sank. With only two Blades on her now, it was easier to get hits in, and she sent the second Blade to the ground only moments later. She was a little surprised no other Blades had come after her to keep up the onslaught, but Sarena was doing an excellent job keeping them back. And those who did get past her repeated shockwaves were mainly focused on Skybreaker.

Jasper slashed the third Blade across the throat, dropping the woman. Behind her, a particularly loud crackle of lightning, combined with a near-blinding flash of green light, made her turn.

Skybreaker tossed aside her staff and reached behind her back. Her hand moved under that thick gray jacket, found something, and pulled. The object was big enough that Skybreaker struggled with it for a moment. But she managed to slip it out of its holster and under the collar of her jacket—the fit was just loose enough for her to squeeze out that terrifying weapon.

Having that strapped to her back explained some of the awkwardness, but Jasper suspected she was still hiding something under that jacket. Her movements were still stiff as she settled the weapon in her arms and took aim.

One by one, Skybreaker took out the rest of the Blades, making them vanish in beams of light that emitted unnerving hums as they came and went. She had to wait about ten seconds between each attack, but her electrokinesis and a few well-aimed kicks kept any Blades from getting to her in the meantime.

Within a minute, the last cyborg Blade was gone. Skybreaker had taken out eleven in total, mostly in groups of two.

"So, given how dodgy you've been, I'm going to assume that does more than simple vaporization," Jasper said.

Skybreaker shot her an annoyed look. "All I know about Starfeller is that it gets rid of people I don't want around. Good enough for me."

"What about your cameras, Subject 12-99-Janus-18?" Starr called. He lifted an eyebrow as Skybreaker and Jasper glanced his way. "And your trackers? Surely you didn't find a way around those yourselves. My tech team is one of the best in the galaxy."

Skybreaker visibly grimaced at Starr's use of what was apparently her full name. She quickly replaced the expression with a mask of confidence. "Your tech team did give my friends some trouble, but it didn't take them long to give me the ability to swap in a fake camera feed and trick the tracker." Eyes narrowing, she added, "And you don't know the galaxy nearly as well as you think."

Thea spoke in Jasper's ear. "Hey, that other team is entering the palace. Care which way I route them?"

Jasper took a few slow steps back from Skybreaker so she could speak quietly to Thea. "They coming in from the rear?"

"Yep. Opposite the protestors."

Perfect. "Just get them to the ballroom as fast as possible." This would be the distraction she needed to get out. "Angel, can you help me with extraction in a minute here?"

"I'm already working on it," Grace replied. "Sounded like things were starting to get rough in there."

Jasper grinned. "Thanks, Angel."

Ahead of her, Skybreaker lifted her chin. "So, what's your plan to kill me now? I already took care of your cyborgs." She seemed rather unconcerned with whether or not Starr intended to keep sending people after her.

"I've got plenty more where those came from," Starr said. At his side, he made a small waving motion with his hand. The remains of his ordinary security team moved in closer around him. It looked like he might be prepping to run himself. That would be the smart thing. He had to know by now he couldn't fend off the protestors without pulling resources from the army fighting the council, and there was the risk the Astronomer would continue to fire on the palace. "And I suspect your next move will be to try to kill me first."

Skybreaker gave him a wicked grin. "You're on my list, old man. But I think I oughta deal with the real threat first."

She whirled to face Jasper. She set the massive gun—Starfeller, she'd called it—on the floor next to her and lifted her fists. They began to crackle with electricity.

Jasper backed away slowly, eyeing the lightning with apprehension. She was relieved Skybreaker apparently didn't want to use Starfeller on her—for whatever reason—but she knew from painful experience how awful that electricity would feel if it touched her.

Jasper lifted her hands as she continued backward. "I still don't get it. Why are we enemies when we could be overthrowing Starr together?"

Jasper swore there was a flash of hesitation in Skybreaker's eyes. Then she was glaring again. "I already told you. The Janus System has to be burned down before it can be rebuilt. And I know you're not going to let me do that."

"I'm not," Jasper agreed. "But we don't have to burn it down—"

Skybreaker lunged. Jasper's mind sped up on instinct, and she dove out of the way in slow motion. As she rolled across the floor, the world picked up again, and Thea spoke in her ear. "You've got incoming."

Skybreaker made another attempt to lunge at Jasper. She probably would have made it, if she hadn't been knocked aside by a speeding motorcycle.

Jasper turned to watch the silent motorcyclist race through the ballroom, drawing confused and startled shouts from the other occupants. She vaguely recognized the villain riding it but couldn't quite recall their name. They'd definitely been in all of the other races, though.

From the ballroom entrance came the roaring of louder engines, and then more motorcycles and larger vehicles were pouring in.

All driven by villains.

The oncoming racers cut between Jasper and Skybreaker as they climbed to their feet. Skybreaker's eyes quickly narrowed.

"Thanks again for sending out that broadcast, Thea," Jasper said, loud enough for Skybreaker to hear. She returned her sword to the scabbard on her back. "Looks like it lured in most of the surviving villains."

Jasper grinned, offered the fuming Skybreaker a wave goodbye, and ran.

Chapter Sixty-Three
Wish Upon a Comet

Grace dropped onto the roof and sprinted across it to where the Comet was parked. Distant rumbles shook the sky above, and the sky partially lit by a distant sun was frequently brightened by massive beams of blaster fire.

She threw the palace another glance before ducking inside the ship. When she'd been over there a few minutes ago, the protestors had just begun shattering windows and making their way inside any way they could. Jasper had mentioned earlier that most of palace security was either in the ballroom or outside, and those outside had already been taken care of. Hopefully, that meant people wouldn't be facing much enemy fire on the way in.

Grace scrambled into the cockpit and started the engines. "Thea," she said as her hands tightened around the steering wheel. "Can you guide me to the ballroom?"

"I'll send a map to the Comet's control screen," Thea replied.

Moments later, Grace was speeding through the air toward the palace. As she neared, she noticed a turret rising from one of its front corners. A massive gun poked out and swiveled toward the crowd gathered around the entrance.

"One of the turret's is about to fire—" Grace started to warn the others.

A cannonball dropped from the sky and smashed into the turret's massive gun, disabling it. "That hit the right spot?" Cutthroat asked, his voice gruff.

"Yep. Thanks." Grace pulled a lever by the wheel and then pushed the wheel forward. The Comet tipped toward the palace below and dove.

She set her sights on a hole already left in the roof by one of Cutthroat's cannonballs, directly over the ballroom. The gap left behind was just wide enough for the Comet to squeeze through. Grace and the ship vanished into a dark tunnel clouded with debris.

Grace pulled up immediately when the lights of the ballroom became visible. She dispatched the landing gear just in time to feel the ship thud against the floor. The Comet skidded across its surface, forcing some of the villains racing through to swerve and change course to move around her.

Grace scanned what she could see of the ballroom through the front window. Skybreaker wasn't far, and she was stalking toward the ship. Yikes. Grace craned her neck, but there was no sign of Jasper. "Hey, Jasper, you around here somewhere?"

"Coming in hot! Open the door!"

Startled—she barely remembered to actually hit the door's button— Grace glanced back out of the cockpit. The ship's door was just open wide enough to fit Jasper when she came diving in. She hit the floor and rolled. "Close it and get us out of here!" she shouted as she staggered to her feet.

The engines roared again as Jasper came stumbling into the cockpit. She dropped into the copilot's seat.

"You okay?" Grace asked as the ship lifted off the ground. Her gaze darted to where Skybreaker had been standing earlier, but the woman was gone.

"I'm great. Wasn't expecting you to come in the Comet."

"I figured it would make better cover on our way out." It would be much safer than Grace just carrying Jasper, even if Jasper could shoot at people who tried to attack. Given the overwhelming numbers of security staff still standing, it wouldn't have been a great chance to take. "And where's Sarena?"

"Ducked into the kitchens to hide," Jasper answered. "Said she'd stick around as long as possible and try to keep an eye on Starr and the elite."

The ship's nose lifted upward, and with another roar from the engines, they shot up.

"That was...brave of her." Grace gave the systems screens a quick check to make sure there were no alerts. Nothing. Takeoff had gone as smoothly as she could have hoped.

"It took a little encouragement," Jasper said. "But her powers are good for escaping if she needs too." After that, she tapped the comm in her ear to unmute it. "Everyone, be careful if you see Skybreaker. She's got that weapon she used on Bruce Wright. She called it Starfeller, but it sounds like she doesn't even know what it does."

"Where'd she get it, then?" Holly asked.

Jasper's expression darkened. "Believe me, I'm dying to find out."

The Comet emerged from the palace and burst into the sky above. The distant sounds of screaming protestors reached Grace's ears. She let the ship hover for a moment as she studied the world below. "Dax, Holly, how are things down there?"

"Good, mostly," Dax replied. "I'm doing some healing right now, so I'm not at the front."

"I'm with people inside," Holly added. "So far, so good."

Aymes chimed in with a warning. "They managed to scrounge up some more upper district security."

"Have they reached the protestors yet?" Grace asked.

"Nope. Coming in from some skywalks just east of the palace."

Grace exchanged a look with Jasper, who smirked. "What do you say we give them some help?" Jasper asked.

Grace pushed the ship forward. "I agree."

It didn't take long to spot the security forces racing across the skywalk toward the palace. Grace armed the Comet's blasters on the lowest setting: painful and disabling, but not deadly unless the targets were incredibly unlucky where they got shot.

She shot Jasper a hesitant glance, and Jasper shrugged. "Fine by me, though I wouldn't blame you for killing them either. But as long as they can't get up any time soon..."

Grace left the setting where it was and began firing.

Once the forces were all on the ground, Jasper spoke into comms again. "Thea, where are the villains?"

"Still moving through the palace, but they'll be heading out the west side pretty soon," Thea answered. "Do we want to do anything else with them?"

Jasper rose to her feet and moved into the ship's rear. To where her motorcycle leaned against a wall in the corner. "We're just going to use them for a little more chaos. I'm going to lead the pack to that block where a few of the upper districts run together."

Grace glanced back. "Where do you want me to drop you?"

"West side of the palace." Jasper picked up the motorcycle and wheeled it to the door. "I'll meet the villains there."

"Why that part of the upper districts?" Holly asked.

Jasper cocked her head to the side. "I have a hunch that the fight between the elite in the palace ballroom was only the beginning."

Sarena spoke up. "I think you're right. The elites that lost the fight to the Fayes seem to be giving orders to outside help."

As they neared the walls of the palace, Grace opened the side door again. The sound of wind shipped through the ship. "Is Skybreaker still inside?" she asked.

"I think she ran off," Sarena replied. "Starr's also gearing up to leave. He's swarmed with security. Some more of those cyborgs showed up, too, though I'm not sure if these ones were Red Blades."

As the wind whipped Jasper's ponytail around, she lifted her chin and mounted the motorcycle. With a grin and a salute directed at Grace, she rolled out of the ship.

Grace leaned forward and peered out the window to the space beneath the ship. As Jasper fell, the motorcycle's wings burst from its sides, catching the air and directing her into a glide toward one of the wide balconies wrapping around this side of the palace. Grace followed, slowing the Comet to avoid passing Jasper.

As she dropped the ship to become level with the palace, the first of the racing villains began to emerge from various windows, shattering them in the process. Some fired weapons first to break the windows, while others plowed right through with their vehicles.

Grace scanned the villains as they fell into pace behind Jasper, following her across Aymes's walkways into the upper districts. Most of them were nothing more than vaguely familiar to her. The villains she'd been focused on the most during the original races had either joined the team, vanished into a spacetime warp, or...

Well, she wasn't sure what had happened to Grim Machine, but he definitely wasn't among the pack of racers.

Grace kept the Comet as low as she could, following the villains as they raced over skywalks and skyways and rooftops. Abandoned vehicles and scattered debris from the battle in the sky above became obstacles in their path. Jasper was particularly skillful in her navigation, manipulating the motorcycle like an extra limb to make jumps and ride railings.

"Where do they think the endpoint is?" Grace asked.

Thea responded. "I gave them half a map in the broadcast and told them the rest would be transmitted during the race. I just marked the finish line as Jasper's destination."

The Comet swerved around the corner of a skyscraper, and Grace nearly hit the brakes on instinct. She did slow the ship considerably for a moment, taking in the view outside the front window.

The upper districts had become a warzone. Blaster fire and bullets cut through the air. Windows shattered and people shouted. And it didn't take more than a few moments for Grace to determine the participants. There were obvious Slicers, as well as members of what looked to be smaller gangs that must have been secretly tied to elite families. The rest must have been from other families' private security teams.

"Looks like they're trashing each other's penthouses on top of all the fighting." There was obvious glee in Jasper's voice. "They forgot that their lives of luxury come from uniting with each other against the lower class."

Good point. With the upper districts in such disarray, it wouldn't take long for opportunists to slip in and steal what they could. As far as Grace was concerned, it would be completely justified, given the way the elite had ruled for so long.

"If they'd just let a little more money stay in the lower districts, allowed laws to pass that let the people live in comfort, they still could have kept plenty of wealth for themselves," Jasper continued. "And they wouldn't have had to hoard it on top of a ticking time bomb of a city. Filled with people constantly on the edge of turning violent against them."

Grace brought the Comet down on a nearby roof. Below, the villains who'd crossed Thea's imaginary finish line had clearly been enticed by the violence and were taking the opportunity to join in trashing—and stealing from—the wealthy estates.

Jasper navigated up a fire escape and joined Grace on the roof as Grace stepped out of the Comet. As Jasper came sliding to a stop at Grace's side, she swept her gaze over the chaos below. Over the villains.

"Let that be their prize," Jasper muttered. "As long as they stay away from civilians, they can steal whatever they want."

Grace nodded, though she hoped this wouldn't end up becoming a war between superpowered villains and protesting masses. But villains were more interested in easy crime than fighting an actual war. She expected most would go back into hiding once they'd filled their pockets. And maybe killed off some of the elite's forces.

Jasper turned her attention to the sky. Her expression darkened. "I think the tide's starting to turn in favor of Starr's army."

"It definitely is," Thea said.

Grace and Jasper exchanged worried looks. "We should get up there, then?" Grace asked hesitantly. Was there really much they could do?

Jasper nodded. "It won't be easy, but if we can start tanking those carriers, it'll make it harder for the cyborgs to attack the council, no matter how powerful their weapons are. Even if we can't kill many of them ourselves, we can still make a difference."

A new voice spoke over the comm network, startling Grace. "Already on it."

Jasper's eyes immediately went wide. "Rose? Where are you?" She began turning in circles, her gaze darting around frantically.

"Like I said. Working on the carriers." A loud thud came from what Grace assumed was Rose's side of the conversation.

The horror on Jasper's face only grew as her gaze lifted up the orange sky. Then, she looked at Grace. There was a tremor in her voice as she said, "We have to get up there."

Chapter Sixty-Four
The Girl in the Rose's Thorns

The cartoon playing on the holoscreen became background noise to Rose as she fumbled with the window. The thundering in the sky outside, all but drowning out the distant screaming and shouting, had finally become too much for her to ignore.

The latch finally gave, and Rose slid the window open. The air that washed over her carried the faintest hint of smoke.

Rose checked the pockets of the green spiked jacket she'd grabbed, the one she'd found at the mall on Iros. She also had the combat boots and collar, too, though the boots still had no bottom from activating her rockets while wearing them. Not much she could do about that right now. In her pockets, she had a handful of knives and small daggers she'd found digging around Jasper's room. She'd also found a blaster that was half-charged and strapped it to her waist.

Finally, before stepping out the window, she slipped a comm from Thea's pile of extras into her ear and made sure it was muted. As she climbed out onto the fire escape outside, she began to pick up on how things were going elsewhere.

The team had their hands full with the protest and the palace, Earthguard was MIA, and… stars, that was a lot of carriers up in the sky.

Rose tipped her head back and studied the black ships with wide eyes. Beyond them were the silver and red-patterned ships of the Interstar Council. Both sides were firing blasters, but Rose could see tiny figures moving from the carriers to the council ships. The cyborg army.

How to get up there without being seen? Rose wasn't sure she could fly all that way, and the chances of getting shot out of the sky were too high.

She climbed from the fire escape onto a skywalk and headed for a staircase moving up between two nearby buildings. She scanned every vehicle she passed, searching for flying cars, and finally spotted one a few stories up from where she'd exited the apartment. It was a clunky old thing with peeling red paint, but the doors were unlocked, and it started up when she turned the key that had been left abandoned on the driver's seat.

The car shot straight up when Rose hit the gas, making her yelp. She'd read up on driving not long after leaving Sky Labs, anticipating the time might come when she'd need to know, but this was her first time actually trying. It was pretty touch-and-go for the first few minutes, but she managed to avoid crashing into anything. Other than a couple of trash cans, that was.

When she neared the city's highest rooftops, she slowed and assessed her options. There was still a considerable gap in the air between her and the lowest carriers. She'd be easily seen if she tried to cross it. She landed the car—harder than she meant to, touching down with a painful thud—on one of the roofs. Then, she threw the door open and stepped outside. Stared upward. *What to do, what to do…*

As she watched, one of Starr's carrier ships was struck by a blast from the council's army. The ship dropped from its position, one of its engines flaming, and descended toward the ocean where debris of other ships drifted on dark, bobbing waves.

Meanwhile, another carrier rose from the ocean's surface and headed to join the rest of the army. The carrier was smoking, and its movements were jerky, but it moved upward at a relatively steady pace. Hastily repaired, perhaps?

Struck by an idea, Rose climbed back into her stolen flying car and took off. She flew toward the ocean and brought the car down on a pier. There, she jumped out of the vehicle again and sprinted to the edge of the pier. Pieces of carrier hulls and engines floated in the water below. And, a little further out, she could see entire ships drifting in the waves.

Good. The intact ships were buoyant. Rose activated the thrusters in her feet and shot across the waves toward the nearest ship. As she neared it, a sliding door along the side facing the air flew open. A man climbed out. Rose flung her legs out, bringing herself to a halt, and dropped onto a floating door that had been separated from one of the other ships. She ducked, and the man didn't notice her as he climbed to his feet atop his ship.

Rose's gaze briefly flitted to the massive blaster hanging at his side. One of those fancy new weapons powered by warp energy that the team had mentioned. The man must have been a cloned cyborg then.

"Anyone else in there still conscious?" the man called into the ship. There wasn't any concern in his tone. The question was a bit monotonous, actually. When the man got no response, he stalked to the growing fire burning at the back of the carrier.

Rose took the chance to leap onto the side of the ship, propelling herself most of the way with her thrusters. She found purchase easily, making use of its complex outer surface to find handholds, and quickly scrambled up onto the top. She slid across its surface and dropped in through the opening.

Rose's feet splashed down in a thin layer of water that coated the bottom of the carrier. A quick glance around revealed four more cyborgs lying about, all either unconscious or dead. It also revealed an open closet full of black tactical gear that would make a decent hiding spot.

Rose sprinted to the closet and settled into place behind the hanging gear, crouching in the shadows that would hopefully be dark enough to prevent anyone from noticing her. The more pressing issue at the moment, though, was whether or not this carrier would be getting back up in the air anytime soon. How long should she give that other guy to repair it? Ten minutes? Twenty?

She started coming up with other potential ways to get up into the sky in case she had to bail on this carrier, but after about seven minutes, a shadow passed over the floor beneath the open doorway, and the first cyborg dropped back into the ship. Rose struggled to keep her breathing steady as she watched him walk to the control panel at the front of the carrier and press a few buttons. There was a roar as the engines came to life. And then gravity was shifting, water was sloshing, and they were rising from the sea.

When they didn't immediately catch fire and crash back to the surface, Rose allowed herself to start considering the next part of the plan: disarming and incapacitating the cyborg. The cyborg that was bigger than her and armed with an incredibly dangerous weapon.

The window above the control panel soon revealed other carriers hovering in the sky that burned with pastels. They'd returned to the warzone. Rose slowly reached for the biggest dagger in her jacket.

The cyborg at the control panel flipped a few switches, and the ship fell into a steady hovering position. He stepped back from the panel and walked to a shelf loaded with grappling hooks and more guns. Rose crept out of the closet slowly, intending to get close before lunging at the man. But she'd taken no more than three steps when he stiffened. She thought she'd been silent, but she realized with horror as he turned around that he'd heard her.

Up close, she could see the cyborg had a very human appearance, though a few quirks indicated he probably had some other species in his blood. A line of sharp, pointed teeth was visible when his lip pulled back in a snarl, his irises reflected an unnatural amount of violet light, and that vibrant lavender hair cropped close to his head didn't seem to be dyed.

He reached for the blaster at his side. Rose felt something in her mind's cybernetics come to life. The man slowed down, and as her legs sprang into motion, she realized she was moving slow, too. The cyborg's blaster lifted. Aimed toward her. She dove to the right as he squeezed the trigger, easily avoiding the blast. She hit the ground closer to the cyborg, rolled toward him, and started to get back to her feet.

She was still getting back up when she noticed the man was moving to fire again. She pushed her body in the other direction this time. The next blaster beam cut much closer to her face than the previous had, but it still missed. Hand tightening around her dagger, Rose continued her excruciatingly slow journey toward the cyborg. She felt she could speed things back up if she really wanted, but the added reaction time was saving her life right now.

Judging by the expression on the cyborg's face as she inched closer, though, he had the same ability. They both moved in slow motion, but their minds were racing. The blaster moved again, attempting to line up with Rose's head. She brought the blade in an arc toward the man's hand. His finger hovered over the trigger.

His jaw clenched as he realized that firing would mean taking the hit to his hand. He seemed to think it was worth it, though, and squeezed the trigger. The blaster was aimed just above Rose's head, where she'd end up by the time the beam reached her. It would have worked, had her mind been operating at an ordinary speed, but now she had the time to halt her motion and start bringing her head back down. As the beam passed over her, missing by less than an inch, her blade sank into the cyborg's hand. He yelped and dropped the blaster.

It then occurred to Rose that while she'd realized the cyborg had the same brain implant as her, he might not have come to the same conclusion yet. It likely wouldn't take long for him to figure it out, though. She needed to end this quickly.

It was easy enough, with the man clutching his bleeding hand and his weapon lying on the ground. He did act quickly to attempt to retrieve it, but he couldn't have possibly moved fast enough. Rose brought the blade down on his shoulder.

While he yelped in pain, she made an attempt at his other arm. This time, the dagger didn't make it far before getting stuck in circuitry and wiring. The blade clanged against metal. Sparks and arcs of electricity danced around the wound.

Rose only spent a moment attempting to free the blade before letting it go and reaching for the blaster she'd brought instead. Rather than firing, she slammed the butt of the weapon against the cyborg's head. It bounced off with a resounding metal clang, and pain reverberated through the arm she'd used.

Gritting her teeth, she tried again in a different spot. The cyborg, focused on trying to free the sparking blade from his cybernetic arm, didn't move to stop her. The blaster found a more vulnerable spot at the back of his head and struck hard.

He collapsed.

The world went back to moving at full speed. Rose returned the blaster to its holster and sprinted over to the front of the carrier, where she stared at the army floating in the air outside. Dealing with them wasn't going to be easy.

Better get started, then, she thought.

Chapter Sixty-Five
Keep It Down Up There

Jasper fired her blasters at every cyborg she saw. Many were shooting at council ships with their much more powerful weapons while hanging from grappling lines, while others simply stood on top of their carriers waiting for a chance to fight. Grace held tight to Jasper as she flew them upward, her wings beating strong currents of wind through the air around them.

"Rose," Jasper said into her comm as she sent a cyborg tumbling off a carrier with a shot to the leg. "Where are you?"

"In one of the carriers!"

"Rose, there are a *hundred* of these damn ships!" Jasper braced herself as Grace brought her low over a roof, allowing her to kick a man in the back of the head and knock him flat on the top of the carrier. She shot at him with the blaster for good measure as they continued on.

Rose stammered. "Uh, I'm—just above that blue building next to the palace. At the bottom of the fleet."

Jasper craned her neck to peer down at the palace. She quickly located the blue building Rose was referring to—a building that shone in shades of aquamarine and came to a sharp point at the top—and moved her gaze up until she found the bottommost layer of carriers.

"Grace?" Jasper glanced over her shoulder.

"I see it," Grace replied. She adjusted her wings, and then they were shooting toward the carrier in question. If Jasper hadn't spent so many years racing vehicles and spaceships at unbelievable speeds, the sensation might have made her throw up.

As they approached the carrier, Jasper could see that its side door was wide open. And she could see Rose inside grappling with a man twice her size.

Jasper readied her blaster, but Rose fired first. And Rose's weapon was packing a much bigger punch. At such close range, it sent the cyborg flying against the wall of the ship with a thud that carried over the wind and, from what Jasper was able to glimpse, some pretty awful burns across his shoulder and upper arm where his shirt had torn open.

Grace landed on the edge of the carrier, and Jasper stumbled out of her arms. "Rose!" she exclaimed, grabbing the girl and pulling her into a quick embrace. After releasing her a moment later, she straightened up and checked her for injuries. Nothing visible. But still… "You've been fighting the cyborgs?"

"I mean, I'm a cyborg too, and I've got some of the newest tech." Rose held up a blaster. One powered by warp energy. "Plus, I got my hands on one of these."

Jasper's eyes widened. "Be careful with that!"

"I am being careful!"

"You're by yourself in the sky fighting an army!" Jasper exclaimed. "That is not what I would call being careful!" Her heart pounded like crazy in her chest, and she forced herself to pause and take a deep breath. Rose was already out here, and they had bigger problems.

Out of the corner of her eye, Jasper could see Grace crossing the carrier to where the cyborg Rose had been fighting was slumped against the floor. A few other bodies were scattered around, too.

"They've got the best tech and blasters, too," Jasper pointed out to Rose, turning to survey the bodies herself. "And they're stronger than you. How have you taken down so many?"

Rose shrugged. "Not that many. This is only my second carrier. Don't get me wrong, they're crazy hard to fight. But they all underestimate me."

"Well, we should keep at it." Jasper lifted her blaster and checked the charge. Eesh. It would probably be a good idea to take a page out of Rose's book and steal one of the warp energy-powered ones.

"There's another thing," Rose said. "When the carriers go down, the cyborgs are repairing them, if they're able to. If we're going to focus on shooting them out of the sky, we need to make sure the engines are absolutely obliterated."

"Got it." Jasper walked to the nearest body and scooped up the man's weapon. She noted that despite the massive hole burned in his shoulder, he was still managing shallow breaths. These guys were tough.

Tougher than her, undoubtedly.

"Let's focus on carriers over the cyborgs, then," Jasper said. "They'll be easier to take down since they can't fight back, and the cyborgs will go down with them. Even if they can survive the fall, we'll at least be getting some breathing room for the council's army."

"What are we waiting for, then?" Rose sprinted toward the open doorway.

"Hey, wait—!" Jasper wasn't fast enough to catch her before she leapt out and activated her thrusters.

Grace caught up to Jasper. "She's stubborn, isn't she?"

Jasper sighed. "And a little unhinged." She shot Grace a sideways glance. "Don't say it."

Grace lifted her hands. "I wasn't going to say anything. You ready?"

"Yeah, let's catch up to that little gremlin before she gets herself killed."

They jumped out of the carrier together, Grace's wings carrying them up to where Rose hovered above. Rose took aim at one of the engines, and Jasper the other. They fired together.

With a spectacular explosion and a whole lotta smoke, the carrier began to sink.

They continued on, flying from carrier to carrier, dodging blaster fire from the other ships. Cyborgs fired at them from roofs and doorways, forcing the three to frequently switch focus. And a few shots were never enough to take the cyborg down. They dodged easily, fired back, and could still pull a trigger even after taking a few hits, unless a direct shot was made to their chest or head.

Rose could dodge with a fair amount of ease herself, but Grace had a harder time turning and moving quickly while holding Jasper. Jasper was forced to stop beams that were coming too close by firing interceptions. When two blaster beams collided, they canceled each other out with an explosion of heat and light. It was a difficult thing to do, but it was made far easier with Jasper's mind working in overdrive to increase her reaction time.

Somewhere above them, a particularly loud explosion rocked the sky. Jasper glanced up in time to see a council ship fall from its orbit and plummet toward them, flaming. Rose and Grace—still holding Jasper—shot off in opposite directions. Jasper's hand tightened around her blaster as if it could do her any good against a falling ship.

Grace led them to another carrier, and they dropped onto its roof. Jasper straightened and turned in time to watch the council ship fall past, close enough for her to feel the heat radiating from those violent flames.

"Rose?" she said, suddenly realizing she wasn't sure where the girl had gone. "Rose, are you okay?"

Coughing came through the comms, followed by Rose's voice. "I'm okay. Landed on a skyway. Area's clear."

"Stay there as long as it's safe. Take cover if you can." Jasper muted herself and nodded to Grace. "Let's keep moving."

While Grace grabbed her and spread her wings, Jasper fired the blaster rapidly at the ship's engines. More fire. More smoke. The ship dropped out from beneath them, but they stayed in the air.

Grace swooped toward another row of carriers, swerving to dodge a spray of blaster fire as she approached. A distant groan of metal made Jasper glance up. Her eyes went wide.

"Incoming!" she exclaimed. "Angel, get—"

One of the falling pieces of ship debris clipped Grace's right wing, sending her and Jasper into a downward spiral. Her hold on Jasper nearly slipped, sending Jasper's stomach into somersaults, but they managed to stay together as they fell through the air.

They were nearly to the top of the city skyline when Grace finally got her wings into a position to catch air. Jasper managed to orient herself and get a look at the several falling ships. One carrier and two more council ships. The carrier was way too close to Jasper and Grace for Jasper's liking.

Jasper unmuted herself as Grace slowed their descent further. "More council ships are dropping," Jasper said. "Did Starr's army suddenly get way better aim?"

Then she spotted the figure falling through the sky behind one of the council ships, lightning crackling around her. She flung out an arm, and the ship's other engine went out in an explosion of flame and green sparks.

Skybreaker.

"Brace yourself!"

Grace's warning came moments before they landed hard on the roof of a steel skyscraper, falling just a little faster than would have been ideal. Jasper gasped in pain as she rolled away from Grace across the slick metal. Next to her, Grace groaned. She sat up quickly, though, to Jasper's relief. Jasper followed suit, and then they climbed to their feet together.

The falling black carrier thudded against the roof they stood on a moment later, sending cracks shooting through the structure and crumpling roof's metal panels. A council ship dropped through the air behind it, missing the building entirely and continuing to plummet deeper into the city.

As it passed, Skybreaker jumped from its open doorway and landed on the crashed carrier's roof. Black smoke filled the air behind her, hiding much of the battle and the sky beyond. Her lightning cracked through the smoke as if it were clouds in a storm.

An explosion behind Jasper made her spin. An engine that had come loose had crashed into the other end of the roof. It rapidly spewed more black smoke, and within seconds, she and Grace were surrounded by a thick cloud that hid the sky and the sun. Everything was dark, except for the glow of various lights in the crashed ship and engine, flames burning within their hulls, and the occasional arc of green lightning racing up Skybreaker's arm.

Jasper and Grace turned to face Skybreaker again, who stood at the edge of the carrier roof, just close enough to be visible. Skybreaker shrugged off the stiff jacket she'd been wearing, now shredded in many places and stained with blood and grime in others.

"I despise Starr from the bottom of my soul," Skybreaker said as she tossed the jacket aside. "I hate him for creating me the way he did, for raising me the way he did. I can't wait to kill him and watch the light drain from his eyes."

"We've got Skybreaker on a rooftop," Grace muttered into her comm. "One block from the shoreline, south of the palace. Black smoke everywhere, a carrier crashed into the roof..."

Jasper resisted the urge to shoot her a glance, not wanting to tip Skybreaker off to what she was saying. It sounded like she had a plan. And for once, Jasper would be the one trusting in it.

Meanwhile, Skybreaker continued her tirade against the governor. "But as much as I want to kill him, right now, we need him. Well, we need his army. And the council's been so damn useless for the past few decades, I don't really care about their attempts to fix things now."

"And what exactly do you need his damn army for, anyway?" Jasper flung out an arm. "Maybe if you'd try running your plans by other people, we could help you make them a little less...unhinged!"

"You have to believe me." There was an odd tinge of desperation to Skybreaker's voice that Jasper thought she must have imagined. "I helped Starr keep his labs and factories secret so that he could get this army built. We need to keep the army around long enough for him to defend himself against what's coming. Then I can kill him."

A massive bolt of Skybreaker's green lightning cut through the black smoke gathering around her, sending a loud crack reverberating through the air. Jasper couldn't help but flinch. "And what could possibly threaten Starr besides us?"

"Someone worse than him." Skybreaker's head cocked to the right. "Someone worse than me."

In the next flash of lightning, Skybreaker spread her wings.

Her *wings.*

Jasper staggered backward before she could stop herself. The wings were massive, extending out nearly a foot more on each side than Grace's did.

Skybreaker started laughing. A laugh that was cold and manic all at once. "I always told you I was the upgrade." She jumped from the carrier to land on the crumpled roof. "Better than you in every way." She strolled forward.

"Jasper," Grace said in warning, seeming to sense that Jasper was going to charge before Jasper herself realized it.

Jasper sprinted at Skybreaker anyway, taking aim with her blaster and firing in rapid succession. Skybreaker ducked and dodged with ease, blocking some of the beams with blasts of her own. But once Jasper had gotten close enough, she tossed aside her blaster and lunged with her hands. Jasper dove out of the way, but not fast enough to avoid being grazed by Skybreaker's lightning. She yelped as her skin burned.

Enduring the pain with gritted teeth, Jasper rolled, jumped to her feet, and drew her sword from her back. As she and Skybreaker began to circle each other, Jasper just caught the words Grace shouted behind her, directed through the comms at the team.

"—ready when you are!"

Jasper smirked. Then, she swung. Skybreaker dodged the blade's arc and threw her leg up. Her foot met Jasper's hand, knocking the sword out of her grasp. Then, she grabbed Jasper by the arm and chucked her. Jasper hit the rooftop about ten feet away and rolled. More pain coursed through her, leaving her with an ache that settled into her bones and lingered.

"Trying to fight me? Really? You can't win a one-on-one." Skybreaker's voice was almost pitying as she strolled toward Jasper. It was certainly condescending. "You know that, right?"

Jasper grunted as she pushed herself up. "There's a plan."

"I've planned for your plans."

"Then it's a good thing this plan isn't mine."

Skybreaker lifted her arms. The air crackled, and the world lit up. Jasper glanced around at the grid of neon electricity arcing around the two of them in a sphere.

"Pretty," Jasper said, daring to let a little sarcasm creep in.

Skybreaker gave her a mad grin in return. "It interferes with signals. No communication with your team. And that technopath of yours won't be able to do anything to me from out there."

Jasper shrugged. "Does sound like something I would ask her to do, if I were making the plan." She shot a glance toward where Grace had been standing, but there was nothing but smoke, now. *I really hope you know what you're doing, Angel.*

The air thundered nearby. The ground beneath them shook violently. Jasper turned and squinted upward through the smoke. A gust of wind cleared it just enough to reveal the council ship crashing into the narrow, cylindrical skyscraper that towered over the building they stood on.

And then the skyscraper collapsing, falling toward them.

Skybreaker grabbed Jasper's arm and, keeping the net of green electricity around them, hauled her toward the edge of the roof. Her iron grip was impossible to break out of, forcing Jasper to move her legs to keep up or risk falling and dragging against the roof as Skybreaker pulled her.

They were nearly to the edge when the skyscraper came crashing down behind them. The next thing Jasper knew, the roof was falling out from beneath her.

The fall took Skybreaker by surprise, too, allowing Jasper to wiggle free from her grasp. She quickly switched her focus to saving herself—hell, maybe sticking to the person with wings would have been smarter. But Jasper quickly spotted a cable swinging through the air. She was barely able to grab it as it passed her, and her collision with it altered its course. Jasper tightened her grip and let the cable carry her away from Skybreaker.

Jasper glanced up as her swing came to the end of its arc. Was the cable attached to a structure still fixed in place, or a piece of falling debris? Well, she didn't appear to be losing altitude, so she assumed the former. Sure enough, she soon came to a complete halt, dangling from the cable amidst smoke and scattered flames.

Jasper coughed a few times as she scanned the air for signs of Skybreaker. She found her on a nearby roof, and thankfully, Skybreaker didn't seem to notice her. She still had that electric net around her.

And, Jasper realized with alarm, she wasn't alone.

Chapter Sixty-Six
Scraping Skies

Grace settled into a crouch on a balcony overlooking the roof where Skybreaker stood, caught between Thea and Dax. Despite being close, the angle made it unlikely that Skybreaker would notice her. The plan was in motion, and all she could do was hope it went well enough for her turn to come.

"Jasper," Grace whispered. "Are you okay?"

"I'm fine, just...stuck dangling from a cable at the top of the city. Could you come get me so we can get Thea and Dax the hell away from that woman?"

Grace grimaced. "Not yet. We have a plan. Just stay there and try not to let Skybreaker see you."

"What? Why not?"

"You'll see."

On the roof below, Skybreaker laughed as she glanced between Thea and Dax. "And what are you two going to do to me, exactly?" Her attention rested on Thea. "If you think you can screw with me with your power, you're going to be disappointed."

"Yeah, your systems are going to be too tough for me to get into quickly, especially with that fancy net." Thea shrugged, her hands moving to rest on the straps of her backpack. "But I expected you'd be able to keep me out."

Skybreaker rolled her eyes. "Sure you did. But I know you've got other tricks up your sleeve, so..." She waved an arm, and her electric net expanded to form a dome over the roof. Thea and Dax both yelped as the net passed through them, but they didn't seem to have been done too much harm by the process.

Grace could still see the three pretty easily through the gaps in the arcs of lightning. Dax shot Thea a glance, and the fact that the glow around his hands was so brief suggested further that little damage had been done by Skybreaker's electricity.

"No drones, no sending out messages, no screwing with my weapons." Skybreaker looked smug. "Go ahead, then. Hit me with your best shot."

"I don't think you want that," Dax said. "So, let's go with this instead."

Skybreaker looked briefly surprised that he'd spoken at all. The surprise was quickly replaced with pain shooting across her face. She screamed and dropped to one knee. Then, gasping, she asked, "Did you just break my leg?"

"Holy hell," Jasper muttered in Grace's ear. "I don't think I realized just how far Dax had come with his powers."

Dax still wore a grimace as pain continued to twist Skybreaker's face, but his jaw was set with determination.

At that moment, Holly jumped onto the roof, wearing Jasper's face.

Holly was dressed in all black, including an overcoat similar to Jasper's that she'd snatched from a store while they'd led the protests up to the upper districts. She also held the sword Grace had taken from Jasper's collection earlier and stashed in the Comet for when the time came.

If Jasper had been worried for the team before, she was terrified now. "What's Holly doing? Skybreaker will tear her apart—"

"She can handle this," Grace tried to reassure her, though she couldn't help but worry herself. "She's got Dax and Thea, and Skybreaker's leg is broken."

"We can't underestimate her!"

"We won't. And you'll be helping, too." Grace adjusted her position and lifted her wings, preparing to take off.

Despite her broken leg, Skybreaker plunged into fighting the moment she saw what she thought was Jasper. Dax backed away a little, avoiding her attention but ready to heal any wounds inflicted on Holly and transfer them to back to Skybreaker.

Skybreaker kept her weight mostly on her good leg, and she managed to make hopping around look surprisingly graceful. Her sword cut quick arcs through the air, bouncing against Holly's defensive swings. Whenever she landed a blow, Dax's hands glowed blue, and the bleeding wound was presumably transferred to the skin beneath Skybreaker's clothes.

Skybreaker picked up on the strategy quickly, and the expression on her face suggested she was frantically trying to come up with a new plan. Assessing, calculating, plotting. Just like Jasper would. Before she could zero in on Dax, Holly moved into a more offensive series of swings, forcing Skybreaker to focus on deflecting the blows.

Time for the next part, before Skybreaker realized just how good Hollixa Faye's shapeshifting was. Grace took to the air, counting on the fight to keep Skybreaker distracted, and raced to where the real Jasper waited.

Grace grabbed Jasper as she passed, and Jasper released the cable she'd been clinging too.

"So, what's this plan, exactly?" Jasper asked, tone still brimming with anxiety.

"Incapacitating Skybreaker and taking her hostage." Grace circled around a building so that they could get close to the fight from the other side without being seen.

"And how are we doing that?"

"We used Dax to weaken her and Holly to distract her," Grace said as they approached their destination. "But you're still the strongest fighter."

"And she's just a little bit stronger," Jasper muttered.

"Alone, maybe," Grace conceded. "But you're going to take her by surprise, and then she'll be facing all of us."

"But she's got those wings now!"

Grace didn't have a response for that. None of them had anticipated Skybreaker showing up with the wings. The reveal had forced some last-minute adjustments to their plans, but all it really meant was that Grace would need to be more involved in the fight. She knew how the wings worked, how they moved and functioned. Their strengths. Their weak points.

She adjusted her trajectory to bring them down to the roof, approaching Skybreaker from behind. Holly broke into more frantic swinging to keep her distracted, and Skybreaker brought her wings around in front of her face to use as shields. Holly took a step back after her sword bounced off of them, breathing hard.

Grace let go of Jasper in time to drop her on the ground a few feet behind Skybreaker. She shot straight up afterward, keeping herself out of Skybreaker's immediate reach while staying close enough to dive in and help if Jasper needed it.

Skybreaker heard the thud of Jasper's landing behind her and whirled, pulling her wings away from her face so that she could see. Jasper was already swinging, bringing the dagger she'd drawn across Skybreaker's chest and slashing open a wound.

"You—!" Skybreaker turned in surprise, taking in the two seemingly identical Jaspers circling her. "What, you dig up another clone somewhere?"

"Nah. You just underestimated my team." It was Holly who said the words, prompting Skybreaker to lunge at her.

Grace swooped in, focused on where Skybreaker's wings disappeared through the slits in the back of her white shirt. Grace grabbed them as close to the skin as possible, holding tight with all the strength she could muster. Skybreaker yelped, and her wings twitched as she tried in vain to flap them.

Unfortunately for Skybreaker, Grace's wings were still free to beat hard against the air, carrying both of them upwards. Unfortunately for Grace, Skybreaker was still maintaining her electrical net, preventing her from reaching out over comms.

"Thea," Grace shouted down to the rooftop before she was out of hearing range. "Direct Cutthroat to me!"

Thea gave her a thumbs up. Grace breathed a small sigh of relief and pushed her wings to move faster, sending her and Skybreaker shooting up faster and moving the net of green lightning away from the rest of the team. Skybreaker thrashed hard in her grasp. Grace's jaw clenched. Her hands were beginning to cramp up, but she couldn't adjust her grip and risk Skybreaker getting her wings into a better position. She scanned the sky above for signs of the Astronomer.

There it was, on the other side of the palace, farther than she'd been expecting. Damn. She took a deep breath and started toward the ship, keeping an eye out for falling debris and blaster fire as she soared. As she neared the ship's deck, she could see Cutthroat waiting with a huge crew of pirates. Cutthroat held chains in his hand.

Grace slowed when she reached the ship and lowered Skybreaker until her feet were just touching the deck. She began to kick violently but stopped moving one leg almost immediately. The broken one. While she hissed in pain and continued to swing the other leg, a few pirates were able to get in and start restraining her.

"Careful, her arms are free," Grace warned as they swarmed. Thankfully, it didn't take long to get Skybreaker in cuffs, and then she was chained to the ship's railing. Once her wings were wrapped in chains, too, Grace released her completely and stepped back.

"What's with all the green lightning?" Cutthroat eyed the crackling sphere warily.

"It's meant to disrupt electronics," Grace explained. "Thea couldn't deal with it while we were fighting, but maybe with enough time she can shut it down."

Speaking of Thea—and the others—the roar of an engine announced the arrival of the Comet. The pirates cleared space for it to land on the deck. Moments later, Jasper, Holly, Thea, and Dax came rushing out.

"Dax, got anything else you can throw at her?" Jasper asked as they approached.

"Nothing major," Dax replied with a shake of his head.

Thea moved to stand near Skybreaker, brow furrowed in concentration. While she worked, Grace turned around to stare at the city's smoking skyline. "How many buildings collapsed?"

Jasper moved to her side. "I don't know, but it was starting to look like dominos for a second there."

From elsewhere in the city, Aymes offered up a response. "Most buildings in the area have good enough construction to prevent the collapse from spreading, though some newer additions at the top of the city have cut corners to save money," he said. "But if ships keep falling into the city instead of the ocean, things could still get a lot worse."

"Got it!" Thea exclaimed. Grace and Jasper turned as Skybreaker's net went out.

Skybreaker cursed. "That system will reboot, eventually," she growled. "You going to keep battling me to get it down when it comes back?"

Thea shrugged. "If I have to."

Jasper took a few steps toward Skybreaker. "Did the same friends that gave you that fancy gun give you those wings, too?"

"Yes." Skybreaker's eyes narrowed. "But I wouldn't call them my friends. And you should be very afraid of them."

Jasper looked surprised that she'd answered at all. Skybreaker glanced up toward the battle raging above. Everyone else followed her gaze, and Grace's heart sank as she realized how much smaller the council's army looked now.

"Still no word from Earthguard?" Jasper asked, though her tone suggested she wasn't optimistic.

Thea pulled a tablet from her backpack and glanced at it. "No, I don't— oh!" She frowned. "There is a signal trying to come through. I think it's from Zoe. But the decryption's still processing..."

"Looks like the council's retreating," Holly said, voice sharp. "So much for defending the values of the alliance."

"Maybe they're going for backup," Dax suggested.

"It won't be fast enough," Jasper replied. "Starr's army will turn their attention to us soon enough. Us and the protestors."

Skybreaker muttered something to herself—Grace thought she caught something about a "change in plans"—while Cutthroat shouted a few orders at his crew. The Astronomer began to sink lower into the city, into the cover of burning buildings and rising smoke.

"Starr's headed for the palace's main landing pad," Sarena announced over comms. Her voice was low. "I'm following. He's got a big security team—mostly more of those cyborgs."

"Hm." Jasper turned so that she was facing the palace. "Maybe we should have chat with him."

Grace's brow furrowed. "About what? His army's winning."

"Yeah," Holly added. "We don't have much to negotiate with."

"Aymes," Jasper said, ignoring their concerns. "Meet us at the palace landing pad. Take Mia and Chloe and drop them off by Rose on your way. Tell them to stay hidden." She turned. "Cutthroat!" she shouted. "Take the Astronomer down to the palace! I doubt Starr will let his army fire at his palace unless he gets really desperate, so we should be safe there for now."

"You heard her!" Cutthroat shouted to the pirates running around. "Get us to that landing pad. Keep the engines online and primed for quick takeoff if things go wrong."

The ship dropped fast. Despite her wings and experience in the air, Grace felt her stomach lurch and grabbed the railing. She shot Skybreaker another glance. Skybreaker was no longer fighting her chains, but she had a murderous glare on her face.

Grace turned to peer over the railing she was clinging to. The palace roof came into view quickly, and then the large landing pad jutting out just beneath the dome at the back of the building. The crowd gathered atop it was easy to spot. Governor Starr stood at its center, with about twenty guards surrounding him.

Jasper appeared at Grace's right. As the Astronomer fell into a hover, its engines dropping to a much quieter volume, she shouted down, "Whatcha waitin' for, Starr? Evacuation? Scared all those people you've been oppressing all your life are finally gonna get their revenge?"

Starr glared up at her.

Jasper laughed at his expression. "Tell you what: call off your army, and I'll call off mine."

It was a long shot, and they all knew it. Starr wasn't in immediate danger, and his army was annihilating everything in its path. "I'm all right," he called back. "But thank you."

The Blades around him drew their blasters, but it was more of a warning. They couldn't hit the ship with any effectiveness at this distance, even with powerful the most powerful blasters in the star system.

Thea yelped in surprise and raced over, tablet still in her hands. "Message is coming through. Earthguard—"

Giant letters flashed across the screen. *We're sending an S.O.S. But I don't think anyone else will show up. Something else is coming.*

Something big.

Most of our ships destroyed.

Grace's heart sank as a new line of text appeared.

Something big is coming.

"Something big is coming," Jasper read, her tone somewhere between confused and alarmed. "What—?"

"I told you," Skybreaker said from nearby, her chains clanging against the railing. "The amount of damage done to Starr's army at this point is too much. We should've left more of them intact. It would've been our best chance at fighting them."

Jasper whirled on her. "Our best chance at fighting who?"

Skybreaker managed a weak shrug. "Well, their leader is a controlling tyrant who declared herself Empress of the Ra System some time ago. She intends to promote herself to Empress of the Milky Way."

A high-pitched whine came from somewhere in the sky above.

Jasper glanced down at Starr. "Looks like you're not the biggest shark in the pool anymore." The words didn't carry any of the glee Grace would have normally expected. Grace's heart skipped a beat. Whatever was coming, Jasper was terrified.

It first appeared as a small crescent shape in the distance, as if a new moon had popped up in the sky. But it was approaching quickly.

Starr lifted his communicator to his mouth. "Send the carriers into lockdown. Put them back in the ocean."

Skybreaker leaned over the railing as far as she could. "No!" she screamed. "Syrus, you have to keep them up there, it's your only chance at keeping her out—"

Carriers were already dropping toward the ocean. But not fast enough. The crescent entered the lower atmosphere, close enough now to make it obvious it was a ship. As it descended further, a blaster emerged beneath it and began firing beams at the carriers. The beams pierced engines with precision, sending carriers plummeting out of their controlled descents.

Grace frowned as she glimpsed something—a smaller ship?—shoot out the side of the crescent spacecraft and fly off into the city's upper limits, disappearing behind a skyscraper. She didn't catch more than a flash of distant sun reflecting off its metal surface.

Then Jasper was grabbing her arm, dragging her away from the railing.

"Where are we going?" Grace asked, confused.

"Astronomer's going to hide. We don't want to make it a target. But we have to see what this is." Jasper glanced up. "Aymes, where are you?"

"Almost to you!" Aymes replied.

He appeared a moment later on a massive hovering platform, large enough for Jasper, Grace, Thea, Holly, Dax, and Cutthroat to all climb on.

Skybreaker yanked an arm hard against her chains, causing them to clang loudly against the railing. "Let me out!" she hissed.

"Keep the chains on, but let's bring her," Jasper conceded, throwing Skybreaker a glance. "She knows more about our new visitors than anyone else."

Aymes waved a hand, causing more chains to materialize and wrap around her. Then, he summoned a blade that sliced through the metal holding her to the ship. Still restrained, but able to walk, Skybreaker joined them on the platform. Aymes added an additional cuff to her ankle, chaining her directly to the platform, before carrying them away from the Astronomer.

The platform came down onto the landing pad where Starr waited and where the crescent ship seemed to be heading. Starr's cyborg security team immediately drew their blasters and took aim, but Starr raised a hand to stall them.

"Let's keep the peace while we greet our visitors," Starr said. "I'm sure they'd be happy to help us deal with Van Terra when the time comes."

"No!" Skybreaker took a step forward, her chains clinking. "Starr, whatever you have planned, it won't work. You can't beat her with your army in the condition it's in. You had a chance at the start, but—"

Starr shot her a curious glance. "Who said anything about fighting? I'm sure our visitors are reasonable people we can negotiate with."

Behind Starr and his entourage, Sarena scrambled onto the rooftop through the door Starr and his team had come through. None of them paid her much attention as she skirted them and joined the team.

"She will not negotiate with you," Skybreaker told Starr, shaking her head. "Not when she can destroy you."

Chapter Sixty-Seven
Jasper Got Run Over By A Reindeer

Jasper's focus was torn between Skybreaker's warnings and watching the flat, crescent-shaped ship approach. She didn't see the smaller ship flying at her until it was too late.

It wasn't moving particularly fast—in fact, it seemed to have been slowing with plans to land on the roof. But it still hurt when it smacked into Jasper and sent her flying into the air.

She couldn't stop the yelp that escaped her throat as she slammed down hard against the ground, alarmingly close to the edge of the landing pad. As she pushed herself up, sending another wave of pain shooting through her, Dax raced to her side. Grace was close behind.

The blue glow from Dax's hands brought relief. It didn't completely wipe away the pain, but it lessened it enough that Jasper could stand without wincing.

"Want me to inflict it on someone else?" Dax asked.

Jasper was surprised that was his instinct. After a quick glance at Starr's forces, she said, "Maybe save it for whoever's coming."

As the three rejoined the rest of the team, the crescent ship settled into a hovering position in the air above them. The smaller ship that had hit Jasper, this one spherical in shape, circled back toward the roof. But a third ship beat it there. A white ship with gray accents and gaps in its plating where blue light glowed from its inner components. A very familiar-looking ship.

Sure enough, as it hit the roof, the ship transformed. Grim Machine emerged from the torrent of shifting metal parts just as the spherical ship that had hit Jasper landed next to him.

"Grim Machine!" Skybreaker shouted. "Free me!"

Grim Machine gave no response. In fact, he stood perfectly still as the door to the other ship lifted from its side and a figure emerged.

"Sorry, Sky," the figure said as she straightened up. "But Grim here knows not to follow your orders anymore." Jasper's brow furrowed at her odd accent.

The woman was unlike anyone Jasper had ever seen. Seven feet tall, if you didn't count the antlers. Massive antlers like a moose's that shone a color somewhere between white and pastel pink. Her skin was lightly furred, also like a deer's, a dark color that looked maroon-brown in the shadows but became closer to purple as she moved into the brighter lights shining from the crescent ship above. Her dusty pink hair was cut in a short bob and bangs. Her eyes were a golden yellow, save for the rectangular, horizontal pupils in their center. Her nose was like that of a deer's, too, and lighter patches of fur like freckles dusted her upper cheeks beneath her eyes. She strolled toward the others gathered on the roof on black hooves.

Her clothes consisted of a shiny white dress with an upturned collar that followed the form of her body down to her mid-thighs. It was made of a thick material that almost looked like metal, though it was far more flexible. She also wore stiff gloves resembling steel that went all the way up to her elbows.

Jasper blinked, still processing the strange woman's arrival. Thea nudged her and pointed to a floating billboard drifting by. The screen had changed to show the woman's face as she walked.

"I'm betting she's put herself on every screen in the city she was able to access," Thea whispered as Jasper turned to watch the woman pass by. Her focus seemed to be entirely on Governor Starr.

Starr waved his hand, and his entourage lowered their blasters. "Greetings," he said.

"Greetings, governor." The woman stopped a few feet in front of him and rested a hand on her hip.

When she offered no other information, Starr asked, "And who might you be, exactly? And what brings you to Kronos?"

"The name's Empress Megaloceros. But please, call me Meg." Meg turned to study the rest of the people gathered on the roof. Jasper swore the woman's gaze lingered on her a little longer than the rest. Well, if this was who Skybreaker had been in communication with, perhaps Meg recognized their nearly identical appearances.

Meg's attention finally landed on Grim Machine, and she issued a command. "Put Starr in cuffs and throw him in my ship."

"Hold on a moment," Starr said, his voice still cool. "Perhaps we can discuss your plans for Kronos. I'd be happy to help you—"

Meg cut him off with a wave of her hand. "I don't have time for this, hon."

Starr's eyes narrowed, but he still didn't look scared or even nervous. As much as Jasper wanted to see him humbled, she was dreading confirmation that Meg was indeed a serious threat. Starr made a gesture with his hand, and his guards raised their blasters again. All aimed at Meg. All fired within seconds of each other.

The air around Meg rippled as the beams struck *something* that had been completely invisible. There were no sparks, no explosions. The beams just vanished when they met the barrier.

"I was a bit surprised to learn how little progress you've made in energy absorption technology," Meg said. "So focused on destruction, were ya? Didn't think you'd need much by way of shielding?" She glanced at Grim Machine. "Go ahead, Grim."

Grim Machine lunged forward. The cyborgs surged to defend Starr from the massive robot, continuing to fire their weapons, but Grim Machine appeared to have the same energy-absorbing shield that Meg had. And it was easy enough for him to toss aside the cyborgs once he was close.

Starr took slow steps backward, eyes wide with dawning horror, too stunned to even make an attempt at running as Grim Machine plowed through his defenses. Grim Machine caught up to him, picked him up with one hand, and slung him over his shoulder. Starr didn't struggle much as he was carried toward the spherical ship and hefted inside. The ship was fairly small, but it would easily be able to fit Meg and maybe two more people alongside Starr.

"Now." Meg turned, her attention shifting to Skybreaker. "Sky, dear, I do have to thank you for all your help. Your intel did pave the way for us to come and finally get the drop on the governor."

Skybreaker glared at her but made no moves. Her mouth stayed firmly shut.

"But I also know you were helping Starr build up his army to fight back." Meg clasped her hands behind her back. "I suppose you were hoping we'd hurt each other enough for the council to finally be able to make a stand against us?"

Skybreaker's silence continued.

"Dax," Jasper whispered. When Dax met her eye, she nodded her head aggressively at Meg. Dax nodded in understanding. One of his fists clenched at his side.

The air around Meg rippled again, and this time faint glowing whisps of blue were briefly visible. Meg turned and lifted an eyebrow. "Now, who did *that*?"

Damn. Jasper's jaw clenched. She hadn't expected Meg's shield to absorb Dax's energy, too, but she supposed it made sense.

When Meg didn't get a response, she shrugged and turned back to Skybreaker. "I'll deal with the rest of ya soon enough. As for you, Sky, I don't think all those people you sent into the warp stream will be too happy to see you."

That got a reaction. Skybreaker's face cycled through confusion and rage and fear.

Jasper grabbed Grace's arm as Grace nervously whispered, "Warp stream?"

"I don't know what that means, but I think we should get out of here," Jasper replied. The question was, what to do about Skybreaker?

She didn't get the chance to figure that out. The crescent ship hovering above the landing pad made a whirring noise. A hatch opened in the bottom, and a wide pillar of light shot out and touched down on the roof.

The light rippled with iridescence, and within moments, silhouettes were appearing within. The first one stumbled out, and it only took Jasper a moment to recognize him as one of the Red Blades that had been fighting in the palace ballroom. One of the Blades Skybreaker had seemingly vaporized with Starfeller.

Meg continued. "Think of this device as a lightning rod for lifeforms in the warp stream. Well, any that entered within range. It should cover the entire Janus System, if our calculations are right."

More cyborg Blades followed. And then came Bruce Wright in his Captain Cora uniform. Jasper's burst of concern at his arrival quickly faded as she realized the state he was in. He collapsed immediately, electric sparks jumping off his body in droves. A bad reaction between his cybernetics and the warp? But why were the Blades okay then?

There wasn't any time to try to figure out what was happening to Bruce. Slicers came pouring out of the light next. And Omic Attom.

Skybreaker hissed. "The weapon was a trap?"

"I didn't tell ya you had to shoot so many extras." Meg chuckled. Then, she lifted an eyebrow as more silhouettes appeared. "Looks like we've got a few stragglers."

Another Red Blade exited the warp stream, this one not appearing to be a cyborg. There was a slight familiarity to his face, but Jasper didn't recall where she'd seen him before until the next figure stepped out.

"Red Boss," Jasper muttered as the man emerged. The other Blade had been the one that had gone with him into the spacetime warp on Radia.

Red Boss glanced around, looking about as confused as everyone else who'd emerged did. But that confusion changed to amusement when he spotted Jasper. "Well, I have no idea what just happened," he said, a wide grin crossing his face. "But I'm going to enjoy tearing you apart, Van Terra." His gaze flicked to her right, and he added, "And your Angel, too."

There was still one more dark outline in the beam behind him. A beep echoed from the ship above, and the light vanished. Jasper yelped as the final man's colorful costume and familiar face materialized. "Ringmaster!?"

So, the beam wasn't just bringing out people who Skybreaker had used Starfeller on. Anyone who'd gone into a warp could come through. Which meant...Starfeller essentially created a mini spacetime warp?

No time to give that much thought now. Jasper turned her head. "Aymes. Free Skybreaker."

Surprise flashed across Aymes's face. "You sure?"

"Yes. Now—!"

Red Boss lunged. Holly tossed Jasper the sword she'd wielded against Skybreaker earlier, and Jasper swung at Red Boss, throwing him off his attack. She shot another glance toward Skybreaker and watched her shake off the chains Aymes had cut through.

Grace drew her own sword and joined Jasper in battling Red Boss while the rest of the team fended off the other gang members that swarmed them. Red Boss fought with ferocity, but he did have occasional moments of slowness that suggested he was still recovering from being dumped out of the warp stream—whatever that entailed, exactly.

Blasters fired, but not as many as there should have been—Thea must have been focused on suppressing the enemies, leaving Holly and Cutthroat to take most of the shots. Sarena's screams pierced the air, joined by Blitz's lasers. Blades and Slicers randomly cried out in pain, bruises and cuts occasionally appearing on their exposed skin. Knives of silvery metal spun through the air to stab others.

Through the fighting, Jasper could barely keep an eye on Meg at the edge of her vision. Meg followed Grim Machine into the small ship she'd arrived in, and the ship moved up to connect to the top of the crescent ship. Jasper contemplated going after them, but she didn't have a prayer of catching up. Moments later, the crescent ship flew off.

Jasper finally managed to get in a wound near Red Boss's neck that sent him staggering out of the fight. She took a few steps back, breathing hard. "Anyone see what happened to Attom?" she asked.

"He ran into the palace," Holly replied as she came jogging over. She swung her leg and delivered a kick to Red Boss's face for good measure, knocking him to the ground in an unmoving heap.

Jasper turned. Skybreaker was dealing with some of the remaining cyborg Blades, having a much harder time now that Starfeller wasn't an option. The fact that one of her legs was broken certainly didn't help.

"Dax," Jasper said. "Heal Skybreaker's leg and give the wound to whichever cyborg's doing the best. And—" Her gaze moved to the edge of the roof, where Ringmaster stood. Rather than joining the fight, he simply watched them with a calculating expression.

"You got any sort of plan, Van Terra?" Cutthroat called to her as he tossed a Slicer over the edge of the landing pad.

"Yeah. I think so." Jasper jogged toward Ringmaster. "Yo, Ringmaster!"

Ringmaster raised an eyebrow as she approached. "Can I help you?"

"You wanna talk to your son?" Jasper shot a glance back at Aymes, who'd formed a massive club of shining metal and was using it to beat back a couple of Slicers.

"You know about that?" Ringmaster lifted an eyebrow. He must not remember their last fight, then. The Blades and Slicers seemed to have picked up right where they left off, but Ringmaster had been in the warp stream much longer.

"Yes," Jasper replied. "He still doesn't, though, and after the way you left, I don't think he'll be interested in a conversation with you without my intervention."

Ringmaster let out a heavy sigh. "I suppose you'll want my help in return?"

"Aymes has come a long way, but his power still isn't on your level." Jasper folded her arms. "If you can get my whole team off this roof, you'll have an opportunity to chat with him."

"You want your white-haired twin, too?" Ringmaster asked, his gaze moving past her.

"Yes. Throw some chains on her, though."

"A 'please' would be nice."

"Please." And after a moment, fearing Ringmaster might not have noticed, she added, "Cutthroat and South Siren are on our team, too. Oh! And—" Jasper unmuted her comm, heart quickening. "Rose? Rose, you there?"

"Yeah, still on this stupid skyway with the androids. What's happening up there?"

"Stay put." Jasper glanced up at Ringmaster. "We have to grab someone else on the way out, too."

Ringmaster sighed again, louder this time, but lifted his hands. "All right, Van Terra. But don't expect this truce to be anything more than temporary. I expect we have some information we could exchange with each other, though."

Nearby, Skybreaker's wings spread, and she attempted to take the air. Golden light appeared in a ring around her ankle and then became solid, joining to a chain fastening to the landing pad. She yelped as she was yanked back down.

At the same time, Ringmaster formed a spaceship out of his power. It had no real engine—it would be controlled by him—but it could fit everyone inside. Jasper hopped on the wing as Ringmaster lifted it into the air and guided it over the thick of the fight with the remaining Blade cyborgs. An opening appeared in the side and a ladder dropped down. While Ringmaster crossed the landing pad to Skybreaker to grab her, Jasper fired her blaster at the last few cyborgs, giving the rest of the team the chance to climb into the ship.

Grace. Holly. Dax. Thea. Aymes. Cutthroat. Sarena and Blitz. Jasper followed them in as Ringmaster and Skybreaker entered from the other side of the ship.

Ringmaster closed up the openings with his energy and made the walls fully solid. "Where's this last pickup?" he asked. The front of the ship became semi-transparent, allowing him to see where they were going as they began to move.

Jasper gave him some directions, then glanced back at Skybreaker. "So, you knew Meg was coming?"

Skybreaker glared down at the chain on her ankle, now holding her to the ship's floor. "Yes. I did."

"A little communication goes a long way." Jasper's eyes narrowed. "If you'd given us a heads up, maybe we could have come up with a better plan."

Skybreaker's eyes rolled. "How many times do I have to tell you? I don't like you. I don't think you're capable of committing to what I have planned. And none of that matters anymore, because Meg is going to kill us all!"

"Why didn't she kill us on the palace roof, then?" Sarena asked. "Unless that was the point by leaving all those people for us to fight."

"Oh, I'm sure she wishes they did beat us. But I don't think she was expecting all you to be there when she unleashed them on me." Skybreaker lowered her head to stare at her chains again. "Doesn't matter. Her armies are coming, and once they settle in, nowhere on Kronos will be safe. She'll find you, and she'll do what she does to everyone she thinks is any sort of threat to her: exterminate them."

Jasper opened her mouth, but Ringmaster spoke first. "That the girl down there?" He pointed through a gap opening up in the bottom of the ship. Rose stood on a skyway below, waving her arms. Mia and Chloe stood on either side of her.

"Yup," Jasper replied.

As they lowered toward the pavement where Rose and the androids waited, Jasper shot Skybreaker another glance. There was a look in her eyes. A look that told Jasper she was scheming.

Ringmaster threw out a ladder. Skybreaker rose to her feet, slowly, as if she hoped no one would notice. Jasper's eyes narrowed.

Skybreaker lunged at Jasper, slamming her into the nearest wall. Her chain snapped to its full length with a clang. Jasper hissed and reached for her blade, but a moment later, Skybreaker was backing away from her. She hadn't been trying to hurt Jasper at all. In her hand was the blaster Jasper had stolen from a cyborg earlier.

Before anyone could get close enough to stop her, Skybreaker aimed the blaster at the chain connecting her to the ship and fired. The blaster beam sliced clean through the chain. Skybreaker let out a short laugh—she looked surprised it had actually worked. But she didn't marvel at the broken chain for long. As Jasper sprang at her, she ducked, then dove for the gap in the floor and dropped out of the ship. The others tried to grab at her, but no one was quite fast enough.

"Ringmaster!" Jasper shouted as she leaned forward to peer out the opening. "I thought you guys could make your constructs invincible!"

"If I were at full strength, sure," Ringmaster snapped in response. "Did you forget I just fell out of a spacetime warp?"

Below the ship, Skybreaker fell past Rose—who shot her a confused look—and continued to fall until she was nearly to the pavement. Then, her wings spread, and she shot off toward the gap between two buildings. The metal cuff and a few chain links still clung to her ankle.

Rose reached the top of the ladder and climbed in. "So," she said as she rose to her feet. "What'd I miss?"

Chapter Sixty-Eight
All Weapons Break Eventually

Janus kept to the lower districts as she soared through Kronos. Now that the battle in the sky had seemingly ended, people were emerging from buildings to assess the damage. The debris littering the streets, the smoke trailing up into the sky. They probably thought the worst of it was over.

Those poor fools.

Janus folded her wings in and dropped into an alley, landing hard on a fire escape. She winced, but the pain faded after a few moments. Her leg had been healed, thankfully, but she still had a few other lingering wounds. Overall, though, she wasn't in too bad of shape, considering everything.

If Meg found her again, though…

Janus sucked in a sharp breath and assessed the electrical net she'd put back up while flying. Its main downside was how obvious it was. Anyone who passed by was sure to notice her. They might even snap a few pictures. Talk about her on the net.

So, she would need to find her target quickly. It had been some time since she visited, but she still knew the way. Breathing hard, she started down the fire escape stairs.

At a glance, the balcony she paused in front of didn't look any different from the others on this side of the apartment building. But in the window to its right, a cord hung down, a smartsphere plugged in at its end. The sphere emitted a soft violet glow that pulsed slowly. Janus climbed onto the window's ledge and tapped gently against the glass. She followed a specific pattern, hoping the man who lived here would accept the code, even if it was a bit old. She probably should have done a better job keeping up her connections with Kronos's underworld over the past month but, well, she'd been busy.

Janus had no doubt the man would be home, at least. He rarely left his small, cramped apartment.

A long moment passed, and then the window slid open. "Janus," the man on the other side said. The Candle Street Tech was a thin, grizzled old emerald-skinned man with a mess of white hair and goggle-glasses that made his eyes look huge.

Janus dipped her head toward him in greeting. "May I come in?"

The Tech stepped aside, giving her space to slip through the window into the dark apartment beyond. Inside, computers and other torn-apart electronics were stacked from floor to ceiling along the walls. In the center of the room was a desk piled high with more devices and monitors.

"What's with that electricity dome you got there?" the Tech asked as he closed the window. With the pull of a cord, he let curtains fall into place, blocking out all but the faintest trace of light. The multi-colored glow of various electronics around the room took over.

"Keeping out tracking signals," Janus told him.

"Well, you're safe in here. Nothing gets in or out." The Tech started across the room to his desk. "All data I transmit and receive goes through cords to a communicator box outside the building."

Janus nodded. He'd mentioned that the walls and even the windows were lined with a material that disrupted signals during her previous visits, but it was reassuring to know the place was still secure. She let the net drop.

"Does that have something to do with why you're here?" The Tech asked.

"Yeah." Janus rested a hand on the desk and leaned against it, trying not to show how weak she felt. "I need my networking systems disabled. I can't have anyone using my equipment to track me."

The tech lifted an eyebrow. "You know to make sure you're completely safe, I'll have to stop all signal transmission. You won't be able to transmit or receive data yourself."

Janus nodded. "I know." No accessing the net through her mind's computer, no sending messages to other devices. It was a sacrifice she'd have to make.

"Well, then, have a seat." The Tech gestured to a chair next to the desk. "I have to wrap up a few things, and then we'll get started."

Janus nodded and settled into the chair. While she waited for the Tech to finish his work at a nearby computer, her mind wandered. How much effort was Meg going to put into finding her? And what about the others? Janus wasn't sure Jasper and her team fully realized how much danger they were in.

Did they think they could just go back to hiding at whatever hole they usually hung out in? Or would they be smart enough to get their asses out of the Janus System?

Janus sighed and sank further into her chair. She'd known her plans would be tricky to pull off, but Meg and Starr certainly would have done a lot of damage to each other had it come to a battle between them. Maybe it wasn't too late—many of the fallen carriers could be repaired, and the cyborgs manning them were as tough as her. But the chances of keeping Meg from taking control here were much slimmer now.

There was still one route Janus could take. Stay here and keep being Skybreaker, but take the chaos up a notch. Destroy everything so that there was nothing left for Meg to rule.

That felt too desperate, though. Sure, letting the two armies fight each other over the city would have caused a lot of destruction, but there still would have been a city to rule afterwards. An entire star system. The easiest way to foil Meg's plans now was to truly leave her with nothing.

Janus sighed. A battle between Meg and Starr would have been so perfect. It would have given her the chance to emerge victorious, with the will to kill anyone who stood against her, the guts to enact an iron rule. The strength, weapons, and power to make it possible. *That* was the only way to keep the people from dividing into classes, from creating an oppressive state...

Did she really still believe that? She had, once, after fully realizing what a monster Starr was. She'd thought that if she had his position, she could force the elite to redistribute their wealth and rebuild the lower districts into something better. Threaten them, hurt them, and even kill them if they stepped out of line. It was the only way to keep the city fair. Balanced. Right?

Even if she had to burn half the system down to get there in the first place?

Janus's eyes drifted shut. She would come up with something. While her body healed and the Tech disabled her systems, she would do what she did best.

Plan.

Chapter Sixty-Nine
Departures

Jasper stared out the semi-transparent windshield of Ringmaster's makeshift ship, her hand tight around a handhold, her knuckles bright white.

"I can't do this much longer," Ringmaster warned.

"We're almost there," Jasper replied. "Astronomer's just around the corner."

Since Skybreaker had fled, the ship had been quiet. Rose and Grace sat in a corner nearby, Grace quietly filling Rose in on the details of the confrontation with Meg.

Less than a minute later, the ship descended on the Astronomer's deck, landing next to the Comet. Once it had settled into place, the ship vanished entirely, leaving its occupants standing on deck.

Cutthroat immediately began barking orders. "Prepare for takeoff," he shouted. "Get the Astronomer to the edge of the Janus System and stay there until you hear from me. Keep cloaking on and electrical activity to a minimum. Find something like an asteroid field or a trash dump to hide in."

After that, they all piled into the Comet. Holly offered to fly, and Dax and Thea moved to sit in the cockpit with her while she got them out of Kronos's atmosphere. Jasper settled onto a bench in the main hold with the rest of the team. After a long moment of silence, she glanced up and realized everyone was staring at her.

Aymes cleared his throat. "So, uh, why is Ringmaster coming with us, exactly?"

"Oh, right. Um." Jasper waved a hand. "He had something he wanted to say."

"I do," Ringmaster said. "But first, I think we can help each other fill in a few gaps. The last thing I remember is returning to Iros. There was a warp in the sky, and I was supposed to be holding the next race in a few days."

Jasper's brow furrowed. "You don't remember actually going into the warp?"

"No, but based on what I'd read in Starr's research, I was able to figure out I'd gone into one pretty quickly after showing up on that landing pad at the palace." Ringmaster glanced around the ship, taking in the Christmas decorations still clinging to the walls. "How much time has passed?"

"A few months," Jasper told him. Then, not sure if he had a good idea of what a month was, she added, "A little over a season. Uh, also, Kiv Astra turned your carnival into a capitalist theme park while you were gone. Sorry."

"I wonder why it affects memory," Sarena said from where she tended to Blitz in his tank.

"It's probably moving the people inside backwards through their own timeline. Your team did come out younger, didn't they?" Cutthroat pointed out with a glance at Jasper. "Ringmaster might technically be a little younger than he was when he went in, even if only by a few days."

"But Meg triggered them getting dumped out of the warp stream," Jasper muttered. She cast a glance toward the cockpit. Holly was focused on the controls, but Thea and Dax were looking at Ringmaster, listening to the conversation intently. "What caused you three to fall out? Random chance?"

Thea and Dax exchanged a glance. They had no idea, of course. Was there anyone in the galaxy who did?

"Why are you really here, Ringmaster?" The frustration in Aymes's voice suggested he already knew it had something to do with him.

Jasper had expected Ringmaster to at least try to get some privacy before talking to Aymes, maybe throw up a wall or something. Instead, the man proclaimed, "I'm your father, Aymes."

A hush fell over the ship. Aymes, whose neutral expression looked close to cracking, finally broke it by saying, "Either he leaves, or I do."

Jasper rubbed her forehead. "I'm more than happy to kick him out, but we're sort of running for our lives—"

"No worries," Ringmaster said. "I'll see myself out." He sent a golden ring flying into the cockpit, where it bounced off the button for the ship's door, drawing a yelp of surprise from Holly. As the door slid open, he added, "But whenever you'd like to talk, Aymes, I'd be more than happy to have a conversation with you."

Ringmaster leaned backwards and fell out of the ship.

Aymes sent a ring of his own into the cockpit to close the door again. Once the roar of the wind disappeared, he turned to stare at Jasper. "Did you know?"

Jasper grimaced. "Uh, in my defense, he got sucked into a spacetime warp right after I figured it out. I wasn't sure whether telling you was a good idea. And then a bunch of other stuff happened…" She cleared her throat at Aymes's cold expression. "I'm sorry."

Aymes swallowed. He looked like he wanted to say more, but Cutthroat took control of the conversation.

"We need to figure out where we're going," Cutthroat said.

"Where can we go that's safe?" Sarena asked. She glanced out the window. "Skybreaker made it sound like Meg was going to start tracking us down pretty quickly."

Thankfully, Cutthroat had a suggestion. "There's a place pirates like to go when they're actively being hunted. Haven't spent much time there myself, but the gasses are supposed to make tracking and radar fail."

"Where's that?" Holly called from the pilot's seat. "Directions would be nice."

"Oxa," Cutthroat said. "It's a moon of Hatu. Well, the remains of one. It's basically just a gas cloud at this point. There's apparently abandoned space station floating at its center, but I've never been that deep inside."

Holly nodded, jaw setting with determination. "I'll take us there, then."

More silence. Then, Grace rose her seat and walked to the corner, where the team had thrown up a Christmas tree…what felt like forever ago now. Grace grabbed the lone gift underneath it.

"Well, it's Christmas, isn't it?" She held the gift out to Jasper. "You willing to open this now?"

Despite, well, everything, Jasper managed a weak smile. She accepted the gift.

Holly put the Comet on autopilot, and she, Thea, and Dax came out to the main compartment and joined the others in gathering around the tree. Once they were settled, Jasper tore aside the wrapping. Her hands froze when she saw what was waiting underneath. A real smile spread on her face this time.

The snow globe had a miniature Earth suspended in its center. Flakes of glitter danced around it like stars, and there was even a mini moon hanging next to it. Earth and Luna.

Jasper grinned. "This is cute. Thank you." She glanced up, and her eyes met Grace's. She mentally cursed as she realized hers were stinging with tears.

To her relief, Thea offered a distraction. "I know we still don't know much about the warp stream," she began. "But if it really does push people backwards through their own timelines...well, I have some ideas on how I might be able to use that to recover lost memories."

Jasper shot her a surprised look. "You think you could restore your memories? And Holly and Dax's?" Her gaze shifted to the other two. Their expressions didn't give away much, but she swore there was a glint of curiosity in their eyes. Hope, maybe.

"Maybe," Thea said. "I just started digging into some of the warp research data we stole from Ringmaster months back. There might be more answers somewhere in there."

"Okay." Jasper rose to her feet. "So, we head to Oxa. Thea does research on the warp stream stuff. Not just for fixing memories, but also to see if it can tell us anything about Meg and her plans." She began to pace. "Once we're safe at Oxa, we can also look into the Ra System. Figure out exactly who Meg is and how she avoided notice from the rest of the alliance for so long."

Sarena folded her arms. "And then what?"

Jasper stopped in the center of the ship and stared out the front window, at the void of space as it passed, at the stars glimmering in the distance.

"We plan."

Thank you for reading
VAN TERRA III: BLACKOUT

To get updates and find out how you can be the first to read new books, find
me at:

www.rorynorth.com

If you enjoyed the story, please help support this indie author!
Tell a friend, leave reviews, request the book at your local library, and talk
about it on social media! #vanterra

More by Rory North:

Villain Complex: After defeating the city's biggest hero, supervillain Julian Godfrey finds himself in over his head when he attempts to train the woman who took on the hero's powers as part of an elaborate scheme.

Plague Saint: In a frozen city in the distant future, Winter Pierce kills the hospital's Plague Saint to save her mother after discovering his corruption. When she steals his identity, she quickly finds herself tangled up in a government conspiracy.

A Drop of Haunted Blood: After a magician kills his family, Felix discovers his latent ability to bind ghosts to his soul and wield their magical abilities.

Be the first to know about new stories and upcoming releases! Sign up for my newsletter at:

rorynorth.com/starchatter